TIME ZERO

Praise for

TIME ZERO

"A powerfully realized dystopian tale . . . Featuring strong characters and crisp writing, this is a solid first entry in a series worth keeping an eye on."   —*Publishers Weekly*

"In *Time Zero*, Carolyn Cohagan brings to life a young heroine who represents countless girls living in today's world. Mina's rights and opportunities are restricted, but she is undeterred. Like so many girls and young women around the world, she has the courage and determination to pursue a new future—not only for herself, but for all girls."
—Alyse Nelson, President & CEO, Vital Voices Global Partnership
and bestselling author of *Vital Voices: The Power of Women
Leading Change Around the World*

"The genius of *Time Zero* is in its subversion of the reader's expectations, not only with its wonderful plot twists, but by the way Cohagan deftly folds the themes of sexual empowerment and religious extremism within the telling of a thrilling love story. I look forward to Book Two!"
—Mark Richard, Pen/Hemingway Award-winning novelist and
producer of *Tyrant* and *Hell on Wheels*

"*Time Zero* could easily be used as a curriculum tie-in for a global studies, religion, or history classroom with nonfiction titles like *I Am Malala*."
—Sarah Tansley, Branch Manager, Chicago Public Library

"*Time Zero* is a social novel wearing the cloak of a thriller, and author Carolyn Cohagan deftly combines these traditions and sensibilities. The pace is breakneck, stakes are sky-high, and the characters are forced to make quicksilver choices. *Time Zero* lights the fire of rebellion."
—Julia Gibson, author of *Copper Magic*

"Topical and sensitively written, *Time Zero* manages to be a suspenseful adventure, a touching love story, and a clear-eyed examination of the treatment of women in organized religion all at once, while still retaining a fresh, youthful voice and humor. I couldn't put it down."

—Andrea Eames, author of *The White Shadow* and
The Cry of the Go-Away Bird

TIME ZERO

by

CAROLYN COHAGAN

SHE WRITES PRESS

Published 2016
Printed in the United States of America
ISBN: 978-1-63152-072-3 pbk
ISBN: 978-1-63152-073-0 ebk
Library of Congress Control Number: 2015958068

For information, address:
She Writes Press
1563 Solano Ave #546
Berkeley, CA 94707

She Writes Press is a division of SparkPoint Studio, LLC.

Book design by Stacey Aaronson

This is a work of fiction. Names, characters, places, and incidents either are the product of the author's imagination or are used fictitiously. Any resemblance to actual persons, living or dead, is entirely coincidental.

All excerpts from *Time Out* magazine were reproduced with permission from *Time Out New York*.

For my father,
who set a budget at the toy store,
but who let me buy as much as I wanted at the bookstore

AUTHOR'S NOTE

The religion that governs the city in *Time Zero* is fictional, yet I've taken its rules from various religions around the world, including those that originate in the United States. Each rule Mina follows is governing the life of a girl somewhere in the world right now.

For more information, please visit:
www.timezerobook.com/religious-rules

All I want is an education, and I am afraid of no one.

—MALALA YOUSAFZAI

ONE

———

HAS ANYONE EVER DREADED A FIFTEENTH birthday more than me?

I lie in bed, staring at the ceiling, and wonder: If I were to stay here, could I prevent the rest of the day from happening? I pull the sheet up over my head and pretend it's still dark outside, that the sun isn't creeping through my window and slowly baking me like a holiday ham. If only the sun were devouring me for real. I would just lie here and welcome the consuming heat, the enveloping flames, and when my parents came to find me, they'd discover a pile of ash in the shape of a girl.

My Offering is tonight. Mother's been planning it for months. She's been running around, excited and anxious, while, as the day's drawn closer, I've become more and more miserable. If only I'd been born a boy.

My bedroom door opens, and Mother walks in. Her hair is pinned in its usual bun, and she's wearing her cleaning clothes. I brace myself for her to snap at me for sleeping in, but she has a strange expression on her face. She sits down beside me on the bed.

"How did you sleep?" she asks.

I shrug.

"You look tired," she says. "That's not good."

Did she really expect me to sleep on the eve of such a depressing occasion?

"I need to tell you something, Mina, but you have to promise you won't get upset. Today is too important for you to go getting all dramatic like you do."

I sit up in alarm. "What is it?"

"It's Nana."

I can't breathe until I hear what she says next.

"She fell."

"But how . . . Does that . . . Is she . . . ?" I can't ask the question.

"She's alive. She's been taken to the Women's Hospital on 14th Street."

I exhale, saying a small prayer of thanks to the Prophet.

"It sounded as if she were trying to *walk down the stairs*," Mother says, using a tone that suggests Nana is some toddler who tried to crawl out of her crib. "I can't imagine what she was thinking."

"I want to see her," I say, rising out of bed and heading for my closet.

"Not today," Mother says. "I have a big list of things for you to do for your party. You can see her tomorrow."

"But she'll wonder where I am!" I say, thinking of Nana lying all alone in a strange hospital.

Mother has never approved of Nana or liked the time I spend with her. My grandmother is my favorite person, which is probably odd for a girl my age. But she's the only one in my life who really listens to what I have to say, and, more importantly, she tells me the truth about things.

"She knows exactly where you are: preparing yourself for suitors." Standing, Mother heads for the door. "Before you shower, I have chores for you. The girl I hired won't be here until noon, so say your morning prayer, get dressed, and come straight to the kitchen."

"No."

The word pops out of my mouth, and for a brief moment, I feel brave, but as soon as I see Mother's face, I know I've been stupid. Her azure eyes narrow into slits, so all I see are her rutted forehead and clenched jaw. She strides toward me, and I don't even see her raise a hand. I just hear the slap and feel a searing pain on my left cheek.

"I won't ask again."

She walks out of the room, letting the door slam behind her.

Tears fill my eyes, but I tell myself they're for Nana, not the slap. I don't want Mother to have the satisfaction. I can only hope that Nana knows how much I want to be sitting beside her, holding her hand, talking about her neighbors, my stupid Offering, or maybe Time Zero.

I stop crying.

The Primer. I have to go and get it.

Nana always warned me this day might come, when something might happen to her, and she told me there was one thing I had to do: get the Primer out of her apartment and keep it safe.

Mother doesn't like Nana, but she would LOSE HER

MIND if she knew how Nana and I were really spending our time together.

My grandmother has been teaching me how to read.

The punishment for teaching females to read is prison. And for me, the girl learning how to read, the penalty is either prison or a public whipping, depending on how long the crime has been taking place. But to Mother, the worst price of all would be the disgrace to our name, which might keep anyone from wanting to marry me.

Nana said that if anything ever happened to her, I had to get the Primer we were using out of her apartment as soon as possible, before the Teachers, the religious authorities, could find it. It's incriminating evidence; plus, Nana wanted me to have it so that one day I could pass on the gift of reading to my own daughter, just as her mother passed it on to her, and her mother before that.

I need to leave immediately. If Nana's apartment is empty, there's no telling who could be there—neighbors, vagrants. She lives in a rougher neighborhood than we do, and anyone could turn her in if they found a forbidden artifact.

I've never snuck out of our apartment before, and the punishment from Mother will be severe, especially on the day of my Offering. I weigh the problem in my mind and whisper a prayer, hoping God might give me guidance, but instead I hear Nana's silvery voice.

Go, Chickpea. Run.

I've always been her Chickpea, a nickname I started to hate a few years ago, when I decided it was a baby name.

What if no one calls me Chickpea ever again? The tears threaten to well up, but I swallow and hold them back. Not yet. I have to get this done.

I quickly get dressed in plain cotton pants and a T-shirt. Grabbing a cloak from the closet, I throw it over my clothes. I take my veil from on top of the dresser and fit the band around my forehead, snapping the back closed just above a modest ponytail. The veil's rectangle of fabric reaches from my temple to my chest, covering my face but leaving the back of my head exposed. The gauzy black material allows me to see out, while no one can see in.

Tiptoeing out of my room into the hallway, I stand at the head of the stairs and see that the living room is clear. A low monotone voice on the radio drifts out of the kitchen: *God created the family to provide the utmost love, comfort, and morality that one can imagine. It is a man's job to support the family, and a woman's job to support the man.*

It's midmorning. Father's at work, and my brother is off training to be a Teacher, so it's only Mother at home, but my disobedience will be the most infuriating to her. I need to accept now that if I manage to sneak out of the apartment, there will be a beating waiting for me when I get home.

But I made a promise to Nana.

I take a deep breath, lift my cloak away from my feet, and race down the stairs and across the living room, not bothering to see whether my mother is standing in the dining room. If she is, she'll start screaming at me soon enough.

I make it to the front door, and there's no sign of her, so my hand reaches for the doorknob. Then I'm turning it and stepping into the hallway. *Am I actually doing this?*

I close the door behind me, hear it click, and pray for forgiveness for disobeying my parents. I run down the hallway, hoping the prying neighbors don't decide to stick their noses out in the next ten seconds. Diving into the stairwell, I sprint down the stairs, seven flights. They are only half-lit, but I know them with my eyes closed, having lived here my entire fifteen years.

We live in a tall building in Midtown, better than most, because my father works in energy. The poor neighborhoods have more guards, more Twitchers, and much less light. Barely anyone on the Lower East Side, in the slums, can afford electricity.

I slow down as I reach the bottom floor, pushing on a door that leads out to a marbled corridor. I try to catch my breath—to look as if everything is normal. Our building has a constant rotation of doormen. The one on duty right now, Rab, is the hairy one who smells like an old armpit. He would love to report to the Teachers that I left home without permission.

Anytime I'm without my father or brother, my leaving home is considered questionable. Luckily, I take Nana groceries every week. I pray that Rab doesn't realize that this isn't grocery day. I keep my head down to avoid looking at his froggy face and overgrown mustache, wishing that in my cloak and veil I looked like every other young girl living in the building, but I know that my fair hair sets me apart.

I feel his eyes following me.

"Peace," he mutters.

"Peace," I echo.

Gliding by him, relieved he hasn't stopped me, I shove open the big glass doors that lead outside. I lift my hand to block the glare of the sun. The heat is so oppressive that when I take a breath, it's like inhaling hot metal. Within seconds, my cloak is sticking to my body, and the synthetic fabric releases a stale, sour odor. I scold myself for not having washed it the day before.

There are two armed men that always guard our building. They've never told me their names, so, privately, I call them Toots and Buddy, names I got from the Primer.

I grab my bike, which leans against the back alley of our building next to dozens of other bikes. I walk it to the street and look up the avenue. Hundreds of women on bikes fly by, their cloaks billowing behind them like bat wings. I climb onto my bike and scoot into the modesty basket, which surrounds the seat and looks like the top of a baby's high chair. The basket assures that no man is subjected to the movement of my hips when I ride.

Tucking the bottom of my veil into my cloak, I pedal into the flock of women. We fly down the avenue as one, mobbing the street, leaving only a scant path for the rare electric bus or taxi, which females are forbidden to take alone.

I'm picking up speed, when a thought flashes across my mind and my foot misses the pedal. *I don't know if any new Ordinances were announced today.* Mother listens to the radio every morning so that we'll know whether the Teachers have declared any new rules. I was so focused on the Primer that I walked out without even thinking about them. *Nyek.* The street curse slips out before I can stop it.

I keep pedaling, but I look to my left and then to my right. I see that the woman cycling next to me is in black, because she's married, and that next to her is a young girl wearing a cloak in the same shade of purple as mine, with a veil the same size as mine. We also wear the same-shaped white canvas shoes. *Praise God. The clothing Ordinances haven't changed since yesterday.*

The Teachers enforce God's laws, as set forth in the Book, but they also regularly dictate new laws, which protect us as a people and test our dedication to the Faith.

My moment of panic has passed, and my legs and shoulders relax into the rhythm of pedaling, until I imagine Nana urging me on: *quickly, Chickpea!* I pump the pedals harder, my tires bumping over the huge potholes and cracks in the long-neglected street.

On the next block, I spot one of the huge posters of Uncle Ruho, our Divine Leader, looking down on me. He has a short black beard, a bushy mustache, and a small, knowing smile. On his left cheek he has a thick, dark mole that my brother says looks like a tick that's filled to the brim. Uncle Ruho is a direct descendent of the Prophet, so God chose him to keep us safe. As long as I've been alive, he's been our leader. His eyes make me uncomfortable. No matter where I go in the city, I feel like they're watching me.

I see that someone has dared to spray graffiti on the

bottom of his poster. The paint is green, and the shape is like an ear, or maybe a leaf. It must have happened just seconds ago, or the authorities would've already covered it up. I look around, wondering if the culprit is near. Does he look guilty? Is he like me, heart beating, palms sweating? I want to look at the graffiti more closely, but I don't dare. What if someone suspects I had something to do with it?

It's time to turn east, toward the market, but a turn west would take me to the hospital where Nana is. *I could just stop by quickly, make sure she's okay.* But I know how upset she'll be if I haven't taken care of the Primer, so I weave through several bikes to get on the east side of traffic. When I see my turn, I swerve and jerk my bike to the left. Through the whirring of bike wheels and flapping of cloaks, I hear several women cursing at me as I almost knock someone from her bike. I yell an apology and make my turn.

I reach the market. The smell of roasted pork hits me first, followed by the seductive aroma of hot pastries and empanadas, alongside hints of mint, basil, and oregano emanating from the spice stalls. The sharp stench of the horses used to cart in vegetables from the Fields lies beneath everything. Men holler loudly, announcing their daily produce. Most days, I like to get off my bike and meander through the stalls, to watch the butcher haggle over a goat shank or the hardware man overcharge for his lightbulbs, but today I'm in too much of a hurry. I hustle through the rest of the market and turn right down the next avenue.

One more block, and I've finally arrived at Nana's apartment. After leaning my bike against a rusted, disintegrating mailbox, I try to walk calmly toward her building. What if Twitchers have already been here? If they've found the Primer, they could be at the hospital, interrogating Nana right now, preparing to take her to the Tunnel.

Before I was born, the Teachers closed off one of the main passages into the city, a huge tunnel for cars that ran under the river. They sealed off one end and turned the rest of it into a prison. Once you're locked up, you have no way out but the front door, and you have to sleep at night knowing there are ten stories of water above you. I had nightmares about the Tunnel growing up. I think it's why I've always hated small spaces and can't stand the thought of being underground.

I can't bear to think of Nana there. I try to keep the fear from fully crystallizing in my mind. The bike ride, the heat, and the anxiety cause perspiration to pour down my forehead and chest. My cloak is drenched.

I approach the guards at the entrance to Nana's building. I'm at her apartment regularly, but if the door guards know she's in the hospital, perhaps they won't let me pass. They stand as tall and motionless as the street lamps next to them. Like Uncle Ruho, they have short beards and stern expressions.

They let me pass without any reaction. I exhale.

Once through the door, I make my way across the empty lobby to the stairwell. No doormen in this part of town. Nana lives on the fourteenth floor, but the elevator doesn't work. She has a bad knee, and it's almost impossible for her to climb these stairs. That's why I bring her groceries every week. I once asked her why she couldn't just come to live with us. Given that Sekena, my best friend, lives with her parents, plus three of her grandparents, and they're all crammed into the apartment next to ours, it doesn't seem like a big deal for us to fit Nana in. When I brought it up, though, Nana just clucked her tongue and said it wasn't part of God's plan.

I wince. If she'd been living with us, she wouldn't have tried to go down the stairs. She could have asked *me* to get whatever it was she suddenly needed so badly.

Seeing no one else in the stairwell, I grasp the bottom of my cloak and pull it up as high as my knees. I jog up the stairs as fast as I can, trying not to imagine exactly where she fell. Panting, I concentrate on the pain in my lungs, hoping it will distract from the fear gnawing at my heart. What will I do if Nana doesn't make it?

Reaching floor fourteen, I pull open the heavy metal door, gasping for air. I curse when I see there's a Twitcher outside Nana's apartment. *Nyek.*

Twitchers are the highest-ranking members of the City Guard. Along with their colossal handguns, always on display, they wear black jumpsuits, black gloves, and thick black helmets. Their mirrored face shields narrow into a point, making them resemble the ants that swarm the streets on garbage day.

This one hasn't seen me yet, which is normal. Twitchers are all wired for down-net; they get constant news and orders sent straight to their helmets and projected inside their visor grid. Standing guard, they might seem to be doing nothing, but watch them long enough and you'll see it—they *twitch.* Even their hands twitch as they type back responses through their wired gloves. They must use up half the electricity in the city. I would never call one a Twitcher to his face. I don't want to get shot.

I approach the guard, lowering my gaze. I wait for him to speak first, because he's male and I'm female.

There's a long pause before he says, "Peace," and through the helmet the voice is distant and metallic, as if he's answering through a pipe.

"Peace," I respond.

"What are you doing here?" he demands.

Me? What is *he* doing here? I keep my eyes down. "I need to enter my grandmother's apartment."

His head slowly moves up and down as he uses the Senscan attached to the side of his helmet to examine me. I don't need to worry about spiritual infractions—my cloak is the proper color and length; my hair is bound; I'm not wearing makeup, nail polish, or perfume; the clothes underneath my cloak are sufficiently modest—but I squirm anyway. I hate being scanned. Does he think I'm bringing a bomb into Nana's apartment or something? Once the Senscan has told him that my DNA matches Nana's, one would think he'd let me in.

Finally, the Senscan's light goes from red to green, which means I've passed. He asks, "What is your reason for entry?"

"She wants her prayer beads." I ask God to forgive my lie.

Another excruciatingly long pause. Part of me wants to turn around and run. His fingers twitch, so I assume he's typing in new information. The Senscan turns red again as he looks me up and down one more time. What's he checking now? All the information that exists about me in the world should have come up on his first scan.

Sekena and I have spent hours speculating about how much the Senscan can see. If it can see through our cloaks, can't it see through our clothes, too? Are Twitchers walking around the city all day, looking at naked girls? Sekena says, "Absolutely not. The Book says seeing a woman's flesh makes a man crazy with desire and turns the world into chaos." So she believes the Twitchers can't see that much, or they wouldn't be able to control themselves. I guess I agree with her, but it's not making me feel any better as the Senscan creeps down my body for the second time.

Finally, the light goes green again, and the guard says, "I'm surprised she would own prayer beads."

Why? What does *that* mean? Was he checking Nana's records, too? I search for something to say. "She uses them every time she prays, and I'm sure they'll help with her healing, God willing."

After pausing again, he says, "There's no light."

At first it seems like a religious message, and then I realize he's talking about the apartment.

He says, "There was a report of looting, so we turned off the electricity to discourage anyone else."

I nod my head. He stands to the side, and I can see that the lock on the door has been broken.

"Keep it quick," he says.

When I enter the living room, the only light comes

from the open door behind me. Nana covers her windows with old cardboard. Even fourteen stories up, she's afraid of being watched.

I expect to see chaos, a ransacked room, but everything seems intact. Glancing to my right, into the kitchen, I can see cupboards flung open and pots and pans on the floor. The looters must have been searching for food. So maybe we're okay.

I can't have the Twitcher watching me, so I shut the door behind me, plunging myself into blackness.

I hear Nana's voice say, *You can do this. You've been in this apartment hundreds of times.* From memory, I walk to Nana's comfy flowered chair. Her scent permeates it, and, for a moment, I pause and breathe her in: warm bread, jasmine soap, and the mint salve she uses on her knee. I want to hug the air that she's left behind.

I shove my hand under the seat cushion, and there it is. *Praise God.*

I pull it out—*gently, Chickpea*—and, after brief consideration, I pull up my cloak and stick the Primer in the back of my pants, praying that the Twitcher doesn't decide to scan me again. I'm about to head for the front door, when I remember the prayer beads.

Nana keeps them with her jewelry, but getting to her hiding spot is going to be a little complicated in the dark. Shuffling around her armchair, arms in front of me, I aim for what I think is the bathroom. I overshoot to the right, stubbing my toe on the wall. I stifle a small cry, then feel along the wall until I reach the door.

Once I've felt the edge of the door, I drop to the ground. Feeling the bathroom tile beneath me, I crawl on all fours until I've reached the cabinet underneath the sink. It's closed, which is a good sign. Hopefully, whoever sacked the apartment didn't think they would find anything worthwhile in here.

I open the cabinet, feeling around with my hands. I touch toilet paper, some sort of metal can, something bristly—the toilet brush, *disgusting*—and then my hand lands on the simple cardboard box I'm looking for. I pull it out and stick my hand inside.

Nana always says that no man will touch anything that has to do with feminine products. That's why she keeps her valuables in a tampon box. She thinks this is especially entertaining now that she is well past her menses. "A man's embarrassment will keep him from considering basic biology," she says. "What dolts."

She loves the word "dolt" almost as much as the word "git," which, she has explained, means "moronic jerk." When she says it, you don't really need the definition. Her delivery tells you *everything*.

I hear the front door open, a voice booming inside: "You've had long enough."

All I've found is a tangle of necklaces and earrings. "Coming now, sir!"

"Why are you taking so long?" All of a sudden, the Twitcher is standing in the entrance to the bathroom, holding a flashlight whose batteries alone must be worth two thousand BTUs. "Looking for fuel to steal?"

"No, I . . . just can't find the beads."

Stepping into the bathroom, the guard snatches the tampon box away from me. Using the beam from his flashlight to sift quickly through the jewelry, he finds the prayer beads in no time. For a second, I'm relieved, but then he pulls out Nana's opal ring and sticks it in his own pocket.

I'm horrified.

"Time to leave now," he orders.

I follow him out, and once we're in the hallway, he shoves the prayer beads in my face. "It will be a good recovery, God willing."

"God willing," I echo. I grab the beads, but I still can't believe he's taken Nana's ring. And what's to stop him from going back inside and stealing the rest of her jewelry? I want to ask him how a man of God can justify such an action, but the contraband I'm concealing is too valuable. Bowing low and muttering, "Peace," I start to walk away from him backward, in case the shape of the Primer is visible underneath my cloak.

He says, "Peace," in response, but he's no longer paying attention to me. He's already receiving new data, uploading information, and plugging back into the world of men.

I reach the exit, spin, shove the door open, and run down the stairs. When I reach the tenth floor, I pause for a moment and look back up the stairwell to make sure he isn't following me. When I'm certain the coast is clear, I try to catch my breath. Am I dizzy from the running or from the number of laws I've broken today?

Looking out the large windows, I can almost see the whole city. It must be close to midday, because the sun is high in the sky, reflecting off buildings in Midtown, so bright that the light sucks the color out of everything, making sidewalks and cars glow white. I can see all the way to the Fields in the Park, to the canals on the West Side and the pig farms on the East.

The Wall blocks my view of the river. Father once told me the Wall is over seventy feet high, reaching around the entire island. It keeps us safe from the Apostates, and brought peace after the Dividing, but I wish I could see the water and the land on the other side. What's going on over there? Is there anyone left? What I would really like to see is the famous statue that once greeted so many immigrants. Nana told me she was called the Statue of Liberty—at least, she was before the Prophet removed her head.

TWO

BACK OUTSIDE, I HOP ON MY BIKE. I PEDAL AS
fast as I can up Park Avenue, new anxiety pooling in my
stomach. Nana always says, "Don't waste good energy on
things you can't control." I can't control my mother's fury,
so I try to think about something *besides* what her first
words will be when I walk through the door.

I choose to think about the first time Nana showed me
the Primer, five years ago. When I arrived at her apartment
that day, she was acting strangely. She was distracted,
almost unfriendly. Nana's not really a hugger, but she
always greets me with a smile and asks how my week has
been. Not that day. She didn't even get up from her armchair. I thought maybe she wasn't feeling well, but when I
asked, she brushed me off and told me to put away the
groceries and join her in the living room.

When I did, she asked me to sit on the couch. She was
sitting tall in her chair, like she had an important announcement to make.

Nana likes to brag that, in her youth, she was nearly six
feet tall. She has silver hair that she keeps short, which very
few women seem to do. She likes to wear pants and men's

button-down shirts that must've belonged to her husband, but she won't talk about him, or much of anything else about her past. When I see Nana interact with my father or any of her neighbors, she scowls and seems pretty unpleasant, but with me she's always good-humored and generous. Sometimes I can hear her swear up a storm under her breath, and I can't believe any woman knows such words.

That day, she asked me twice if I'd locked the front door, then told me to pull down all the blinds even though she'd already covered the windows with cardboard.

Finally, when she seemed satisfied that we had absolute privacy, Nana reached under the cushion of her chair and pulled out the Primer. I couldn't have been more shocked if she'd pulled out a snake!

As usual, Nana could read my thoughts. "Don't be afraid, Chickpea."

Using her cane, she came to sit next to me on the couch. The Primer was crisp and brittle with age, and Nana handled it as though it were made of cobwebs and might blow apart at any moment. I had so many questions, but I didn't speak. I sensed that, for Nana, this moment was sacred.

The front cover of the Primer is made from thick, shiny paper, but it's torn and the right corner is missing. I now know the big letters on the front spell "Time," followed by another word that's forever lost, a victim of the tear. All that remains is the letter "O." Nana and I have spent hours speculating about that second word—"Time Over"? "Time Off"? or, my favorite, "Time Odd"? We'll never know for sure. So we settled for "Time O," or, as Nana says, "Time

Zero." This also became our code for the time before the Prophet.

Nana began to turn the pages, slowly, allowing me to look at each one. Some of them had squares cut out of them. I learned later that the Primer is what people used to call a *magazine*, and that, many years ago, Nana's grandmother cut out any pictures she thought were sinful.

Nana just kept flipping the pages, showing me word after indecipherable word, until she got to a page in the middle, and I gasped. Nana's grandmother had left a picture there, and it showed a New York of the distant past, when electricity flowed abundantly to everyone who wanted or needed it. The city was lit up like its own galaxy.

I couldn't contain my questions for one more second. "Nana, why—"

"Hush," she said. "Today is a very special day, Chickpea. It is THE day. You are finally old enough, and I can begin what I was put on this earth to do."

And then Nana turned to the next page and did something that shocked me down to my toenails. She began to read!

This wiener dive offers the best Jersey-style dogs this side of the Hudson: handmade smoked-pork tube steaks, deep-fried until they're bursting out of their skins. While you can order them wrapped in bacon and drowning in chili ($4.75), we're partial to the classic ($2.75) with mustard and kraut.

When she finished the passage, she looked so proud—smug, even. I wasn't quite sure I believed her, because the words made no sense to me. "Smoked-pork tube," "Jersey-style dogs," and "dive"? Was this English?

"Nana, what is this? Are people eating dogs?" I asked, worried not only that we were performing a forbidden activity but also that she was making me hear about barbaric people.

She grinned. "No, no, dear. Don't worry about what it means yet."

She turned to another page.

> This is as close as cinema gets to a fairground ride: it's shiny, noisy, and exhilarating. Whedon directs with a sledgehammer, bashing the audience, Hulk-like, with action piled upon action, explosion after explosion.

She stopped and said, "Today I begin to teach you how to read, just as my mother taught me, and her mother taught her. I would have taught my own daughter, but . . ."

"You didn't have one," I finished for her.

Nana's face contorted briefly, and I wasn't sure if it was a look of pain or disappointment, perhaps both. She only has one child, my father, and they aren't close. When I was little, before I was allowed to travel to Nana's on my own, my father would bring me. He would politely say hello to her and leave. He'd then return two hours later, picking me up in the same formal way.

I understand now that Nana had been waiting, all that time, to teach me.

It's so strange to learn that someone has plans for you that you know nothing about. I'd never thought I was special or interesting in any way. And all along, Nana had been counting down the days until I turned ten, when she could start sharing her secret with me.

I felt a tingle of excitement, like I was finally an adult, like life was finally starting. But there was still a part of me that was terrified. "Nana," I said, "aren't these words written by Apostates? If I read them, won't God be mad?" An Apostate is someone who doesn't believe in the Prophet, who doesn't believe in God, or who has betrayed Him in some way.

She closed the Primer, looking me straight in the eye. "God *never* said women shouldn't read. He never said that one of his creatures was built for education while another one was not. That's a rule that a *man* created, and it wasn't about his quest for Paradise; it was about his quest for power. You understand?"

I shook my head. I didn't understand what could be powerful about reading. It couldn't make me rich, make me taller or stronger, find me extra food or batteries or water, keep my parents from arranging my marriage, or make my older brother any less repellent.

"Ignorance, Mina, is the enemy of change."

Nana was always talking about "change." I sensed she meant something more than just our being able to ride in a taxi alone. When most people talked about "change," when they said they wanted perfect health or an easier life, it reminded me of the way in which the Heralds talk about Paradise—it's not anything you can expect to experience in this life; you just have to hope you'll see it in the next.

But when Nana talked about "change," I sensed she was talking about something real, as if it were a person she'd met once whom she expected to see walking through the door again any minute. When I'd ask her to get specific, though, she'd stop talking.

"Ignorance is the enemy of what kind of change, Nana?" I asked that day.

She opened her mouth as if she were going to answer, but instead she opened up the Primer and pointed to a word. "Start here today."

If anyone else on the planet had approached me about reading, I would've told them to suck pavement, but this was Nana. If she'd asked me to, I would've taken up a sword and faced Satan himself.

I'M STILL ON MY BIKE, WISHING THE WOMEN pedaling in front of me would move about a hundred times faster, when I hear the deep chime of the Bell sounding from every direction. Not now!

The Bell means everyone has to stop whatever they're doing and pray. It'll delay me at least twenty minutes. I contemplate not stopping. *I'll just keep pedaling as if I didn't hear.* But then I could be stopped by a Teacher, or a Twitcher, and they could discover the Primer. I have to stop.

The Bell continues to sound, a clanging that blares down the sidewalks, reverberates up the avenues, and bounces off the abandoned skyscrapers. I'm heading across 17th Street by now, but Union Square is the closest prayer center, so I turn around. The Bell used to come from speakers that were attached to the street lamps, but people always stole the batteries or the wiring, so now the speakers are built right into the helmets of the Twitchers. Three times a day, the Bell is projected straight from their heads. It must make them even more twitchy.

I arrive back at Union Square to see hundreds of people streaming out of the local businesses. Boys and men get out of stopped buses or taxis, and, like me, the girls and women walk up with their bikes. Despite the sweltering heat, the men prefer to profess their faith in the open air, so they gather all over the square.

I spot some male Convenes preparing to pray, which is unusual. The Convenes are a different sect from mine, the Deservers, and their members usually like to stick to their own prayer centers. Today they stand out here, with extra long beards, tatty clothes, and thick East Side accents. They make me nervous.

Mother says Convenes commit most of the crimes in the city, and that if it weren't for Uncle Ruho, they would've overrun us long ago. Father disagrees. He feels bad for them, not only because they're poor, but because so many of them are sick. A lot of Convene children have died, and the women can't seem to get pregnant anymore. My grandpa Silna thinks God is punishing them for questioning the leadership of Uncle Ruho. I don't really know what to think.

The men in the Square are giving the two Convenes a wide berth.

I walk my bike to the women's prayer center on the north edge of the Square. Men and women aren't allowed to pray together. The Prophet said that if a man watched a woman pray from behind, it might give him "impure thoughts." I wear the cloak and veil for the same reason. If a man were to see my bare arms and legs or my face, he could become so aroused that he wouldn't be able to function. Supposedly, if all women walked around uncovered, society would fall into complete disarray. Having seen myself naked, I can't say I really understand this fear.

I place my bike on a stand and walk into the prayer center. It's a red brick building, six stories high, that has big windows overlooking the Square where the men are praying. I guess there's no danger of *us* having impure thoughts while we watch *them*.

There's a very old, chiseled sign above the doorway of the center that says BARNES & NOBLE. It's my secret that I know that. There are old metal stairs inside that used to move when electricity was like sunlight and everyone could have it. Now, we clomp up the stairs, hoping that today isn't the day they decide to collapse from decay.

Uncle Ruho lives in a building even older than this one, called the Cloisters, at the northern tip of the island. Father says it looks like it's been there for a thousand years. I thought he meant it was falling apart, but he said no, it was beautiful, full of lush gardens, stained-glass windows, and wall-size tapestries—a castle meant for a king. When I was little, people, my mother and neighbors included, were always gossiping about who Uncle Ruho might marry, but now he's older than my father and the subject seems to have become taboo.

The Heralds live in the Cloisters, too. After being handpicked by Uncle Ruho from the top one percent of Students at the Lyceum, they take vows of celibacy. They're promised lifelong residency at the castle, and they're responsible for leading prayer services all over the city. Most importantly, they become part of Uncle Ruho's inner circle.

I'm not sure how Twitchers are picked. They go to the Lyceum, hoping to be Teachers or Heralds, but instead of becoming religious scholars, they end up patrolling the streets with handguns. Perhaps their instructors find them antisocial?

Twitchers come and go from the Cloisters, but Father says there's not enough space for them to live there, too. Sekena thinks they take off their helmets at the end of the day and head home, just like anyone else, and that maybe some of our neighbors are Twitchers. But I'm not sure. After a long day, I think a Twitcher without his uniform would still twitch a *little*.

In the Barnes & Noble, hundreds of empty shelves line the walls. Nana says this place used to be a bank, and that's where they piled up the money—which used to be drawings on bits of paper, which is weird. I don't understand how paper was useful to anyone, like BTUs. Maybe they burned it for fuel?

The wonderful thing was that women used to be able to come inside the Barnes & Noble and say, "Give us some money, please," without permission from their husbands, and the bank would give them as much as they wanted. Imagine.

What would I have done with all that money? The Primer is full of suggestions.

Do this: Go kayaking in Puerto Rico for a tour of PR's bioluminescent bay, full of plankton that sparkle a brilliant blue when disturbed—you can't swim here, but your paddles and boat will glow.

I loved this word, "bioluminescent," from the first moment I saw it. I like to say it to myself when I'm stuck at home, washing my brother's laundry. I often wonder, if I had enough money, could I maybe find this Puerto Rico?

I reach the second floor, which is covered in a huge, patterned rug that was probably very beautiful at one time but is now threadbare and smells like cheesy feet. But the room is spacious, the ceiling is high, and light streams through the massive windows. I wait my turn to wash my hands and face in one of the many pails. I must be pure before I pray. Removing my veil, I gratefully splash my face with the cool water and then go find my place on the rug between two girls my age.

Matrons comb the floor. They're checking us for infractions, just like the Twitchers, but because they're women they aren't allowed access to any computers—so, no Senscans. They have to use their eyes. They look for fingernails that are too long, cloaks that are too short, or hair that is not properly bound. Matrons wear chocolate-brown cloaks and carry little silver tubes capable of giving you a shock that'll make your tongue wobble.

My head is down when I hear the first *zap* of a tube, and a young woman cries out in pain. The Matron growls, "I can see the shape of your brassiere through your cloak! Are you trying to court Satan?!"

"No, Matron," the girl says, whimpering.

"Then you need heavier clothes," the Matron declares.

While the Matrons police the room, my hands begin to tremble, so I fold them in my lap. Nana and I have broken the rules by reading in her apartment, but I've never broken the law in public. Once, I accidentally wore my hair too loose—my elastic band was old—and a Matron gave me a quick zap. I learned then that pain could reach into the marrow of your bones. If I'm caught with the Primer, the shock of a Matron's tube will only be the beginning. I try to fill my mind with images of a sparkling blue sea full of glimmering plankton.

I hear the Herald outside start to lead the men in prayer. This is our signal to begin. The Matrons must stop patrolling to pray, so I'm relieved, for now. Standing, I take the hands of the girls next to me, and we create a large ring. Together we pray.

"Lord, forgive me. Lord, make me strong. Lord, keep me safe. Lord, allow me into Paradise to be near you." We repeat this over and over, these words I've been saying three times a day since I could speak. They're automatic, and, as I repeat them, a calming energy fills my body. *It's going to be fine. I'm not going to get caught. I am safe.* Breathe in. Breathe out. *Nana is safe. She's in the Lord's care.* My heart slows down, and, for the first time since I left my apartment, I stop sweating.

Before I know it, we're finished, and we give thanks to the Prophet for Her wisdom and for bringing us the Wall. I smile at the girl next to me, releasing her hand. She smiles back, eyes twinkling. We're both filled with God's love.

The Heralds say, "When God looks down upon the Earth, He is warmed by the faith that radiates out of Manhattan"—because we all pray together, in the same way, at the same time, all ninety thousand of us.

Life here can be difficult, but it's nothing compared with life outside the island. Outside, there are nothing but Apostates who crave violence and want to destroy us. I must remember to be more grateful.

After we've snapped our veils back into place, the other women and I start to pour out of the prayer center, eager to escape the eyes of the Matrons. Before I can reach the exit, I hear a commotion, and suddenly everyone is shoving forward to find out what's going on. As I emerge outside, I see a pale man with a belly standing on a trash can, and he's yelling and pointing to someone exiting our building.

"That woman is Satan's whore! She's nothing but a mongrel slut, and I demand justice!"

All the women look around, wondering which woman

has dared to dishonor her husband. The man spits, hollering, "Delia Solomon is an adulteress!"

The women standing where the man points scatter like flies avoiding a swatter. A tiny woman in a black cloak is left behind. Her dark hair shows a few streaks of gray. "No, treasured husband, never. I've never betrayed you, n-n-n-never invited Satan into our bed." Her voice trembles, and her small hands clutch at her cloak in dismay, and I believe what she says. I look around, waiting for someone to speak on her behalf.

Bellowing more loudly, making sure all the other men can hear him, the man says, "My brother saw her! He followed her to the market and saw her share looks and insinuations with another man, some sort of sex slave she has hypnotized with her sin!"

A crowd of men has now gathered around the shouting man, and they all have the same hard, hateful expression. Then I hear someone say, "You must have two witnesses to the sin!"

And the accuser says, "My brother is the first, and I am the second. I saw her strumpet herself at the bewitched man! She is a Saitch!"

Everyone gasps in horror, and many women shake their heads in disbelief. A Saitch is the worst possible thing you can call a woman, because it can describe someone possessed by the Devil but can also refer to a woman's private parts. I've never heard it said in public before.

The men are now whipped into a frenzy, and a beefy one not far from me yells, "A Saitch must be put down! The Book says she must be stoned!"

"Yes! Yes, we must stone her!" another shouts.

"Destroy temptation wherever it festers!"

"Let not rise a lewd woman!"

"The woman who sins against her husband sins against her people!"

Wait! What about a trial? The Book also speaks of trials! I look around and spot a Twitcher watching from the edge of the Square. Why isn't he intervening?

Opening my mouth, I imagine speaking on Delia's behalf. Then I picture these men discovering the Primer, and I know I could be stoned right next to her.

The words stick in my throat.

The first rock is thrown, and I see it hit poor Delia in the arm.

She turns to run away, but the beefy man shoves her back toward her husband, tearing away her veil in the process. Her brown eyes are so large with fright, she looks like an owl, her head turning left and then right, searching for a sympathetic face. She falls to her knees, clasping her hands in prayer. "Please, darling, please. I did nothing. God sees I am loyal."

I hope that the sight of her face will bring mercy, make it harder for these men to think of her as an anonymous creature of no worth. But a second rock comes from somewhere behind me and narrowly misses Delia's neck. She begins to cry.

A rock hits Delia's forehead with a dull thud, and I see blood pouring down from the wound. With horror, I think of the first crack of an egg. The women around me scream, jostling and pushing to leave as quickly as they can.

We have to help her. That could be me. I would be terrified, praying so hard that just *one* person would speak up for me.

Temporarily forgetting about the Primer, I grab the wrist of a woman next to me, who is trying to flee. "Wait!" I say, pleading, but she wrenches herself away with surprising force.

"I can't," she says, remorse in her voice.

Shrieking and crying build around me as the women try to leave, each of them determined not to see Delia's fate. Hundreds of men, even boys, are trying to get closer to the disgraced woman, to join in on the punishment, so we are squeezed back.

I search the faces of the men moving forward, looking for a hint of sympathy. Spotting an old man with soft eyes, I push toward him. "Help her," I say, as loudly as I dare. "You must—"

Eyes narrowing into slits, he spits on the ground, thrusting a hand out to grab me.

Lunging out of reach, I trip backward over someone's foot and land on the pavement. The crowd keeps shoving and pushing above me. Someone steps on my hand, and I cry out in pain. *I'm going to be crushed to death.*

Two arms snatch me up from behind. I thrash and kick. Is it the old man? A Twitcher? The stranger carries me through the crowd, holding me out in front of him like a rag doll.

"Put me down!" I say. "What are you doing?" I scratch

at the bare hands under my armpits and hear my captor curse. I'm happy he knows I won't go easily, and his lack of gloves means he can't be a Twitcher.

He drags me away from the mob, across 17th Street and into an alley. My skin seems to shrink against the bone as I realize that the situation is much worse than being arrested.

I continue to writhe and kick, but the man is too big, too powerful, for me to break free. I'm ready to fight to the death. If I'm raped and I survive, my parents would rather force me to marry my assailant than admit that dishonor has been done to our name.

The stranger sets me down next to a garbage bin, and finally, I see my enemy.

I gasp. It's just a boy!

He wears a uniform—an olive jumpsuit with black boots and a gun on his hip. Not government, maybe private militia. He's tall and broad, like a man, but he can't be more than seventeen or eighteen.

He examines the back of his hand. "Ever think of having those nails trimmed? It's like I was trying to bathe a cat."

This is perhaps the last thing I expect him to say.

"You broke the skin!" He holds his fist forward to show me, and I flinch. He realizes I'm frightened of him, and I'm sorry I let him see my fear. He pulls back the fist. "I'm not going to hurt you."

I imagine how I must look to him—a heap of purple cloth on the ground, a square of fabric placed dully on top. If only he could see the fuming eyes boring holes into his head and the clenched fist longing for a knife to plunge into his leg.

He smiles. "Okay, I forgive you the scrapes. You were only protecting yourself. But I needed to get you away from that mob. Sorry I tripped you."

"That was you?" I say, surprised to hear my own voice.

"I know you were trying to help that woman. But a mob like that . . . they were only a few seconds from turning on you."

"Why didn't *you* do something?" I know I should be grateful to him, but I can only feel anger. "You're a man!"

"Maybe it seems that simple to you," he says, looking at the ground. "But there were probably two hundred other men there, all of them ready to kill or cripple anyone who disagreed with them. No matter how wrong a mob may be, it's still a mob." His words are certain, but his face betrays shame, even pain, at his decision to leave Delia behind.

"Why did you bring me to this alley?" I ask, wondering if I can outrun him.

"If anyone saw us talking," he says, pointing to the street, "we could be forced to marry, and although you seem nice . . ."

"You didn't *have* to talk to me," I say. "You could've rescued me and walked away."

Now he blushes a little. "Yeah, well, that's true. But you were struggling so much, I knew you thought I meant you harm, and if I didn't talk to you, I wouldn't have a chance to explain myself."

"You've risked a lot to prevent a misunderstanding that would've cost you nothing."

He looks at me intensely, like maybe if he concentrates deeply enough, he'll be able to see through my veil. "The truth is . . . I . . . what you did was very brave."

"But I . . . didn't do anything. None of us did!" I think again of the rock hitting Delia's head, the sound it made, and the blood pouring down her face. Thinking of the terror in her eyes, I burst into tears. "They k-k-killed h-h-her."

"No, please don't do that. I, uh, are you in pain? Are you hurt?"

I sob uncontrollably, shaking.

"Breathe. You just need to breathe."

I nod at him but can't stop, feeling as if no air is reaching my lungs.

Looking completely helpless, he checks to make sure no one is coming, and then he kneels down, putting his arms around me. "Shhh. It's okay. It'll be all right. Shhh," he says, patting my back over and over, like I'm a baby.

It's the first time any male besides my father or brother has ever touched me—a severe breach of law—but the thudding in my chest seems to slow down. I gulp for air. The shuddering stops little by little.

"Yeah, that's it. That's right," he whispers, his voice deep and soothing.

Finally, I seem to be able to breathe normally, so I lean back and he releases me. Hearing me sniffle, he searches his pocket and finds a handkerchief. I take it, lifting up my veil slightly so I can wipe my nose.

I catch him sneaking a look at my face, and his eyes widen.

Embarrassed, I return the handkerchief and rise to my feet. I can still feel the Primer scratching at the skin on my back. *Thank the Prophet.* I could have lost it back at the Square.

"Are you okay? Did they hurt you?" he asks.

Realizing that my right hand is throbbing, I look down to see that it's swollen and pink where a shoe crunched it. He steps toward me, reaching for it. "I've studied first aid, as part of my job. Let me see."

I slowly raise my hand, amazed at my boldness. What if one of my relatives were to see us?

He takes my hand gently, like it's made of freshly blown glass, and slowly turns it around, examining it, allowing me to really look at his face. He has a bit of stubble on his chin where he's trying, and failing, to grow a beard, but mostly his olive skin is smooth. His hair is light brown, and his eyebrows are a little bushy, but they only make his eyes more striking. Jade green, they seem to have a light shining behind them, like the water in the fountain at Lincoln Center. They lit it up once to celebrate Uncle Ruho's birthday, and I've never forgotten it. It was . . . *bioluminescent.*

He presses my hand. "Does this hurt?"

I shake my head, and he does it again in a different place, and then another, and then another, which makes me squeak with pain.

"Okay, it's not broken, which is lucky. But when you

get home, put ice on it, for the swelling, and maybe take some ibuprofen for the pain. Can your family afford it?" he asks with concern.

"Yes," I say. He doesn't let go of my hand.

Hearing a noise outside the alley, I panic. "I have to go."

"Yeah. I have to get back to my boss." Releasing my hand, he looks around in dismay. "I dropped the figs. *Nyek.*" Looking up at me, he adds, "Excuse my language."

"If you're going to keep rescuing girls from mobs," I say, smiling under my veil, "you should really work on your vocabulary."

He looks ashamed, but then a second passes and his mouth breaks into a wide grin. He laughs, his chest shaking, while no sound comes out of his mouth. "What's your name?"

I hesitate. It's really stupid to give a stranger my name. He could change his mind and report me to the Teachers for talking with him. He could force me into marriage for letting him touch my hand. But, somehow, looking into his eyes, I know that he won't. I can't explain why. "Mina."

"Mina," he repeats. "I'm Juda."

"Thank you, Juda. For helping me." I walk to the entry of the alleyway. Thoughts of Nana, the Primer, and Mother waiting angrily for me at home start to flood my mind, and I can't believe how long I've been away. I have to go! My legs are reluctant.

"Mina!" Juda says.

I turn.

"Meet me again."

I'm shocked, but I feel warm and dizzy. "How? We can't—"

"Meet me here tomorrow, at noon. Stand outside the alley, and I'll find you. We'll stroll in the market. No one will know we're talking. My friends do it all the time."

Feeling like a crazy person, and before I know what's happening, I say, "Okay." And then I run to find my bike.

THREE

Twenty-five minutes later, I let myself into our apartment. I've been gone for nearly two hours. I'm dead.

I expect to see Mother standing directly in front of me when I open the door, but the living room is empty. I rush to the stairs, thinking maybe I can make it to my room without seeing her, but I hear the kitchen door open.

"How DARE you leave this home without permission! You have SHAMED this ENTIRE family!"

I keep walking, but she grabs my ponytail, yanking me back, and it's like my hair is being torn out at the roots.

"Perhaps you're not even my daughter. You're more likely the daughter of some PROSTITUTE or other filth, if you're so willing to go wandering around the streets dishonoring your father and me!"

She jerks down on the ponytail, forcing me to my knees. I know it's useless, but I say, "I'm sorry."

"How could you do this to me? The day of your OFFERING? GUESTS are coming to this house! I've NEEDED you ALL day to cook and clean. You're the most SELFISH GIRL to ever walk the earth!"

"I wanted—"

"Do you know how important this day is? For your future? For OUR future?"

I don't answer.

"You went to see her, didn't you? When I expressly told you not to."

I knew my mother would assume I went to see Nana. "Yes," I say, wishing I'd been able to.

She tugs harder on my hair, and it feels like skin is being ripped off my skull.

Leaning down, she says quietly into my ear, "I told you I'd let you go tomorrow." Her whisper scares me more than the shrieking.

"I know."

"But you went anyway."

"Yes."

She sighs. "Then you're not going to visit her."

"Tomorrow?" I ask, my skin growing cold.

"Ever." She releases my hair, and my head seems to snap forward. Does she mean it? She can't just leave Nana lying alone in a hospital bed.

I turn to her, seeing her face for the first time since I entered the apartment. Her cheeks are scarlet; her hair is frizzy and coming out of its bun.

"But she doesn't have anyone else!" I say. "What will she—"

"You should have thought of that before you disobeyed me," she says. "God will send you to burn in hellfire, Mina. The Devil will boil you alive in his vat full of liars and blasphemers."

I disobeyed my mother in order to obey my grand-mother. Will God understand, or will he only see that I disrespected my parents and make me suffer for an eternity?

I did what Nana wanted—I got the Primer—but I can't believe the price. Would Nana really have wanted me to save it if she'd known it would mean I'd never see her again? Or if she'd thought it would keep me out of Paradise?

Mother smoothes her bun and says, "Go upstairs and shower right away. Wash your hair and use your nice shampoo. Then put on your good dress, the one that matches your eyes."

Desperate to get away from her, I sprint up the stairs as fast as I can, but not before she yells, "You haven't heard the last of this, Mina!"

I get inside my bedroom, shut the door, and wait for my thumping heart to return to normal.

My room is small and simple: a single bed with plain sheets, a closet for my few items of clothing, and a vanity table for my hairbrush and barrettes. I'm not allowed to have anything on the walls. There's just the medium-size window that allows me my little patch of sky.

Where will the Primer be safe? Mother gives me little privacy.

If I had tape, I could stick the Primer to the bottom of the table, but that might cause me to tear the pages later; plus, it would be hard to remove quickly. I could put it in the laundry hamper with my dirty clothes, but who knows when Mother might decide to do my wash, instead of leaving it to me? That leaves the bed or the closet.

Opening the closet, I scan the contents and my eyes land on a shoebox on the floor. Mother bought me a pair of red flats last year, but a new Ordinance was decreed that stated only Teachers could wear red, so the new shoes stayed in the box. I crouch down, pulling it out. The flats inside are surrounded by pink tissue paper.

Taking the shoes and tissue out of the box, I quickly pull the Primer out from inside the back of my cotton pants and curl it gently inside the shoebox. I'm covering it with the pink paper and the shoes, when a voice comes up behind me.

"'Scuse me. The lady . . . Mrs. Clark . . . told me to do yer nails?"

I nearly jump out of my skin. I turn my head to see a girl just a little older than I am standing in my room. I replace the lid on the shoebox and stand up.

"What?" I ask.

"Yer nails . . ." She points to her hands and makes a buffing motion. She's a Convene. I can tell from her accent. Mother probably hired her to help with the housework for the day. The girl's face is unremarkable, her skin dull, but I can see that under her cleaning clothes she has a strikingly curvy figure. She looks at me with eyes that are tired and weary, as if she's already seen too much of life.

"Yeah, uh, what's your name?" I ask.

She looks around the room, like she'll find the answer on my walls. After an awkward silence, she finally says, "Katla."

I remove my veil. "Hi, Katla. I'm Mina. Nice to meet you."

She continues to give me her tired stare, every word I say making her more exhausted. I hope she's not ill. I would be worried about myself, but so far, no Deservers have caught whatever it is that the Convenes have. Like Grandpa Silna, the Teachers assume they've angered God, but Father says it must be something genetic.

I remove my cloak and canvas shoes, so I'm in just my T-shirt and pants. "I need to shower and change," I say, "before you help me with my nails." I grab a towel and head for the bathroom down the hall, but Katla just stays in my room, staring at the wall, and I realize she's not going to leave. But there's no part of me that wants to leave her alone in my room with the Primer. What if she saw me hiding it?

"Why don't you go ask Mother which dress I should wear?" I suggest, even though I know perfectly well which one Mother meant. Katla nods without looking at me and meanders out of the room, in as much hurry as a worn-out turtle.

I go into the bathroom to turn on the flame on the hot-water tank. This is the biggest extravagance we have. The tank is fueled by some sort of gas, and Mother and Father argue about it often. Father says one tank of gas costs as much as two months' rent, but Mother says she doesn't care, she's *not* going to bathe in cold water "like an East Side peasant!"

I have to confess, there have been a few times when we've run out of gas, or I haven't had time to wait for the tank to heat up, and I've taken a cold shower. It was *awful*, especially when it was cold outside. I felt like I just couldn't get warm all day. Most Convenes, like Katla, have probably never had a hot shower in their whole life. I don't know how they do it.

While I wait for the water to get hot, I look in the mirror. My cheek is still flushed where Mother hit me this morning. The cold water I splash on my face makes it feel better.

Father says that Mother means well, that she acts the way she does because she has a lot of anxiety. Things have been better since Father got his promotion. He's now the deputy chief energy engineer for the city, and the day he told Mother about it, she fell to the ground and started praising God. She's so dramatic.

There were times in my childhood when she was really sweet. Like the time she traded our salt rations and got me a doll for my sixth birthday. Or the time she made a cake in the shape of a train for my brother.

Father says she was really beautiful, too. She used to have blonde hair like mine, and she has much better cheekbones than I do, and her eyes are deep-set and cerulean blue. Father says the first time he saw her without her veil, on their wedding night, she was so bright and pretty that she was like the sun, and so he became a sunflower, turning his face wherever she might go. It's hard to imagine them that way now, so in love. Father works most of the time, and when he's at home, he stays in his office all day.

I see a little green light flicker next to the tank, and I know my water is ready. Now I have just enough hot water to wash my hair and rub a soapy washrag everywhere else. Because Mother told me to, I'm going to use the special shampoo—it's in a tall green bottle, and there's a pretty woman on the front, but all the words have been blacked out, which means it's a Relic, something from Time Zero. It smells delicious, like crisp apples. Mother gave it to me for my thirteenth birthday, but I was told it was only for very special occasions.

Massaging the shampoo into my scalp, I'm aware of a dull pain in my right hand. I smile thinking of Juda holding it, examining every inch for damage. What if he knew my Offering was tonight? How could I have said yes to meeting him tomorrow? What was I thinking?

My smile disappears as I admit to myself that not only will I not be able to meet him tomorrow, I'll probably never see him again.

When I emerge, clean and steamed, Katla is waiting in the hallway with the dress. It's knee-length and royal blue, with what Mother calls a "sweetheart neckline." It has a little pink bow on the chest. It's really dumb. I hate it, and I can't believe I have to wear it now. But it will be covered with my cloak, so it could be worse.

It's worse. The dress doesn't fit me properly anymore. I guess I've grown since the winter. The hemline is hitting me an inch higher than it should, the shoulders are too tight, and, worst of all, the stupid sweetheart neckline is now way too small and my breasts are threatening to pop out. I can't breathe!

I show my mother, assuming that when she sees the

terrible fit, she'll tell me to change at once. Instead, she tells Katla to do my hair. After all the money that she and Father have spent on this day, I can't believe she's content to let me wear this ill-fitting dress. Maybe it's part of my punishment. At least she didn't notice my swollen hand.

Katla brushes out my hair, one hundred strokes, each yank harsher than the last, and twists it up into an elaborate bun with a dozen sections twirled into tiny curls, using what seem like a thousand pins to hold it in place. She then buffs and files my chewed, neglected nails, making my hands look long and feminine and less like those of a ten-year-old boy. Lastly, she uses some beige-colored powder I didn't even know Mother owned to cover the pink mark on my cheek. Frowning at the result of the powder, she pinches the other cheek.

"Ow!" I say.

"Better," Katla says, shrugging. "Now they match."

I'm about to leave the room, when I remember my manners and say thank you to her for all her hard work. It's not her fault I'm miserable.

I return to the bathroom to look in the mirror. I don't recognize the girl in blue staring back, with the pin curls and rosy cheeks. I look like that birthday doll Mother gave me. None of this is even for my suitors, who won't be able to see anything but the fancy hairdo once I'm in my cloak and veil. But their mothers or sisters might get a glimpse of me in the kitchen, where men aren't allowed, so Mother is leaving nothing to chance.

One time, Mother went to the market, visiting the

most upscale butcher, to purchase a pound of steak, which cost a fortune. Unwrapping the package at home, she discovered she'd been swindled into buying a pound of raccoon meat. Mother is going to a lot of trouble to make me look nice for my Offering, but I worry that if I *do* attract a husband, he'll get me home and discover he's ended up with a gussied-up raccoon.

FOUR

THE OFFERING IS MEANT TO BEGIN AT SIX.
When I walk downstairs at five thirty, I barely recognize
our apartment. Mother has set up a long buffet table in the
living room, covered with food and drinks. Fifteen candles
are set in large, ornate holders made of silver and amber and
are spread throughout the room, causing the light to flicker
off the walls. I grimace with guilt when I realize that,
among other things, Mother and Katla must have spent
hours today polishing the silver candleholders.

I can't remember the last time we had so much food in
the house. There are pastries and cakes, *cheese*, and even
what look like two or three kinds of meat. The smell of
warm bread, cinnamon, olives, grilled chicken, and ham,
mixed with the sandalwood candles, makes my head swim.

My father has arrived home, and he stands gaping at the
food. He must be thinking the same thing as I am: Where
did my mother get the money for all of this? My father
makes a good living, better than most, but almost everything she has set out is an extravagance. The pastries alone
must have used up our sugar ration for the year. And I can't
imagine where she found apples for the tart I see. Or how

she found the hard cheese. There are only a few cows left in the city.

My father acknowledges my arrival with a nod of his head.

He's shorter than my mother, but he's always seemed larger than life. He has a gray goatee, which he scratches when he's thinking, and his serious face can be very intimidating, unless you've seen him smack his lips over bread pudding or roar laughing at one of his own awful puns. His eyebrows are still black, and they keep close guard over his dark brown eyes. Everyone says I have his tall forehead, but luckily I didn't get his nose, which he likes to say looks like an old potato. He wears the black tunic and black cotton pants of a married man.

"Your mother has created quite a display," he says.

"Yes," I say. "The guests will be impressed."

"That's certainly your mother's intention."

Turning from the food to look at me, he takes in Katla's handiwork. "Lovely," he says. "You look just as your mother did when we got married."

"Thank you, Father," I reply, although I can't believe my mother would've ever worn an unbecoming dress.

His expression becomes grave. "You behaved very badly today."

I say nothing. There's no use denying it.

"I can't imagine what you were thinking, Mina. With every year, you seem to get more foolish."

I look at the floor, pained to know my father thinks I'm a fool. In many ways, I'd rather he knew I was a liar.

He's a scientist, and he's always shared a lot of his work and ideas with the family, especially at dinner. Not many daughters can say the same. He's never been around as much as I would have liked, but I'll always be grateful for his knowledge.

"I think maybe I was too indulgent with you," he says. "You've become willful. You won't be able to behave this way with your husband, Mina. You'll bring shame on the family—"

"Then don't make me get married," I say, jumping in, the answer more obvious than the simplest mathematical equation.

His eyes are gentle. "It's your time."

I think of the Primer up in my room, the pages full of possibilities that it would take me a lifetime to explore.

"Why can't *I* decide when it's time?" I ask.

He smiles, reaching for my hand. "Your mother was scared, too. She didn't feel ready. But she understood that it was all part of God's plan. And you'll feel that way, too. I promise."

If Mother hadn't been ready, if maybe her parents hadn't arranged her marriage to my father when she was my age, then perhaps she would be a nicer person now. I want to say this to my father, but I don't dare. I need an ally in other matters.

"Father," I say, in my most respectful tone, "Mother says I'm not allowed to go see Nana in the hospital. But Nana is your mother, and don't you think that she'll recover more quickly if she knows that a loved one is by her side?"

He smiles at me, raising an eyebrow, and I can see that

he is not fooled for one moment. "Your mother has punished you, and I do not disagree with her decision."

My body deflates.

"However," he says, "I would recommend you make a wonderful impression on a variety of eligible men this evening and then ask her again tomorrow. She might have a new attitude." He winks.

He's right, of course. Nothing would make my mother happier than if I managed to get several marriage offers tonight. I tell myself that I will try my hardest to actually win someone's heart.

I PUT ON MY CLOAK AND VEIL AS EARLY AS possible, not wanting anyone to glimpse my ridiculous dress. People turn up promptly at six o'clock, and Mother happily switches into hostess mode.

When she considers the room to be full enough, she signals to the Herald to begin. Brother Ozem, whom my parents have known for years, reads from the Book. Standing regally in his gold tunic, he recites a passage in honor of my Offering that I find really embarrassing, about how a daughter is as "delicate as a fresh egg," and how you must keep her inside to keep her "unbroken."

When Brother Ozem has finished, the guests immediately descend on the food. I watch with my mouth watering, knowing that my mother will be furious if I eat before the men. It occurs to me that I haven't eaten all day, and I'm suddenly starving. I'm so focused on the apple tart that I don't even notice that the front door has opened again and my older brother, Dekker, has arrived. But then my mother makes a sound like a yelping goat and leaps toward him. It has only been three weeks since she last saw him, but she does this every time she sees him, her only son.

"My Little Love!" she cries. She doesn't have to wait for him to speak first, since she's his mother.

"Peace, Mother. I've brought you a gift." Seemingly from nowhere, he produces an orange. He's always shared Mother's flair for the dramatic. Several guests gasp, and Mother coos like a dove.

"Oh-h-h-h-h. Dek-k-k-k-ker. An or-r-r-r-range! How extravagant! What an exceptional Student you must be to receive such favors!"

"One does not strive to be an outstanding Student, Mother, only to stand out in the eyes of God."

My mother sounds like she might faint from her son's devoutness. "I'm so proud of my Little Love." Dekker is nearly six foot two, and you'd think he would've grown tired of this nickname, but there's nothing about my mother's fawning attention that ever bothers Dekker.

She turns to the guests and announces, "This is my son Dekker, on leave from the Lyceum for the night. He's a top Student there. All the Teachers say so."

I roll my eyes, but thankfully my veil keeps anyone from noticing.

Mother brings Dekker over to where I'm hovering by the buffet. "Dekker," Mother says, "say hello to your sister on this auspicious occasion."

Snorting with laughter, he grabs a piece of ham with his grubby fingers. "Yeah, right. Okay. Congratulations, Mina. May you attract a real winner." He shoves the whole slab of meat into his mouth, chewing it with a grin on his face, as if he's said something witty.

Mother's expression is hidden under her veil, but I see her dig her nails into his arm.

"Ahhh," he says, flinching, the smirk finally disappearing.

"Not today, Dekker," Mother says quietly. "Too important."

"Where is Sekena?" I ask. My best friend is the only person I want to see right now, the only one I want to talk to.

"She wasn't invited," Mother says, in a tone suggesting I should already know this.

"What?" I say, wanting to flip over the entire buffet table in response.

"This is your night," she says. "You don't need any competition."

Dekker picks up a hunk of cheese obviously meant to be sliced into many pieces and gnaws on it. A few morsels spill onto his new tunic, which is the same light blue that all Students wear. Mouth full, he says, "That girl is hardly competition. She's like some sad little Chihuahua who fell into a bottle of bleach."

"How can you talk that way about Sekena?" I say, ready to plunge my own nails deep into his flesh. "You've known her since you were—"

"Mina," Mother says, her voice hissing in warning.

I stop talking. I can't afford to make her any angrier today.

"I think it's time for you to mingle with your guests," she says.

I nod and walk away, taking deep breaths under my veil. I remind myself that Dekker is under a lot of stress right now and doesn't mean what he says. He's not worth getting worked up over.

I survey the room to see who else has arrived.

Standing in the corner with a cup is Tonis Plander, a boy almost as rich as he is dumb, but not quite. He spills some juice on his sleeve and looks around to see if anyone has noticed. He then dips his head to suck the liquid off the fabric with his mouth, and that causes him to spill the rest of the juice down his pants.

I turn away, spotting an old friend of Dekker's, Xavier Pog, who isn't half-bad-looking. Unfortunately, he's only as tall as my shoulder and laughs like a choking donkey.

There are a few boys huddled in the corner whom I've never met, but they seem too young to be here as suitors. They're probably the younger brothers of some of the guests. They watch Katla, who's picking up after people. They whisper about her and giggle like gits, as Nana would say.

Mother talks into the ear of a man who lives in our building. Mr. Yun is an architect who must be at least forty. He's a widower who makes good money, so of course Mother invited him. He's looking at me in my cloak and veil like I'm a present and he hasn't decided whether he wants to unwrap me or not.

Feeling a little queasy, I head for the kitchen. Mother will be very annoyed that I've left the room, but I need some air.

Much to my despair, my mother's sisters have decided to hold court around the kitchen table. I spin on my heels, hoping to walk right back out, but it's too late. Their conversation has stopped, as if the taps have been shut on three spouting faucets.

"Mina!" Purga says. "Come here!"

I reluctantly approach my aunties. They like to gather in here, with a pile of food, where the men aren't allowed. They can shed their veils and speak their minds. I should have known better than to come in.

"Let's see your face!" Sersa says.

I reluctantly unsnap my veil.

The three of them "hmmm" and "ahhh."

"Skin is pretty good," says Kilya.

"She's too pale!" says Sersa.

"She's blonde. What do you expect?" asks Purga.

"Too bad about her father's forehead," adds Sersa.

"Yes, but those *eyes*!" counters Kilya.

"She's gotten so tall!" Purga says.

"The lips *are* nice," says Kilya, as if this is a point they've been arguing about. "She's a woman now!"

You'd think they hadn't seen me in years, as opposed to last week at Sunday service. But my aunties relish on-the-spot assessments.

"Has she started her menses?" Sersa asks.

"You came to the celebration!" Purga screeches. "It was

right here in this very apartment only last . . . last . . . How long ago was it, Mina?"

I feel myself flush. "Last summer," I mumble.

"Yes, yes, of course," says Purga. "Remember, Sersa? We taught Mina what it means to be a woman, and then Kilya ate so much that she made a burp we thought would blow a hole in the Wall."

All the aunties burst into laughter.

"Like I said, last summer. That's wonderful. That means when you get an offer, you can get married right away, dear," says Sersa.

"I'm in no hurry," I say.

Sersa sniffs. "Well, look who thinks she has all the time in the world! I can tell you, she doesn't get her arrogance from *our* side of the family."

Kilya leans over and whispers something in Sersa's ear. Sersa laughs.

Purga then says to me, "It's all right, dear. You're just nervous." She then says to the others, "Did you see that spread of food? Daughters are *so* expensive."

"What do you mean? We got a year's worth of batteries and lightbulbs when we married off Lille," says Kilya.

"Yes, but first you had to make her known to the best families," says Sersa. "It's all so exhausting. Praise be to God for my four sons."

"I'm so relieved," says my mother, who is suddenly standing in the doorway of the kitchen. "I was afraid a whole five minutes were going to pass without Sersa mentioning her *four* sons."

The other two aunties snicker, but Sersa glares at Mother and says, "Don't feel too bad, Marga. Dekker is better than *nothing*."

Mother is the oldest of her sisters, and although she was the first of them to get married, she was the last to have children. For many years she was made to feel ashamed for her inability to reproduce, and now the aunties love to talk about their already-married children in front of her.

Mother grabs a pitcher of water from the counter behind me. With her back to Sersa, she says, "Mina is going to make a match that is worth more than all of your sons put together."

The sniggering stops.

Mother continues. "Zai's boss is coming today, and he's bringing his son, Damon. Every Deserver in town knows he's the most eligible man in Manhattan. And who here has a daughter of marriageable age? Oh. I do." She turns and walks out of the room.

The aunties turn back and look at me, but I'm as surprised as they are.

"Mina, you've got your work cut out for you today, sweetie!" Purga says.

"Marga is dreaming," says Kilya, "if she thinks they're going to land Damon Asher."

"She's crazy," Sersa adds.

"It's going to take a lot more than Marga's fruitcake," says Kilya, shoving a piece in her mouth.

"Shhh. You're upsetting Mina," Purga says, noticing that I've started to tear up.

Sersa attempts a smile. "You're a good girl. No one thinks you're not up to the task."

"Even in a cloak and veil, you can make a big impression. It's all in the hands." Kilya holds out her hands and holds them up in different poses. "And the tilt of the head." Turning and tilting her head slightly, she freezes, looking like a confused squirrel.

Purga says, "I'm sure Damon will think you're fresh and adorable!"

I nod, smiling, as if they've given me wonderful advice. I can't tell them the truth: that I'm worried about Nana. I don't want to be left alone in the world, with no one to talk to but my aunties and my mother.

"I'd better get back to my guests," I say.

Purga says, "You'll get married to a powerful man and have lots of baby boys, God willing."

"God willing," they all repeat.

An awkward silence fills the air as they wait for me to respond appropriately, so I echo, "God willing." Then I put my veil back around my head and leave the kitchen.

FIVE

THIRTY MINUTES LATER, I STILL HAVEN'T TALKED to one potential suitor. Mother will be very annoyed, but all the candidates are lingering on the edges of the room, seeming even more anxious than I am. I'm not allowed to initiate conversations with men, so what can I do?

Mother is busy with Grandma and Grandpa Silna, her parents, and as much as I don't enjoy standing alone, I really don't feel like seeing them right now. Grandpa Silna is very stern and never has much to say beyond quoting the Book, and Grandma Silna says even less. She just stares at the ground, nodding at whatever her husband says. Come to think of it, it's pretty amazing that she produced my aunties, who never seem to stop talking.

I decide to get some food while I can. I grab some slices of cheese and bread and stand in a quiet corner, putting small pieces of each under the veil and into my mouth. I've always hated eating with the veil on. Thank goodness I don't have to wear it when it's just my family.

I've managed to eat a small amount, when Dekker comes sauntering up.

He's got a pastry in each hand. "I'd offer you one of

these, but I doubt you could fit them under the ol' 'shower curtain.'" He gestures at my veil.

"How's the Lyceum, Dekker?" I ask.

Looking at him, his smooth skin and blue eyes, his short little brown beard, I think he could be almost handsome, if he didn't look so put-out all the time.

"You heard Mother. I'm a top Student." He turns away from me, wiping his hands on his tunic.

He's lying, and I know it. And after all of these years of his being such a creep, I really shouldn't care. But it hurts my heart, because when we were little, Dekker and I were best friends. We did everything together, and he thought I was the funniest person on the planet. All I had to do to make him laugh was fall down. I was great at it. He would say, "Play dead," and, no matter what I was doing, I would freeze and fall over, and he would bust a gut laughing. All day long we talked and made up games, and neither of us could fall asleep if we weren't in the same room.

And then Dekker turned six and was sent to school. He cried and cried when my parents said I couldn't go with him, and I promised we would still play like always as soon as he got home.

But when he walked through the door after his first day, he had changed. He didn't want to play with me. He didn't even want to talk to me anymore. And he wouldn't tell me why. Finally, at dinner, he told Father to explain to me that his Teacher had educated him in the ways of the female, and that girls were worth half as much as boys, and that women were the cause of all evil on Earth.

And that was it. We were never really friends again. Dekker might get so bored at home that he would play with me for a while, but, soon enough, he would feel the need to remind me of my inferiority and we would end up in a fistfight. Mother always took Dekker's side. Little girls weren't supposed to get in fights. We were supposed to obey our older brothers in all things.

So now, even though he's in trouble, he'll never lower himself to talk to me about it.

Around two weeks ago, a letter came from the Lyceum. It was on the Teacher's official stationery, and Mother was very excited, but she can't read, so she had to wait for Father to get home to learn the contents. He opened the letter in his office and then refused to tell my Mother what it said. She was furious, but I could tell from his tone that the news was bad.

The good thing about no one's knowing that you can read is that no one bothers to hide anything—Dekker had *A Is for Apple* and *Animals of the World* textbooks in his room that I looked at as often as I could after Nana introduced me to the Primer.

The day after the letter from the Lyceum came, I waited for Father to leave for work and for Mother to be in the shower, and I ran into the office and found the letter still sitting on Father's desk. It was a warning that Dekker was on probation and in danger of being kicked out of the Lyceum.

The Lyceum is the only place for higher learning, and because it outgrew the building it was in, the Teachers decided to take over a massive old museum on the Upper East Side, on Fifth Avenue. It has these huge rooms and galleries they can use for group prayer. There are probably four thousand Students there, eating, sleeping, and praying every day.

Dekker started attending only six months ago. He was rejected four times. You have to recite the first six chapters of the Book by heart to get in. I heard him practice so much that I know them by heart, too. It would make him really angry when I corrected him sometimes. But I couldn't help it—it was all I'd heard, all day, every day, for two years!

So, one morning a few weeks ago, one of the Teachers sent Dekker to fetch some textbooks, and he got lost in the museum and ended up on a floor where he wasn't supposed to be. He discovered several rooms full of art that had been removed from the museum walls. It seems one painting in particular caught his eye—a nude woman brushing her hair.

The Teachers found him sitting in front of it *three hours later*.

I couldn't believe it. I mean, I'm sure Dekker had never seen a naked woman in his life. His jaw probably hit the ground and then bounced back up to the ceiling. But *three hours?*

Dekker is on probation for the rest of his time at the Lyceum. If he makes any more mistakes, even the tiniest infraction, he'll be expelled.

Becoming a Teacher is the only hope Dekker has of getting married and having a family. My parents can't afford a bride price. Teachers are supported financially by Uncle Ruho and the government, and they're considered a great catch for women, since being married to a religious scholar practically guarantees a slot in Paradise. If he flunks out, however, Dekker will be alone forever.

I reach out and put my hand on Dekker's back. I want to tell him that everything is going to be okay, like Juda did with me earlier today.

But he flinches and jerks away, as if my touch causes him pain. The Teacher's Taser canes rarely leave physical marks, but they say if you pass by the outside of the museum, you can hear the screams. What did the Teachers do to Dekker?

"No one gave you permission to touch me, Mina!" Dekker hisses.

"I'm sorry. I—"

"I'm glad it's finally time for Father to give you to another family."

Now it's my turn to flinch. "Why do you hate me so much?"

"Women aren't worth hating. Women aren't even worth thinking about."

"Really?" I snap. "Not even when they're *brushing their hair*?" And the second it's out of my mouth, I regret it.

Dekker's eyes bug out in surprise. "What did you . . . ?" Stepping in closer, he grabs my upper arm. He tries to see my eyes through the veil. "How do you know about that?"

My mind races for an explanation. Father would never have told me, and Dekker knows it. If Dekker discovers I can read, my parents will for sure never let me see Nana again.

"I overheard Mother and Father talking," I say, deciding it's my only option.

"Mother doesn't know," he says confidently.

"She's just pretending for the guests," I say. "Did you expect her to share it with everyone?" I keep my voice steady and confident. It's just like when I was seven and stole the colored pencil he'd gotten at school. I convinced him he'd lost it on the way home. It was either that or take a beating from Mother for stealing.

He keeps glaring at me, and I can feel a little bead of sweat running down my forehead. Then he looks away, and I know I've won.

He lets go of my arm. "What did she say when she found out?" His face becomes soft and nervous, a completely different Dekker than he was a second before.

Should I take pity on him? "She, uh, didn't believe it, actually. She told Father she thought it was some sort of misunderstanding and that you had, uh, probably been off praying during the time you were missing."

His face relaxes. Does he really believe that nonsense? Nana always says, "We believe what we need to believe."

"Don't worry," I say. "I'm sure she's not mad."

He snorts. "Of course not. I'm her Little Love."

I add, "Too bad the Teachers don't feel the same way about you."

His eyes flash with anger. "We had an interesting lesson in theology last week. The Book says that a husband is free to beat his wife not only when he *knows* she is being disobedient, but when he *suspects* she is being disobedient." He leans in close to my face. "I hope you marry a *suspicious* man."

I look deep into the eyes of my only brother and wonder how that little boy who loved to laugh turned so bitter. "The crazy thing," I say, "is that I still hope all the best for you."

He blows air out through his lips. "Which is why women will always be inferior to men. You know nothing about survival."

He walks away, and I let him. There's nothing left to say.

Father shuffles up next to me. "Mina, your mother is asking for you."

Brushing some crumbs off the front of my cloak, I let him lead me across the room. My mother hovers by two men who are drinking cups of tea.

"Mina!" Mother says, a little too loudly. "Come here and meet your father's boss, Mr. Asher."

I take a small step forward, and, although I keep my head down in a respectful way, I manage to get a good look at Mr. Asher. He's strikingly handsome for an older man, quite tall, with salt-and-pepper hair and big, broad shoulders —not like I pictured him at all. Father has complained about him ever since they started working on the water plant together. He doesn't think Mr. Asher has any idea what he's doing.

"Peace," Mr. Asher says in a low, warm voice.

"Peace," I repeat.

"And this is his son, Damon," Mother says, with a flutter of excitement that I find humiliating. "He brought you some lovely fresh figs. Wasn't that thoughtful?"

I turn toward Damon, head still down, waiting respectfully for him to speak. Glancing upward, I see he's probably twenty or so, attractive, but with a face covered in pockmarks, like someone who's picked at every pimple he ever had. He's managed to cover most of the bad skin with a short, neatly trimmed beard, and he wears a tunic covered in hand-stitched embroidery that must have cost a fortune. He's several inches shorter than his father. "Peace," he says, barely looking up from his cup of tea.

"Peace," I say.

Damon looks as if he'd rather be anywhere but here right now, like perhaps getting his beard plucked out one hair at a time.

Seeing him look around our apartment with a frown, Mother says apologetically, "You must be used to extremely sophisticated homes."

"Yes, I am," he says matter-of-factly, sipping his tea.

What a skeeze pig. My mother cleaned all day and probably used our meat ration for three months just to impress him, and he's acting as if he's drinking his tea in a stable.

"We're so sorry," I say, "to have disappointed you. Perhaps my next fifteenth birthday will be more to your liking."

Damon looks confused, while I see my father stifle a smile. My mother quickly changes the subject. "Mr. Asher, is your son also interested in building water plants?"

"Is there any other business worth being in?" Mr. Asher replies, with a charming grin.

"I agree," my father says. "Without clean water, the entire island faces certain extinction."

A long silence follows this grim pronouncement. Father looks at me guiltily, knowing that he's brought the conversation to a standstill. Grinning goofily, he adds, "An engineer told me a wonderful joke the other day."

Oh no.

"I don't think—" Mother tries to stop him, but it's too late. He's already begun.

"Parallel lines have so much in common," he says. "It's a shame they'll never meet!" He raises his eyebrows, waiting for the laughter, but Mr. Asher and Damon stare at him blankly.

Not wanting to abandon Father, I laugh, although I don't exactly get the joke. He looks at me apologetically, signaling with his eyes for me to say something.

I rack my brain to find a simple, ladylike topic. "Was it difficult to find figs this time of year?" I ask Damon.

He shrugs. "Not for me."

"Of course," I say, in a way that suggests I was being a silly girl.

My mother then asks Damon about his time at the Lyceum. Damon obviously belongs to the exclusive group of Students who study at the Lyceum because it offers a great education, not because they have any interest in becoming Teachers. They just want to graduate and start making gads of money at whatever their fathers do.

I try to concentrate on Damon's answer, or at least to take on the posture of someone who is listening. But he's droning on and on about himself and how well liked he was at the Lyceum. *I'm sure the Teachers adored your money*, I want to say. My mother is dreaming if she thinks Damon Asher would ever have anything to do with me in a million years. His father only brought him tonight to be respectful to my father, as a gesture.

If I'm honest, none of the other boys seem that interested, either. What's the worst thing that can happen if the evening ends and I have no offers? Mother will be angry, Father will be disappointed, and I'll be destined to live out my life in solitude and poverty. When Father dies, we'll be thrown out of our apartment, because Mother and I aren't allowed to inherit property. We'll be forced to rely on Dekker.

I need to go talk to some of the other suitors *now*.

"Mina. Damon asked you a question," Mother says.

"I'm sorry, what?" I say.

"Your mother says that your brother brought you, um, an orange today." Each word out of Damon's mouth seems to bore him more than the last. "I asked if you . . . like oranges."

I shrug, just as he shrugged at me earlier. "Sure."

Mother says, "Excuse us for one moment." She grabs my hand, pulling me away from Damon.

Murmuring angrily, but so quietly that none of the guests can hear, she says, "You may not take the future of this family seriously, but *I do*. You're not even paying attention to what he's *saying*." She plants me by the buffet table. "I want you to stand here until I tell you otherwise."

She goes back to the Ashers and takes her place by my father. Within seconds, she's laughing at something Damon has said that I guarantee is not the least bit funny.

"Sir, your driver wishes me to remind you that the car battery is only good for another thirty minutes," an oddly familiar voice says across the room.

I look up and, at first I think I'm hallucinating from all the craziness of the day, because standing there, in the middle of our living room, is Juda.

"What a shame," says Damon, feigning disappointment. "I guess we have to go."

"Oh no," says Mother. "Surely not. You just got here!"

"You heard my guard," says Damon, gesturing at Juda. "My car needs recharging. Let's go, Father."

What is he doing here? Is God punishing me because I lied to my parents? What if Juda says something? I can't even imagine what my punishment would be if it were known that I talked to this boy. But, even as I fear the repercussions, I feel giddy with the thrill of seeing him again.

I jerk my eyes back to the floor. There's no reason he should recognize me with my veil on. I stand there, still as a statue, trying to be as inconspicuous as possible. A second later, I cover my right hand with my left, afraid Juda might notice the slight swelling that lingers on my skin.

Noticing a warmth spreading through me, I assume it's because Juda is near. I'm embarrassed to think he has such an effect on me, and I try to ignore it, but then the warmth gets more and more intense, spreading up the back of my legs. Then it becomes a scorching heat. My cloak has caught fire!

The flames grow in a flash, shooting up my legs and onto my back. My skin feels like it's exploding. I scream as I feel myself start to burn.

My mother springs toward me, screeching, "Mina!" She pulls my cloak off over my head as quickly as she can and throws it on the floor, and Dekker douses it with a pitcher of water.

I frantically search my dress and hair for more flames, sure that the fire isn't finished with me. Grabbing me, Mother says, "It's okay, Mina! You're safe."

I stare up at her, still in shock. "What . . . what happened?" My cloak now lies in a heap on the floor, hissing and steaming, as if it's angry it couldn't consume me.

Dekker looks at me. "I was reaching for my tea, and I knocked a candle off the table. Sorry," he says, using the same sheepish expression as he did when he forgot to feed our goldfish and it died.

Mother asks, "Are you hurt?"

I turn around to show her my back, which feels like it's still on fire, burning through to the bone.

But Mother clucks her tongue and says, "Nothing serious. God is kind."

I'm about to disagree with her, when I realize that when she pulled off my cloak, my veil went with it. I'm standing among our guests, completely exposed, wearing the blue dress that's a size too small. I feel naked, and I'm humiliated. I feel crippling shame that these men and boys have seen under my veil, until I realize that all of our visitors have averted their eyes, out of propriety.

All of them except for Juda and Damon.

Damon leers at me as if I'm in my underwear, staring at my legs and then slowly moving up to my hips, my waist, and my breasts, which I know are pouring out of the too-tight dress. He then looks me square in the face, saying, "Blue eyes. Very nice," which causes several of the other men to look.

Juda, on the other hand, has a look of pure shock on his face. He has recognized me now, and there's nothing I can do about it. I want to say something to him, anything. And for a moment, it looks like *he's* going to say something, and my heart stops, but then he comes to his senses, turning his eyes away like all the other guests.

"Mina, you should go to your room now," my mother says.

I want nothing more than to run upstairs, but when I turn to take a step, I find my back is searing with pain.

Juda says, without looking at us, "Mrs. Clark, I've had some medical training. May I offer advice on how to handle a burn?"

Mother, having not noticed Juda before now, says, "We have it under control." Her tone suggests Juda is something she's found on the bottom of her shoe.

Despite my pain, I want to apologize for her—even if it's just with a look—but he's facing away.

Damon steps forward, finally averting his own eyes. "I hope the injury is nothing serious. It would be a crime to damage such beauty." He makes a little bow. "I hope to see you again, Miss Clark."

Mother, her voice radiating happiness, says, "Mina?"

"You honor me," I whisper, despising Mother for not seeing how much pain I'm in. "Good night."

"Good night," he replies. "Peace."

"Peace," I say, wondering how much longer I can keep the tears from coming.

"We'll pray for a quick recovery," Brother Ozem says, as he opens up the Book.

Mother grabs my elbow and rushes me up the stairs.

We reach my bedroom and open the door, and there is Katla, sitting on my bed, holding a bowl and a jar on her lap. Placing the containers on the floor, Katla rushes toward me. She and Mother take off my dress. Mother lifts the skirt section, and Katla holds the bodice as far away from me as possible, and then they pull the dress up over my head.

I cry out as the fabric peels off my back.

"Shhh. It's okay," Mother says. She throws the dress in the corner. "Lie on your stomach on the bed."

Wearing just my underwear, I do as she tells me. Katla sits down next to me.

Mother goes to the door, saying to her, "Soak her back in milk for fifteen minutes, and then apply the honey."

She leaves. Katla picks up the bowl from the floor and, using a cloth, starts to apply cold milk to my back in gentle dabs. It's agony at first, but soon the cold of the milk starts to soothe my skin.

Only when the pain becomes more bearable am I able

to see things clearly: Katla was sitting in my room. Waiting with milk and honey. Waiting for me to be burned.

SIX

I'M DREAMING ABOUT THE SEARING DAYS, during which we fast and pray. I've been fasting all day, and I'm so parched with thirst, I'm running through the streets, searching for water. I turn a corner and see thousands of men, and they are eating, but I can't see *what* they're eating, and suddenly I'm terrified. Then they all turn, seeing me at once. I'm not supposed to be here. I turn and run, but I can barely move my legs, and I feel hands upon my shoulders and then teeth on my back.

I jolt awake. The singed skin on my back tightens, and I groan.

A smell of honey fills the room, and the memory of last night comes rushing back. I bury my face in my pillow and breathe deeply, wishing I could make it all go away.

A tapping at my door makes me look up. I expect to see Mother, but instead, it's Sekena! My dark mood lifts a bit.

Sekena and I have known each other since we were little. Her family lives in the apartment next door, and Sekena and I have spent half our lives playing in the stairwells and hallways of our building.

She smiles, shedding her cloak and veil and throwing

them on the foot of the bed. She's wearing pink cotton pants, a pink top, and bright blue canvas shoes. Sekena doesn't pay much attention to the clothes Ordinances because she hardly goes out.

Standing over me, she inspects my back. "It looks good."

"How would you know?" I say, grumbling at her optimism.

"Mom said it would be bad if it was covered in blisters, and very bad if the blisters were open or oozing," she says.

"No blisters?" I ask.

"Nope! And you smell delicious."

"Ha-ha."

"Like the strata cake on Searing Days."

Yes. They're made with honey. My dream . . .

"Will it hurt if I join you?" she asks.

"No," I say, and I carefully scoot my body over to make room for her.

She lies down next to me—she's on her back; I'm on my stomach. I can't count the hours she and I have spent staring up at my ceiling, just talking and laughing.

Sekena has wispy strawberry-blonde hair, and she's crazy pale, with big green eyes and freckles, and she laughs a bit like a horse, and I love her with all my heart.

"Mom said I had to wait to come over until I was invited, but then I knew I'd be waiting until winter," she says, teasing. "And I couldn't wait that long to hear about him."

"Who?" I ask.

"Damon Asher, of course!"

I moan, putting my face in my pillow. Sekena ignores my theatrics, exclaiming, "Mina! You're finally going to be a woman!"

I love Sekena, but she's very devout, and her greatest dream is to marry a Teacher or an energy farmer and have lots of babies, all boys, God willing.

I almost snap at her but don't have the heart. When Sekena was tiny, she got floppy-baby syndrome because Mrs. Husk, her mother, never went outside, therefore never exposing herself or Sekena to sunlight. Her mother was too afraid of the Twitchers, of accidentally breaking the Ordinances, to leave her apartment. So her milk didn't have enough good stuff for Sekena. The doctors did what they could, and Sekena takes all sorts of vitamins all the time, and she sits in front of a sunlamp every day, but she has bowlegs and bad bones.

Her parents will throw her an Offering party, but chances are she won't have many suitors, so even being with someone as horrible as Damon seems like a dream to her. I tell myself to stop being so crabby.

"I'm sorry you missed my party," I say. "Mother didn't tell me you weren't invited until it had already started. I was so mad." I look in her eyes, the most sincere I've ever known.

"That's okay," she says, but I can see she was disappointed.

"Was your mom upset about it?"

She smiles and shakes her head.

"Liar," I say.

She giggles. "She was mad. But your mother came over this morning with leftover cakes and told us all about it, so Mom's completely forgiven her, of course."

We lie there in silence. How many more times will we get to hang out like this? All at once, it feels as if my childhood has gone by much too fast. I've spent so many bored hours in this apartment, staring out the window or up at the ceiling, longing for my life to begin, and now, what I wouldn't give for a few more years of that boredom.

After a while, Sekena says, "I can't believe you were exposed in front of all those men! So humiliating." When I don't say anything, she adds, "But I suppose . . . Damon Asher got to see something he liked!" She grins, raising an eyebrow.

I turn my head away from her and finally give voice to what's been haunting me since last night. "Mother did it on purpose."

"Did what?"

"Set my cloak on fire."

"But that doesn't make any sense—"

"She didn't do it herself. She had Dekker knock a candle onto me."

"Why would they do that?"

"She wanted the suitors to see me without my cloak."

Sekena shakes her head. "Your mother has done some rotten things, Mina, but that's crazy." She props herself up, considering it more. "She'd never commit such a horrible sin."

"When we got upstairs, there was a girl waiting for me with a salve all prepared."

Sekena's eyes get huge. In a nervous voice, she says, "Did your father know?"

The question kept me up half the night. "I don't know. I can't remember seeing him." In my mind, I see the faces of Damon, Juda, Dekker, and my mother, and that's it. Maybe Mother got him out of the room before it happened.

"What are you going to do?" Sekena asks.

"What can I do? It's over." As usual, my mother has gotten exactly what she wanted, and there's nothing I can do about it.

"You have to get married and get out of this apartment," Sekena says, as if she's a doctor prescribing the perfect remedy.

"Why does that have to be the only way to leave?" I ask, knowing that it's a useless question. "I wish I could live with Nana."

"Your mother told us about her. I'm really sorry."

"Thanks." Deeper depression sets in. "I'm not allowed to go see her. I made Mother angry yesterday."

Looking back at the ceiling, Sekena says, "Whatever you did, don't you think a burned back makes you even?"

I smile. "I like the way you think, Miss Husk."

She smiles back.

I wish I could tell Sekena about the Primer, explain why I got in so much trouble. When we were little, I told her everything, from what I had for breakfast to what I thought Paradise looked like. But as we grew older, I found it harder and harder to share my secrets. I could tell her about Mother and about the candle, because Sekena already thinks my mother is doomed to burn in the fiery pits of Hell. And she's probably right. But I can't tell Sekena things about me that would make her worry about my soul. I can't tell her that sometimes I wonder whether God really exists, or that sometimes I'm not *sure* that I want a family. I certainly can't tell her that Nana taught me to read. Not only would she be terrified for my soul, she would fear constantly for my physical safety. Sekena is the kind of person who stays up at night praying for people she doesn't even know who are imprisoned in the Tunnel.

I miss being able to tell her everything. I would love to be able to tell her about Juda and the market yesterday.

I gasp as I realize that I'm supposed to meet him today at noon.

"What is it?" Sekena asks.

"Nothing. My back stings."

I wonder if he'll even be there after everything that happened last night. I hate the idea of his standing there, waiting, thinking that I don't want to see him. But, at the same time, I realize that I hate the idea of his *not* showing up even more. . . .

"So, what does he look like? Is he short? Tall?" Sekena says.

"Who?" I ask, wondering if she's somehow reading my mind.

"Damon Asher, dummy."

Trying not to show my relief, I say, "Um, tall, I guess."

"And . . . ?"

"And male."

She pinches me and I laugh, but I can't sustain the jovial mood for long. I say somberly, "I don't want to marry him."

"Who wouldn't want to marry one of the richest men in town?"

I roll my eyes. She sounds just like our mothers. How can she not understand?

"Sekena . . ."

"Yes?"

"Don't you ever want *more*?"

"More what?"

"Never mind."

"Peace, Mina," says Dekker, walking into my room. "How's—" He stops in his tracks when he sees Sekena and immediately turns his body around, staring at the floor. "Forgive me. I didn't know you had female company."

Sekena jumps up, grabbing her cloak and veil. She looks mortified as she throws the cloak over her clothes and snaps the veil into place. "Forgive *me*, Dek—Brother Clark. I was just leaving."

"No! Don't go," I plead, annoyed that Dekker is chasing her away.

"I need to get home for breakfast anyway." She's about to slip out the doorway, when she turns to me and, in a stern tone, says, "Remember, Mina, you *already* have more."

Then she scoots past Dekker and is gone.

"How do you feel?" Dekker says.

"How do you think?" I say, icily.

He walks in and looks at my back, and I hate how exposed I am. "Don't touch me," I say.

"I'm not. Jeez." He leans in closer, grimacing. "It looks like raw chicken."

"Can you leave, please?" I ask.

"I'm about to go back to the Lyceum."

"Good."

He straightens up. "Before I left, I wanted to say . . ." He looks at the floor, and I wait for him to finish the sentence. Then he stares out the window, as if he's suddenly seen the most fascinating view.

"Maybe you wanted to say you're sorry? For setting me on fire?" My temper is short today.

"It was an accident," he says, defenses rising.

"Was it?" I say, glowering at him, daring him to tell me the truth.

Mother asked him to do it, and he obeyed her blindly, like he always does. But I'm enraged that he can't take responsibility for it now.

His fingers pick at a loose thread on the side of his tunic as he wavers between truth and pride. He takes a deep breath, beginning again. "I wanted to say that I didn't want—"

Mother walks into the room. "Time to change your dressing."

Dekker looks at her, relief on his face. Turning back to me, he says, "May God offer you a speedy recovery and an auspicious outcome for your Offering. Peace, Mina." Then he walks out the door.

"Did you say goodbye to your brother?" Mother asks, sitting on the edge of the bed. "He won't be home again for quite some time."

"I don't know how I'll survive," I say.

"Dekker's going to be a great and powerful man one day. You should show him respect," she says, moving right over my sarcasm.

I'm in no mood to argue with her about Dekker.

She begins to change the dressing on my back, which is just a square of plastic wrap that's been stuck over the honey. She's gentle as she pulls off the old one, but it stings as if she's peeling off skin. She wads the plastic up into a tight little ball, throws it into the trash can, and then begins to apply a fresh layer of honey to the burn. The smell makes me sick.

She tries to make small talk with me, but I'm not listening. She's midsentence, saying something about Auntie Kilya, when I interrupt her, asking, "Where did you get the money for the food?"

"What food?" she asks innocently, concentrating on my burn, but I know she knows exactly what I'm talking about.

"For the reception. And the Convene girl. How did you pay Katla?"

"That little thief. I'm missing two silver forks."

Katla cleaned all day, made me presentable, served food, took care of guests, and then nursed me into the night. I'm sure she didn't touch Mother's silverware, but I wish she'd stolen the whole drawerful. "Answer the question, Mother."

"I don't like your tone," she says, a warning in her voice. The Bell sounds from the street, temporarily muffling the rumble of the buses and taxis. Mother is skipping prayers to nurse me. After several minutes, she sighs, saying, "I've been putting rations aside."

"So, you were stealing from Father?"

She stops reapplying honey and smiles. "Hardly. I just started a little 'investment' fund." When I don't smile back, she adds, "Don't be self-righteous, Mina. My mother did it for me, and you'll do it for your children."

"Why didn't you just ask him for the rations?"

"Men can't see into the future like we can. Your father would only have seen the immediate cost of the cheese, whereas I can see that marrying Damon Asher would be like acquiring a dairy farm." She taps my nose with her finger, winking.

Suddenly all the anger I've been repressing rushes up like a bad breakfast. "Looking into the future? Is that what you were doing when you set me on fire?"

"It worked, didn't it?" she says, almost purring.

She's proud! She thinks she did a clever thing. I close my eyes and say, "I hate you." The words are out before I have time to think about them, but they feel more true at that moment than anything I've ever said.

I open my eyes, bracing myself for her slap. I'm lying there, back exposed, a layer of skin missing. She could hurt me in terrible ways right now.

She doesn't move. Still smiling, she leans over and picks up a pair of scissors from the floor. She stares at the long, sharp blades, seeming to study her reflection in them. Then she picks up a long roll of plastic on a tube, pulling out a few feet and cutting off a square. She puts down the scissors, and I understand that she has made a new dressing for my back.

She speaks in a low, calm voice as she applies it. "I hated my mother, too, you know. It wasn't until I had my own children that I finally understood what she sacrificed for us. It's okay for you to hate me now, because I'm keeping you safe. With Damon Asher, you won't starve; you won't be raped on the street and forced to marry a stranger; you won't be forced to sell your body. The Ashers are powerful, and they will protect you. And that's all that matters to me." She stands to go.

"All that matters to you is the money, so you can brag to Auntie Sersa."

"Careful, Mina. I've put up with your insolence today because you're in pain. Don't push me."

"What if it had burned my face? Then no one would want me."

Her voice rises. "Then you could join the beggars in the market! Is that what you would prefer?"

"I want to be alone," I say. This conversation has not gone as I planned. Now she's angry and will never agree to let me see Nana.

She goes to the door. "I'll be back in a few hours to check on you, but it looks good. I don't think there's going to be a scar."

We stare at each other. I look at her face, which seems a little sad and yet irritatingly confident.

"I don't agree," I say.

SEVEN

THE NEXT DAY, MY BACK FEELS GOOD ENOUGH for me to stand up and walk around, but I hole up in my room anyway. Annoyingly, when Father gets home from work, I'm expected to come down for dinner.

I sit with my parents, chewing but not tasting the food, wondering how quickly I can return to my room.

Father, chin raised, announces, "I have news."

"The Ashers. They made an offer!" Mother says.

"That is not my news," he says, beaming in a way I rarely see.

"A raise?" she says, trying to be coy, but I can hear the longing.

"No." Seeing that she's out of guesses, he says in an academic tone, "I'm being presented with an award."

"That's wonderful!" I say, happy for the first time in days. "Congratulations!"

Father spent over a decade designing a water plant that's powered by algae. The most amazing part is that the algae live off old sewage water, so not only is the dirty water recycled, but the waste itself also powers the plant.

Mother never wants to acknowledge this, especially at

mealtime. I've heard her tell my aunties that Father is working on "very important fuel development for Uncle Ruho," and I always wish I could add, *Yes, Auntie Sersa, the fuel comes from algae, and the algae feed on our turds!* I can't even imagine the smack I'd get for that.

"What kind of award?" I ask.

"Significant Contribution to the Community," Father says.

"I'm happy for you, Father," I say.

"Mina, do you know what they say when I walk around the East Side?"

Bracing myself for a joke, I say, "No. What?"

"They say, Mr. Clark, *water great guy!*"

I roll my eyes but laugh anyway.

Not laughing, Mother says, "Who's giving you this award, dear?"

"Jordan Loudz."

Dropping her fork with a *clang* on her plate, Mother says, "That's inappropriate."

"I don't see why," Father says.

"What will people say if you start associating with Convenes?"

Jordan Loudz would be the leader of the Convenes, if they were allowed to have a leader. I guess I'd call him . . . their spokesperson. Father's water plant was built on East 14th and services the whole Lower East Side. The Convenes no longer have to haul horse carts full of filtered water from the West Side. Women don't have to carry huge, heavy buckets on their heads back to their homes. Taps carry a constant flow, as they do in our home (as Deservers, we get our water from the Inwood Hill Holy Spring, at the northernmost tip of the island). I'm not surprised the Convenes want to give Father an award. Convene women have stopped him in the streets to give him gifts of fruit and bread as a show of gratitude.

"Convenes are good enough to serve our food and wash our dishes," he says to Mother, "but not to speak to. Is that it?"

"They're rising up, Zai. You can't believe what I hear. They call us 'cockroaches' and 'a virus.' Disgusting things."

"If everyone's going to act like you, then we deserve it."

I'm shocked to hear Father speak to her this way. He's the head of our household because he's the man, but he doesn't cross Mother often. She stares at him, open-mouthed. Standing, she says, "If I'm so abhorrent, then perhaps I should eat in the kitchen."

"Don't be ridiculous," he says, exhausted by the conversation.

Pouting, she grabs her plate and leaves the table.

"I have other news," he says.

She doesn't stop, determined to make him work for her forgiveness.

Wiggling his eyebrows at me, he announces grandly, "Mina has had two marriage offers. One from the Planders and one"—he pauses dramatically—"from the Ashers."

"*Ooooohhhhhhhhhooooohh!*" Mother squeals, spinning around so quickly that her fork and knife fly off the plate. I stop eating, my spirits plunging.

He adds, "I've turned them both down, of course."

I wish I could take this as a sign of hope, but it's customary for a girl's parents to say no to a marriage offer at least twice, to prove that their daughter is of great value.

"Oh, Zai, what was the Ashers' offer?" Mother asks, prancing back to the table.

"Four hundred thousand BTUs, variable sources."

Mother frowns. "I thought it would be better."

"It's a first offer. The second one will be better, and the third better still. Don't fret."

"And what did you say to Mr. Plander?" Mother asks.

"I haven't turned him down, yet," Father says. "We'll get a better price if there's a bidding war."

"Of course we will," Mother says, her face glowing with pride. "What wonderful news! God is kind."

"God is kind," Father echoes.

"But I don't want to marry Damon," I say, and Mother's head whips toward me.

"We've already discussed this," she warns.

"What's the problem?" Father asks.

"The problem?" I say. "You met him. He's rude and spoiled." I know Mother won't listen, that she can't see what I see. Surely my father can understand. "You know I'm right."

Father sits back, making a triangle with his index fingers and thumbs and placing it on his belly.

Mother jumps in. "Zai, ignore her. Is Damon an Apostate? A murderer? A thief?"

"For all you know, he could be," I say. "You don't know anything about him."

Screeching so that every apartment on our floor must

hear, she says, "He's from one of the best families on the island! You can't make one claim of substance against him!"

Father asks earnestly, "Do you think we'd give you to just anybody?"

"After meeting Damon Asher, yes. Yes, I think you would," I say, leaning back and crossing my arms in front of me.

Mother slams her fist on the table. "Mina Clark!" she yells, but Father holds a hand up to her.

"Mina," he says calmly, "you've always been strong-willed, but I can't have you speaking to your mother this way." I open my mouth to speak again but then think better of it. His face is very serious, and I see none of the humor or light that I'm used to. "Damon may not be your first choice for a husband . . ." He sees my dark face and adds, "Or even your second, but it's common to be anxious about your parents' choice for you. It's part of growing up. You're not old enough to understand everything that goes into our decision. But you *are* old enough to understand that Damon's father is my superior, and to refuse this offer of marriage would be a terrible insult. Do I need to explain to you what would happen to this family if I were to lose my job?"

I shake my head and then watch as my mother's face goes white as chalk. She thought by marrying me into the Asher family she would secure my father's job for life. It never occurred to her that she could endanger it.

"Good," he says. "Now, can we please continue with dinner?"

I get up from my seat. I pick Mother's silverware up off

the floor. I walk to the kitchen to get her more. The room spins around me as I realize that this is actually happening; there's no way out of it. I'm going to have to spend my life as Mrs. Damon Asher.

I SPEND SATURDAY IN BED, SULLEN AND ILL-tempered. Because of my back, my parents leave me alone. But the next morning, I'm forced to get dressed and go to Sunday service.

We walk to the prayer center at Lincoln Center, Father's favorite. Saying goodbye, Father leaves to worship with the men outside, near the fountain, while Mother rushes me to our building. I know why she's in such a hurry—she wants time before prayers to tell everyone that I'm under contract. I drag my feet, dreading the attention the news will bring.

We enter the women's center, which juts out over the street like a pointy elbow. The outside is all angles and glass, but once you're inside, it's all warm, curvy wood, like being at the center of an almond. There are hundreds and hundreds of seats and a stage with a speaker, which pipes in the prayers of the Herald outside. We remove our veils here, so Heralds aren't allowed inside.

To my surprise, after we wash our hands and faces, Mother leads us to two seats at the back of the room. I expected her to search out her friends immediately, but she sits down, pulls out her prayer beads, and clasps her hands together piously.

I'm relieved, until I see Auntie Sersa marching our way. Auntie Purga and Auntie Kilya are right behind her.

"Mina!" Purga says. "Thank the Prophet you're okay!" Reaching me, she throws her arms around me, causing me to flinch. She and the other sisters were still in the kitchen when my "accident" occurred, but I'm sure their husbands told them everything.

"We've been worried sick," Kilya says.

Mother doesn't acknowledge their arrival, continuing to look down.

Touching my hand, Sersa says, "How *horrible* for you, dear. Revealed in such a *humiliating* way." As she says this, she looks not at me but at Mother. She's obviously delighted at my mother's social debacle.

"We've prayed that the Offering wasn't a total failure," says Kilya. "Perhaps some of the suitors left before the unspeakable incident occurred?"

I wait for Mother to speak, to tell them smugly of the offer from the Ashers. But she says nothing.

Kilya says, "Don't be sad. The Prophet has a plan for each of us."

Mother says softly, "I am thanking God and the Prophet for sparing Mina from the flames, and you are interrupting."

The aunties are taken aback, but they can't possibly be as astonished as I am.

I can't believe she's going to let them revel in her failure, in *my* failure. They'll tell everyone at today's service how I was exposed in front of all those men. The Clark name will become a laughingstock. I open my mouth, ready to announce that I am under contract to Damon Asher, but Mother's hand reaches out, gripping my knee in warning.

Obviously disappointed that Mother won't engage, Sersa says, "Peace and health to your family." She then signals for the other two to follow her.

As soon as they're out of earshot, I say, "Why didn't you tell them?"

"Because I wanted to say a prayer for my beautiful daughter," Mother says, pushing a few stray hairs out of my face. I pull back from her, out of habit, and she stops.

She glances toward the aunties, and I follow her gaze. Sersa is whispering to a woman who lives on the second floor of our building. The woman whispers something to Sersa, whose eyes soon look like they might pop out of her head.

Sersa gapes at Mother and me.

Mother's head goes back down in prayer, but after a few seconds, I see a tiny smile pull at the edge of her lips.

She didn't tell her sisters about the Ashers because she knew that somebody else would. Her satisfaction would be greater if she got to watch the aunties hear it from other people, because then they couldn't be suspicious or accuse her of bragging. Mother probably spent all of yesterday telling everyone in our building about the contract. She knew word would spread quickly.

I should have known that Mother could never be humble. But can I condemn her for the sin of pride? I'd been thinking myself how good it would feel to tell the aunties about Damon. There's something about Sersa—she makes you feel like you have to prove yourself constantly. Having her as a sister can't be easy. Today, Mother was two steps ahead of everyone, and I imagine that was how she had to be throughout her entire childhood.

The Herald begins the service, and so we stand and join hands. Mother's prayer is extra fervent today.

AFTER THE SERVICE, FATHER IS PLEASANTLY surprised by Mother's giddy mood. She doesn't complain or criticize either of us the whole walk home. She's in such a good mood that I decide to ask her about visiting Nana. Her answer gives me hope: "When your back is fully healed, perhaps we can go see her." I would much rather go alone, and seeing my mother is hardly the thing Nana needs to make her feel better, but I'll take whatever I can get.

When we get home, I go straight to my room and remove my cloak and veil. I'm wondering if Sekena is home from Sunday service yet, when I hear a knock on our front door.

My mother answers, and I can tell from the trill in her voice that she's happy with the visitor. It must be someone more important than Sekena. Then I hear the voice of the guest and my heart stops.

It's Juda.

I tiptoe out of my room so I can stand at the top of the stairs, just out of sight. Juda greets Father.

"Good morning, Mr. Clark," Juda says. "I have a delivery from Mr. Asher."

"Of course," Father answers. "If you'll wait a moment, I'll have an answer for you."

It must be the second marriage proposal. It will be a higher offer, and my father will refuse a second time, as custom demands. I'm a leg of lamb, haggled over at the market.

Slowly peeking around the corner, I see Juda standing at attention, at the entrance to Father's office. My mother must have gone in with my father to see what the new offer is.

Juda's eyes suddenly flick up to meet mine. His body goes tense. This is the second time he's seen me without my cloak. But this time my mother hasn't made me into a tramp. This time I'm wearing a T-shirt and cotton pants and my hair is in its usual ponytail. This time it's actually me.

I smile, making a tiny waving motion with my hand, and then immediately feel idiotic. Maybe he's appalled at my immodesty.

But he smiles back, and I'm relieved. I'm thinking of what to do next, when my parents come out of the office. I dart back out of sight.

"You can give this to Mr. Asher with our blessing," says my father.

"Thank you, sir. Peace."

"Peace."

"Zai," says my mother.

"What?"

"Give the boy something for his trouble!"

"Oh, yes, of course."

"No, thank you, sir. I volunteered to be the go-between," says Juda.

"That was generous of you," my father says.

"I've been with the Asher family a long time. I have a personal interest in Damon's marriage to Miss Clark."

What does that mean? He wants it all to go smoothly? He wants to make sure the Ashers don't overpay? He wants to make sure I'm good enough for Damon?

I stomp back to my bedroom and slam the door, hoping Juda can hear. What a dirt-eater. Why did he smile back? Here I was, thinking he cared for me, and he was just looking after the interests of the family he works for. I should have known. *Nyek.*

I spend the rest of the day thinking about what he said, and it irritates me more and more. Why did he volunteer to come to our apartment? All he'd have to do would be to tell Damon that I spoke to him in the market and let him touch my hand, and that would be it. The marriage would be off. So is he just coming here to taunt me?

Determined to find out what's going on, I start to scheme. There's going to be a third proposal, and this is the one that my father is supposed to accept. Juda will most likely deliver it, so it will be my only chance to speak to him. But my parents will be in the apartment the whole time, so how can I get him alone?

MONDAY PASSES, AND THEN TUESDAY, AND I can't believe we haven't heard anything. Is there a chance there won't be a third proposal? Maybe the Ashers didn't like Father's second counteroffer, or maybe Juda decided to inform on me after all. I can't believe I want the contract to speed up. As soon as it's signed, it's only a matter of weeks before the wedding will occur. But I've become fixated on talking to Juda, and I've come up with a plan I think will work.

My mother is antsy, too, and she fills the time by teaching me recipes I already know, wanting me to master the dishes before I become a married woman. I try to pay attention, but I'm distracted. Mother notices, but she thinks it's about wedding-night nerves.

She says, "The first night is bad. But after that, if you make friends with Damon, it can get better. You must pray and think about the sons he'll give you."

I smile and nod, hoping she won't bring it up again.

I've already talked about all that with Nana. After I started my menses, all the aunties came over for the celebration and started to talk about what it meant to "be a woman." A few of them had married men twice their age, total strangers for whom they felt no attraction. They sat around and told horror stories of their wedding nights. Then they laughed and expected me to feel comforted!

I was terrified, and that afternoon, I ran crying to Nana. She held my head in her lap and stroked my hair and let me cry my eyes out. When I'd finished, she held my chin in her hand and said, "Listen to me. Never cry about this again. The man who becomes your husband will have power over your body, but he will never have power over your mind, unless you let him. Understand?"

I thought I did understand, until I met Juda. I feel so crazy today that I'm starting to feel like he *does* have power over my mind. So does that mean Nana would disapprove of him? I'm confused.

I want nothing more than to see her and discuss everything that's happened in the last week, but Mother insists that the burn on my back needs more time. My singed skin *does* still hurt and forces me to sleep on my stomach. A hot shower is torture. But I would never admit these things to Mother. She wants to keep me away from Nana, but I think she's also happy to keep me close, where I can't break any rules that might threaten my engagement.

Juda finally returns Wednesday morning.

Hearing the knock on the door, I race to my room, surprised by the early hour of his visit. He must be trying to catch Father before he leaves for work. I throw on a cloak and my veil, preparing myself, then creep into the hall, close enough to hear but not near enough to be spotted.

There's no noise, so I've missed the greetings. Mother and Father must be in the office. I very slowly peek around the corner, and, sure enough, Juda is standing outside the office door. He's looking straight at me, as if he were waiting for me to appear. He smiles but then makes a confused face, but it's lighthearted.

I guess it's because of the cloak. He's wondering why I have it on. I smile, but he can't tell because of my veil.

I lift my hand, daring another little wave. He moves his hand a tiny bit; mostly it's his fingers, but I can see he's waving back. Then I move back out of view. It's important my parents don't see me.

A minute passes, and then Mother comes out of the office, loud and excited. "This is tremendous! Such a wonderful day!"

I hear Father say, "Yes, yes. It's all worked out rather well."

Juda says, "So it's all moving forward, sir?" His voice sounds funny.

Too excited to let her husband answer first, Mother says, "Yes. Yes! It's all signed. Take it to Mr. Asher immediately! Don't delay!"

"Of course, ma'am. Congratulations." If Juda is shocked by Mother's lack of deference, he isn't letting on.

"Peace," Father says.

"Peace," Juda responds.

"Peace!" Mother says.

And then I hear the front door open and close.

I count to ten, which feels like a hundred, and then I walk down the stairs to the living room.

Mother says, "Mina, congratulations! Your father has signed the marriage contract!"

"This is a very big day for me," I say, trying not to overact my part. "I'd like to go discuss this life change with Sekena." I head for the front door.

Looking smug, Mother says, "I'm glad you finally came to your senses."

"The Husks will be quite excited," I add. I open the door.

"Wait!" Mother says, and I know I've failed. "Come here."

"Yes?" I ask, shutting the door and walking to her. All this waiting and planning, *for nothing*.

She inhales deeply, and I can see I'm about to get a

lecture. Was I so obvious? Or maybe something about Juda gave my feelings away?

"It's not appropriate," she says, "for you to go bragging to Sekena about your successful match. The poor girl won't do half as well as you, and you'll just make her feel bad."

"Of course, Mother."

"You can tell her you're under contract. Just be humble and grateful, and don't discuss BTUs. It's in poor taste."

"Yes, Mother."

She crosses the room and opens the door for me. I smile under my veil.

"Don't be long," she says.

I nod. *I can't believe it worked!*

The door closes behind me, and instead of turning left, toward Sekena's apartment, I turn right and run down the hall. For the first time in my life, I praise God for our useless elevator. I throw open the door to the stairs and look down into the stairwell. I yell, "Juda!" and then start running down.

Soon I hear, "Mina?" echoing back up toward me, and my heart leaps. He's still here!

I run four flights, wondering how far he might have gotten, and then I almost barrel into him on the third-floor landing.

He's standing there, shocked. "What are you doing? Are you crazy?"

As I catch my breath, I say, "I said I was going to the neighbors'. It's fine." I might be overstating things. "I've got a *few* minutes."

"You're insane!" he says, hissing in a low voice.

I pull my veil up over my head, because he's already seen my face plenty of times and I want a clear view of him. "What did you mean the other day when you said you had 'a personal interest in Damon's marriage'?" The question sounds angrier than I wanted.

"Isn't it obvious?" he says.

I cross my arms in front of me. "I guess you wanted to make sure he was getting a good deal on his bride."

Juda throws up his hands. He turns away from me, and I flinch when he slaps the wall next to him. "You've got to be the strangest girl I've ever met. If you're so sure that I'm on Damon's side, what are you doing here right now?"

I open my mouth to speak but realize I don't have an answer for him.

He keeps talking. "Did you go to the market that day when we were supposed to meet?"

"No, I couldn't. I—"

"Of course you couldn't! You were injured. But I still went!"

"You did?"

"Yes, because I'm an idiot. I knew it was a waste of time. I knew you wouldn't be there. But when I thought about the tiny chance that you might show up, and then me not being there . . . it didn't feel right. So I went. And then I stood there, lurking like a moron, for forty-five minutes."

Is it possible for a heart to rise up in joy and sink in disappointment at the same time? He was there. We could have had an afternoon together. "Thank you."

"For what?"

"For going." I smile, and he looks relieved.

His voice becomes gentler. "Are you okay? How's your back?"

"Much better."

"What a horrible accident. I wish I could've done something to prevent it."

I'm relieved he thinks it was an accident. What would he think of my family if he knew my own brother threw a candle on me? "Yes, it was horrible."

"Mina, I did volunteer to deliver the contract. But it wasn't to look after Damon." He looks chagrined. "I was trying to look after *you*."

"What? How?"

"I guess I thought . . . I don't know, maybe I could find a reason to invalidate the contract. Or I could find something wrong with you or your family that I could take back to Damon. God knows I would have thrown the contract down the gutter if I'd thought it would help."

"You could've said that we spoke in the market. That would've been enough."

"Yeah, that would save you from Damon, but it would ruin you, your family, your reputation . . ."

He's right. My name would be destroyed. I would be unmarriable.

His face conveys his misery. "Out of all the men you could marry . . ."

"It was my mother. She—"

"I know. It's just that Damon is . . ." He looks at me like I'm a dog about to be put down.

"What?"

"Don't trust him. Ever."

"He's going to be my husband, Juda. Forever is a long time."

He looks down and shakes his head. "It's not right. It's just not right."

"It just is." I've been so despondent about this marriage, completely convinced that it's the worst thing that could happen to me—but looking at Juda and at his big green eyes, I don't want to say anything that would bring him pain. I could never tell him how terrified or unhappy I am. What good would it do?

Besides, standing on this stairwell with him, at least for this tiny moment, I feel like everything might be okay.

"You need to go," he says.

"Yes," I say, and then neither of us moves.

"Someone could walk down the stairs any second," he says.

"Yes," I say. "Father will be leaving for work soon."

Again, neither of us moves.

He takes a step closer, reaching out and brushing my cheek with his index finger. His touch is light as a feather, but it sends a little current of electricity down my body. He whispers, "Mina, who has eyes like the ocean and the personality of a bull, turn yourself around and go back to your apartment." I stare at him a moment longer. "Go," he says, voice deepening.

I smile, and finally my feet start to move up the stairs. I murmur back to him, "Juda, who has eyes like the fountain at Lincoln Center and the manners of a wild boar."

"You're the one who never gives me a proper greeting," he says.

Still walking up, I say, "You're the one who carried me like a sack of potatoes."

"The bull and the boar," he calls after me. "I think they can be friends."

I start running up the stairs, smiling so wide it doesn't feel like my face can contain it. He was there. He went to the market and waited for forty-five minutes! I have to pull myself together before I knock on Sekena's door.

EIGHT

I PRACTICALLY FLOAT PAST MRS. HUSK TO FIND
Sekena sitting on the floor of her pink bedroom, eyes
closed, facing her sunlamp. She's wearing a pair of bright
orange pajamas covered in lemon-yellow daisies. The
sunlamp hums loudly, casting a tangerine glow on her face
that almost matches the pajamas. In our household, hot
water is our biggest luxury. For the Husks, Sekena's sunlamp keeps Mr. Husk working an extra job.

Removing my cloak and veil and tossing it in the
corner, I see Sekena open her eyes to give me a once-over.
She says, "You're in a very good mood today."

I'm *desperate* to tell her about the stairwell, sure if I
open my mouth, the only words that'll come out will be
"Juda, Juda, Juda."

But Sekena will blow it out of proportion. She might
even tell her mother, if she thinks Juda is some sort of
delinquent who could endanger my life. So, sticking to my
original plan, I say calmly, "I'm engaged. Father just signed
the contract." I grab a bunch of pillows from her bed and
join her on the floor.

Flipping off the sunlamp, she claps her hands in

excitement. "Ohhh! That's incredible news! I can't believe it happened so quickly. God is very kind." She looks at me, noticing my goofy grin. "You seem to feel very differently about Damon than the last time I saw you." Her smile suggests she knew I would come around. "When do you think the wedding will be? Next month, I suppose?" Her jaw drops open. "He's so wealthy, maybe his family will want *two* months to plan an elaborate event!"

The thrill of my brief moment with Juda fades as Sekena starts to talk about the wedding. I've been so busy waiting for Juda to deliver the last proposal that I've been in complete denial of the actual situation. I'm *engaged*. This marriage is going to happen.

Sekena is still talking, a dreamy look in her eyes, as if she can see a golden band being slipped on her own finger. "What kind of dress do you think you'll wear? I bet your mother saved hers, knowing her, don't you think?"

Mother has shown me the dress, which both she and Grandma Silna wore, many times since I was a girl. It's blue, of course, the color of the Prophet, with long sleeves and a wide neckline passing just below the collarbone. The heavy fabric reaches to the floor, and, besides a thick belt holding a fake sapphire, the design is quite plain. The dress, and all it represents, has always depressed me.

Glancing at me, Sekena cocks her head like a little sparrow. "What's wrong?"

I hug a pillow. "Do you ever think about a love match?"

Since marriages are arranged after an Offering, love matches are extremely rare. Besides fathers and brothers, we seldom interact with boys before we're fifteen. But I've heard of it—girls falling in love with a neighbor or maybe a distant cousin and then convincing their parents to let them get married.

Sekena doesn't even consider the matter. She just says, bluntly, "Love matches end in poverty and divorce."

"That's your mother talking."

"But it's true. Remember that woman who jumped off the building next door? My mother told me she was in a love marriage."

"No," I say, knowing that she means Mrs. Kasan. "Mr. Kasan beat her every day."

"Who told you that?"

"Father. Mother told me she did it because she was in a love marriage, just like your mother said, but he wanted me to know the truth."

"Why?"

"Mr. Kasan beat her for not giving him children. He said the problem was that she wasn't pious enough. Father wanted me to know that there are physical reasons why women can't have children, and that sometimes it's even the *man's* fault."

"Why did he want you to know that?" The shock in her voice suggests she thinks it was inappropriate for Father to tell me such a thing.

"Father is a scientist. He gets angry when people don't understand how things work."

But the truth is, I, too, sometimes wonder why he told me the story. If I can't bear children, Damon and the Ashers most certainly won't care about the scientific explanation. *I will be at fault.*

Sekena takes in the information about Mrs. Kasan. "I still don't think a love match could work. How would I know if Father approves? If your family selects for you, then you know you have their blessing, so you know you have Uncle Ruho's blessing, and then you know you have God's blessing. If you choose someone just because you *like* them, it's selfish. You're not thinking about Uncle Ruho or God."

Now I feel like a terrible person. Why can't she just be my best friend, for once, and not so perfectly proper? I ask, "If you could marry *anyone*, who do you think it would be?"

We used to ask each other this question all the time as children, before we understood how the Offerings worked. It's been years since either of us has brought it up. Why talk about something that can never happen? It's like discussing what I would wear if I walked on the moon.

Sekena bites the inside of her lip in an expression I recognize as deep thought. After a minute of silence, she says, "Hmmm . . . weeell . . . if I *have* to say someone—"

"You *have* to say."

"And this would be considering what we just said about family approval, of course . . ."

"Of course." I'm so glad she's taking the conversation seriously now.

"I guess it would be . . ." Her pale, freckled face turns a deep scarlet, and then, in a voice so soft I can barely hear, she says, "Dekker." And then she grabs one of the pillows and buries her face in it.

"DEKKER! Are you KIDDING?" I say, almost yelling.

"Shhh. My mother will hear."

"But Dekker is . . . is . . ." A million words enter my head: *Gross. Mean. Rude. Disgusting.* "Why *Dekker?*"

"You said I had to say someone. You didn't say I had to say *why.*"

"But Dekker smells."

She giggles, and then I start to giggle, too. What did I expect? Dekker is one of the only boys Sekena has ever met in her life who she's not related to. What would she think if I told her the story of him sitting in front of that nude painting? Is there a red deeper than scarlet? Because that would be the shade of her entire body.

"How about you?" she says.

"Hmmm?"

"Who would you marry if it could be anyone?"

Juda's face flashes in front of me. "I don't know."

"No fair! You have to answer."

I consider it and say, "It seems like the whole point of a love match is that it's someone you've met and know and have a connection with. And then you build on that and actually get to know each other, and by the time you get married you feel like the other person is a part of you."

"Where did you hear all that?" she asks.

"Uh, Nana and I talk about it sometimes," I say, worrying that I've said too much.

"Wow. That's weird."

"Yeah. Pretty weird."

"Have you ever met anyone like that? That you had a 'connection' with?"

I'm in dangerous territory now. "I . . . I think maybe I have."

Sekena bolts upright. "Praise be to God. You're talking about Damon! I knew there was a reason you were smiling when you walked in!"

"No, I—"

"It's okay, I won't tell! What happened? Did you see him again after your Offering?"

Sekena's expression is full of hope and excitement, so I say, "He's very handsome." Thinking of Damon's smug face, I want to punch Sekena's pillow.

"This is really exciting. Your parents have made a match for you *and* you think it might be a love match? It's a dream come true!"

"Yeah."

"So what's wrong?"

She knows me too well. I think about Juda again. "What if he doesn't like me as much as I like him?"

"What? Of course he will. You're a perfect woman— devout, beautiful, obedient."

I laugh, but it comes out as more of a snort.

"Well, you're devout and beautiful, and you're getting better at being obedient," she says with a happy shrug. "And once you're running your own household, I just know you're going to want to serve your husband as best you can."

I wish I could be so confident. Then I wonder if Juda is looking for an obedient wife. Probably. Aren't all men?

"Wow," she says. "There's going to be a lot to do before the wedding."

"Mm-hmm," I say, not really paying attention.

"You'll get to go to a bathhouse, which I hear is amazing. And your mother will probably pay for someone to style your hair, but, you know, you'll have to get rid of your hair everywhere else."

"*What?*" I'm listening to her now.

She nods emphatically. "Yep. I was at my cousin's wedding last year, and I was there when they got her ready. They used hot wax, which is not even the worst method. My cousin heard about some poor Convene girls who use chewing gum."

"Now I know you're lying!"

"I'm not," she insists. "Ask your mother!"

I think this is the last conversation on earth I want to have with my mother. She won't tell me the truth, and she'll make me feel like a degenerate for asking. "Please, Sekena, if it's true, promise me that you and your mother will help me before the wedding, and that you'll keep my mother as far away from me as possible." The idea of Mother wielding hot wax makes me shudder.

Sekena becomes dead serious, or as serious as someone can be in flowered orange pajamas. "I promise."

I lean over and hug her. "Thank you. You're a great friend." I may not be able to talk to Sekena about everything, but I don't know how I would survive without her.

We say, "Peace," and I let her get back to her sunlamp.

When I leave the Husk home, I look down the corridor and am surprised to see a strange man walking out of the front door of our apartment. He's short and wears a uniform. He's not a Teacher but looks like he belongs in a government building, like some of the people Father works with. He walks down the hall, pushing through the exit door with a grunt.

Thinking about why he was in our apartment makes me feel dizzy and anxious. Does he know about the Primer? About my reading? Did someone see Juda and me talking in the stairwell?

I want to turn and run back to Sekena's room, but I know that eventually I'll have to go home. Plus, I can't handle the not knowing. I open our door and walk inside the apartment, looking left and right for my mother, expecting her to pounce immediately. Instead, she's seated on the couch in the living room.

"Come sit down," she says, in a voice that sounds not angry but agitated.

I sit as far away from her on the couch as I can. She looks worried, so I'm guessing someone saw Juda and me talking and she thinks my marriage contract is in danger.

"I have news, dear."

Dear? Why is she calling me "dear"? The room seems to tilt.

"I'm afraid that . . . your nana has died."

My body goes rigid.

"The hospital just sent word. Nana is . . . gone."

"You're lying," I say, my mouth barely moving. "You're making this up to punish me."

I'm waiting for her to say that she knows about Juda and me, that she knows about the Primer, anything but this. . . .

"I'm . . . sorry." She leans forward, reaching out a hand, but I recoil, so she leans back, crossing her hands awkwardly in her lap.

Pressure builds inside me. Something in my core is fighting to make the news not true, and this something lurches inside my stomach, making me want to vomit, and then it moves to my head, pounding on the inside of my skull. It feels like a demon, but I think it's my soul, screaming in protest, trying to punch its way out of my body, and when it does, I'll be nothing but sludge and blood and guts on the floor, and that's fine. Because I don't want to live here on this planet anymore.

I didn't go to her.

I didn't see her.

She died alone.

And it's my fault.

Sound emerges from my throat, more animal than human. Tears flood my eyes, then run down my cheeks, and soon I lose control, my lungs trembling with each breath. My whole body starts to shudder. The sobs keep coming and coming, but I don't want to stop crying, ever, because as soon as I do, I have to face a world without Nana.

Looking toward the ceiling, Mother says, "She's in Paradise now, a garden of perpetual bliss, God willing."

"Leave m-m-me alone," I manage to say.

Mother stands, smoothing her hair. "Yes. You need space." She walks toward the kitchen, and just as she gets to the door, she says, "One million BTUs. In high-density liquids."

Wiping my nose on my sleeve, I look at her in confusion.

"That was the final bride price. You did very well. You should be proud."

As she walks into the kitchen, I pull off my shoe and sling it at the door. Why couldn't Mother have died instead?

I fall back onto the sofa, sobbing once more, knowing that without Nana I don't have the strength to face my future. A life with Damon? Being the mother of his children? Looking at his stupid face across the dinner table every night until I die? Nana would have understood my misery, would have comforted me and given me the support I needed to survive. And now I'm alone, abandoned, in a world that thinks I'm worth nothing more than "high-density liquids."

I'm not sure how long I stay there crying. It feels like days.

I don't remember walking up the stairs or through my door, but I find myself in bed. Once I'm lying down, my body gives over to exhaustion and I fall into a hard, dreamless sleep.

NINE

I WAKE UP THE NEXT DAY, BODY LIMP AND wrung out, as if I've been fighting an illness.

I can't bring myself to go down for prayers or breakfast. Mother eventually brings up a tray with some toast, but I leave it sitting by the door.

I miss lunch, too, staying in bed, staring out the window, listening to the traffic below. How does my father feel today? Is he as sad as I am? Is that possible? Nana was his mother. I wish he'd come talk to me.

I find myself remembering the weird things, the things that made me tease her.

She hated feet. She thought they were ugly and smelly, and she felt a little bit sick when she looked at them. She wouldn't visit a person if they made people take their shoes off at the door. I always had to keep my socks and shoes on when I went to her apartment.

She also hated raisins, in anything. If you gave her something, like a cookie, without warning her that there were raisins in it, she'd give you the silent treatment for at least ten minutes.

I smile, thinking of her grumpy moods. She liked to tell

me how important it was to be difficult. "Never let anyone think you're easy to please, Chickpea. It's just another way of saying you've got no opinion and no self-worth."

Remembering her voice makes me start crying again.

Nana would be disappointed in me for staying in bed all day. She wouldn't want me to fall apart. She would want me to pull myself together, to be dignified.

When I stand, finally, I feel a bit dizzy.

I'm not ready to go downstairs yet, but I've thought of one thing that might make me feel better.

I shut the bedroom door. I go to my closet, grab the shoebox, and get back in bed. I take off the lid and slide the Primer out from under the shoes, then situate myself under my blanket in such a way that I can look at the Primer but Mother won't be able to see it if she comes barging through the door.

I open the Primer, slowly turning the pages, realizing I've never looked at it without Nana. I wipe my eyes on the corner of my pillowcase.

Nana always loved the food section, where they talk about different restaurants and which ones are the best. She liked imagining the meals, and after we read a section, she would make me close my eyes and imagine them, too.

> We enjoyed an inspired take on *poutine*: fries topped with duck gravy, cheese curds, shredded duck confit, and crackly skin. A cod entrée offered a neat rectangle of flaky fish over verdant vegetables—fava beans, asparagus, green onion.

Nana's mother told her about ducks. Ducks used to live in the Park, but then I guess everyone decided they made nice gravy. And then no more ducks. It seems like the worst thing that can happen in life is for people to decide you're desirable. It's better to be invisible, for no one to know that you exist at all.

I flip numbly through more pages, past my favorite sections, the ones about books and movies and music—all once so common and limitless that people needed to be guided and instructed on what to select. What happened to it all: the stuff that people made, the information that people had? Is it up in the museum next to those paintings that Dekker found?

I turn another page, and my hand freezes.

Stuck between pages seventy-one and seventy-two, there's a leaf. It's about three inches long and an inch wide, and it's deep green. What's it doing *here*?

I take it from inside the crease and rub it between my fingers. I sniff it.

It's *fresh*.

Did Nana put it here? No one else knows about the Primer, so she must have, but how did she get it? She has a few herb plants in her kitchen, but I'm certain this leaf didn't come from any of those.

"She fell down the stairs." That's what Mother said the day Nana had her accident. Nana was going out, even though she wasn't supposed to leave her apartment. I stroke the leaf against my face. Where were you going, Nana? What was so important that you would climb down fourteen flights with your bad knee? Why didn't you ask me to do it for you?

"Mina, the Ashers have sent an invitation!"

I look up to see Mother opening the door. I quickly shove the Primer under the blanket.

With a big, satisfied grin on her face, Mother looks a lot like Auntie Sersa discussing one of her sons. "They want you to join them for dinner tonight!"

She can't be serious. "What about Nana?"

The grin remains, but her eyes go blank.

"What about the funeral, the arrangements?" I say. "I want to help—"

"Yes, well, we're waiting on the paperwork from the government. It could be weeks before we can bury her."

Weeks?

"The island is small. You can't just go burying everyone willy-nilly, wherever you like." She claps her hands. "You need to take a cold shower—hot will be bad for your back—and wash your hair. We need plenty of time for it to dry properly. We'll have your father take you over in a car. You can't arrive all sweaty." She looks at my face, which I hope conveys my total contempt for her plan. "Come *on!* Out of bed!" And, before I realize what's happening, she leans over, grabs my blanket, and whips it in the air.

"No—!" I cry, but it's too late. The Primer flies off the bed, fluttering down to the ground like a wounded pigeon.

Mother's expression changes from happiness to confusion.

"What is . . . ?" She bends over and picks it up, and for

a moment she looks like a small child trying to put a name to an object for the first time.

Then, when she realizes what she's holding, her eyes narrow, her head snaps back, and her entire body contorts with rage. "SHE PROMISED ME! THAT LYING SAITCH PROMISED ME!"

I sink into the corner of my bed. I've never heard her speak this way.

"My HOME! Apostate FILTH! IN MY HOME!" She starts to tear the pages out of the Primer.

"No!" I say, reaching for it.

"Don't you DARE!" she spits at me, as she continues to destroy the magazine, shredding the pages as quickly as she can. Tiny pieces of paper float down around her legs like confetti.

My father, who's just arrived home, comes running into the room. "What's happening? Is everyone all right?" He looks like he expected to see one of us on the floor.

"LOOK, Zai!" Mother holds up the remaining pages. "LOOK WHAT MY MOTHER DID! After everything that happened . . . she corrupted our daughter!"

"Keep your voice down, Marga. I could hear you from the hall!"

Mother surges toward me, and I cover my face for protection. "How long was she teaching you?" I don't say a word. "HOW LONG?"

"Six months," I lie.

"Who else knows?" she asks.

"No one," I say.

"Marga, stop this!" Father says, his voice pleading.

Pointing at me, she shouts at Father. "No wonder she's so DIFFICULT, so outspoken!" Then she points at him. "This is YOUR fault! I told you Mother was dangerous, but you wouldn't listen!"

Her eyes are crazed, like she's no longer in the room with Father and me. It's a look I've seen before, and, with horror, I realize that it's the same expression Delia Solomon's husband had before he demanded that a mob stone his wife to death.

"Our daughter is going to HELL!" Mother says, her finger still wagging in his face.

Father steps forward and grabs Mother's arms, pulling them down by her sides. His voice gets louder. "ENOUGH, Marga. Enough. The *neighbors* can hear you."

The mention of neighbors finally breaks through, and she stops speaking. Her breathing is shallow and fast, and I wonder if she's having some sort of attack.

Father continues, "Ura made a promise to us, and she broke her promise. Now she has to answer to God. That's it. It's over."

Mother's breathing slows down as Father pats her hand. He says, "Now go get something to clean up this mess."

Mother glances at the pile of torn paper, clucking her tongue, as if someone else were responsible for it, and then she walks out of the room.

Father looks at me and asks, "Are you all right?"

Still cowering in the corner, I don't say anything.

We stare at each other as I wait for him to explain what

just happened, all the things my mother said. But he only says, "I'm sorry about your nana." And then he leaves.

I look down to see that my hands are balled into fists, my nails cutting into the flesh of my palms. I release the fists and see that, in my right hand, I'm still holding the leaf. I've crushed it, but it's still whole. I shove it under my pillow just as Mother returns with a broom and dustpan.

She begins to sweep up the shredded paper, a fake little smile on her face. I pull my knees into my chest, afraid she'll decide to punish me further. But she just keeps sweeping, and the odd smile doesn't change.

"Mina, darling, you aren't going to say anything about this to anyone, are you?" Her voice seems to have gone up an octave.

I'm confused. Does she mean about the Primer? Of course I won't say anything. "No."

She pushes the scraps into the dustpan. "That's a good girl. Never speak of this again."

She picks up the dustpan and dumps the contents into my wastebasket, throwing away the remnants of the Primer as if it were fluff she had found under my bed.

At least Nana didn't have to see this.

She comes over to the bed, sitting down beside me. She touches my hair, but instead of yanking it, she strokes it.

"Your bride price was very good, but remember what your father said about his boss? If Mr. Asher feels that he's been swindled, he may decide that he doesn't want to employ your father anymore, and then where will our family be? We'll have to move to the East Side, with the Convenes, and beg for food on the streets."

As she pets me, I want nothing more than to slide out from her grasp, but I feel completely frozen, as if she's paralyzed me with her venom.

She continues, talking in her new, singsong voice, "The last thing we need now is for the Ashers to discover that Nana was educating you. So you'll go to their house and be a nice, *simple* girl. You'll talk about the weather, the food, and all the babies you want to have. And nothing more. Understand?"

I nod, detecting a desperation in her voice that I've never heard before.

"We're going to be just fine." She nods her head over and over and then walks out of the room, forgetting the broom and dustpan.

I SPEND THE REST OF THE DAY GETTING READY. Numbly, I go through the motions of washing my hair and putting on a dress, but I can't imagine that life is really going to continue, that anyone expects me to walk outside this apartment and speak to people in a normal manner.

First Nana. And now the Primer. Generations of women in my family have hidden and saved the Primer for almost a hundred years, and my mother destroyed it in a matter of seconds. Everything that meant anything to me has been taken away.

My mother disappeared into her room and left me to

get ready on my own, but just as Father and I are about to walk out the door, she emerges. She can't help herself. She has to inspect me before I present myself to the Ashers. She nods at my dress—long and gray, with a high neckline. Not that I plan on taking off my cloak tonight, but, after my Offering, I don't want to take any chances.

After looking me over from top to bottom, Mother holds me by the shoulders and says, "Listen to your new mother-in-law. Obey her in everything. Do not express an opinion. Do not ask questions. Be docile and pretty and pious. Do you understand?"

I nod.

She shakes me a little and adds, "I never want to hear about Nana again. You're not allowed to mention her in this house. Do you understand?"

I nod again, but it's hard to bite my tongue. Does she think she can just erase Nana, that if we don't talk about her I'll stop *thinking* about her?

Mother says, "You can still be a good girl, God willing."

"God willing," Father echoes.

They wait for me to say it, too, but I stay silent.

Father says it's time for us to go, but I think of something I want.

Pretending to need the bathroom, I race up to my room and thrust my hand under my pillow, grabbing the crumpled leaf and shoving it into the pocket of my dress.

Downstairs, Father hails a cab. I've never been in one. Women aren't allowed to ride in them alone, and Father has never deemed it necessary to use one before. The cab that stops for us is rusty and dented; if it were a can of baked beans, I would throw it away. But Father gestures for me to get inside. A sticker is plastered to the window: DON'T WASTE WATER. DON'T WASTE FOOD. GOD IS WATCHING.

Dekker would know what kind of car it is, but I have no idea. Dekker is fascinated by cars. For over a hundred years, everyone had one, and the fuel that ran them caused all sorts of wars, and I think they also have something to do with why we can't eat fish. Either way, their allure escapes me.

The cab driver, an Asian man who doesn't look at either of us, reaches for his radio as we slide into the backseat. I hear the name Jordan Loudz just as the station is switched over, so the driver must have been listening to illegal Convene radio. The regulation Teacher broadcast now drones through the speakers: *Women are our greatest assets. They are the vessels of the future. Protect your women.*

Father tells the driver an address, and when the man hits the accelerator, my body is pressed against the seat. I flinch as my tender back hits the leather. We're soon flying across Central Park South.

Knowing my time alone with Father is limited, I turn and ask him the question that's been tormenting me. "Why was Mother calling Nana *her* mother?"

My father doesn't answer. He stares out the window. Perhaps he's just going to ignore me, but I press on. "Grandma and Grandpa Silna—those are Mother's parents."

He turns and looks at me and, in the voice he uses

when explaining very simple scientific facts, says, "Nana was Grandpa Silna's first wife. *She* is Marga's mother."

I blink several times, trying to understand. "Then why would you say she was *your* mother?"

He sighs. "Because my parents are dead, and I thought this was best."

Everything I know is backward. Next he's going to tell me that this cab swims underwater.

"Your mother would prefer people thought her mother was Grandma Silna," he continues, "and I respect that, but the Prophet said we should look after our families. So I claimed Ura—your nana—as my kin, and we continued to look after her."

"Did Mother and Nana have a fight?"

Father plays with his goatee, and it's a habit I know well. He's unsure of how much he wants to say. He needs more prompting if I'm going to get the full story. "I'm about to be married, Father. Soon I'll be giving you grandchildren. What should I tell them? That my mother *shunned* her own mother and that she lied about it my entire life?"

"No!" he says, and then, looking at the driver, lowers his voice. "After today, you shouldn't talk about it ever again."

"I won't. If you tell me why Mother is ashamed of Nana."

He picks a piece of lint off his pants and rubs it between his fingers. He then says, in a voice so low I can barely hear it, "Because Nana was in the Tunnel."

"That's not true!" I say, not bothering to whisper, since what he said is so absurd.

"Ura went to prison," he says, looking me in the eyes, "because, when your mother was little, Ura tried to teach her to read."

The cab jerks to a stop at a light, throwing me forward. I fling out my hands to keep from smashing my head on the seat in front of me. Seconds later, we're speeding forward again and I'm hurled backward.

I want to throw up. Why would Nana have kept all this from me? I thought we told each other everything. What could be more important than my knowing that she once taught my own mother to read, just like she was teaching me? And that she went to the Tunnel for it?

Father continues to speak. "Your grandfather remarried while Ura was in jail. He wanted help raising your mother."

"Auntie Sersa, Purga, Kilya . . . ?"

"Your mother's stepsisters."

Mother has always seemed to be outside the aunties' tight little circle, but I just assumed it was because she couldn't stand Auntie Sersa. In reality, though, they had different mothers. Is that why Sersa is so competitive?

My stomach continues to churn as the cab hurtles up Madison Avenue. "Can Mother still read now?" I'm amazed to think she might experience the city the way I do, secretly reading signs that are meant only for men.

"Oh, no," he says. "She was quite young when it happened. She barely remembers it."

I'm disappointed. As much as I know that Mother

disapproves of reading, at least we would finally have had something in common.

We come to a screeching stop somewhere on the Upper East Side. "How did Nana get caught?" I ask, but Father is busy paying the cab driver. They haggle for a while, and then Father hands him a bag of batteries.

Standing on the sidewalk, I ask again, "Who turned Nana in? A neighbor?"

He stares at me, eyebrows knitted together, his expression telling me he doesn't want to answer.

"Was it Grandpa Silna?" I say, shocked by the idea. I've never been close to my grandfather, but I've never thought of him as a heartless man.

"That's enough, Mina."

"But you just said the Prophet told us to look after family. How could someone turn in his own wife?"

"Sometimes things . . . just happen," he says, hesitant in a way that's unusual for him, a man of science. "Now we must close the subject. Not one more word. Your mother will be very upset with me for sharing as much as I have."

I touch his hand. "Thank you for telling me the truth."

He smiles briefly, turning his face away to check the address. Ushering me past two apartment complexes, he stops at a beautiful building with a revolving door and a spotless sidewalk. Stranger than the clean entrance is the complete lack of people. There aren't any guards by the doors.

"Where is everybody?" I ask.

"Welcome to the Upper East Side," Father says, "where

the people are wealthy enough to afford security cameras."
He points up at a camera placed discreetly on a street lamp.

The striking building and its clean, spookily quiet
surroundings have finally reminded me of what's waiting
for me tonight: Damon Asher, his parents, and probably
Juda.

Father puts an arm around me. "This is an important
evening. Forget about Nana. Forget about your mother.
Look at me." I stare up at him. "You need to think about
the future tonight and be on your best behavior. I know
you're upset with your mother, so if you can't do it for her,
do it for me. I still have important things to do for our city
—more water filtration that could save thousands of lives—
but only if Uncle Ruho lets me. And he may not let me if I
anger his *chief energy engineer.*"

Father cannot say "chief energy engineer" without
sarcasm. He is substantially more qualified than Mr. Asher,
and no one knows why Uncle Ruho chose Mr. Asher to be
in charge, but Father would never dare ask. As long as he
can create fresh water for people, Father will suffer whatever slights come his way.

"Mr. Asher *must* be satisfied with his son's new fiancée,"
he says. "Understand?"

I nod. Father rarely asks me for anything.

So much has happened. Only yesterday, I got to talk to
Juda, and in those brief minutes my happiness felt
indestructible, as solid and impenetrable as the Wall surrounding the city. Now, life couldn't be worse. I have to
go into this building and pretend to be happy about marry-

ing a boy I can't stand. And Juda will probably be there, watching me fake it. And, through all of it, I can't even say that my heart is shattered because Nana is gone. And no one in my family cares but me.

Everyone has their own idea of who I should be with the Ashers. My father has asked me to be on my best behavior. My mother has begged me to discuss babies and the weather. And Nana, wherever she is, would want me to be bold and difficult. I have no idea what *I* want yet. I just know that it's going to be a very long night.

TEN

—————

THE ASHERS LIVE IN THE PENTHOUSE
apartment, which is particularly extravagant when you
consider that no one lives on the thirty-three floors beneath
them. I suppose the long elevator ride is their way of flaunt-
ing the amount of electricity they can afford. The elevator
has gold striped wallpaper, a gold ceiling, and a cream
carpet.

Don't rich people get dirt on their shoes?

The doors open with a *ping*, and Father leads me down
a private hallway with more cream carpeting. The high
ceiling glimmers with gilt-framed mirrors. The muffled
noise of our feet breaks a cold silence, and I feel like I'm in
a place of worship. We reach a towering ebony door with a
gold knocker. Father knocks twice, making a dull *thunk-
thunk* sound.

A guard opens the door, but it's not Juda. I don't know
if I'm relieved or disappointed. I wonder where he is. Does
he work for Damon all the time? I'm much too nervous not
knowing if or when he might pop up.

We step inside the foyer. A boat-size chandelier dangles
from the recessed ceiling, throwing its twinkling light over

a black floor so shiny I can see my reflection in it. White orchids spill out of white vases placed on long, black, lacquered tables that line the white walls. The only color in the room is one chair covered in bright coral.

I hear *click-click-click*, and soon a woman in a cloak is walking around the corner toward us.

My father says, "Peace."

She responds in a monotone voice. "Peace."

"I am Mr. Clark, and this is my daughter, Mina."

She doesn't look at me. "God is kind for bringing you here in safety."

"God is kind," Father agrees. "I will be back at ten o'clock to pick up Mina." He's anxious to leave. He has never liked social situations.

"Peace," the woman says, releasing him.

"Peace," my father says. The guard opens the door, and Father darts out without looking at me.

The mysterious woman then pulls off her cloak and veil and surprises me with a giggle and a big embrace. "Mina, darling, I'm so happy to meet you! Damon and Mr. Asher told me all about you, but I had to see you for myself." She smells like lilies, but the scent is overwhelming and too sweet. *Perfume*, I think. *Forbidden.*

"Mrs. Asher?" I ask.

She laughs. "Of course! Did you think I was the maid?"

Mortified, I say, "No! I—"

"Come this way," she says, with a goofy smile.

My first thought is that Mrs. Asher is the most beautiful woman I've ever seen. She's short and voluptuous, with smooth caramel skin. Her hair is thick and dark, and her eyes are a deep amber. She's much younger than I was expecting, no more than thirty-five. She wears lots of chunky gold jewelry and a chocolaty cashmere wrap dress the exact shade of her shiny hair. Cashmere! In this heat!

And that's when I first notice it. It's cold inside the apartment. Air-conditioning. The Ashers have *air-conditioning*. Despite Mrs. Asher's kind smile, I'm suddenly afraid. I've never been around this kind of wealth.

"Would you like to take off your cloak?" Mrs. Asher asks.

I look at the guard in the room and shake my head. She giggles. "He doesn't count. And you're family now. You should be comfortable." She reaches out for my cloak. The truth is, I would be more comfortable if I stayed in it, but she's insistent. She pulls up my veil.

I'm grateful for my demure gray dress as I hand over my cloak. She looks me up and down, and I can see she was determined to get a good look.

"You're as lovely as Damon said. And those eyes! Like blue topaz. Come this way."

I follow her across the marble floor. She's wearing high heels! Like Nana told me about. I've never actually seen anyone walk in them before. The loud *click-click* of her steps echoes through the enormous apartment, and the way Mrs. Asher has to walk—it's kind of embarrassing; her big bottom is just swaying back and forth and back and forth. It's mesmerizing. I notice the guard is watching me watching her, and I look away quickly, but not before he smirks. I'm humiliated.

Does she wear forbidden shoes like that all the time? Even outside? Will Damon expect me to wear them?

We reach the living room, and there's a big white leather couch surrounded by white leather chairs with silver metal legs. There's a glass table in the middle, displaying a white leather–bound copy of the Book next to a weird white sculpture that looks like a scoop of mashed potatoes. I look around and see that there are more of the white plastic sculptures all over the room. There's an enormous mirror on one wall, making the room look much bigger than it actually is, and a white bearskin rug on the floor.

Mrs. Asher folds herself onto the couch and then motions for me to join her, but I don't want to sit anywhere. Everything is white and perfect, like nothing's ever seen a piece of dust. I'm confident I'll ruin something. Knowing I can't stand all night, I finally sit on the front edge of a chair and place my hands in my lap.

Mrs. Asher looks at herself in the mirror and runs a hand through her hair, causing her gold bracelets to clink together. The gold hoops in her ears catch the light, but they can't compete with her chunky necklace. It's all very striking, but I would guess that Mrs. Asher is not wearing the jewelry for its beauty alone. Nana once told me that the wealthiest women in Manhattan always wear real gold so that if their husbands decide to divorce them and throw them out onto the streets, they at least have something of value on their bodies.

I decide a woman wearing as much gold as Mrs. Asher must not have much trust in her husband. What kind of son does that man produce? Looking at my own bare fingers and wrists, I decide to ask for something gold as soon as possible.

"So, Mina, your father is a very clever man. He has revolutionized energy production. What do you know about this fungus he grows?"

"Uh, it's not fungus. It's algae, actually."

"Ah! Algae, of course. And algae makes gasoline?"

"Not exactly. It makes an oil that can be turned into fuel."

"Amazing." She then yells into the hallway, "Ray, bring us some Dom!" I'm not used to hearing a woman bark orders at a man, even if he's a servant.

Looking back at me, Mrs. Asher says, "My husband has told me about this whole new water supply. He says it's very clean, but . . . I don't know about you . . . I don't want to drink water that used to be something in the toilet."

"No, that's not—"

"Uncle Ruho is very excited about this algae, though. What will he want to fuel next? Cars . . . trains . . ." She arches an eyebrow. "Roller coasters? Who knows where the lunacy will end!?"

I don't know what to say. I'm not used to this kind of talk, especially from strangers. Nana and I sometimes talked about Uncle Ruho, but I've never heard anyone else question his judgment. And there are servants and guards all over the Ashers' apartment. It makes me uncomfortable, and then I wonder if she's testing me.

"Have you met him?" she asks now.

"Who?"

"Uncle Ruho!"

"No. My father did, once." Wanting to commend him on his work on the plant, Uncle Ruho blessed Father with a few seconds of his time last year. "Father said he was very majestic." Mrs. Asher stares at me, eyebrows raised, waiting for more. "Father also said he was, um, shorter than he expected."

She cackles with laughter. "Yes! He's a little troll of a man. It's no wonder he can't find a wife!"

I smile politely, trying not to grimace at the blasphemy.

An elegant man in a white suit comes in, carrying a tray supporting two skinny glasses filled with a liquid through which bubbles rise in streams of gold. He hands one to me and one to Mrs. Asher. I very carefully take mine in both hands. It's cold, and when I smell it, it tickles my nose.

"What is it?" I ask.

"Try it," she says. "Tiny sips at first."

I do as she says. The drink is strong, and I choke a bit. It's not refreshing at all.

"One more sip," she insists.

Not wanting to be rude, I take another sip, and this one tastes a bit better; the little bubbles seem to rise up from the glass and into my head. I become alarmed. "Mrs. Asher?"

There's a glint in her eye. "Yes, darling?"

"Is this alcohol?"

"No, Mina."

Relieved, I take another sip.

She continues, "It's champagne. Men drink alcohol, but real ladies drink only champagne. This bottle was smuggled in from France, many years ago, and cost forty-five thousand BTUs, so you should savor every drop."

My head spins. "But alcohol is forbidden!"

She giggles, tips back her glass, and finishes her drink in one long gulp.

I put my glass of champagne down on the glass table. "When will Damon be home?"

"Any minute! And he'll be furious about the champagne, don't you think?"

I leap up, looking for a place to throw away my glass.

She roars with laughter. "No, no, no, Mina! We have hours, dear." She motions with her hand for me to come back to my seat. "I wanted a little time alone with you."

She then signals for Ray to refill her glass.

"A toast, Mina. To your engagement!" She raises the glass and waits for me to raise mine.

"I'd rather not," I say.

She smiles, and her beauty is overwhelming. "I insist that you celebrate with me!"

I lift the glass, making a toasting gesture, and then press it against my lips.

Mother told me to obey my new mother-in-law. Uncle Ruho says that alcohol is forbidden, that it interferes with our ability to properly worship God. If I disobey God, he may not allow me into Paradise. If I disobey Mrs. Asher, I'm insulting her in her home and possibly creating an enemy for the rest of my married life.

I reason that I can beg God for forgiveness tomorrow, but an unhappy mother-in-law is forever. Saying a quick prayer, I drink the champagne. I feel it rushing down to my toes. Is that possible? Does liquid go all the way to your feet? My stomach is a little woozy, but in general I feel quite good, less stressed than when I first arrived. I notice that my back has stopped stinging as much.

Mrs. Asher laughs, clapping her hands like a delighted toddler. "Good!" She turns to Ray. "Refills!" He refills our glasses, and she sweeps her arms around the room. "This is your new home. Isn't it grand? Everything a young girl dreams of?"

I look down at the rug. The bear's face is glaring up at me with a horrible grimace. She sees me staring at it and says, "It's extremely rare. Polar bears have been gone for decades."

I smile, like this is wonderful news. She drinks more of her champagne, watching herself in the mirror. She sticks her chest out a little and tosses her hair. I look to see if Ray has noticed, but he's staring off into the distance, eyes as glazed over as the polar bear's.

"This building used to be a hotel. It was very chic, and many famous people stayed here. Presidents. Movie stars, even."

She means during Time Zero. I bet she doesn't know anything about it—doesn't even really know what a movie is. Or maybe she does. If she has champagne, maybe somewhere in this apartment she's hiding Relics—actual movies, or "discs" that hold music. Wouldn't that be exciting!

For a brief moment, I imagine sitting with Mrs. Asher and showing her the Primer. She would "ooh" and "aah" as

I showed her all the places that used to serve people food, and she would laugh at the ridiculous ways everyone spent their time—paying to see a man sing a song, or traveling miles for a special bowl of noodles.

At the thought of food, my stomach gurgles like a busted pipe, and I look down, embarrassed, wondering if Mrs. Asher heard it.

She answers my silent question by turning to Ray and saying, "Bring Miss Clark some snacks."

Within seconds, there are two identical long, thin green boxes in front of me. One says CRACKERS, and the other says COOKIES. I open the one that says CRACKERS and quickly eat five in a row.

"Better?" she asks, and I nod, feeling steadier.

"Leave us alone, Ray," Mrs. Asher says, without looking at him, and he glides out silently. "I understand if you're nervous. I remember the first time I had to meet my in-laws. I was terrified. My mother-in-law, Mrs. Asher, was a real *chupacabra*."

I give her a blank stare.

"You know, a 'goat-sucker'?"

I giggle.

"She never had one kind word for me, and before she would let me marry her dear, sweet baby boy, she had to make sure for herself that I was a virgin."

I look up at the ceiling, then down at the floor. Anywhere but at Mrs. Asher.

"That's right. She took me into the bathroom and shoved her wrinkled hand right up inside me."

The room spins. I take another gulp of champagne.

"Oh dear, little Mina's gone green." She bursts out laughing. "Don't worry, sweetie, I'm not going to check. I have better things to do." She then says, as if to reassure me, "Besides, Damon will show us the sheets the morning after your wedding."

I'm mortified.

"You wouldn't believe the stories from the old country. Girls would do amazing things to pretend they were still virgins. Like, they would soak sponges in pig's blood and then put them inside themselves on their wedding night. Can you imagine?"

Why is she telling me this? Am I supposed to react? I hear Nana's voice: *When in doubt, say nothing.* I keep my face neutral.

"Mr. Asher never had to worry. I was only thirteen when he bought me off the street."

"B-b-bought you?" Now I know she's telling me too much. It must be the champagne. The way she tittered when I first arrived—has she been intoxicated this whole time?

"Oh, yes. Don't let the packaging fool you," she says, motioning to her dress and hair. "I come from Convenes."

Nana taught me that when the Teachers took over Manhattan, they ordered anyone who didn't follow the Prophet to leave immediately or die. Some people were too sick or poor to leave, or had nowhere to go, so they stayed and converted. Although the Teachers allowed the new believers to live, they were treated as if they were equal to the dogs that roamed the streets.

After a few years of being looked down upon by their neighbors, new converts started to convene on the Lower East Side, rarely venturing to other neighborhoods, and that led to their name, the Convenes. But I've heard people like my grandfather joke that the name actually comes from the fact that the group decided to convert because it was "convenient."

The Prophet gave the Deservers our name because we followed Her unquestioningly from the beginning, recognizing Her divinity as soon as it manifested. She declared we *deserved* unhampered access to Paradise. Deservers like to think that Convenes are all jealous of our stature, but they seem to look down on us just as we look down on them. Father once told us a joke they have:

Question: Why can't a Deserver walk into Heaven alone?

Answer: Because he needs a servant to carry his ego.

Mother didn't like this joke.

It's impossible to believe Mrs. Asher was once a Convene. I can't picture her in any surroundings other than the beautiful, white, air-conditioned penthouse she sits in now.

Enjoying my astonishment, she says, "My sisters and I used to walk the streets, looking for horse dung we could sell for fuel. I don't think my parents really considered someone taking notice of me, since I walked around all day covered in dirt and shit."

I wince at her language as if Mother were in the room.

"But my husband has a 'talent for seeing potential.' He followed me back to my parents' house one day and offered to buy me on the spot. I was only eleven. My parents said I was too young, and I was so relieved. I thought they were looking out for me. But, two years later, on the very day I hit puberty, they got in touch with him, and he came to get me that night. My parents took his money, said goodbye, and put me in the arms of a total stranger. I haven't seen them since."

She gives me a rueful smile, but I see little tears in the corner of her eyes.

"I'm sorry . . . ," I begin.

"Why?" she says, snapping at me, her brown eyes going dark. "Don't you think your parents just did exactly the same to you? Maybe they call it a 'bride price,' but it's the same thing. They *sold* you. And now they're at home celebrating and eating a big fat meal. So drink up!"

I want to fight with her, tell her she's wrong, but I'm sure Mother *is* celebrating right now, bragging to our neighbors about what a fabulous price she got.

"A toast, Mina. At least we're not in the street, collecting shit, right?" She takes another drink and waits for me to do the same.

I look down at the glass in my hand, now half-empty. I'm frightened by the change in her mood, and, not wanting to make her more angry, I drink it down.

I slump down a little in the chair, suddenly exhausted.

"I think we're going to be friends, Mina, don't you?"

"I hope so," I whisper. I really do.

Mrs. Asher seems farther away. Once again, I'm struck by her beauty, but now I can think only of what a curse it was. Maybe if she'd been plainer, she would still be at home with her sisters. Or did they all get sold, too?

I let out a little burp.

I just burped in front of Mrs. Asher! My mother would be *destroyed*. This is hilarious to me. I burst out laughing.

Mrs. Asher starts to laugh, too, and the two of us just sit there, giggling at my burp. I'm amazed at her lack of formality.

Then she catches her breath, saying, "What's wrong, Mina? Don't you like our cookies?"

I find it hard to focus on the unopened box in front of me. "I love cookies, but these have ginger, and I *hate* ginger." Mother grows it at home and puts it in *everything*.

Leaning forward, Mrs. Asher narrows her eyes on the cookie box. She looks back up at me.

"My husband gave those cookies to me as a gift," she says. "And I've been wondering what kind they were. But the picture on the box looks like a hundred different cookies, so how could I guess? How could I possibly know what the ingredients were, unless"—she pauses—"I could *read*?"

She leans back, a nasty smirk on her face. "Clever little Mina! How full of secrets you are."

Trying to think quickly, I say, "We eat the same kind at home. I recognize the box."

"Really? Your family has access to cookies from England?"

My family could never afford such a thing, and Mrs. Asher knows it. I have no reply.

She takes a triumphant sip from her glass.

Be calm, I tell myself, trying to slow my pulse. My first instinct is to drop to my knees and beg her not to tell the authorities. But I'm frozen in place, head swirling. *She's drinking alcohol, so of course she won't summon the Teachers.* I continue to study her face, that sneer, and I see her expression contains no disapproval—it's all self-satisfaction.

And then I understand. She's been waiting for this moment all along—some mistake, a transgression, anything she could hold over me. Now I know why she's been filling me with champagne. She doesn't want to be my friend. She wanted me to let my guard down.

And I fell for it. *I'm so stupid.* I gave myself away over *ginger.* Nana would have known better. She would have known from the first moment that Mrs. Asher was the true *chupacabra.*

I want to scream at her, *You wear perfume and high heels!* but I swallow my outrage, because I don't know what Mrs. Asher is going to do next. She's spread out on the couch, in wonderful spirits, like a mosquito who's been buzzing around for hours and has finally sucked its victim dry.

She leans forward again, opening her mouth to speak, when we hear noises coming from the entrance hall—male voices.

Eyes widening, she says, "Pull yourself together." She looks in the big mirror on the wall and pats her hair. I jump up, unsure what to do, so I look in the mirror as well.

I look awful.

My eyes are bloodshot, my hair frizzy and wild. I can't believe how quickly the alcohol has turned me into such a mess—a terrified mouse. I quickly pull out my elastic band and pull my hair back into a new, controlled ponytail. It helps a little.

"You look scared stiff, Mina," Mrs. Asher says. She looks calm and elegant. She comes over to me and hooks her arm through mine. Then she leads me toward the foyer. "You must learn to smile in the face of adversity. It does wonders."

I plaster a weak grin on my face and let Mrs. Asher drag me to the men.

ELEVEN

We're walking down the hallway, about to arrive in the foyer, when a large body blocks us. It's Juda.

I make a small, embarrassing yelp of surprise.

Ignoring me completely and forgoing the traditional greeting, he speaks directly to Mrs. Asher. "Mr. Asher has brought guests home. He asked me to fetch your cloaks."

He hands Mrs. Asher our cloaks and veils, and she says, "He knows I hate surprises, Juda." She leans in close to him, whispering, "Go tell Ray to clear the glasses in the living room."

Juda's face remains neutral, but his eyes reveal alarm, and I'm sure he knows that we've been drinking alcohol. I'm not surprised to learn this is a regular habit of Mrs. Asher's, but I'm ashamed for Juda to know that I had anything to do with it.

He hurries toward the kitchen, and Mrs. Asher hands me my cloak and veil. I throw the cloak over my head, only I can't seem to find the opening for my head. Mrs. Asher has to help me, and I can see she's stifling a laugh, but it doesn't seem so funny to me. Once it's on, I add the veil and readjust my ponytail.

I was unprepared to see Juda. The champagne has

already caused one big mistake tonight, and I can't afford another. Having Juda stand near me for just those few seconds has made my heart race as if I've been running up and down the hall.

Stop it, Mina. Pull yourself together.

Taking a deep breath, I look at Mrs. Asher. I can still see that luscious hair, though, in black cloak and veil, she manages to appear ordinary, even dutiful. Her voice, slightly muffled now, says, "Follow me and stay quiet."

There's a group of men talking near the front door, and they grow silent as we approach. I keep my head down modestly, but by looking at feet, I can count six men. I hear Mr. Asher say, "Gabriella, may I present Captain Memon, the head of the City Guard?"

In front of me, Mrs. Asher bows. Sneaking a look, I see a huge black man dressed like a Twitcher—but he's holding his helmet under his arm. I've never seen a Twitcher without his helmet before. A long wire connects the helmet to the back of his uniform.

The man is as old as Father, but his chest and shoulders bulge with muscles in a way that suggests he could crush every man in the room. He manages to make even Mr. Asher seem small. His expression is professional and stern, his charcoal eyes icy. He isn't holding a gun, like every Twitcher on the street. At his waist is a long dagger sheathed in an ivory holder encrusted with emeralds and pearls.

Dread bubbles in my throat. Not only is the captain of the City Guard in charge of every Twitcher in this city, but he also oversees the Tunnel and all public executions.

Mr. Asher says, "And, Captain Memon, may I present the fiancée of my son, Damon."

Moments pass before I realize he's talking about me. I'm frozen. Mr. Asher raises an eyebrow. He's signaling for me to move, but my legs won't obey. I finally lean forward, walk a few steps, and bow.

"She's as lovely as an unplucked plum," Damon says. I hadn't even noticed him, but he's hovering by the doorway.

"I would expect no less for the Asher family," Captain Memon responds, but his deep, gravelly voice makes the compliment sound forced.

"Yes, she'll make a good wife," Mr. Asher says. "Please, Captain Memon, you and your men make yourselves comfortable in our living room. The servants will bring you tea."

"I'm not here for tea, Max. I want to discuss your contribution to the Convene problem. The time for politeness has passed."

"Of course! And we will. But there's no reason to stand uncomfortably in the hallway while we discuss it. Please, let me take care of you and your men."

Captain Memon grumbles a bit but allows Mr. Asher to lead him toward the living room. Then Memon stops, turns to him, and says, "The results have slowed. How long do you expect us to watch as the Convenes die slow, lingering deaths? Or their women become infertile? Perhaps it's time for you to make a new investment in the future of our city?"

He then continues to the living room, flanked by his four men.

Since when have Uncle Ruho's men cared so passionately about the Convenes? And Mr. Asher is giving money to help cure the mystery disease? Surely Mother would change her tune if someone as powerful as Mr. Asher were helping Convenes. I'm delighting in the idea of telling her about it, when suddenly Mr. Asher is right in front of me, his face only an inch in front of mine.

"How much did you have?" he whispers.

"Wha—?" I ask, terrified. "Uh. She . . . uh . . ."

Whirling around to his wife, spit flying from his mouth as he speaks, he says, "You fool. Mina is drunk!"

Mrs. Asher wags him away with her hand. "Pshaw! She's fine. It was just a little sip."

"She's as wobbly as an eighty-year-old man. We're lucky Memon didn't notice, or we'd all be heading for the Tunnel!"

If Captain Memon knew I'd been drinking, he needn't bother to sentence me. He could just grab the dagger at his side and slice off my head.

Damon is angry, too. "Mama, what did you do?"

Mrs. Asher snickers like a girl caught wearing her mother's jewelry. "We were just having a little fun—isn't that right, Mina?"

All I want to say is, *No, she made me drink it, and I hate her, and she's a chupacabra*, but I can't, not now that she's learned my secret. After a painful silence, I say, in a very tiny voice, "Yes, we were just having a little fun," and that's when I see that Juda has joined us in the foyer. He's heard my words. I see him frown.

He's disappointed in me.

Mr. Asher snaps his fingers in my face. I wave him

away like a fly. He seems very annoying right now. "She's had more than a sip. She's pickled! She can't be around Captain Memon!"

I try to respond. "I—"

"We can't send her home like this," Damon says, his voice nasal and whining. "It'll ruin everything."

I glance at Juda again. Perhaps now is the moment we've been waiting for. If I go home drunk, my parents will never allow me to marry into the Asher family. "I should go home!" I blurt. "Father will be waiting."

"Quiet," Mrs. Asher tells me, and then to her husband she says, "She should stay here. Send a message, Max. You'll think of something."

Mr. Asher then spins around much too quickly and says to Juda, "Bring me pen and paper, and then prepare the guest room."

Juda brings him stationery and a fountain pen laid out on a tray. He won't meet my eyes.

I hold my breath as Mr. Asher writes out a letter.

"What will you say, Father?" Damon asks.

What *can* Mr. Asher say? It's not proper for me to stay the night here before Damon and I are married.

Mr. Asher doesn't stop writing. "I'm explaining that Mina seems to have come down with a cold, and that I don't think she should be moved until her fever is gone."

"Well done, Father," Damon says.

Mrs. Asher laughs with glee. "Very clever, darling."

Mr. Asher finishes the letter and signs it with a flourish. "Do not patronize me, my dear," he says to Mrs. Asher. "I have no intention of forgetting why we are in this mess in the first place." He walks the letter to the door guard, saying, "Deliver this immediately to Mr. Zai Clark on Columbus Circle."

Nodding, the guard disappears out the door.

Mr. Asher tells his wife, "Mina is to go straight to bed to sleep it off. And that goes for you as well. I don't want to see you again tonight."

Mrs. Asher opens her mouth to protest, but Mr. Asher says, "Don't. You've already tested me enough tonight."

Pursing her lips, she stomps off. *Click-click-click.*

Mr. Asher is starting to head for the living room, when Damon says, "Father, what about the *gift?*"

Mr. Asher seems exhausted by his entire family. "Oh, yes, well, go ahead and give it to her. I must tend to our guest." He walks away, tense, like a man going to attend to a bad-tempered Rottweiler.

Approaching me, Damon says, "I have an engagement present for you, my flower."

Damon looks at Juda, who cringes slightly and then reaches into his uniform pocket and pulls out a white box. He hands the box to Damon, who opens it and holds it out to me. Damon says, "Please accept this bracelet as a token of my affection."

I look inside the box, and, lying on a bed of burgundy silk, is a diamond cuff, twinkling in the light reflecting off the chandelier above. I cannot begin to imagine its worth. The next thing I know, Damon is on one knee, unfastening it and putting it on my wrist.

Perhaps Damon is more generous than he first appeared and is just shy, or bad at expressing himself. Sekena sometimes gives me a hard time for being too quick to judge people.

He turns the cuff so that the clasp is facing down. "It looks beautiful on your lovely wrist." He kisses my hand, a forbidden act I'm sure he wouldn't have tried if his father had still been within sight. "Now you should go to sleep, like Father said."

"What about dinner?" I ask. I've only had a handful of crackers, and I'm starving.

He hesitates. "You need to go straight to your room. I'll have Ray bring you something later." He turns to Juda. "Take her to the guest room. I'm joining Father."

Juda walks down a hallway to the left. I assume I'm supposed to follow him, so I jog to catch up. As soon as we're out of earshot, I say, "Juda, I didn't want to drink the—"

"Shhh," he warns.

I stop talking, and soon we reach a lacquered black door. Juda opens it, gesturing inside. He says loudly, "The guest room, Miss Clark."

Stepping inside, I turn around to try to talk to him again, but he shuts the door in my face.

Well.

Trying to ignore the sting of his rudeness, I examine the room.

It's yet one more luxurious interior. The enormous bed could accommodate my entire family. It has a glossy black frame with four posters that almost reach the ceiling. The pearly white bedcover looks untouched by human hands.

There seem to be twenty pillows sitting at the head of the bed, and I don't understand why. How many pillows can one person use?

The floor here is crisp, snowy marble, not black like the hall. Besides the bed, there's a vanity table with an enormous mirror, a large wardrobe, two chairs, and a desk. The desk holds another one of Mrs. Asher's plastic mashed-potato sculptures. This one looks like a vase. The whole room is pristine and cold, not like a place that's actually lived in.

It's also completely quiet. The door is thick and heavy, and I'm sealed away from any noise from the rest of the apartment. We're so high up in the building that there's no sound from the street, either—no people, no traffic. They probably can't even hear the Bell up here. It's just the silence of the marble speaking to the silence of the plastic.

I'm inside a tomb.

I pull my cloak and veil up over my head and throw them over one of the chairs. Then I crawl onto the bed, and I can't believe how soft it feels, a cloud wrapped in silk.

I drift off, my body finally relaxing. All I want is sleep. I don't want to think about the day, all that's happened. I'm grateful for the numbness of the champagne. I'm almost able to forget—about Nana, the Primer, Mrs. Asher. I just shove it all to the back of my mind. But, deep down, I know it's like ignoring the presence of a bug or two, when one secretly knows that the walls are about to collapse from an infestation of roaches.

TWELVE

I WAKE UP ON TOP OF BLANKETS IN A PITCH-black room, with no idea where I am. Several seconds later, I remember that I'm at the Ashers'. I don't know what time it is, but something tells me I've only been asleep a few hours. My head is pounding, and my tongue feels thick and dry, like I've been chewing on a bearskin rug.

My wrist hurts. I look down to see that my new diamond cuff has been cutting into my skin as I slept. I use my other hand to try to release the clasp, but it seems to be stuck. *Nyek.*

I need to pee. Badly.

I roll across the enormous bed and stand, which makes my head throb even more. I sit back down on the bed. Wasn't Damon going to send me some dinner? I guess he forgot.

I wait until I feel steadier, before shuffling to the door. I turn the knob and pull, amazed by the door's thick, solid weight. When it's finally open, I find I'm staring at Juda's back.

He turns, surprised to see me standing there.

"Hi," I say, embarrassed. I slept in my dress and must look like death. "I, uh, need a bathroom."

He nods and walks me across the hall, pointing to a door.

"Thanks," I say.

I look up and down the hallway. No one else appears to be awake. I go into the bathroom, wondering if Juda is going to stand outside and wait for me.

I pee quickly and wash my hands. I stick my head under the faucet and gulp down water. I can't remember the last time I was so thirsty.

As I use a fluffy towel to dry my face and hands, I look in the mirror over the sink, and, as I suspected, it's pretty bad—there are dark circles under my eyes, and my hair is sticking up to the left. I take out the elastic and try to smooth it down.

Finally, I step out of the bathroom, smiling at Juda. He looks away.

I know I shouldn't be hurt. He's doing the right thing. I'm going to marry his boss, and there can't be anything between us, not even friendship.

We return to the guest room, and Juda opens the door for me without a word. Stepping inside, I whisper, "You're doing the right thing."

He doesn't say anything, but he also doesn't shut the door on me this time, so I keep talking. "By ignoring me. I want you to know I understand it's the right thing to do." But as I say it, my voice catches and tears threaten to come. The thought of coming to live with this family is hard enough, but how can I bear it with this new, hardened version of Juda near me all the time? I'm saying that it's the right thing, but the truth is, his coldness is agony. In a flash of anger, I say, "Maybe it would be easier for both of us if you just quit."

"You're right."

I'm shocked he's spoken. "What?"

The all-business, stone-faced Juda melts to uncertainty in front of my eyes. "I thought I could handle it. I tried to prepare myself. But tonight—seeing how she treated you, seeing you with the bracelet—I can't do it. I can't stay. I'm going to tell Damon tomorrow."

"Tomorrow?" Panic rises in my gut. "I didn't mean it. I was just mad because you were ignoring me. Please, *please* don't leave me."

"I'm not *leaving* you, Mina, because I'm not *with* you," he says, resentment in his voice.

"Tomorrow?" I repeat. It's too soon. There's so much I wanted to tell him, so much I wanted to ask. How can he just disappear? "Will I see you again?"

He hesitates but then shakes his head no.

I throw my arms around his waist. I don't care if anyone sees. I just don't want him to go.

"Mina, you have to get ahold of yourself. Someone will catch us." He takes a step deeper into my room, easily carrying me with him. "It's all right. Everything will be okay."

"No, nothing is all right. Nothing is going to be okay, and you know it." I'm talking into his chest. I'm enveloped by his scent, a combination of soap, sandalwood, and a sharp hint of gasoline.

He pats my back to soothe me, as he did on the first day

we met. My skin is tender, but I try not to wince, because I
don't want him to let go of me. I look up at him. Having
never been this close to him before, I can now really appreciate his height. His shoulders seem as wide as the door.
He's radiating warmth, and I can hear his heart underneath
his uniform. It's beating quickly.

Something occurs to me. "You knew you were leaving.
Why were you standing outside my door in the middle of
the night?"

He furrows his brow and looks as if he's struggling to
find the answer, and, just when I think he's about to say
something, he bends down and kisses me instead.

At first, when his lips touch mine, I'm consumed with
how unlawful it is, how much trouble we'll be in if we're
caught. Soon, though, I'm thinking about how surprisingly
soft his lips are. He kisses me once, twice, three times—and
then his mouth opens and it becomes one long, ongoing
kiss that spreads through my body like a fever.

I close my eyes, and he pulls me in tighter and lifts me
slightly off the ground. His breath deepening, he stops
kissing me for a second and says, "Mina, I . . . ," and then
there's a sound from the hallway.

We separate as if we've been slapped.

"Get in bed," he orders, looking around the room.
"Now."

I obey without question, leaping onto the perfectly
made bed. Juda disappears into the wardrobe on the far
wall, before I have a chance to blink.

Just as my head hits the pillow, Damon walks into the

room. He's wearing silk pajamas with an animal print. Tiger? Leopard? I really don't care. His slippers match.

He smirks at me. "I saw your open door."

I turn away, raising a hand to cover my unveiled face. "I went to the bathroom."

"I thought maybe you were out scrounging for food."

"I should have been. You said you would send me dinner." I lunge toward the chair where I placed my cloak and veil, but he blocks my way.

"Father decided it was best not to. He thought you needed to learn a lesson."

I would love to tell Damon what I think of this lesson, but what I really need is for him to leave.

Still refusing to look at him, I say, "It's inappropriate for you to be in my bedroom."

"Interesting," he says, "that you should be so caught up in the rules *now*."

I hear him shut the door. My body tenses.

"I didn't know it was champagne!" I say.

"Here I thought you were such a good girl, so faithful and compliant." He circles the bed, trying to make me look at him. Sitting down on the mattress, he says, "But you're just a little lush, aren't you?" He slides his hand toward me.

"I have begged God's forgiveness for my transgression." I scoot to the far end of the bed. He seems entertained by my discomfort.

Flicking out his hand, he grabs me by the calf. "I found you beautiful when I first saw you, Mina, but I never imagined you would be so full of . . . *sin*." He yanks me toward him by my leg, which causes my dress to pull up toward my hips. He leers at my bare legs, then leans over to kiss me. I hold him back, and he laughs. He likes this game.

I wonder how much Juda can hear from the wardrobe.

I try quoting the Book. "Do not practice fornication; it is debauchery and a wretched path to follow."

"It's hardly a sin when our marriage contract is already signed," he mumbles, stroking my knee.

Thinking of another strategy, I look deep into his eyes. "Damon, *darling*." Tasting the word "darling" on my lips for the first time makes me sicker than the champagne. "Haven't you ever waited for anything? Like that first, succulent morsel of lamb after a long day of fasting? Isn't it the best lamb you've ever tasted?"

His leering smile is wicked. "I enjoy lamb whenever I'm hungry." He leans in again, and this time he doesn't allow me to hold him off but pushes down my arms, shoving his mouth onto mine. His cold lips taste like garlic and beef. He thrusts his tongue deep inside my mouth until I can't breathe. He starts to make horrible moaning sounds, and I can't believe he's experiencing pleasure when I'm so obviously disgusted by him.

I try to push him off me, but he just leans into me harder. He weighs so much. He gropes at me, running his hands up and down my chest and legs. A different, more frantic panic washes over me.

"Please," I beg. "No."

I know that when we're married, I'll have to submit, but I'm not going to give in one second earlier than I have to. And how can I suffer this humiliation, knowing that Juda will have to listen to the whole thing?

His hand goes underneath my dress. "Damon, NO!" I say in a commanding tone.

He instantly sits up, grabbing my hair and yanking back my head, much harder than my mother did, as if he actually wants to snap my neck. "A *woman* is not allowed to speak to me that way!"

I can't move. Cold, hard fear replaces the panic. Tears are running down my cheeks.

Damon keeps one hand on my hair, pulling it harder, jerking it painfully from the roots, while he takes the other hand and starts to unbuckle his pants.

"Please, Damon, not like this . . ."

"I think this is how you wanted it all along," he mutters.

And that's when I see Juda.

He's come out of the wardrobe, and he's holding a chair above his head. I try to say, "No!" because he'll be killed for striking his master, but it's too late. The chair comes smashing down over Damon's head.

Damon collapses in a heap on top of me. I can't breathe.

I wait for Damon to roar up in anger, but he doesn't. He just lies there.

Juda rolls him off me. "Are you all right? Did he hurt you?"

"Is he d–d–dead?"

Juda looks like he doesn't know who I'm talking about. He leans into my face. "Mina? Are you all right?"

"Y-y-yes, I'm fine. What have you done?"

"He was touching you. . . . He was going to—"

"You killed him!"

Juda looks at Damon. He leans over me, placing two fingers on Damon's neck. "He's just unconscious."

Thank the Prophet. "Juda, you have to get out of here!"

He stares at me as if I'm speaking another language.

I jump out of the bed and shake his huge shoulders. "Now, Juda. Run, before his parents come!"

Finally, the reality of what he's done seems to sink in, and I see fear in his eyes. "You have to tell them that I came from outside your room," he says. "So they won't punish you, okay?"

"Yes, yes. Just go!"

He heads for the door.

"Juda," I say, and he stops, and I think of the thousand things I want to say, but the only thing I can manage is "thank you."

He nods and smiles weakly.

And then he is gone.

THIRTEEN

I LOOK AT THE SCENE IN MY ROOM AND WONDER if there's anything I need to move or change. Noticing that the door of the wardrobe is open, I rush over to close it.

Damon, who's still spread out on my bed, lets out a whimper and begins to move. I run to him, ready to play my part.

"Damon! Are you all right? Are you hurt?"

He raises his head, looking at me in confusion. "Did *you* do that?"

"I . . . I . . . uh." What can I say? He'll see the splintered chair on the floor soon enough and know that someone else was here, but I can't form the words in my mouth—*Juda did it*. I can't bear to be the one who seals Juda's fate.

But it doesn't matter, because a second later, Mr. Asher, in purple silk pajamas with a matching robe flowing around him, sweeps into the room, a befuddled hawk roused from his nest. His gray hair sticks straight up, and I feel embarrassed to see him in his nightclothes. "What's going on? Juda just ran out of the apartment!"

Damon holds his head. "Good. He must be chasing the man who just assaulted me!"

"He wouldn't speak to the door guard on his way out." Mr. Asher moves his head back and forth in quick, tiny motions, as if he's having a spasm. "The door guard said he appeared to be fleeing!"

"That's ridiculous!" Damon says. He tries to stand, wobbles, then sits down again. "Juda wouldn't dare strike me."

"Are you all right?" Mr. Asher asks. "Do you need a doctor?"

"No. I'm fine," Damon says, irritated with the question.

Mr. Asher spots the debris on the floor. "Did Juda attack you?" His voice is full of incredulity.

Damon shakes his head, confused, and Mr. Asher looks at me for the first time. "Cover yourself!" he says, his voice shifting from bewilderment to disgust.

I put on my cloak and veil as quickly as I can, but I'm already shamed.

In the same tone he uses with his servants, he says to me, "Tell me what happened."

But before I can say a word, Damon answers. "I decided to bring Mina a snack, since she missed dinner. We were sitting here, talking, when suddenly I was hit from behind."

I open my mouth to contradict him, but then stop. Damon is the firstborn son, and I am a woman. My word is worth half of his. To call him a liar would be an enormous insult to his father and the entire family. I dig my thumbnail into the flesh of my forefinger, waiting for Mr. Asher to accept Damon's explanation.

But Mr. Asher looks around, seeming to note the lack of food in the room. "You were . . . *talking* when Juda hit you?" From his tone, Mr. Asher seems suspicious of his son's story, allowing me a flutter of hope.

Damon nods, stubborn.

Mr. Asher's nostrils flare. "Juda has worked for this family for nearly ten years. He's never laid a finger on you, not even when you belittled him or struck him. He's never stolen so much as a grain of rice. Why do you suppose he would suddenly attack you, unprovoked, after all this time?"

"Maybe you should check the safe."

"I don't think I need to," Mr. Asher says, stepping in toward Damon. "I think the reason is sitting right here in front of us." He gestures at me dismissively.

Damon looks at me, surprised.

"I think the best explanation is one of the oldest," Mr. Asher says. "Jealousy. It must be."

"That's ridiculous. Juda has seen me with plenty of beautiful women, and he's never batted an eye."

I'm supposed to ignore the implications of this remark. A new bride has to be as pure as a downy chick emerging from its shell, but the rule doesn't apply to the groom. On the contrary, society expects him to enjoy his freedom before he shackles himself to one girl. Propriety usually forbids the discussion of any such activity around the bride, but I think propriety was thrown out tonight with the remaining champagne.

Mr. Asher strokes his brow as if to contain the pressure building behind his wrinkled forehead. "I believe we may have come to the core of the problem. Despite Miss Clark's questionable behavior in our home this evening, she is not a working girl from the Theater District! Perhaps you had a problem differentiating the two and Juda was upset by your confusion? Am I getting closer to some version of the reality of what occurred here this evening, Damon?"

I should be shocked that Mr. Asher has mentioned the Theater District in front of me, but I'm too busy concentrating on the edge of disdain for Damon's behavior in Mr. Asher's voice. It makes me believe that all is not lost for Juda.

I wait in the heavy silence for Damon to answer.

"Well, Damon?" His father looks more tired than he did when he first entered the room.

Through gritted teeth, Damon says, "I think you and I should speak alone, Father."

"Why? Mina is aware of what happened here this evening, is she not?"

"Fine," Damon says, growing more furious by the second. He purses his lips, glares at me, and then looks at his father. After an excruciating silence, he says, "If Juda was jealous, it's because she led him on, not because I acted inappropriately."

"That's a lie!" I say, etiquette forgotten.

"Now, now, Mina," Mr. Asher says. "Be careful, dear. Don't say anything you might regret." He takes a deep breath, giving me his full attention. "I now find it necessary, Mina, to ask if you ever lowered yourself to become a temptress. Did you or did you not try to seduce or enthrall Juda?"

"No!" I say. Feeling my cheeks flush, I thank God I

have the veil to cover my face. *Did* I try to seduce him? Was that what I was doing when I met him in the stairwell? When I let him kiss me? Have I committed a horrible sin, and now it's time for my punishment?

"And did you think it was appropriate to allow my son into your bedroom, in the middle of the night, with no supervision and no veil?"

"No, sir," I say quickly. "But it wasn't like that—"

"I think there are several guilty parties here," Mr. Asher says. "I must confess that you have been an enormous disappointment to me, Miss Clark, and I've always been fond of your father. First, you become inebriated in my home, and then you lure my son into your bedchamber before your wedding night. I feel I've been deceived as to the true nature of your character. Perhaps it would be best for me to call off the engagement."

His words should fill me with joy. Isn't this exactly what I wanted? To be away from his disgusting son forever? But it will mean the end of Father's career. His dream of ensuring fresh water for everyone in the city will be destroyed if there's no marriage.

"No," I say. "Please." I look to Damon. "Please tell him the truth."

Using the nasal, whiny voice he produces when dissatisfied, Damon says, "Father, you're overreacting. There's no need to cancel the engagement—"

"Overreacting! Look at this sinful behavior! And Juda, our best guard, a good, decent boy, has fled into the night!"

"He can't get far," Damon says, with an attempt at

reasonableness. "Why don't you wait until he's captured before you decide about the marriage?"

A deep sadness settling on his face, Mr. Asher makes more tiny shakes with his head. "We have spoiled you, and you have no respect. I should have known that something like this would happen."

"I respect you, Father," Damon says, but even I can see he's lying.

Mr. Asher walks to the door. "I'll use my contacts within the Guard to look for Juda. We won't alert the Teachers yet. Not until we know the full story. I'll make my decision then."

Smiling, Damon says, "Thank you, Father," simpering like a boy who's received an extra scoop of ice cream.

"Thank you, Mr. Asher," I say.

Facing me, Mr. Asher says, "You are not to leave this house until Juda is recovered. If he tells us that you behaved in a manner unbecoming to a Deserver, I will send you to the Tunnel without a second thought. Is that clear?"

I nod, head spinning. If Juda is caught, what will he say? That we met in the Square? That I led him into my bedroom? If it means saving his own life, why wouldn't he?

Mr. Asher and Damon walk out of my room. Hearing a soft *click*, I realize they've locked me inside.

I look around the room, as if I'm going to find another way out, but of course there is none. I think about yelling for help, but who would hear me? Mrs. Asher? The servants? All people who take orders from Mr. Asher.

What's left for me to do?

Dropping to my knees, I begin to chant my daily prayers, and I have no intention of stopping until Father or the Prophet Herself comes through the door to save me.

FOURTEEN

I HAVE NO WINDOWS OR CLOCKS, SO I CAN'T BE sure, but I think I've been locked in this room for nearly twenty-four hours. I haven't even been allowed out to use the bathroom. I got so desperate this morning that I finally just peed into Mrs. Asher's weird white vase. It didn't seem to be serving any other purpose.

I'm *starving*. I've had nothing to eat or drink. How can they treat me this way?

I've heard tales of girls who betrayed their families, who spoke against the Prophet or who made eyes at a brother-in-law, who are locked inside dark rooms and abandoned. The girls either starve or go mad. Is that what's happened? Have they found Juda and already sentenced me? Yes. That must be it. I've been left in this room to wither away, and no one—not my parents, not Dekker, not even Sekena—will ever know what became of me. If only I could get word to Nana; she'd know what to do.

My ears ring. Sharp pain starts at my temple, stabs down through my jaw. Nana is dead. She can't help me anymore.

The funeral. They have to let me out of here, or I'll miss Nana's funeral!

I'm determined not to cry, because surely I'll become
thirstier if I waste tears. My mouth is so dry that my tongue
is starting to swell.

How could Juda betray me like this? Juda, Juda, Juda. I
say his name over and over again until it becomes a mush
of nonsense in my mouth. Juda, Juda, Juda. You are the
Devil who tempted me. *I hate you.*

Yes. You're the Devil. You were sent by God to test
me, and I failed. God knew me, knew my innermost
thoughts, and created you so that I would stray from my
family and commit sin after sin—talk to you and touch you
and think about you, *oh God, how I think about you and want
to smell you again, sandalwood and soap*—but I shouldn't
want to, because you are the *Devil.*

The door swings open, and Mrs. Asher walks in,
holding a tray of food. I'm sure she's a hallucination. "Get
up," she says.

The smell hits me. Roast lamb and potatoes—I swoon, it
smells so good. She places the tray on the desk, next to the
vase. Sniffing the air, she crinkles her nose. "On second
thought," she says, lifting the tray back up, "it would be
better for you to get out of this room. Clean yourself up,
and then join me in the dining room."

I watch as she takes the food out of the room again. If I
were stronger, I would rip the tray from her hands, but I'm
sitting on the floor. I've been down here since my prayers
last night.

I stand. The room spins, so I lean on the wall.

Mrs. Asher left the door open. Strange to see it wide

open after it has sealed me in for so many hours. I drag myself through the doorway and cross the hall. I can't remember the last time I was so pleased to see a bathroom. After I relieve myself, I notice that Mrs. Asher has left a large, fluffy towel folded by the sink. "Clean yourself up," she said.

My stomach rumbles. I wish she'd allowed me just one bite of potato.

A porcelain bathtub as big as a taxi stands on gold claw feet at the far end of the bathroom. I turn the faucet, shaped like a gold swan, and scalding water pours out immediately. *Figures.*

After a few minutes, I climb in, moving as slowly and stiffly as Nana did with her bad knee. I can't believe how good the hot water feels and the cold porcelain feels nice against my scorched back. I had planned to splash myself quickly and get right out so I could get to my food sooner, but I find I'm paralyzed with relief. My muscles begin to melt. I wonder if I'll have the strength to climb out of the tub again.

There's a gentle knock on the door, and before I have a chance to say anything, I'm shocked to see it opening. I was sure I locked it. A figure slips inside, and I stop breathing. It's Juda! He puts his finger to his lips, and I nod, understanding everything. He didn't escape at all—he hid inside the apartment! He crosses over to me and then, without undressing, he steps into the hot water, sitting down across from me. I giggle, because it's like bathing with Sekena when we were toddlers. He giggles, too. And then he gets very serious, staring at me, and I remember I'm naked. And

I want him to stop looking, but also I don't. Goose bumps run down my body. He leans forward—

"Mina? Mina, your food is getting cold!" Mrs. Asher yells outside the door.

I jerk awake. How long have I been in the tub? I blush at my thoughts of Juda and then remember I'm mad at him. "I'll be right there!"

I quickly use the perfumed soap lying in the dish, and the shampoo next to it (both Relics). I rinse and then, pulling the plug, let the glorious hot water drain away. I carefully climb out and dry myself with the towel. The gray dress I've been wearing is truly disgusting. I dread putting it back on.

It's only now that I see a fresh cloak hanging on the back of the bathroom door. It's purple, the color appropriate for a single girl. That was thoughtful. Either that or Mrs. Asher doesn't want to be near the stink of my dress.

I happily grab the cloak and slide it over my naked body. I've never worn one this way, but it's actually quite comfortable.

I leave the bathroom and head for the dining room, which I remember having seen across from the living room where I sat with Mrs. Asher.

Mrs. Asher motions to the table, where my dinner is, and I sit, grabbing the fork and knife. I'm about to dig in, when I think better of it and look at her, making sure I'm allowed to eat.

She gives me a small nod and a smile, seeming pleased that I looked to her for permission.

I eat quickly and with desperation, and although I want to inhale the entire plate of food, my stomach seems smaller. I actually feel full after three little potatoes and a quarter of the lamb. But I want to save the rest of the food in case Mrs. Asher changes her mind about letting me out.

I point to the living room. "Mrs. Asher, what is that white sculpture?"

She turns to look, and I quickly stick two potatoes in my left pocket.

"Which one, dear?"

I look, and of course there are at least three white sculptures in the living room. "The one on the right."

"That's by a pre-Dividing artist named Sharun. He was brilliant."

I decide there are more useful things than potatoes on the table.

"And what about the one on the left?" I point back at the living room.

She looks over again. Deciding the knife is too close to her, I grab the fork from the other side of my plate and quickly shove it into my pocket.

"That's a knockoff Sharun. But who can tell?" She turns back, saying, "Are you finished?"

I nod, praying she won't notice the missing fork. But she has something else on her mind. "Mina, you're going to do something for me today."

"I am?"

"Yes." Reaching into the sleeve of her dress, she pulls out a folded envelope. "You're going to read this letter for me."

"But Mr. Asher—"

"Is not here. He and Damon are out searching for Juda."

Juda is still free. *He hasn't told on me.*

She examines the letter with suspicion and disdain. "My husband has kept this letter in his desk for many years, and I would like to know what it says." She sees my reluctance. "My son believes the best way to get the truth about Juda out of you is to starve you until you talk. If you'd like to eat again anytime soon, you'll read this to me now."

She slides the letter across the living room table until it's within my reach. I stare at it, wondering whether this is some sort of trap. She has fooled me before. Perhaps if I read this letter, Mr. Asher, or Captain Memon himself, will jump out of the kitchen and announce my execution.

Mrs. Asher clenches her jaw, her breathing unsteady, while her right hand taps on her thigh. She's worried that she herself is going to get caught.

It's not a trap.

Wiping my hands on a napkin, I take the letter carefully out of an old, crinkled envelope. I begin to read out loud:

My dearest Max,

My brother Mal has been kind enough to write down my words for this letter, but do not worry—he is entirely trustworthy. I want you to know that I have thought long and hard about your offer, but I'm sorry, I cannot accept. I do not wish to be the second wife in your household. I do not believe I have the correct temperament to share a husband with another woman. I shall raise our son here in my family's home, and he will have the guidance of his grandfather and uncles, and he will know his father was a man of honor. I think of you often, with much love and respect.

With sincerest affection,
Rose

After I finish the letter, I continue to stare at the page. I don't want to look up.

I don't know any man who has more than one wife. Only the wealthiest of men can afford to, and although the Book condones the practice, the Prophet never did, so most people look down on it. I can only imagine Mother's reaction if Father tried to add a new wife to our household —Mother would claw the woman's eyes out.

The letter I'm holding is proof that not only did Mr. Asher invite a woman to be his second wife, but he fathered a child with her. I wish more than anything I'd refused to read it.

Her voice surprisingly calm, Mrs. Asher says, "Give it back to me," reaching out her hand.

I pass her the letter, noticing that the blood has drained from her face. Rising, she crosses to my side of the table and yanks me up from my seat.

"But you told me to read it!" I say, my voice becoming loud and defensive as she digs her fingers into my arm and pulls me back toward the guest room.

"Please," I say. "Don't make me go back in there."

We reach the open doorway. She shoves me inside so hard that I trip, falling on my knee. I cry out as she shuts and locks the door. Sitting on the floor, I hold my leg, knee throbbing. "Let me out!" I holler. "The Prophet can see you!" I scream more loudly. "God can see you!" But it's no use. If the Prophet can see us, She has decided to do nothing.

FIFTEEN

I'M SURPRISED WHEN THERE'S A KNOCK ON MY door less than an hour later. "Come in," I say, doubting I can be heard through the ebony door. Mr. Asher appears. "Peace," he says, averting his eyes.

Responding, "Peace," I fetch my veil.

"Why don't you join us for a bite to eat?" he says, not unpleasantly. He gestures toward the dining room.

Confused, I walk out of the room. I am barefoot and naked under my cloak, since Mrs. Asher never returned my gray dress and shoes. Mr. Asher follows me, and when I reach the dining room, I see that Damon and Mrs. Asher are already seated and waiting.

Damon, not acknowledging my presence, looks irritated.

Mrs. Asher, veil-free since she's only with family, wears a tight smile. She says, "You must be *starving* after your long day *in your room.*"

She doesn't want me to mention the lamb and potatoes. She doesn't want the men to know about the letter. Her piercing eyes don't leave me for a moment.

"Yes, I'm famished," I say, knowing that her secret could incriminate me as well.

Mr. Asher claps his hands together. "Then let's eat!" He takes his place at the head of the table, whips his napkin onto his lap, and smiles at Ray, who scampers off to the kitchen.

Within no time, Ray has returned with a stew that smells like heaven. As Ray spoons the meat and vegetables into his bowl, Mr. Asher says, "I have explained to Damon, Mina, that starvation is a barbaric tactic and is no way to obtain information. It weakens only the mind, not the resolve."

Next to me, Damon snorts in derision.

After Ray has filled Mr. Asher's and Damon's bowls, he tends to Mrs. Asher. Then he stands over me and scoops large chunks of beef and vegetables into the bowl in front of me.

Mr. Asher thanks God and the Prophet for the bounty of food and for Their grace, which allows his family to continue to prosper.

As the others begin to eat, I pinch the bottom of my veil and pull the fabric away from my face, allowing just enough space for me to pass the spoon up to my mouth. I dislike eating with the veil on, but the broth is salty and delicious and easier to eat than the lamb I had earlier.

Mr. Asher keeps speaking. "No, starvation is not the way. Captain Memon agrees with me. I spoke to him today, in fact."

I stop slurping the stew.

Using his knife to tear into a large piece of beef, he continues to talk. "He said there was a much simpler way to go about these things. And once he explained, I felt very foolish for not having thought of it myself." Chuckling a bit, as if at his own shortcomings, he takes from his pocket what looks like a piece of silver pipe. He places it on the table and then goes back to concentrating on his dinner.

I stare at the silver pipe, broth threatening to surge back up my throat, as I realize that it's one of the Tasers that the Matrons use.

Mr. Asher doesn't say another word. He leaves the tube sitting next to his hand as he continues to eat.

Mrs. Asher doesn't look up. Damon says, "Even if Mina confesses, Juda still has to be punished. He hit me!"

"Yes, Damon," Mr. Asher answers. "We've heard all about your suffering. But if Juda was manipulated, then we might try to find it in our hearts to forgive him—"

"I don't care if the Prophet showed up in his bedroom closet! He struck me, Father, and the punishment is *death*."

Without warning, Mr. Asher stands up and roars, "You will not blaspheme in this house! And you will not dare to pronounce judgment and sentencing where it is not your place! Do you understand?"

Damon slumps, motionless, like he's been hit over the head with a chair a second time.

"Max, what's the matter with you?" Mrs. Asher says. "He was assaulted and he wants justice! Nothing more!"

Mr. Asher starts to lecture her about the importance of a trial when it comes to the death penalty. I listen to them talking, but it's as if I'm underwater and the three of them are hovering above me, still able to breathe air. I'm drowning in my own fear, knowing that at any second they'll stop talking and Mr. Asher will hold that silver Taser rod against my flesh.

I have to do something. I was willing to do everything in my power to make this marriage happen, to save Father's job, but I won't just sit here obediently and wait to be tortured.

But I have nothing. No means of escape. My mind kicks and thrashes under the water, grasping for the tiniest bubble of hope.

And then I have it.

"Mr. Asher," I say, almost in a whisper. I'm still so dehydrated, speaking with any volume takes great effort. "MR. ASHER," I repeat, more loudly, cutting off his conversation with his wife.

"How dare you interrupt me!" he says. His hand reaches for the Taser, and I know my time has run out.

"Why don't you tell us about Rose?" I say.

Mrs. Asher's head snaps around to face me, her eyes blazing fire.

Mr. Asher's eyes go blank, as if he's trying to connect two words from separate languages. But then he becomes irate. "What do you . . . How dare you . . . What is this child talking about?"

Mrs. Asher looks away from him, trying to remain composed, but her face turns puce and the tiny lines around her mouth and eyes grow hard. It's like watching a piece of pottery bake and then crack.

Gaping at both of them, Damon says, "What's going on? Who the hell is Rose?"

"No one!" says Mr. Asher, his anger becoming defensive.

But Mrs. Asher turns to Damon and, in a low, hateful voice, says, "Your father's lover."

"What?" Damon looks at his father, amazed.

Mr. Asher examines me with loathing and rage. "What does SHE know about it?"

"Who cares?" Mrs. Asher says, leaning forward, raising her voice. "You're the liar. Not her. Maybe we should use this on you!" She snatches the Taser rod from his hand and starts waving it in his face.

Mr. Asher grits his teeth. "Give it to me, Gabriella. It's not a plaything."

"That seems to be what you know about, Max. Playthings!"

Mr. Asher says to Damon, barking like a soldier, "GET THE ROD FROM YOUR MOTHER."

Jumping up, Damon is around the table in seconds. He grabs his mother's hand, forcing the wand from her grip in no time.

"Take Mina back to her room," Mr. Asher tells him.

"But, Father—"

"Now!"

I stand, not wanting to be yanked from my seat ever again. Damon says, "Let's go," heading toward my room. I follow, and we're in the hallway when we hear the sound of a plate smashing. Then Mrs. Asher yells, "If you were going to treat me like shit, you should have left me living in shit."

I smile underneath my veil. Grabbing my wrist, Damon

says, "What have you done?" His grip grows stronger. "Why did you mention that woman?"

I say nothing. Releasing my wrist, he slaps me across the face. The pain of it is shocking.

The force of the blow has unsnapped my veil, and I hold the fabric up against my eyes, not wanting him to see the tears forming.

"Tell me!" he says, growing impatient.

"No!" I say, matching his tone. I re-snap the veil. Then I smooth my hair, like Mother does when she's regaining her composure.

"I want to know what's going on," he says, holding up the Taser.

Before he can grab me, I turn and run toward my room.

I get there first, but he catches the door before I can shut it and walks in after me. He happily shuts the door behind us. There's nowhere left for me to go.

"How did you know about the name Rose?" he asks in a voice that is mockingly sweet, but he doesn't wait for an answer. He approaches fast and sticks the silver rod straight into my side.

The sound is like fifty matches sparking at once, and the shock that runs through me is worse than any pain I've ever experienced—as if my muscles have been stripped of skin and are being stung by wasps. As I convulse, my teeth seem to shove up into the soft tissue of my brain. Then my legs go out from under me, leaving me crumpled on the floor.

Damon is laughing. "That was amazing. Wow!"

After a few seconds, my convulsions stop. The pain felt like it was going to kill me, but now it's just a nausea filling every pore.

Grinning down at me, he says, "I think you should probably tell me everything now about Rose, about Juda, and anything else you feel like talking about. Because I could do this all night."

"Yes . . . yes . . . anything," I say, trying to buy some time. I need to get upright. "It was a letter. . . . Your mother . . . made me read her a letter . . . about your father." Taking a few deep breaths, I pull myself into a crouching position.

"What? What do you mean? You mean you can—"

"I can read." I stand up slowly while he absorbs the information.

He looks me up and down. "I can't believe how close I came to marrying you," he says, as if a bad taste has entered his mouth. "Father was about to bind me to an Apostate!" He raises the Taser again.

"I have the letter. If you want to see it." I put my hand in my pocket.

"Give it to me," he says, leaning forward with anticipation.

I whip the fork out of my pocket, lift it as high above my head as I can, and then ram it down into his shoulder.

He screeches in pain.

Grabbing the Taser rod he's dropped to the floor, I look up to see him pry the fork out of his skin, blood dripping down his arm.

I spin the silver tube in my hand, frantically searching for the ON switch. Spotting a small button at the base, I press it and feel the rod vibrate.

"You Saitch! I'LL RIP YOUR THROAT OUT!"

He lunges for me, and I stick the Taser straight into his crotch.

He freezes, his face a solid mask of rage. His body starts to flail, like he's a fish that's been dumped from its bowl. Still, I hold the Taser to him. Drool runs down his mouth.

Then his enormous body hits the floor with a *thud*.

He lies there, shuddering, tears running down his cheeks. Several seconds go by, but he doesn't regain the use of his limbs. I've hurt him much worse than he hurt me.

Maybe I should feel sorry for him. The Prophet would want me to recognize that he's just as human as I am and to offer him forgiveness. But I cannot. Even in stunned pain, his face is hateful.

I lean over him and whisper, "You're a liar. And you're half the man that Juda is. I know it. Your father knows it. And you act like a miserable *git* because *you* know it."

He can't respond. He can only whimper. His whole body is curled in on itself, his eyes glazing over like they're covered in wax.

Placing the Taser in my pocket, I rush to the bedroom door and open it carefully. No one's in the hallway. I walk quickly but softly to the foyer, and I can hear that the Ashers are still fighting in the dining room. They haven't heard anything above their own yelling.

I'm reaching for the front door, when suddenly it

swings open, almost knocking me down. The door guard is as surprised to see me as I am to see him. His eyes go wide. I look down and see blood on my hand and cloak.

Heat surges through my veins as I prepare to be restrained, but then a lie spills from my lips: "Mrs. Asher has stabbed her husband. He needs help."

Looking appalled, the guard runs toward the shouting in the dining room.

I run out the door and sprint down the hall, spotting an exit. I barrel through it and down the stairs, when I remember—I'm on the thirty-third floor! I can't possibly run down the whole stairwell before the Ashers realize I'm gone.

Racing down a few more flights, I shove through the door to the thirtieth floor. I dive for the elevator buttons, punching the down arrow.

This floor has no air-conditioning; the air is torrid and stale. Wallpaper peels off the walls, exposing glue that looks like hardened mucus.

Hearing a *ding*, I pull out the Taser, holding my breath, as the elevator to my right opens.

It's empty.

I leap in and hit LEVEL 1. Waiting for the elevator to move, I'm sure time has stopped. Finally, after what feels like two lifetimes, the doors slide shut and I begin to descend.

What if the electricity is cut? Can the Ashers trap me in here? I feel faint at the thought. I hear another *ding*; then the doors open and I find myself on the ground floor.

───

No door guards wait here—only cameras, pointing out. The rich don't expect their trouble to come from the inside. I dash through the lobby, pushing into the giant revolving door and out again, and then I run like demons are grabbing at my heels.

SIXTEEN

MADISON IS A LARGE, BUSY AVENUE, LANES
jammed with bikes, buses, and taxis all trying to head
north. As I head south, the brutal roughness of the sidewalk
scrapes my bare feet, and I can only pray that I don't step
on something sharp or nasty. I don't have time to be
cautious. I have to keep sprinting.

I fly across 74th Street. Pedestrians stare at me as I
charge by, but no one stops me. Where am I going? I want
to go home. I want to run to my parents: to tell them
what's happened, to hear the soothing words of my father.
But I can't. I've shamed him. I ran away from my fiancé's
family. I assaulted my fiancé. No one will care what they
did to me. All that will matter is *my* behavior toward *them*.

My mother will turn me back over to the Ashers, rather
than dishonor our family publicly.

The same will be true of all my relatives—my aunties,
Grandma and Grandpa Silna. No one will give me safe
harbor now.

I reach 72nd Street, stopping to let traffic cross in front
of me. My lungs scream. I can't catch my breath. I wait
with a large group of pedestrians—women in their cloaks

and veils, like dark ghosts, and men with impatient frowns. A Teacher stands tall and proud in his red cloak, the Book resting in the crook of his arm. A little boy standing with his mother gapes at my naked feet.

I look behind me for signs of Mr. Asher or his guard, but I can't see much beyond the mass of people. The light changes. I'm moving with the crowd, when, without warning, a piercing alarm fills the air and everyone stops walking, looking around for the source. It's deafeningly loud, and the little boy starts to cry. I cover my ears, but the siren only gets worse. With horror, I realize why.

The alarm is coming from me.

The diamond cuff on my wrist is emitting an ear-splitting scream.

I pull at the bracelet, desperate to get it off, but I can't unlock it, and it's too small to slip over my hand. As they realize the source of the screeching, the people around me begin to back away.

Just like they did in Union Square. *Right before the stoning.*

My stomach seizes as if I might be sick. I keep trying to unlock the cuff, hands shaking, but it's no use. I look up at the women around me. "Please. Please help me."

They turn their heads away.

I can't just stand here. I should keep running. But, just as the thought passes through my head, a hand lands on my shoulder. I turn to find a Twitcher standing behind me, his helmet shield an inch from my face. I can't be sure whether he's speaking to me or not; I hear nothing but the siren. He twists my arm behind my back, and pain shoots up my shoulder.

A second Twitcher appears. He grabs my other arm and places a thin metal reed into a hole in the side of the diamond bracelet, abruptly stopping the alarm. After seeming to exhale all at once, the people around us start walking down the sidewalk again.

The first Twitcher stands facing me on the sidewalk, and I see his Senscan move up and down. Instead of turning green, the scanner's light flashes red. The Twitcher says, "Seems we've caught a bride mid-flight."

The other snickers. "Not a Deserter, then. A 'Dreader.'"

They both laugh. "Why are women so dramatic?" Twitcher Number One asks, sounding tired. "Let's take her to the Lyceum. The Teachers can have a nice 'chat' with her until Mr. Asher wants to pick her up."

After the other one nods, they start to pull me uptown. I resist, relaxing my body into dead weight, but the one on my left twists my arm again until I'm forced to stand and walk normally.

The Lyceum is on 80th and Fifth, and it will be full of hundreds of Teachers, each of them carrying a Taser cane. I don't want to "chat" with any of them. I have to escape before we get there. I still have the Taser rod in my pocket, but there's no way to reach it with my hand behind my back. Plus, how can I take down *two* Twitchers?

Dekker will be at the Lyceum. What if he sees me? The chances are slim—the Lyceum is huge—but if he does, I wonder what he'll do. Will he acknowledge me? He'll probably escape the room as quickly as possible. If only I could get him alone, tell him everything that's happened, maybe I could make him understand. Maybe he could help me escape. . . .

I stumble, and the Twitcher to my right jerks me forward. We pass 74th—only six blocks left. I can't go back to the Ashers'. I can't. The Tunnel would be better. I'd rather be in a place that acknowledges that it's a prison than with a family that pretends it's something else.

75th Street comes and goes. I have five blocks to think of something. What can I do that will make these Twitchers so angry that they'll turn around and take me to the Tunnel, instead of the Lyceum? Speak against the Prophet? Confess some horrible sin? But if I admit to a crime they consider reprehensible, they might execute me on the spot. How is one to know?

I open my mouth, ready to confess that I once touched a boy's hand and spoke to him without my family's permission, when there, standing on the sidewalk in front of us, is the boy himself: Juda.

I'm sure I'm hallucinating, like when I was in the bathtub. But then he speaks.

"Peace," he says to the Twitchers, who want to keep walking but stop because Juda has blocked our path.

They respond, "Peace."

Juda doesn't look like a man on the run. Instead, he looks exactly like he did when he arrived at my Offering. He's wearing his uniform, hair perfectly combed, hands held calmly at his sides. Eyeing me, he says, "This is the

fiancée of my employer, Damon Asher. We've been searching for her all day. I have instructions to return her to his
home immediately."

The Twitcher on my left says, "When a chip is acti-
vated, it's protocol to take the runaway to the nearest
Teachers for penance."

Juda doesn't flinch. "You know as well as I do that she
could easily get held up in the system, and it could take
days, if not weeks, for her to atone and be returned to the
family. Damon's father, Mr. Maxwell Asher, is Uncle
Ruho's chief energy engineer. He would be very displeased
if this delay were to occur. And it would be very unfor-
tunate if your names were in the system as being the cause
of such a holdup, don't you agree?"

A long silence follows. I try not to look at Juda. I try
not to have hope.

Turning his head away for a moment as if he's heard a
sound, the Twitcher on my right seems to type on an invisible keyboard. He tells his partner, "Headquarters says there's
another graffiti leaf over on Park. I said we'd take care of it."

The other Twitcher then does exactly what I've been
dreading: he scans Juda. I hear the hum and watch the red
light, fearing the moment when it will start to flash like it
did with me. Juda stays calm, ignoring the Senscan, but I
can only imagine that inside he is preparing to run.

The light turns green. *I'm flabbergasted.*

The Twitcher holding my right arm shoves me toward
Juda, saying, "If there's a hole in the record, you'll be to
blame, not us, Mr. Alvero."

This is the first time I've heard Juda's last name.

Juda says, "Thank you for your wisdom. Peace."

"Peace," the Twitchers say, heading east.

Saying nothing, Juda grasps my elbow and starts walking south. We don't turn our heads. We don't look behind us. I wait to hear the yelling—to feel the bullets slam into my back.

"Why hasn't Mr. Asher turned you in?" I say, still stunned.

"I don't know," he says. When we've gotten a block away, we turn west. "Your word plus mine equals one and a half testimonies. He probably realizes that the Teachers would have to believe our story and not Damon's."

And if they only have me, my word is worth half of Damon's.

"Damon wants revenge," I say, lengthening my strides to keep up with him. "He's not going to let you walk away."

"I know. I don't think we have long. When those Twitchers learn that I'm wanted, too, they'll reactivate the alarm on your collar."

My *collar*? My extravagant engagement gift—I should've known.

"Where are we going?" I ask.

"To the Fields," he answers.

The Fields are where we grow most of our food, a big block of land in the middle of Manhattan. I've never been inside, but I would go anywhere Juda told me to right now. I'm so happy to see him, I think I might cry. I grab his hand, but he quickly shakes it away.

"No," he says, a slight snarl in his voice.

I pull my hand back as if he's bitten me, and he quickly changes his tone. Keeping his face looking forward, he says, "I'm sorry. I meant . . . we can't attract attention."

He's right. I only touched him because I don't believe this freedom will last. Any second, the Ashers or the Twitchers will come drag me away. I want every second with him to count.

As we approach Fifth Avenue, he says quietly, "We're going to cross the street, and then we'll enter the Fields at 72nd. There's no reason for a single girl to be in there, so just go along with whatever I say."

I nod, and we continue across the street. A huge fence lines the perimeter of the farmland, and a closed gate stands here at 72nd. A sign warns, FARMING PERSONNEL ONLY. Examining me, Juda asks, "Can you rearrange your cloak at all?"

Seeing that my cloak is spattered with blood, I pull out the fabric around my sleeves, and by crossing my arms in front of me, I'm able to cover the stain. He frowns at my bare feet, but I can't do anything to hide them. I look like a beggar.

He approaches the side of the enormous gate, producing a card from his pocket. He slides the card into a small box I hadn't noticed, and, after a little *click*, the heavy gate swings open, revealing a cornfield that reaches as far as the eye can see. I gasp, taken aback. The beauty of the waving stalks astonishes me.

Juda takes me by the shoulder, a little brusquely, leading me inside.

The corn is planted in perfect rows, evenly spaced, crisp and neat. Each stalk is over seven feet tall, and the evening light bouncing off their tassels is golden, as if there were a spotlight on each one.

The air here seems fresher and smells earthy. For a moment, I forget everything and just want to race through the dirt and run my hands across the long green leaves.

I'm thrown out of my daydream when I spot a man with a shotgun standing just inside the gate. He's not a Twitcher. He's wearing a soiled tunic and work pants, and he seems to have been out working in the Fields.

Juda says, "Peace," and the man nods in return.

"What's this?" he asks, motioning to me.

Juda smirks in an unfamiliar way. "Entertainment for the boys who've been harvesting in the meadow."

The man leers at me as if he can see through my cloak. "Why doesn't that ever happen when *I'm* working over there?"

"It's all about timing, brother," Juda says, his voice both friendly and mocking.

The man laughs bitterly, motioning for Juda to move on through.

Juda pulls me roughly ahead into one of the cornrows, and soon the stalks have engulfed us completely. The cool dirt soothes my feet and feels wonderful between my toes. When we're out of sight of the gate man, Juda releases my arm, giving me a warm smile.

Relief trickles through me, and I start to ask him where we're going, but he puts his finger to his lips. I look around, not seeing anyone, but if he says someone is listening, I believe him.

Instead of saying anything, I stand on tiptoe, lift my veil, and quickly kiss his lips. His eyebrows shoot up, and then a lopsided grin spreads across his face. I mouth the words "thank you."

Nodding once, he signals for me to follow him. He heads west, straight at first and then weaving in and out of the rows, walking with purpose. I can't imagine how he knows where he's going. Every row looks exactly like the last. I could be lost in here for days.

After walking for about ten more minutes, he finally turns toward a clearing. When we emerge from the corn, the sun is lowering to the west. I squint at the orange glare. Wheat grows far into the distance, sloping up hills, disappearing into ravines, and turning pink in the light of the fading day.

"Wow," I whisper, before I can stop myself.

Just then, I hear the clang of the Bell, the sound ringing across the wheat stalks and then disappearing into a thicket of woods to the north.

Tense, Juda pulls me back into the cornfield and makes me crouch down low, gesturing for me to be quiet.

No need. I'm still as stone. Men are walking through the wheat, all dressed like the gate guard but with wide-brimmed hats, and all headed in the same direction. A prayer center must be close by. We were lucky not to be walking near it.

I look at Juda. His face is a mask of concentration. On

second thought, luck had nothing to do with it. He knows where he's going. I try to relax and trust him.

After a few minutes, when the men are gone, he signals for me to stand. We head back into the clearing, toward the trees. The sun is disappearing. As we enter a thick cluster of maple trees, the night becomes darker, cooler.

Before long, I see a building—or what used to be a building. Instead of grass, I now walk on old, cracking concrete, which forms a path up to the crumbling structure. Approaching an empty window to look inside, I see a cavernous room with a stone floor, its rusted-green copper roof collapsed down the middle. Grass and ivy snake in-and-out of cracks in the stonework and up thick marble pillars. I'm astonished to see a tranquil lake visible through the columns. This must have been quite a grand place, once.

Walking to the empty doorway, I'm excited to step inside, when Juda says, "Be careful." He points to shattered glass on the floor, and I stop dead.

Indicating my bare feet, he asks, "May I lift you?"

I try to be casual as I say, "Yes," but I'm sure he notices my voice getting higher.

He encircles me as he did at the Ashers' right before he kissed me. I hope he's going to kiss me again, but instead he scoops me up into his arms and carries me across the crunchy floor.

Trying not to be disappointed, I inhale his Juda smell. He's been on the run, but he still smells like sandalwood and soap. He walks me through the room and down two steps, until we're at the water's edge.

"It's beautiful here," I say, watching the last of the light sink into the dark lake. Thick trees rise up from both shores and bend inward, their bowing branches like hands protecting the precious water.

An odd chirping fills the air, and before I can ask him about it, Juda says, "Crickets."

I smile, finding the sound strangely soothing.

"You need to get wet."

"Excuse me?" Is he about to throw me in the water?

Checking the floor for glass, he places me back on the ground with great care. "Your wrist—the collar. Submerge it. It will disarm it temporarily, hopefully long enough for us to break it off."

As soon as I understand his meaning, I kneel on the edge of the floor and stick my hand in the cold water, but soon I realize I actually need to lie down if I want to get my arm elbow-deep. Rearranging myself, I plunge my arm in, sending ripples across the calm lake. I see the diamonds sparkling under the dark water, and I imagine them attracting little fish that will come and gnaw off the bracelet.

I'm surprised to look over and see Juda lying next to me, scooping water into his mouth.

"Is it safe?" I ask.

"They use it to water the Fields. It's probably the cleanest reservoir in the city."

I happily use my free hand to ladle cold, crisp water under my veil and into my mouth. Until now, I didn't know water could be delicious. I slurp handful after handful, until

Juda stands, saying, "That's probably long enough," pointing toward the cuff.

His eyes dart along the perimeter of the lake. Understanding he's afraid of being seen, I stand to leave. He puts his arms out, ready to carry me again.

"I'm a bit wet," I say.

"I know." He smiles. "I told you to get that way."

Picking me up, he turns back into the ruins. This time, he heads for two swinging doors on the northern side. Putting his shoulder against the right door, he pushes it open, revealing a decrepit kitchen. "This used to be a restaurant," he says. "There are *three* kitchens."

"Three?" I try to remember a restaurant next to a lake in the Primer, but I can't think of any. This one must have been enormous.

"There are some old nails and stuff in here, so I'll, um, just take you to the other side."

The old kitchen has a partial roof, even less than the last room. He carries me past several rusted, decaying stoves and a huge, open refrigerator with collapsed shelves. We reach the far end and face another door. This one is solid and looks as if it's made of thick metal.

He says, "You should be fine from here."

No, I wish I could say. I don't want him to put me down. He places me on my feet and I stare at him, knowing he can't see my eyes through my veil. His uniform has a mark where my wet arm must have been, and I can see his skin through the fabric. I step in closer, wanting to touch that wet patch of skin.

His thoughts are elsewhere. The door moans when he pushes down the heavy handle.

"What's in there?" I ask, peering into the pitch black, all thoughts of being held by Juda disintegrating.

"No Twitchers," he says, striking a match.

I wonder where the match came from, but before I can ask, he's produced a lantern, and I can just make out the top of the staircase where they were resting.

I realize what he wants me to do.

"I'm not sure I can, uh, go down there," I say. "I really don't like being underground."

He sighs. "I don't have anywhere else safe for us to go."

My chest tightens. Not only do these stairs lead underground, but they're next to a lake. For all I know, we're going to a room that's under the water, just like the Tunnel. All my childhood nightmares involved being caught in one of the Tunnel's prison cells and then drowning. . . .

My mind spins with other options. What about Nana's apartment? Or maybe Sekena could help us? Or perhaps I should try contacting my parents, just once?

"Juda, maybe there's another way."

Despite my veil, he seems to look me straight in the eyes. "Mina, there may be other options for you tomorrow, but right now the sun has set and Twitchers will be hunting for you soon, if they aren't looking for you already. I'm sorry you don't like spaces below the ground, but you're just going to have to trust me that it's safe. I slept here last night and—"

"I trust you; it's just . . ."

"What?"

"The air . . . I'm afraid of running out of air."

He probably thinks I'm being a baby.

"There's a vent. I can show it to you as soon as we get down there. Would that help?"

I nod, but I'm skeptical.

"Do you think you can give it a try?"

I hesitate but nod again.

"We'll go slowly. Just tell me if you need to come back up." He gives me a supportive smile and takes my hand.

Then we step down into the blackness.

SEVENTEEN

WE REACH A TINY ROOM, EVEN SMALLER THAN I feared—a simple square with metal shelves reaching from floor to ceiling. I counted fifteen steps from the top. Juda flicks a switch, and, to my utter amazement, the space floods with light.

Industrial gray paint coats everything—the walls, the ceiling, the floor, the shelves. Whoever made this room wasn't worried about making it cheerful. A large bundle of clothes nests in the corner, tins and jars of food are stacked on the shelves, and two buckets of water rest near the wall.

"I don't see the air vent," I say, starting to panic.

"It's over here." He hops over to the corner, pointing up. I walk over, turn up my head, and see a long aluminum tube that doesn't look like much to me.

"It's hard to see it at night, but in the morning, you can see blue sky. I promise."

"Tell me something you're afraid of," I say sharply, more like an order than a request.

"What?" he says, confused by my change of tone.

"I want to know something that bothers you as much as being underground bothers me." I hate feeling so insecure around him, like he's seeing me at the age of five, cowering under the blankets. I need to know that something makes him feel vulnerable, too. His puzzled expression tells me he doesn't understand this need for empathy right now, so I change the subject. "So where's the electricity coming from?"

"Over there." He points to a black box in the corner. "It's some old model battery people used to use in emergencies."

"Uh-huh. Hmmm." I act fascinated, the room still closing in. "If you don't mind, I really need to take off my veil so I can breathe better."

He turns away, out of habit. "Of course. Go ahead."

I give the veil one quick jerk, causing the button in back to snap open. I inhale deeply, enjoying that first unencumbered breath. "You can turn around. You've seen me without it before."

"I know," he says. "I didn't want to be presumptuous." He turns back around but looks at my feet, as if he's become shy at the sight of my face. "You can take off your cloak, too, if you'd be more comfortable."

Now it's my turn to be embarrassed. "No, that's okay . . . um . . . huh . . . I don't have anything, uh, on underneath."

I expect him to laugh, but instead his ears turn crimson while he searches for a response.

"This is where you've been hiding?" I say, deciding to help him out.

He nods.

"Why is this place even here?"

"I'm not sure. My mom thinks it must be some sort of war room—like where you would run if the Apostates were coming." Our eyes meet. I smile, and he smiles back, and our moment of awkwardness seems to be over. "And . . . we . . . uh . . . these food cans have been down here for decades."

I study the food tins, all Relics that Nana would have found fascinating. "Your mom knows about this place?" I ask.

"Yeah, she showed it to me. She works in the Fields."

I'm amazed. "She has a *job?*"

"Yeah, since I was little."

I was raised to believe it was illegal for women to work. "But . . . how?"

"It took too long for the farmers to leave the Fields, have lunch, and come back, and none of the men wanted to cook—they thought it was demeaning—so Uncle Ruho let a few women inside to make the meals. But they do it in exchange for food, so it's not considered 'work.'"

"And your father doesn't mind?"

Turning away, he rearranges the cans on the nearest shelf. "He died when I was little."

"I'm sorry," I say, wishing I hadn't brought it up.

He shrugs, his back still turned. "I never knew him, so it's not like I have anyone to miss."

The silent air seems thick between us.

I finally say, "You're using your mother's gate pass?"

"Yeah."

"You're very lucky she's willing to help you."

Sticking a hand in his pocket, he smiles impishly and

pulls out a rusty nail. He then holds up a can of Relic spinach he just took from the shelf. "It's time to get that collar off."

I hold on to one of the shelves while he works on the lock of the bracelet. He inserts the nail into the same hole that the Twitcher used for his long, reedlike key.

"It's much bigger than what the Twitcher used," I say. "Will it work?"

He's concentrating deeply. "Shhh."

Pushing the nail in as far as it will go, he lifts up the can of spinach. "This may hurt. I need to hammer it in further."

"Okay," I say, closing my eyes. "Do it." Hearing the *thwack* of the can against the nail, I brace myself for the pain, but none comes.

"*Nyek,*" Juda says under his breath.

My eyes fly open. The punctured spinach can is squirting nasty green juice down his robe. I laugh before I can stop myself.

"It's not funny," he says, clearly annoyed. "If the alarm goes off again, people will find us. Even down here."

I stop laughing.

He holds the can away from us both. "Oh . . . it really stinks." The spinach must've spoiled years ago, leaving behind a liquid that smells like rotten eggs swimming in cat poo.

I bite my lip to keep from laughing again. It's like when I was little—if I started laughing during prayers, Father would scold me, which just made me want to laugh more.

"You need something harder than a c-can," I say, coughing to cover my giggle.

"Thanks," he says dryly. He looks around the room but can't find anything suitable. "I'll be right back," he grumbles. He heads up the stairs.

"Wait!" I say.

"What?"

"Nothing." I can't say it. *Please don't leave me. I'm not ready to be alone down here.*

He keeps walking.

I hear the slam of the door, then silence. Although Juda is large and takes up a lot of space, the room feels smaller without him. I instantly regret having laughed at him and resolve to apologize the moment he returns. He's just trying to look after me. And if the cuff goes off and gets us caught, it will be my fault. He didn't have to come get me. He could have stayed here much more safely on his own.

After an unbearably long five minutes, I hear the door open again. "It's me," he says.

I'm grateful he knew I would be on edge.

He comes down the stairs, big rock in hand. "It took me a while to find the right size. And I decided to rinse off, for both our sakes." Smiling, he points to his wet uniform where the spinach juice was. "Shall we try again?"

"I'm sorry I laughed—"

"No apologies," he says, waving away my words. "If you were covered in rotten spinach scum, I'm sure I would be laughing, too."

"You have my advance permission to *howl* if and when I'm covered in rotten spinach scum."

He grins. "Accepted."

I smile, putting my hand on the shelf where it was before.

He reinserts the nail. "Ready?"

I nod.

He whacks the nail with the rock, and it's like bird claws digging into my wrist. I wince. The cuff doesn't budge.

"Again?" he asks.

Taking a deep breath, I say, "Yes."

He hits it harder this time, thrusting the metal of the bracelet deep into my skin. I cry out, and he says, "I'm so sorry."

"It's fine. Keep going. We have to get it off." Looking into his eyes, I wish I could tell him how much more I've suffered, that watching my mother tear up the Primer hurt me a hundred times more than this. I want him to know that, despite not liking being underground, I'm not the delicate flower he thinks I am. "Don't hold back. I can tell you're afraid of hurting me."

"Okay," he says. His face ruddy, perspiration beading on his forehead and cheeks, he holds the rock higher. This time, he brings it down with true force. When it strikes the nail, I think my wrist might crack, but instead the collar splits apart. As the bracelet lands on the floor, the diamonds spill across the concrete.

"YES!" Juda cries. A grin blossoms on his face.

"You did it!" I say, jumping up and down, rubbing my wrist.

"Thank the Prophet," he says, exhaling.

As a few of the shiny stones roll toward my feet, it

occurs to me that they probably *aren't* real diamonds. I'm resisting the urge to grab the rock from Juda's hand and grind them all to dust, when suddenly, what remains of the cuff starts to scream. We look at the crushed bracelet in horror—the vanquished beast has risen from the dead. The alarm echoing inside the tiny space is like an ice pick through the ear.

Grabbing the remaining pieces, Juda throws them into the bucket of water in the corner. The siren stops immediately.

Unable to speak, we just stare at the bucket, then at each other.

"Do you think anyone heard?" I whisper finally.

He shakes his head. "The guards seem more concerned with protecting the crops than with exploring abandoned buildings. They're all praying right now, anyway. Plus, it only went off for a second. . . ."

The more he talks, the more worried I feel. We're the ones who should be praying.

"Do you want to sit down?" he asks.

"Yes," I say, feeling like I'm about to pass out.

He goes to the pile of clothes, separating out more than half of what's there and making a second stack. "You can sit on these."

I happily lower myself onto the makeshift cushion.

"Don't worry. They're clean," he says.

"I wasn't worried."

The cleanliness of his laundry is the last thing on my mind.

When he lowers himself onto the smaller pile of

clothes, his enormous size makes the whole image pretty ridiculous. He looks like a bear trying to relax on a pincushion. I can't help but smile.

"I never promised comfort," he says, laughing. "I said there would be no Twitchers, but I'm all out of silk sheets and down pillows."

I grin but can't hold it for long, feeling ashamed. "I never wanted silk or down."

"I know you didn't." He searches for something else to say.

"It's Mother," I say. "She was always so worried about the whole family and the future—"

"Doesn't the whole family include you?"

I stop talking. Mother's caused me a lot of pain through the years, but knowing I may not see her again makes me feel more forgiving. I'm picturing her and Father's lives if he loses his job, which surely he will after my disappearance. Will anyone else hire him, or is Mr. Asher so powerful he'll be shunned? Will Dekker have to drop out of the Lyceum? Will Mother and Father be able to stay in our apartment?

Not ready to discuss these things with Juda, I ask, "How were you able to save me from the Twitchers? How did you even know where I was?"

"I was watching the building, trying to figure out how to bust you out."

"You were?" I'm astonished.

His face screws up as he slowly inhales. "I'm *sorry* I left you behind. I should never have done it. I don't know what I was thinking."

"You had to leave. I knew—"

"No. I didn't." His shoulders tense. "As soon as I got outside, I knew that it was a terrible mistake . . . that Damon would never admit what had happened . . . that you were in horrible danger." He drops his head, eyes boring into the floor. "So now, I need to know . . ." He takes another big breath. "Did they hurt you?"

"It doesn't matter. I told you—"

He cuts me off, looking up, his words slow and fierce. "Did . . . they . . . hurt . . . you?"

I think of the day without food or water. Of Mr. Asher sitting at the dinner table with a Taser rod by his plate. Of Damon shocking me and smacking me in the face. And part of me is desperate to tell Juda all of it, to let him console me, to share my pain. But one look at his eyes is enough to know that I can't. He'll storm out of here, searching for revenge. He'll get himself arrested or killed.

I stare right into his jade eyes. "No. They didn't hurt me."

He studies me for a while, and I'm not sure he believes me, but I think he can sense that he needs to pretend that he does, for now. "Will you ever be able to forgive me for leaving you behind?"

Leaning forward, I take his hand. "You saved me from Damon. He wasn't going to stop. He was going to hurt me very badly. You struck him, knowing it could mean your life. There's nothing to forgive."

"Thank you." His shoulders lower, and the muscles in his face relax. He leans in as well, with a curious look. "I have another question."

"Anything."

"How did you escape?"

I pull the Taser rod from my pocket, setting it down on the floor in front of me.

He eyes it. "Who did you use it on?"

I look down coyly. "I hope Damon can still reproduce."

After a pause, Juda bursts out laughing, cackling wildly. "Mina, you never cease to amaze me."

"The feeling is mutual," I say. "I was sure you'd be in the Tunnel by now."

I like making him laugh. He has a dimple on his right cheek that I've never noticed before. I'm still holding his hand, and I wonder if he wants to kiss me. Or maybe I should just kiss him?

"I would have been caught the first day if it weren't for my mother."

"Tell me about her." We're so close I can feel the warmth of his breath.

"Tomorrow," he says, releasing my hand. "I think you should get some sleep."

"But I'm not tired." Did I say something wrong?

"You need to stay strong for us to be safe, and for that, you need sleep."

I rearrange the clothes pile and lie down, trying not to let him see my disappointment. I thought boys *always* wanted to kiss and touch. My aunties warn me about it all the time.

I lean on my elbow, trying to look casual, even though my entire body aches. My back stings if I recline, my bruised knee complains when I straighten my leg, and every one of my muscles seems to be angry about the shock from the Taser. Even if Juda wanted to touch me, I'm not sure what part of me doesn't hurt. "Just tell me one thing about your mother," I say, distracting myself.

He fixes his pile, too, lying down across from me. "Okay. One thing." He frowns a little as he concentrates, and when he smiles, I know he's thought of something. His face is so open and expressive. I realize it's one of the first things I noticed about him. He doesn't wear the same stony face the other men have.

Lying there, he looks so relaxed—flat on his back, feet crossed, hands under his head. I've only ever seen him upright, usually standing at attention next to his boss. How funny. This suits him so much more. He looks so much younger and happier, which seems crazy since he—I mean, *we*—are on the run.

"When I was little," he says, "we couldn't afford many things, which always bothered my mother. She was upset she couldn't give me the treats and toys that other kids got. So, one year, a while after the harvest, she notices that there are these ears of corn that the pickers somehow missed. The husks are all dry and brown, the cobs have gone really hard—"

"Don't tell me you ate them!" I interrupt.

"Just listen," he says, grinning. "So she brings home this armful of old, stale corn, and while I'm sleeping she shucks all the corncobs and paints little faces on them. There's a mama corn, and a daddy corn, and a little baby corn, and even a grandma and grandpa corn. When I wake up, she's turned the kitchen table sideways, and she's sitting behind it, and she does this whole puppet show—"

"With corn!"

"Yeah. It was the greatest." His smile is larger than I've ever seen it, giving me a knot in my stomach because of how beautiful I think he is.

"It sounds terrific."

"I can't even remember what happened to the corn family. . . . It seemed like we had them for a really long time . . . like, years. Is that possible? Does corn last for years?"

I shrug, trying to imagine my own mother, on her knees, acting out a silly puppet show for my benefit, but I can't. I can only imagine her yelling at my brother and me to clean up the mess all that shucking would make. "It must have been nice to grow up with a mother like that."

"Most of the time, yeah." He jumps up and flicks off the light switch, leaving only the amber glow of the lantern between us. "You should close your eyes."

"Okay. I'll try."

As we lie there in silence, I can hear him breathing. I want to keep talking to him, to ask him a million more questions. I decide I didn't say anything wrong earlier, or he wouldn't have told me the corn story. I guess there are times when boys want to kiss you and times when they don't. I don't have enough experience to know the difference.

Breaking the stillness, he says, "Rats."

"What's wrong? Did you forget something?"

"No. Rats. I hate 'em. Have since I was a kid. And, um,

before I would come down here, I made my mother come down and make sure there weren't any."

I grin so wide it hurts my face. "Thank you," I whisper.

"You're welcome," he says, rolling over. "Good night."

EIGHTEEN

FRESH FRUIT IS THE LAST THING I EXPECT IN this depressing gray room, but when I wake in the morning, Juda offers me a jar filled with sweet pieces of apple, peach, and blackberry.

"You said all the food down here was rotten," I say, confused.

Pointing to the tin cans, he says, "All the stuff that was already here. My mother's been bringing other things by." He hands me a fork, says a quick prayer, and offers me the first bite. "Fruit salad is her specialty."

I happily sink my teeth into a juicy peach and then a crisp, tart apple. I then choose a ripe berry, deciding this may be the most delicious breakfast I've ever had. "It's so good! Where did it all come from?"

"It grows all over the city. You just have to know where to look," he says. "My mother spends her weekends foraging."

"That's amazing." I certainly can't picture my parents out in the city, hunting for a blackberry bush.

"I didn't think it was so amazing when I was a kid. She'd drag me from Wall Street to Columbus Circle in search of a pear."

"Right now, it seems totally worth it," I say, licking my fork as I hand him the jar. He grins, helping himself to several bites. We keep eating until there's nothing left. "Is there any more?" I ask.

"Not today." He places the empty jar next to several others I hadn't noticed before, up on a high shelf.

My stomach gurgles. "Maybe we could eat something else?"

"Okay. But something with more substance, so we'll be full longer." He looks at the shelf below. "This'll work." He sits back down, holding a small container of brownish-gray meat. "It's squirrel. Nice and filling."

I wrinkle my nose.

"You don't like squirrel?"

"We . . . uh . . . don't eat a lot of it." More than half the city eats squirrel, but it's really considered the meat of last resort.

"Of course," he says, embarrassed.

"Mother is silly about it, really," I say, afraid I've insulted him. "When we can't afford ham or even goat, she'll serve us spinach and carrots with no meat. She just can't wrap her head around the idea of squirrel. But I've always wanted to try it." I smile.

"You're a terrible liar," he says, laughing and opening the jar.

I laugh too, as a sharp, gamey smell fills the room. "Ooh-wee! That smells strong!"

"I know. It tastes better than it smells. The thing about squirrels . . ." He holds the open jar forward for me to examine. "They eat nuts—acorns and walnuts—so their meat is really nutty and sweet. I actually like it better than ham." Spearing a big hunk of the gray-brown meat, he shovels it into his mouth. "Mmm," he says as he chews. "Delicious."

Tree rat is all I can think, but I need to repress my judgment, because I know it's my mother's voice talking.

Suddenly, and with great relief, I remember the potatoes in my pocket from yesterday, and I offer one to Juda. I eat mine, but he places his on his knee while he continues to eat the squirrel.

"Convenes are raised on this stuff," he says as he swallows. "We're taught to hunt squirrel before we're taught to speak."

I smile, gnawing on my potato, but my expression must be too forced for him to believe it.

"Did you not know I was a Convene?" he asks, amusement in his eyes.

"Of course I did."

"I think we've already established that you are a *terrible* liar."

I groan. "How was I supposed to know? You don't have a long beard. And your accent has disappeared."

"I'm not very good at growing a beard of any kind." He strokes his stubble. "And Mrs. Asher made me work on my accent as soon as I started working for Damon."

"But she was a Convene once."

"Exactly. She doesn't want to be reminded. Ever."

I'm embarrassed. Despite his lack of accent or beard, I

feel like I was still supposed to know. I mean, what did I think he was? A Deserver who's been working since he was a boy? Who has a mother who works in the Fields? I guess I didn't really think about it. If only Mother could see me now: I've run away from my rich fiancé so I can sit in a basement and eat squirrel with a Convene.

He offers me the jar, but I'm not quite ready. If only the meat were hot, I think I'd be able to stomach it. To divert attention from my squeamishness, I ask, "What was it like to grow up on the East Side?"

"Hard," he says, taking a bite of his potato. "At times it could be *very* hard. A lot of families didn't have any fuel, any electricity. People died every winter—children, the elderly—just because they couldn't get warm. And it was hard to look over to the west and see buildings with the lights on and know they had heat when you didn't."

I feel ashamed. I've never been cold in the way he's describing.

"But in general, Convenes are much happier," he adds.

"Really?" I've never heard that before.

"Yeah. Neighbors are nicer. Everyone knows one another. There just seems to be more . . . trust, I guess. You don't worry about being robbed when you have nothing worth stealing."

I remember Mother's certainty that Katla had stolen our silverware.

"At least they *used* to be happier, before the plague. I can't really say now."

I've never heard it called a plague before.

"My friend Shad," he says, becoming more quiet, "he lived across the street from me growing up. He died last year."

"I'm so sorry," I say, and I am. I can't imagine losing Sekena.

"Sometimes I wish . . ." He jams his fork back into the jar, frustrated.

"What?"

"That I still lived there, that I was helping."

"Then you'd be sick, too." I hope his family is okay.

"*ALL* of us Convenes are going to get sick. Haven't you heard? *God hates us.*"

"That's not how disease works, and you know it." Father has explained germs to me.

"Why aren't the Deservers getting sick, then?"

I have no answer for him.

"Even if Deservers do start getting sick," he says, "you'll find a way to buy yourselves out of it."

I don't like the way he's talking about Deservers, like we're a bunch of rich creeps with one brain. And nothing he's saying makes sense. "What do you mean? Money can't heal people. You need science." Father complains about this a lot—how people think if you throw money at a problem, you can make it go away.

"Science isn't fast enough for people like the Ashers. I mean, how do you think they're powering an air conditioner?"

"I have no idea." I've never known people who had one before this week.

He puts down the squirrel meat. "It's coming from outside Manhattan."

"What is?"

"Diesel fuel."

"That's ridiculous. Everyone outside the Wall wants us dead. Why would they give us fuel?"

"I guess everyone has a price."

"But then . . . then . . ." It's like he's just told me you can eat sidewalk cement. "Then why doesn't Uncle Ruho just buy as much fuel as the whole island needs? Or send people for proper medicine for the Convenes?"

"It would be Apostate fuel. Apostate medicine. It goes against God and His plan for us." Sarcasm gives his voice a dark edge. "If we take their medicine, then we might as well pull down the Wall, let in the Apostates, and give up our belief in the Prophet." Juda believes in God and the Prophet, as far as I can tell. He said a prayer before we ate our breakfast. But the tone he's using suggests that he finds the logic around not using the fuel and medicine to be ludicrous.

"So why are the Ashers allowed to use the fuel?" I ask.

"They're rich—they think they're allowed to do whatever they want. One time, no kidding, I saw Mr. Asher invite over a Herald and have him say a blessing over a container of smuggled car batteries. So maybe he thinks he can pray his way out of it."

"I don't believe you. The Twitchers would catch them. Batteries, maybe, but Uncle Ruho would know if huge barrels of oil were coming over the Wall."

"My theory is that they're coming *under* the wall. Besides, who says Uncle Ruho *doesn't* know?"

My face turns hot. I wish he would stop talking. "So now it's a big conspiracy?" Why did my father spend his entire life finding an alternative energy source if Uncle Ruho could just leave the island at any time and say, *I'd like some gas now, please*? "But the people—they would rise up if they knew!"

"They're already rising. Haven't you seen the green leaves around town? Sprayed all over Ruho's face?" His voice has gone from bitter to excited. "Rumor is that it's some sort of rebel group."

Painting leaves doesn't seem like much of a rebellion to me. I remember the Twitcher yesterday mentioned one—they left me to find "a graffiti leaf over on Park."

"I bet it's a group of Convenes." Juda holds up the jar of meat. "You know, if you're going to survive without your family, you're going to have to try new things."

"Fine," I say, grabbing the jar. Snatching my fork from the floor, I poke a piece of meat, trying not to think of a rodent with beady little eyes. I count to three and take a bite.

"See? It's good!" Juda says.

I finish chewing and swallow. It's gamier than goat, but he's right. It tastes nutty. "It's not as bad as I expected."

"You'll learn to love it."

"You said rebellion 'group,'" I say. "How do you know it's more than one person?"

Something about "graffiti leaf" is poking at the edges of my memory, but I can't figure out what it is.

"I don't. You just hear about people getting arrested, and yet the leaves keep popping up."

Juda offers me a second bite of squirrel, and I'm hungry enough to take it. I chew on the meat, wondering if Nana ever ate squirrel. It seems like something they would serve in the Tunnel. Then I remember: "Nana left me a leaf!" I shove my hand in my pocket, only to remember that I'm wearing Mrs. Asher's cloak, not my own. I can't believe I lost it. The Primer and now this. Can't I keep any part of her?

"That's a weird coincidence," he says.

"Maybe it's not." Nana never went out, because of her bad knee. The leaf I found was fresh. If I didn't bring it to her, how did she get it? She was definitely up to something.

"So why did she give it to you?" he asks.

I stare at the floor, trying to piece it all together. "Maybe she wanted to tell me something about this person —or the people—who are painting the leaves around the city." I'm frustrated with myself, like I'm missing something obvious that Nana thought I would understand.

"Where did you find it?"

I'm relieved he asked, since I don't want to keep anything from him. I tell him about the Primer and Nana's teaching me how to read. I fight not to get emotional as I describe our lessons.

He gets a funny smile on his face.

"What?" I ask.

"That explains a lot."

"What does?"

"Why you're so . . . different. You're smart and defiant. And you want to do things your own way. She must have taught you that." I'm amazed he sees me this way. I feel like the whole world tells me what to do and I always comply. "So she told you to get this Primer thing, and you did, and then the leaf was inside it?"

"Yes."

Extending my mind back to the time before the Ashers', back to my bedroom, when I was lying on my bed, looking through the Primer, I concentrate on the pages and images, trying to recapture the moment of surprise when I first saw the leaf. Was I reading about food? No. Movies? No. Then I think, *Top Live Shows.* Music! "It was between pages seventy-one and seventy-two," I say.

"Wow. Good memory."

"I know the Primer pretty well," I say, shrugging. "That's what happens when you only have one thing to read."

Nana must have counted on that. My blood starting to circulate faster, I think of the pages again. I see flowers on the left side and a photograph on the top right. I murmur, "'Pere Ubu frontman David Thomas sings in "Musicians Are Scum," a spicy standout on the avant-punk album *Lady from Shanghai*, "Why don't you get in line"—'"

"What are you doing?"

"Shhh. 'Since 1975, the Ubu starting lineup has gone through more changes than the New York Knicks, with Thomas the stalwart eye of the hurricane.'" Is something in there supposed to help me?

"You're kind of scaring me," Juda says.

"It's how they talked in Time Zero." The words go on and on about these people called Ubu—and how they are "the most mutable band in avant-punk." Nana could never explain "mutable" or "avant-punk," but I always loved the sound of the words and the way they felt in my mouth. I imagined telling someone, *Hi, I'm Mina, and this is my friend Avant Punk.*

"What's Time Zero?" Juda asks, interrupting my train of thought.

"That's just what Nana and I call the time before the Prophet." Remembering that right at the end of the page it says, "Bowery Ballroom, Sept. 12," I ask Juda if he thinks it could be significant.

"Uh, Bowery Ballroom. That's a prayer center."

"Maybe Nana wanted me to go there."

He raises an eyebrow skeptically. "You think the leaf is a reminder to pray?"

"No," I say, irritated. He's obviously not taking this seriously.

I turn away from him, trying to imagine what else about these musicians could be important to Nana, but then I realize that I've forgotten about the other side—the flower page. I picture it again, but all I can remember is a bunch of roses and lilies and stuff. The page didn't have much for me to read, so I always just wanted to flip by it, but . . . Nana would always make me stop and look at it.

I breathe more quickly. I'm getting close. I can feel it. Nana made me stop, look, and concentrate on this page *every time.* What else was on it? All I can see are the flowers.

No. Wait. There's an announcement. "'At *Macy's*!" I blurt. "'There's a flower show at Macy's!'"

"I have no clue what you're talking about," Juda says, his mouth half-full of squirrel.

"It was a picture of beautiful flowers with big letters saying how it was time for the yearly flower show at Macy's. And then, at the bottom, in little letters, it said, 'The Magic of Macy's.'" My mind is reeling now. "I always thought Nana stopped on that page because she liked the flowers, but it must've been because she wanted me to remember what was on it! She wanted me to go to Macy's!"

"That building was bombed out years ago. There's nothing left."

"No. It's where she wanted me to go!" I say in a petulant voice. Jumping up, I start pacing around the room. "The leaf was supposed to be a clue that I'd recognize, but I was too worried about Damon and you and my marriage to think about it. And it was really smart of Nana, if you think about it, because if she'd written it down for me, like, 'here's where this secret group is hiding,' then anyone who found the Primer would have found the group!"

"Mina, you need to calm down." He stands up to face me. "You're acting like you're going to go running out the door and down to Macy's, and you know you can't do that."

"Not right this second. But eventually . . . maybe . . ."

He pleads with me. "Even if this crazy group is down there, why would your grandmother put you in that kind of danger?"

"Maybe she only meant for me to do it if she died."

He throws his hands in the air. "So she knew she was going to fall down the stairs? And she went out and found a leaf first? That doesn't make any sense."

"Maybe not at first, but—"

"STOP IT!" he says, so loudly his voice echoes around the room and admonishes me multiple times. He tries to soften his tone. "Please be realistic. You're safe *here*."

Impatience bubbles inside me. I've figured out what Nana wanted me to do, I know it in my bones somehow, and now Juda wants to stop me from doing it. "We can't stay here forever," I say. "And you know that every day we're here is another day we put your mother in danger."

He looks like I've slapped him. "She wants us here."

"Juda, if we get caught, they'll punish her for letting us into the Park!"

"I'm extremely careful. We won't get caught." A new tension has entered his voice, and exasperation is making a vein throb in his forehead.

"You can't control everything. You have to know it's not realistic to stay here."

"I don't want you back out there."

"In the streets?"

"In the world!" he says, blurting it out before he can stop himself.

I laugh, but I don't think it's funny. "Then we might as well be locked up in the Tunnel."

"So being here with me is like prison?" he says, voice cracking.

"No, of course not. But we can't stay holed up in this little room for the rest of our lives!"

"What choice do we have?"

I can't believe he's saying this. "We still have choices. This city is huge! The Ashers won't search for us forever."

"You don't know Damon."

The tiny room narrows in on me. Sleeping here for one night was one thing, but now Juda seems to think that I'll spend a lifetime in this hole in the ground. Is he as crazy as the Ashers? As bad as my mother? "I need air," I say, walking past him to the stairs.

"Don't go out there," he says.

I start up the steps.

"Mina, I order you to stop!"

I freeze out of habit, my head lowering in automatic deference. But as I realize what I'm doing, I'm filled with fury. "You order me? Under what authority?"

He shifts uncomfortably. "My authority as a man."

I look up, my eyes narrowing. "The only reason I've trusted you, listened to you, until now is because I thought you were different. I thought you actually cared about what I had to say and that you didn't believe you were better than me just because of what's between your legs. But I guess I was wrong. At the end of the day, you're just as bad as Damon."

I storm up the remaining stairs and out the door.

NINETEEN

BURSTING OUT OF THE STAIRWELL, I DART
across the derelict kitchen, gasping for fresh air, but I stop
dead and stifle a shriek when I see a veiled figure standing
in front of me.

"God in Heaven, you nearly gave me a heart attack!"
she says.

I scared *her*? I look around, expecting other people to
swarm in.

"Relax," she says, her voice assertive. "I'm Juda's mother."

Still trembling with the shock, I say, "I'm sorry. I . . . You
surprised me." As she walks toward me, I see that she wears
the black cloak and veil of a widow. Not even her hair or
hands show; nothing of the woman underneath is revealed.

"Sorry about that," she says. "I brought you a few
things." She holds up a little cloth bag in her gloved hand.
"But we should go down to where it's safe." She gestures
toward the metal door behind me.

Back down with Juda? It's the last place I want to go. "I
came up to get some air."

"I understand." Approaching, she puts a hand on my
arm. "But you can't stay up here. Not on your own."

She's not exactly ordering me, but the confidence in

her voice suggests she's used to getting her way. If I break free, where am I going to go? I don't know my way around the Fields. I'd probably be spotted in seconds. I watch, unhappy, as she opens the metal door.

Juda stands right behind it.

"Ma?" he says, a gasp of surprise in his voice.

"We're coming down," she tells him.

"Do you need help?"

"Why would we?" she asks, pushing past him.

Juda scurries after her. When we reach the bottom, he stands in the corner, looking everywhere but at me. The tension in the room is worse than the smell of the squirrel, which sits half-eaten in the middle of the floor. Juda's mother doesn't seem to notice the strain between us.

She raises her veil, finally revealing herself. Her face is softer than her rough voice, though deep creases around her mouth and between her eyebrows betray a certain intensity. Her skin is brown, and her eyes are darker than Juda's, but I'm relieved to see they hold the same warmth. She's shorter than I am, with a surprising little potbelly.

She looks around the room, pursing her full lips. "It's a mess. The secret to living in a small space is to keep things very tidy at all times. You know that, Udi!"

"Yes, Ma," he says, bending to pick up the abandoned squirrel meat. I feel a bit sorry for him, knowing how clean he's kept it until now.

"Do you have fresh water?" she asks.

"Yes," he replies. "Right here." He points to a bucket. "Would you like a cup?"

"No, no. I was thinking Mina might like a wash and a change of clothes," she says, holding out her bag.

"How did you know I was here?" I ask.

"Juda told me this morning when I came by."

She's already been here today? How long was I asleep?

She juts her thumb at Juda. "He's been worried sick about you, you know."

I smile tightly, not quite ready to give up my anger at him.

"Look through the bag. Use whatever you want. There's soap, a nice sponge—you'll see. Use whatever you want." She places the bag on the floor, claps her hands, then looks at her son. "Let's give Mina some privacy, eh?" She moves back to the stairs.

Juda follows her without protest, probably happy to avoid any conversation with me.

"Where will you go?" I ask.

She smiles. "Don't worry about us. We know the good spots, and we're quiet, like angels on clouds. Come, Udi." She walks up the stairs, Juda traipsing behind her.

I stand there gaping after them, half-wanting to run up and yell at Juda some more and half-wanting to beg his mother to stay and take care of us. Instead, still disconcerted, I pick up the bag and sort through it.

There are two cloaks, one purple and one black, several changes of underwear, a cotton T-shirt, a simple pair of cotton pants, and—*praise be* to Mrs. Alvero—a pair of shoes, simple canvas slippers. I try them on. They're a little tight, but they'll certainly do. I also find soap, a sponge, and a comb. It really was very thoughtful of her. My only regret is that there's no bra, mine being somewhere back at the Ashers'.

I take out the soap and sponge and, using the bucket of water, proceed to give myself a very cold sponge bath. I kneel on the ground to wash my hair, lathering it with the bar of soap, figuring it's better than nothing, and then I rinse it over and over again. Seeing no towels in the room, only washcloths, I use two on my hair and then one to dry my body a few inches at a time. I'm shivering in the concrete room, thinking of Mother's fights with Father about hot water and how she thought it was more important than a weekly ham. I'm starting to see her point.

Soon, though, I'm putting on clean clothes and feeling enormously improved. The cotton pants have a drawstring, which I'm sure is why Juda's mother chose them—they're big but adjustable. The T-shirt is white and soft and feels great next to my clean skin. I run the comb through my hair and then hang the washcloths from the shelves. Drying might take a long time down here, without any sunlight or breeze. I hope they don't get moldy.

Once I've tidied up, I lie back down on my pile of clothes from the night before. There really aren't a lot of places to go in the room—it's stand or lie down—and I must fall asleep for a little bit, because the next thing I know, Juda and his mother are in the room with me.

"Nice and clean!" his mother says. "All better?"

I sit up. "Yes. Thank you so much for the clothes."

She waves away the gratitude—something I've seen Juda do—then tosses off her cloak and plops herself onto the floor. She crosses her legs underneath her, looking more comfortable than I would expect, like a plump cat who's assessed the situation and quickly found the best spot in the room. She wears the same tunic and pants as the farmers, but hers are clean and neatly pressed. She wears a wedding ring on her left hand, with a pretty matching chain and gold heart around her neck. She squints, saying, "Juda told me about your fight."

I flush. "It wasn't a fight, exactly—"

"Sure it was. And I'm glad you know how to stick up for yourself."

I blink. She likes how I spoke to her son?

"But you behaved badly."

Here we go.

"You can't just go running out the door when you have a disagreement. It's too dangerous. You understand? You have to trust each other. Udi trusts you, enough to put his life in danger and bring you to his hiding spot. You trust him, because you stayed here overnight, which most unmarried girls wouldn't dream of doing. Let's be honest, he could've only wanted to 'unbuckle your belt,' as they say."

I feel myself turn a deeper crimson. I glance at Juda, whose face is purple with embarrassment.

"You've already put a lot on the line for each other, which means you can't go running around every which way, putting *yourself* or each *other* in danger, right? Do you both agree or disagree?"

I still can't imagine reacting any differently than I did to Juda's piggish behavior, but I know she's right in theory, so I say, "Agree."

She glares at Juda, until he mumbles, "Agree," and then she stands up. "Fantastic. Now, I have to get to work. You should be fine for the rest of the day, and I'll check on you again in the morning." She walks to the stairs. "Mina, if anything happens, I packed a black cloak. That way people will think you're married and won't give you a hard time about being together. We just have to pray there are no new Ordinances for a while, and that the length and style remain allowable."

"Thank you, Mrs. Alvero."

She comes back over and gives me a little hug. "Take care of yourself. And don't call me Mrs. Alvero. Call me Rose!"

She hugs Juda, who says, "Goodbye, Ma. Peace."

"Peace," she says, climbing up the stairs.

As soon as the door has shut behind her, Juda turns to say something. When he sees my face, however, he asks, "What's wrong?"

Sure I've gone white as a corpse, I grasp for something to say. But all I can think of is the name I just heard. Did his mother really just say "Rose"? I want to pretend I didn't hear it. I want the moment to go away.

"Mina, are you all right? Are you going to be sick?"

I shake my head, drifting over to the stairwell, as if I can summon his mother back to tell me that I misheard her. I sit on the bottom stair.

Juda hunches over me, placing his hand on my forehead. "Maybe the squirrel was off. But I feel fine—"

"It's not the squirrel."

"What is it?"

Mr. Asher had an affair with a woman named Rose. I look away from him, afraid that somehow he'll be able to read my mind. He told me yesterday that his father was dead, and I know he believed it. He had genuine pain in his eyes —eyes that, God help me, now that I think about it, resemble the olive green of Mr. Asher's.

"Maybe you're dehydrated," he says, going to a bucket and scooping out some water with one of the cups.

His mother doesn't want him to know. All this time, Juda's been working under his father's roof . . . so she must have wanted him there. What else did the letter say? Rose wanted to raise her son among her own family. The beginning said something about a brother—Sal or Tal?

I sip the water. "Thank you. That's helping."

He sits by me on the stairs. "Should I bring my mother back? Maybe you need a doctor."

"I . . . uh . . . it's just a girl thing," I say, unable to come up with anything better.

He stands right back up and sputters, "Oh . . . uh . . . okay. Well, that's good. I mean, not good that you feel bad, but good that it's not something serious."

I would laugh, if I weren't so miserable. "Udi?"

He shrugs. "Nickname. It's how I said my name when I was little, I guess."

"Your mother's great." I breathe a silent prayer, grasping at the tiny chance that I could still be wrong, and say, "Is she your only family?"

"When I was little, we lived with my grandfather, but then he died and we moved. And my uncle Jiol helps out my mother when he can. And then there's Uncle Mal, her baby brother, who runs a butcher shop. His meat has gotten us through a lot of winters."

Mal. That was the name. *Nyek.*

I now think back to Damon and Mr. Asher fighting about how Juda's punishment should be handled—how Damon was insisting on death and Mr. Asher wanted to wait to hear Juda's explanation. Mr. Asher wanted to protect his other son. It all makes sense now.

Juda's mother lied about his father. My parents lied to me about my grandmother. Why is everyone so deceitful? I don't understand why people think their children can't handle the truth.

"How about you?" he asks. "Is there anyone besides your nana that you're close to?"

I shake my head.

We sit in silence while I struggle with my conscience. How would I feel if someone told me I was related to the Ashers? They may be despicable, but they also have more BTUs than most banks. Maybe this information would have mattered to Juda a week ago. Now, it's useless. He destroyed his relationship with them forever when he struck Damon. Which he did for me. But maybe, if he knew the truth, he would want to go back and mend things. Is it my right to take that option away from him? I resolve to tell him the truth.

Tomorrow.

Juda kneels down on the floor in front of me, his face soft and sad. "I'm really sorry about what I said earlier. I was angry, but . . . I was scared, too."

I'm so focused on my new revelation about Juda's relationship to Mr. Asher that I've forgotten about our fight. "Of me?"

"No. I was scared of you leaving, of losing you again and not being able to protect you, and I just blurted out the first thing that came into my head, and it was stupid. Please forgive me."

I smirk. "Did your mother tell you to say that to me?"

"No. Well, maybe some of it. I told her we fought, but I wasn't stupid enough to tell her exactly what I said. She might've slapped me in the head." He grins.

He's so close to his mother. What will he do when he learns that she lied to him?

Taking his hand, I stroke his palm. Things for us just seem to get harder and harder.

He leans forward, as if to kiss me, but then pauses to look into my eyes. I'm afraid he might see that I'm keeping a secret, so I lean in to meet his mouth. He responds by kissing me deeply.

My mind finally stops spinning, so that the only things that exist are his feel and his taste. I wrap my hands around his head and run my fingers through his hair. He leans closer, resting his hands on either side of me on the stair. He begins to kiss my neck, sending a shiver down my spine.

I whisper, "I'm sorry I ran away from you."

He doesn't stop kissing my neck. "Promise you won't do it again?"

"I promise."

"Good," he says, running a finger down my arm. My skin seems to melt under his touch, as if my body is liquid and will flow whichever way he leads it.

I remove my hands from his head and move them to his shoulders, which are tense from leaning into the stairs. He shifts forward, causing his muscles to move under my fingers, making me want to touch every part of him. His breath has gotten deeper and faster, and when his mouth meets mine again, there's a new urgency, and I feel myself being pushed back against the stair.

This must be what my mother means when she says, "When a boy and a girl are alone, they become hungry for nothing but each other, and only the Devil will make them full."

His right hand leaves the stair and wraps around my waist. He pulls at my shirt, grabbing a handful of cotton fabric, and I know he'd rather be touching the flesh that's just underneath. I know because I'd rather be touching his skin, too.

I pull away from him, alarmed by my own desire.

He looks surprised that I've stopped and then ashamed. Standing, he walks away from the stairs. "Sorry, I—"

"Don't be," I say quickly.

"Now you'll think it's what my mother said, that I brought you down here for—"

"Don't be silly. You brought me down here to save my life."

He sits on a clothes pile, his back to me. He says nothing, and I feel awful. I didn't mean to upset him. How did we go from everything being so perfect to everything being tense and awkward? "I'm sorry," I say.

"No," he says emphatically. "Don't apologize. It's . . . you were right."

"About what?"

He turns to look at me. "About staying here. We can't hide here forever. We'll drive each other crazy." He looks away again. "One way or another." He lets out a long, low sigh. "Promise me, if there's nothing there, we'll come right back."

"Where?"

"Macy's."

My breath catches. "Of course."

"And if we run into danger on the way, we turn around."

"Yes."

I wait, as he seems to be fighting against making the final decision, but finally he stands and says, "If we leave now, we can be back by dark."

TWENTY

WE WAIT UNTIL AFTERNOON PRAYER IS OVER, SO by the time we cross the Fields, it's almost two o'clock. We walk side by side along Central Park South, our determination to look natural of course guaranteeing that we're stiff and awkward. I wear my veil and new black cloak, even hotter than my purple one, but the new, comfortable canvas shoes protect my damaged feet. *God bless Rose.*

Juda wears the simple black tunic and pants of a married man, reasoning that the Twitchers will be looking for a private guard in uniform. He was, however, unwilling to leave behind his gun and decided to conceal it underneath his waistband. At first, I thought this was a bad plan: if we get scanned, the Twitchers will immediately see the gun—a "pistol," as Juda explained. But then he pointed out that if we get scanned, our names will come up and we'll be sunk anyway. So I gave in.

How funny—less than two weeks ago, I was conspiring just to speak one word to Juda, and now here I am, pretending to be his wife. I feel a thrill knowing that he can reach for my hand whenever he wants, that we can speak in public, that people will even assume we've had a *wedding night. . . .*

But I'm naive if I don't admit that I've put myself at great risk. By pretending to be Juda's wife, I've given him total power over me. As long as we're around strangers, I must do whatever he commands. When we were in the bunker, discussing the marriage charade, the whole scheme felt like a game, but now that we're in the street, surrounded by other men, the decision seems reckless.

I remind myself of everything Juda and I have already been through, that I trust him and have no reason to believe he would take advantage. I glance at him. His searching eyes and tight jaw tell me this is not a man who is pondering his new position of power. I stop worrying about him so I can focus on where we're going.

To reach Macy's on 35th Street, we decide to walk down Broadway, instead of 6th. Juda thinks there will be fewer Twitchers in the Theater District, a neighborhood I've never seen. Nana once warned me away, saying, "It's where women end up when they have nothing left."

The buildings start changing as soon as we pass 44th. Windows disappear from the storefronts, blacked over or replaced by signs that say WARM GREETINGS FROM 7:00 UNTIL MIDNIGHT and EXOTIC FLOWERS: 24 HOURS.

Why don't the signs advertise the truth? WOMEN FOR SALE. Do men really feel better if the signs say WARM GREETINGS?

Hulking doormen hover in doorways, and every so often a man dashes out of a building, head down. With a sinking feeling, I realize I'm the only woman in sight. We were supposed to blend in, and instead I feel like a pear in a crate of bananas.

A man grimaces at me, spitting on the ground as we walk by.

"Are you sure it's okay for me to be here?" I ask, noticing other men glaring at me.

"Yes," Juda says, putting a protective hand on my arm. "You're just a reminder of the wives waiting for them at home. Don't worry."

Hearing yelling, I turn my head to see a man being shoved out a door into an alley. The man—a Convene, judging from his accent—is angry that the woman in the doorway doesn't want his business. The woman, who wears a minuscule pink nightgown that perfectly matches her huge magenta lips, tells him to go to Hell. Wild brown hair tumbling down her back, she glares at him, her eyes surrounded by thick black eyelashes that look like two spiders resting on a doll's face.

Juda gapes at the woman. He sees me watching him and looks away, ashamed.

We pass a few more theaters.

"Do you like makeup?" I ask.

"I don't know—"

"What about forbidden underwear?"

He's silent.

"You must. All men must. Why else are they paying for it?"

"Mina, I don't—"

"Please explain it to me. I want to understand."

My mind is spinning now. Men will stone a woman for wearing makeup one day and pay a woman to wear it the next. I have to be a virgin to be a bride, but Damon can visit the Theater District every day and be a groom. Men don't allow their wives to be educated, but then they complain that their women are dull and use it as an excuse to come here and have a "warm greeting." I want to scream.

"PLEASE. Explain it," I repeat, more loudly this time.

Juda looks around uncomfortably. "This may not be the best time to talk about it."

I see that several men walking nearby are listening to our conversation. The doorman from the nearest business takes a step forward, blocking our way. He puffs up his chest to emphasize the fact that he's built like a bus.

They've all heard me raising my voice at my "husband." They eagerly await Juda's response.

Under my breath, I whisper to Juda, "Berate me."

Through gritted teeth, he says, "No."

"Do it," I murmur, "or they'll beat me instead." I have the Taser in my pocket, and Juda has his pistol, but if we use either, Twitchers will come running.

The doorman takes another step toward us, and I tell Juda, with as much urgency as I can manage without raising my voice, "*Now.*"

Juda looks down and sighs, and then, before I know what's happening, he's an inch away from my face, yelling, "DON'T SPEAK TO ME THAT WAY OR I'LL CUT OUT YOUR TONGUE AND FEED IT TO THE WHINY SAITCH YOU CALL A MOTHER, UNDERSTAND?"

I'm so shocked to hear him use such foul language, and

by the crazy look in his eyes, that I can't respond. He grabs my arm and shakes me. "Do you HEAR ME?!"

The men surrounding us begin to laugh; one says, "The women for six blocks heard you." They break apart, moving on down the sidewalk. The lumbering doorman goes back to his doorway.

Keeping his hand on my arm, Juda pulls me down Broadway.

For several blocks, neither of us says a word.

When we reach 37th Street, he drops my arm, saying, "I wish you hadn't made me do that."

"Well, I wish," I say, snapping back, "you hadn't been so good at it." I know I'm admonishing him for something I told him to do, but I can't stop myself.

He's taken aback. "You thought that was me?" He makes a sound that's half laugh, half cough. "That was Damon. I've been watching and listening to him every day for nearly ten years."

I smile, relieved. Of course it was Damon. Juda even imitated the nasally, stuck-up voice. "Do some more."

He turns down his mouth and juts out his bottom lip. "But I don't *want* the silk pajamas. I want the silk *robe*. And if you can't tell the difference, then you aren't worth the manure you were raised in."

I stop smiling. "How did you live with those awful people for so long?"

He cringes. "I pretended it didn't matter, that it was just a job and that I didn't care about the people they affected." He pauses. "That changed with you."

"Have I said thank you enough times?"

"Please stop. I wasn't a nice person. As long as I ignored the things Damon did, it was the same as if I was doing them myself. So *I* actually owe *you*. You set me free from the Ashers for good."

Nyek. If Juda learns the truth of his birth, his blood will bind him to Mr. Asher forever. He can never have the freedom he deserves.

I wish I could talk to his mother about it, ask her why she lied to him in the first place. She seems like such a smart, strong woman. How could she have fallen for a man like Mr. Asher? How did they even meet? He's not hanging out in the Fields, that's for sure. He found his wife when she was just a child, roaming the streets with her sister. Maybe Rose was young, too, easily impressed by his money and power. Although, when the time came, she turned down the offer of his name and fortune. And the letter I read seemed genuine, tender.

The idea of being close to Mr. Asher in any way makes me shudder. And then to decide to send Juda into his house, forcing him to be close to Mr. Asher and his mean wife and bratty son? I don't understand it.

I'm worried that the longer I wait to tell Juda the truth, the madder he's going to be. Every minute we spend together counts as time that I'm lying to him. What if I tell him and he decides he doesn't like me anymore? The thought is agony.

Interrupting my train of thought, Juda says, "I'm sorry."

"Why?" I ask.

He points across the street. My mouth goes dry.

We've reached 35th Street, and there's a huge building, a whole block wide, that must've once been the Macy's from the Primer. But, as Juda warned me, it's completely bombed out. The top has been blown off, and the remaining floors have collapsed in on themselves. No one could possibly be inside. "I should have listened to you," I say. "I'm sorry I made you come all the way down here."

"I knew you wouldn't be satisfied until you saw it for yourself." His voice is kind.

I nod, trying not to be too disappointed. What did I really expect? A big party going on, with everyone waving green leaves in the air?

Walking alongside the wreckage, we see more exploded windows and debris. "What happened?"

"Apostates did it, probably when the Teachers were taking over the city."

I wonder what it must have looked like in Time Zero. Surely I've passed this block of ruins before. I just never paid attention to it, since I didn't need anything from it.

"Mina," Juda says, urgency in his voice.

A Twitcher is headed our way. We keep walking as if everything is normal. As he passes, I know I should look down at the sidewalk in deference, like a good woman, but I'm frozen, staring right at him. Is his little red light moving up and down, scanning us, telling him we're "wanted"?

The red light doesn't move, so my breath returns to normal. Juda takes my hand to rush us away, but I turn around, wanting to get another look at the Twitcher.

But he's disappeared.

"Juda," I say, "look."

Reluctant, ready to flee, he stares at the empty sidewalk while I inspect everywhere around me, afraid the Twitcher is camouflaged and ready to pounce, like a praying mantis.

"Something's wrong," I say.

"Exactly. Let's go." He tugs on my hand. "We have to get out of here."

I let him pull me along 35th Street. We make a left onto Sixth Avenue, and I realize with relief that Juda doesn't intend to take me through the Theater District a second time. It wasn't an experience either of us wants to repeat.

Crossing 36th Street, I'm still puzzling over the Twitcher. Besides his disappearing act, there was something else strange about him, but I can't put my finger on what it was.

I picture him marching past us. I think of his helmet, his uniform, his gloves . . .

I stop walking. "He was carrying a bag," I say. Juda looks at me, confused. "Think about it. In all your years, have you ever seen a Twitcher carrying a *bag*?"

Juda squints, concentrating. "Maybe he was on his way home? Or . . . maybe it was a toothbrush, so he could stay over with another Twitcher?"

I don't smile. Before I saw Captain Memon's face under his helmet, I wasn't a hundred percent sure Twitchers were human. I turn to walk back toward 35th Street.

Groaning, Juda catches up. "You want to search for a Twitcher?"

"I don't think it *was* a Twitcher. Not a real one."

"And you're willing to risk your life on a *bag*?"

Not answering, I keep walking until we've arrived back at the remains of Macy's. I find the approximate spot where the Twitcher disappeared. Pointing toward the massive pile of debris, I say, "That's the only place he could've gone."

"We can't just start poking around in there. It could collapse on us."

"Fine." I start walking toward the rubble alone.

"Wait," he says, sighing. "At least let's find a safe way inside."

I nod, happy he's come around, even though, to be honest, I'm not entirely convinced myself about this plan. An armed Twitcher could be waiting for us inside the demolished building—but something in my gut tells me otherwise.

All we see is smashed concrete and deformed steel bars, not even one foot of surviving floor. Juda stares at the rubble for a long time.

"Look at the junk in this pile," he says. "It's stone, concrete, metal beams, and *wood*."

"So?"

"The fire from the bombs should've burned up any wood."

Without warning, he approaches the debris and starts to climb, finding several wood beams sticking out that make a nice series of steps. "Someone has done a great job creating stairs while keeping the look of wreckage." He finds three more wood steps and is quickly at the top of the rubble. He then ducks under a beam and disappears.

I wait a few seconds, surprised when he doesn't return right away. "Juda?"

I hear only the sound of scraping metal, then banging.

My breath catches. "Juda?" I say, releasing a little squeak at the end of his name.

"I'm here," he says, his voice muffled. More time passes, I hear more scraping, and then finally he says, "I think you should join me."

Checking down the street to make sure no one is coming, I lift my cloak slightly and start to clamber up after him. Juda made it look easy, but the cloak means I can't see my feet. I use my hands to grab at the wood beams above me, but then fabric starts to get caught around my legs. I make clumsy progress up the pile.

Juda pops his head out from under the beam. "Give me your hand," he says.

Annoyed that he has to help me, I offer him my hand, and he helps me balance while my other hand holds up my cloak. This way, I'm able to climb at a decent speed. "Watch your head," he warns as I reach the top. He pulls me under the beam, and now I find I'm in a cave. Sunlight shines through several beams crisscrossing above us. A floor has been created with sheets of rusted metal.

"Someone built this," Juda says.

Yes. The beams above us are a very deliberate ceiling. "But it doesn't explain where the Twitcher went," I say. "There's no way out."

"Don't be so sure." He lifts a large sheet of corroded metal. I approach slowly, not sure what his odd expression could mean. But when I get next to him and look down, I understand.

He's found a stairway that leads underneath the demolished building. And on the underside of the piece of metal that he's holding, someone has painted a green leaf.

TWENTY-ONE

I START DOWN THE DARK STAIRWAY, BUT JUDA grabs my shoulder, saying, "I'll go first. There's probably a Twitcher down there."

"I'm *sure* it wasn't a Twitcher. If I'm wrong, then I should accept the consequences."

"We can argue about it all night, but there's no way I'm letting you go unarmed into a dark pit in *front* of me."

I don't want to waste any more time. I just want to get down those stairs and find out what Nana wanted me to see. So, instead of fighting him, I say, "Fine."

"What happened to your fear of being underground?"

He's right. As soon as I saw that leaf, I was ready to dive into this hole. "Nana matters more," I say with a shrug.

We walk down a few more steps; then Juda changes his mind and climbs back up to replace the metal cover. "Wait," I say. "We won't be able to see anything."

"This is the way we found it. We shouldn't leave their entrance exposed."

Panic sets in. If he slides the metal sheet over our heads, this will be a hundred times worse than walking down into the bunker. There, we had the lantern and Juda knew exactly what we were walking into.

I rack my brain for an argument that might leave us even a sliver of sunlight, but I know that Juda is right—we have to cover our tracks.

The horrible scraping of metal on metal echoes the screeching protest in my head as the world slowly goes dark. My eyes search for something, *anything*, to focus on, but there's nothing. A black cloak seems to cover my eyes.

"Stay still." Juda places his hands on my back, then slides them down to my waist, giving me the chills. Slowly, he circles around me so he can position himself on the stair below, but he doesn't let go of my waist, so I know he's still facing me. I can hear his breath and feel its heat.

I want to reach up and touch his arms again, like in the bunker, when I could feel the muscles moving underneath his skin. His big hands make me feel small and delicate, something I never felt before he started touching me. This complete darkness is like playing under the blankets when I was little, like nothing that happens in here could ever be real—Juda and I could touch on these stairs all day, and no one would ever know or care.

I put my hands on top of his hands, ready to find his lips, when he says, "There'd better not be rats."

I cover my mouth with my hands so I won't laugh. "You okay?" he asks. "Your breathing is weird."

"I'm fine," I say, pulling myself together.

He lets go of my waist, turning around. "Put your hand on my shoulder, and don't move until I do."

I wish he hadn't mentioned rats. The darkness here is like staring into a hole, and I feel light-headed. Maybe the

Apostate's bomb created a crater and we're about to fall into it.

Shaking off the thought, I continue to descend, slowly letting each foot feel the stair so that I can anticipate the size and shape of the next one.

We keep climbing down, the blind leading the blind, and I'm grateful for Juda's sturdiness in front of me. At least I can't go tumbling forward into the abyss. We continue down for a long time, descending much deeper into the earth than we needed to for the bunker. "Can you see anything yet?" I whisper.

"Nothi—"

Suddenly, a blinding light is thrown into our faces. Juda freezes, and I bump into his back. He throws up one arm to protect me while his right hand reaches for his pistol. Growling like a provoked animal, he speaks into the darkness, "Who are you?"

Silence.

"Answer me!" Juda says.

I stick my head around him. "We're here about the leaves!" Shielding my eyes with my hand, I try to see whom I'm speaking to. "We don't mean any harm. We just . . . uh . . . ." Then I remember exactly why we're here. "Someone sent me."

After a moment, the harsh beam drops and a new light goes on; this one illuminates the entire space. We're in a small room filled with boxes. And in the center of it, blocking the only door—a Twitcher.

"Stand back, Mina!" Juda cries.

"No," I say. "It's okay." I look at the Twitcher, who holds the bag that I saw. "Isn't it?"

The Twitcher cocks his head so that his helmet turns sideways, studying me. Then he takes a gloved hand and un-clicks two latches at the base of the helmet. Air whooshes out.

I'm in shock, Juda, too, for underneath the Twitcher helmet is not a man but an Asian girl with hard brown eyes; high, sculpted cheekbones; and short, spiky blue hair. She's older than I am, maybe twenty or twenty-one, and while her hair might be playful, her expression most certainly is not. "Who sent you?"

"My grandmother?" I say. I'm annoyed with myself that I make it sound more like a question than a statement.

"He's not welcome here," she says.

"Why not?"

"He's a man," she says, as if I'm an idiot.

"I'm not going anywhere without him," I say.

"You're not going inside *with* him," she says.

"Why?" I ask. "He doesn't want to hurt anyone."

She looks at his gun. "Suuure," she says, the contempt in her voice dropping the temperature in the room a few degrees. "He only *wants* to make women better listeners. Or make them better wives. Or better servants of God. Men never *want* to hurt anyone."

"No, that's not what I meant."

Juda turns to go. "Forget it, Mina. I'm not wanted here. We should leave."

"*Mina? Mina what?*" the girl asks, very attentive now.

"Clark."

"*Nyek.* Wait here." She turns and disappears behind the door.

Juda raises his eyebrows. "What was that?"

I shake my head.

"She's nuts," he says.

"Maybe, but we have to see what the group is about, at least."

"I think I can tell you . . . ," he says, grumbling. Then he smiles. "But you were right. It wasn't a Twitcher."

I smile back, feeling uneasy. I hope there are other people here and it's not just this one strange girl with crazy blue hair painting those leaves.

Several more minutes go by. I sit down on the stairs.

"Did you see what was in her bag?" Juda asks. When I don't answer, he says, "It looked like a dead chicken."

"Really?" I say.

He nods.

"Maybe she *despises* chickens," I say, trying to lighten the mood.

"Only the male ones, I would guess," he says.

I laugh and the door opens, bringing back the girl. Her face is even angrier than it was before. I stop laughing.

"You can both come in, but *you* . . ." She points at Juda. "You don't talk to anyone, and you keep your face *down*. You got it? *You* are the subservient one here."

Juda nods, clearly wanting to march right up the steps and back to the Fields.

"I'm Rayna," the girl says, with irritated force, as if she hates her own name—or most likely because she has to deal with Juda in any way.

"I'm Mina," I say.

She looks at me like I'm a moron, and I remember I already told her my name. Then Juda says, "I'm Juda."

"Speak when spoken to," Rayna says, without looking at him. She opens the door, motioning for us to follow. I go first.

It's an unlit corridor with low ceilings, and only Rayna's flashlight shows the way. The smell in here is stale, moldy, and rancid, and I bet the floor is peppered with mouse droppings. It seems like there's less air to breathe than there was in the last room. Or is it that my lungs feel smaller?

I'm becoming aware of the layers of earth above us, how this ceiling could collapse and bury us alive. I try to take long, deep breaths, but my heart beats like a clattering spoke.

Rayna knows the way well. She walks quickly, so it's hard to keep up with her, and the farther behind we fall, the less light we have. The floor is solid but dirty—every pebble and fragment seems to punch through the soles of my thin canvas shoes. Debris crunches each time I step forward.

I'm concentrating on the long beam of light that flickers ahead of us, when, out of the corner of my eye, I spot a body. I freeze and shriek, and Rayna spins. "What's wrong?!"

"There's a woman!" I cry. "By the wall!"

As she shines the light to our left, I see it again—a naked figure frozen on the floor. "There!"

"Don't be stupid," she says, kicking the figure with her

boot. As it rattles and spins, I see that it isn't real but made of plastic. "It's a doll. They were called *mannequins*. You know, for selling clothes?"

"Oh," I say, mortified.

"Can we keep going now?" Rayna asks, using the same voice my father reserves for dimwitted children. Is the whole group going to be just like her?

Juda leans in and whispers, "We can leave anytime."

Rayna keeps walking. As we continue down the corridor, her flashlight allows brief glimpses of shelves stacked with more of the "mannequins." I'm a little embarrassed to be looking at these naked women with Juda behind me, even if they are plastic. The figures seem completely out of proportion—the breasts enormous, the waists tiny, and the legs much too long. Did women in Time Zero look like this? What happened that made us so short and fat?

I'm relieved when Rayna stops walking. We've reached the end of this disturbing crypt. Opening a door, she invites us to enter the next room, a cavernous space filled with electric light. Dozens of women lounge on jewel-toned pillows placed atop luxurious rugs. The smell of freshly baked cookies and black tea fills the air. The conversation stops as soon as we walk in. I take in the women's faces, which are alert and curious.

Then my stomach drops as if the floor beneath me has collapsed. I reach my arms out to steady myself, but I can't seem to find the wall. I hear a loud rushing sound, like someone has opened a faucet in my head, and my whole body starts to tremble.

"Mina? What's wrong?" Juda rushes forward and wraps his arms around me. But I wrench myself from his grasp, tears streaming down my face, and run across the room—to embrace Nana.

TWENTY-TWO

I'M SURE SHE'LL DISAPPEAR BEFORE I CAN touch her. As I'm about to reach her, several large women rise to block my path. "What are you *doing*?" I say, trying to shove by. "What's going on? NANA!!"

I hear Nana's voice through my yelling, calm and certain. "Be still, Chickpea. Everything's fine."

Hearing "Chickpea" has an instant effect, and I back down. One of the women says, "We didn't want you to approach her too fast. That's all."

"Why?" My hand balls into a fist. "Is she hurt? Did you hurt her?"

"I'm much better now," Nana says. "Let her pass, ladies."

The women surrounding her sit back down.

"This is my Mina, everyone!" Nana says to the room. She's trying to shout, but her voice has lost a lot of its force. "The one I told you about!"

A few women holler and whistle, and an exuberant clanging of pots and pans soon joins the uproar. I wince, concerned the racket will attract a hundred Twitchers. I guess the collapsed Macy's muffles sound, but I notice a few other women also seem unnerved by the commotion.

Nana is nested in a pile of bright silk cushions that I can now see are propping her up. The rest of the group, probably around forty women, sits on ornate rugs and pillows—there's no furniture to speak of. They're all smiling as they whoop and clap, happy to celebrate my presence. But underneath the smiles, some of the faces look haunted, while others look angry, like Rayna's. Some of them are girls my age and younger. I see no boys.

When the commotion dies down, Nana says, "Come here so I can get a proper look at you" and reaches out her arms. I kneel beside her, still nervous she'll disappear, and she embraces me, pulling me close and kissing the top of my forehead. Her soft skin smells like warm bread, as always, but I also detect something sharp and antiseptic.

"Look at you." Nana brushes tears from my eyes. "You've become a young woman."

Her salt-and-pepper hair, usually short and carefully groomed, hangs around her face in shaggy disarray. Her hazel eyes no longer sparkle, and the skin around them is puffy and dark.

"How can I have become a woman?" I ask, tempted to roll my eyes. "I saw you less than a month ago."

"The eyes. They tell me everything." Women around her nod, as if this is common knowledge.

"Mother told me you were dead!" I say.

She looks as if she's about to say something about Mother but changes her mind. "I would have been if it weren't for the Laurel Society."

"Who?"

"This is Ayan." She gestures to her right, and a tall black woman with a shaved head steps forward and bows. Given her sharp nose, square jaw, and mysterious eyes, Ayan's lack of hair does nothing to distract from her beauty. She wears the same type of tunic and pants that my father does, but hers are emerald green. Wooden bracelets climbing up her arm make a clacking sound as she moves, but she's all elegance and poise.

"Welcome. We're happy to see you," Ayan says. "Your grandmother is an old friend."

"Thank you," I say to Ayan, and then to Nana, "How did you get here?"

"I was in the hospital with a broken hip," Nana says. "But I wasn't getting very good care."

"The doctor was examining her through a hole in a sheet," one of the women says, with anger and disgust.

The Teachers won't let women have an education in order to become doctors, and then they won't let male doctors look at women.

"A young man set the bones and put me in a cast, but he didn't do a very good job. The pain was excruciating. Luckily, Herra"—Nana points to a slight woman in the corner with a pixie-like face—"was bringing food to another patient and saw me there. Ayan arranged to smuggle me out."

"With a broken hip?"

Nana smiles. "Ayan thinks of everything. She gave me a sedative, so not only did I not feel the pain of the journey, but she also disguised me as a corpse that needed to be disposed of."

"How's your hip now?" I ask.

"Regina reset it, but I'm afraid the first few days were crucial," Ayan says.

"What does that mean?" I ask, trying to suppress my panic.

"Don't you worry, Chickpea. I'm going to be fine," Nana says, taking my hand and stroking it.

"Don't baby me, Nana. I want to know."

She just smiles at me, and it's Ayan who answers. "She might not walk again."

"Oh." I absorb the news. I remind myself that only an hour ago, I thought Nana was dead, so I should be praising God for her life. I try to feel grateful, but I can't. I want to collapse into Nana's arms and weep and do whatever I can to take away her pain.

My eyes start to fill with tears again. Nana grabs my chin. "None of that. I'm exactly where I want to be—inside the Laurel Society with my Mina. You were so smart! You followed my clues *perfectly*. I couldn't be more proud. This is a time for celebration, not sorrow."

I nod, trying to be brave.

"You brought a friend," she says.

Realizing I've completely forgotten Juda, I twist to see where he's gone. He hovers by the door, staring down as though there were nothing more interesting in the world than his feet.

"Come meet Nana, Juda!" I say.

"I would be honored," he says, his deep voice echoing through the cavernous space, "but I don't want to insult our hosts by looking upon them without their veils."

Until now, I hadn't even noticed that all the women were uncovered. No wonder Juda is so captivated by his shoes.

Ayan says, "None of us ever wears the veil inside. We consider it oppressive. We give you permission to look upon us."

Several seconds go by, as if Juda's deciding what to do, but eventually he raises his head and finds my eyes. He walks over, carefully not looking anywhere but straight ahead, and stands by Nana and me.

"Nana, this is Juda."

"My goodness, you're big," she says.

He does seem to loom over her like a refrigerator.

He kneels on the ground, looking more shy and boyish than I've ever seen him. While Nana looks him up and down, the other women size him up, too.

"Thank you for helping to bring Mina to us," Nana says.

"I'm very happy for her that you're not, um . . . that you're well," he says, squirming. "She speaks of you often."

"He's delivered the girl. It's time for him to go." I look up to see Rayna standing over us, scowling, her hand resting on the pistol that's part of her Twitcher uniform.

I look at Juda, expecting him to be taut and ready to argue, but instead he looks completely submissive, with his hands in his lap and his eyes on the floor. *Smart.*

"I couldn't have found you without him," I say to Nana, wanting to tell her everything about our journey but not knowing where to begin. I turn to Ayan. "He's wanted. The Teachers are looking for him, and it's my fault! You can't just throw him out."

"Watch me," Rayna says, lurching toward him.

"No one is leaving tonight," Ayan says, her voice soft but commanding. "The boy stays." The other women murmur in surprise.

"You've got to be kidding!" Rayna says. "No one here—"

"I've made my decision," Ayan says, cutting her off but not losing her cool. "It's final."

Glaring at Juda, Rayna storms away, like a hyena denied her share of the carcass.

Ayan continues, "But he will not join us for dinner. And he will have separate sleeping quarters. Understood?"

She looks at me, not at Juda, for confirmation. I look at him, and, although his pose is still compliant, his jaw is tense. He'd be much more comfortable if he returned to the bunker, but I'd never forgive myself if he were caught on the way.

"Well?" I ask him, my voice sounding more pleading than I want it to.

He gives a quick jerk of the head, which I assume is a nod, so I say, "Yes. We understand."

"Good. Dinner is in an hour," Ayan says. "Herra will find a room in back where Juda can wash."

Juda rises to go with Herra, and I pull him aside. "Thank you," I whisper.

"For what?" he says.

"For staying with me."

"I didn't do it for you."

My heart sinks, but I try to keep my face from changing.

"If I went back onto the streets without you," he says,

"I wouldn't be able to tell the difference between a real Twitcher and a fake one. I'd be doomed." A huge, beautiful smile takes over his grim face, and, once again, I want to pull his body toward me and kiss him hard.

Herra leads him away. When I turn back to Nana, she's frowning at me, as if she could hear my thoughts about Juda. I feel my face start to burn.

Nana turns to a plump woman sitting next to her. "Regina, Mina's going to help with my bath tonight. She and I have a lot to talk about."

Regina nods, and when Nana smiles at me, I realize that, for the first time in my life, there are some things I might not want to discuss with my grandmother.

TWENTY-THREE

Rayna comes over and, without discussion, lifts Nana into her arms. Nana relaxes right into her, so I assume this happens often.

"Follow us," Nana says.

Watching Rayna be gentle with Nana and so mindful of her pain makes me start to reconsider my first opinion of the blue-haired girl.

We leave the big room, cross a hallway, pass through a swinging door, and enter a large restroom, all shiny black-and-white tile, with a checkered floor. It still has all its stalls and sinks. It must be almost exactly as it was when the Macy's was still standing.

A dull, unpainted wood chair sits awkwardly in the middle of the room, and I wish I could remove it. Its presence ruins the perfection of the clean black and white lines, like a twig atop piano keys. Rayna gently places Nana in the wood chair and says to me, "Use the bucket and sponge in the corner. The water's not hooked up."

I nod. "Where does the electricity come from?" This room, like the last one, is brightly lit.

"That's none of your business," she says, and then walks out the door.

"Should I be worried about her?" I ask, once Rayna is gone.

"What do you mean?" Nana says.

"Is she going to go beat up Juda?"

Nana laughs. "No. She'll obey Ayan."

I know Ayan said Juda was being taken somewhere he could wash, but what if instead Herra put him in that horrible corridor with the plastic bodies and he's just sitting there in the dark? I'm sure Rayna would love to use my Taser on him. I can imagine her smiling while she does it.

"Rayna's pretty crazy, huh?" I say.

Nana's mouth tightens. "Rayna suffered many horrible things before Ayan found her—things you and I probably wouldn't have survived."

I think about Damon in my bed, one hand forcing my head back, the other clawing under my dress. I imagine Nana means even worse things than that.

"Before you judge people," Nana continues, "no matter how odd or irritating they may be, you have to force yourself to ask, 'Who treated them so terribly that they became this way?' Someone who is angry all the time most likely grew up in a family infused with anger. Or they suffered something so terrible, so painful, they can't move past it. When people are unpleasant to you, Chickpea, it can be very hard to be sympathetic to them, but if you can manage it, you'll hang on to your humanity. And you won't overlook the people who need you the most."

Now I'm confused. "You mean, if someone treats me badly, I'm supposed to be nice in return?"

"I'm not telling you to be a doormat. I'm not telling you to act grateful when someone spits on your toast. I'm just telling you not to be judgmental. Try to put yourself in that person's shoes, and see if you can figure out what's making them be such a pain in the rump. That's all."

I can imagine being sympathetic to Rayna, but I don't know if I'm capable of it with Damon, the one who tried to hurt me the most. My hatred for him increases daily, so much that it frightens me a little. Maybe I *do* understand how Rayna's rage could seep into every interaction of her life.

"I'm sorry I called Rayna crazy," I say.

"Fetch the bucket," she says with a smile, so I know my lesson is over.

I walk to the corner and pick it up. The water inside is so cold, I expect to find ice cubes in it. This room is cool and dank—from being so deep underground, I suppose. I now worry that undressing Nana might be dangerous. I don't want to leave her cold and exposed. She seems frail, something I've never thought before.

"Quit looking at me like I'm one of your dolls that's lost its stuffing," she says in a prickly voice that tells me she's not going to listen to any of my concerns. How is she able to read my thoughts so easily? "I can bathe just fine on my own, but I wanted some time with you alone. So just help me freshen up—we'll do my hands and feet."

Nana doesn't seem to mind the cold water. While I bathe her, she asks questions, one after another, so I tell her everything: about the Twitcher who stole her opal ring; my

Offering party and the candle; my engagement to Damon; Mr. and Mrs. Asher; the night Damon came into my bedroom; and how Juda saved me. I tell her about the Primer last—how I hurried to retrieve it, but that Mother destroyed it.

I'm ashamed to tell her the last part—that after all the years she kept the Primer safe, I'm responsible for its ruin. But she just smiles with satisfaction. "It served its purpose perfectly. It got you here, didn't it?"

"Yes, but—"

"Every time I left the house, I put the leaf on page seventy-one, knowing that if anything ever happened to me, you would come and find Ayan."

"Why couldn't you just tell me about this place?" I say, thinking how close I came to missing her clue.

She leans forward. "Once, when you were seven years old, you visited me and I said, 'There's a shoebox in my bedroom with a mouse in it. His name is Goliath. But, whatever you do, don't open the box, because he'll escape and run through the wall to the apartment next door and get eaten by the neighbor's cat.' And how long did it take you to open that box?"

I shrug.

"You didn't even last a day," she says, leaning back. "You were determined to get a look at Goliath, even though I told you it would cost him his life!"

I feel bad, even though I don't remember the mouse.

"Children can't be told about a special place until it's *time to go* to the special place. It would have been too dangerous for Ayan and the others to have you poking around outside for hours at a time."

"Well, you should've told me about Mother," I say. "You lied to me!"

"Mina, you're scrubbing too hard!" she says.

I look down and see that I'm rubbing the same spot on her arm over and over. The skin is glowing red. I stop immediately and switch to her feet, slipping off her socks and washing her ankles. It occurs to me that she and Mother have similar feet, even though Nana's are larger. And they have the same nose. I can't believe I've never noticed before.

"I made a promise to your mother a long time ago that I wouldn't tell you about the past," Nana says, "hers or mine. It was the only way she'd agree to let me see you. And seeing you was the crucial thing."

"But you could've told me," I say, "as soon as I was old enough. I wouldn't have said anything."

"Oh, Chickpea. I'm sure you would have tried not to, just like you tried not to open Goliath's box. But think about how you felt when you found out. Didn't things seem different?"

I remember the day Mother tore up the Primer, when Father explained that he wasn't related to Nana. I'd been so confused, and I felt so betrayed by everyone.

"You would have gone home and tried to act as if everything was normal, but you would have been furious, which is only fair, and as soon as your mother sensed your anger, she would have figured the whole thing out and banned you from seeing me. I couldn't risk it." She stops me from washing her legs and puts her finger on my cheek. "You're too important to me."

I pull away, grabbing the soap to lather up the sponge.

I didn't actually meet Nana until I was six. The first time I met her, I was terrified. My father took me to her apartment and dropped me off without much of an explanation. Nana told me that she was my grandmother, but she wasn't like Grandma Silna, who smiled all the time and had nothing to say but, "Aren't you a pretty little thing!"

Nana wore men's clothing, and she walked with a limp and used a cane. When she spoke to me, she didn't use the voice that people normally use when they speak to young girls, the one that's so sweet flies should stick to it. She spoke to me as if I were another adult. We spent that first day discussing our hatred of housework and our love of bananas (I had only ever had one, but she had gotten an entire bunch as a wedding gift), and by the time Father returned to pick me up, I wanted to stay with Nana forever. She became the person I told all my secrets to, and I thought that I had become the same for her.

"Couldn't you at least have told me about prison?" I say, becoming huffy.

"It's not something I particularly enjoy talking about," she says, in a tone that's sharper than I'm used to hearing from her. "And I expect a more respectful manner, Mina."

My head jerks up. "And I expected honesty."

She doesn't reproach me for talking back. Instead, she sighs as if she's anticipated this conversation for a long time.

"I hated it when my parents didn't tell me things," she says.

I stop scrubbing her feet. "I guess I just don't know why you bothered."

"With what, Chickpea?"

The use of my nickname is supposed to be soothing, I know, but I don't want to be comforted right now. "With any of it. If I was just going to be married off to some horrible man, why did it matter if I could read? Or if I was strong? Or knew anything about Time Zero? I would've been happier if you'd left me ignorant! Then I wouldn't have wanted anything from my life."

"But look what you did! You stood up for yourself. You got away from a vicious boy who didn't deserve you, who didn't even deserve to speak your name!"

"And now I'm on the run, wanted by the police! And Father's going to lose his job! Is that what you wanted?"

The light disappears from her eyes, leaving her looking more tired than ever. "No. That's not what I wanted. Give me your hand." Reluctantly, I put down the sponge and give her my right hand. "I always knew the day of your Offering would come, and when it did, I planned . . . I'm so sorry, Chickpea. I didn't mean for any of it to happen this way."

I still feel anger, but it's at Mother, and Damon, and the Ashers, and the whole world that's making us hide underground in this cold room. I'm not angry at Nana. How can I be mad at her for falling down the stairs?

I lay my head on her lap. "I didn't mean it. I'm glad you taught me how to read."

"I know."

"And *you* didn't want me engaged to Damon."

"No."

"And it's all okay, really, because if I hadn't needed to get the Primer, I never would've met Juda."

Nana is quiet. I look up.

"You need to be very careful there, Mina."

"I am—"

"The boy has helped you, and he seems important right now, but I promise you, he's not. You *have* to be selfish and think only about what's good for *you*."

Why would she say that when she doesn't even know him, hasn't even had a conversation with him? My head spins with the dozen different ways I want to defend him, but before I can fully form a thought, I blurt out, "That's not fair!"

"I don't care about fair. I care about keeping you safe."

"I *am* safe with him." After everything I told Nana about what he's done for me, I expected her to be praising him, not dismissing him. "He's smart and strong and kind and—"

"So are most husbands. Before you marry them."

I have no response.

"Relationships are hard work. You get frustrated with one another. You get sick of each other's company. And it's hard to see the other person's point of view. It takes a lot of time and effort to listen and get to know someone else. So if one person has the power to shut down the conversation and say, 'You *must* do as I say, because I have the *authority*,' he'll do so eventually—inevitably. It's too exhausting and hard for him to do otherwise."

I stare at the black-and-white floor, now spattered with water. Grabbing a mop I see leaning against the wall, I start to sop up the tiny puddles. When Juda and I had our fight and I wanted to leave the bunker, he *ordered* me to stay. Later, he claimed he'd done it because he was scared of my leaving, but at the time he didn't seem to have the patience to listen to what I had to say. He made the choice that took less energy.

"Are you telling me that men behave the way they do because they're lazy?"

She lets out a laugh that is sad and world-weary. "It's very hard to get anyone, man or woman, to make a choice that's going to involve more work than they're used to. And sometimes it's about fear. If the woman is not forced by law or a threat of violence to stay with her husband, then she must stay because she loves him. Then he must be love-worthy. And what's scarier to a man of violence or cruelty than needing to *earn* someone's love? He can't even love himself."

I wring out the mop in an empty bucket under a sink. Neither of us speaks. What if Damon actually had to earn a girl's love and not rely on a wedding contract? He's about as charming as a roach. And he survives in the same way, crawling out at night to take whatever he wants, resistant to any outside force. "I know the kind of man you mean," I say. "I think Juda is different."

"I once thought a man I loved was different." She rolls down her pant legs. "It was the greatest mistake of my life."

I assume she means her ex-husband, Grandpa Silna. He turned her in for teaching my mother how to read.

Before I can ask her about him, the door swings open and Rayna's blue head appears. "Time for dinner."

"Thank you," Nana replies. "We're almost ready."

I put her socks back on her feet and roll down her shirtsleeves. Rayna crosses the room, lifting her once again.

Frustrated that our conversation had to stop when it did, I tell Nana, "I have more questions."

She says, as if she didn't hear, "You're in for a real treat. Gray is a wonderful cook."

I have no choice but to follow the two of them out the door.

TWENTY-FOUR

BACK IN THE MAIN ROOM, THE WOMEN SIT IN small circles, chatting and laughing. Smiling, Ayan motions for me to sit, too. I plop myself into a mound of pillows, trying to lean against them so that I look as graceful as she does. Within seconds, though, my neck and back are aching, so I sit up and cross my legs in front of me.

A smell hits my nostrils. I feel my eyes grow huge. Chicken.

Several new women appear, carrying enormous trays of food. So many women seem to be living here—I wonder if there's anyone left to cook dinner in the city tonight.

Someone lays a plastic tarp in the middle of our circle, and the dishes are placed on top. There's fresh, hot bread, beans, roasted eggplant, sautéed spinach, and a thick orange soup. There's a whole roasted chicken (probably the one from Rayna's bag). I see a butter dish, salt and pepper shakers, and bowls of sugar and cinnamon—items my mother only serves on holidays. I think I must be drooling.

I expect a prayer, but no, everyone just dives in. As soon as I taste one bite, it's hard not to knock the other women out of the way. I realize I'm *starving*. I devour a chicken leg, and when I'm finished, I lick the bone over and over.

I look up to find that everyone is watching me. I'm sure I turn a deep crimson. Was I eating like a pig? "I'm sorry. I guess I'm pretty hungry."

Ayan says, "We're privileged to nourish you. And we don't put value on being ladylike here."

As if to prove the point, Rayna lets out an enormous belch. The entire room bursts out laughing.

I laugh, too, and then ask, "Where did all this food come from?" as I shove more of the warm bread into my mouth.

"When you help the women of this city, they make sure you have everything you need," Ayan says. "This is a grand feast, Gray. Your cooking talent knows no bounds."

Gray, a tough-looking woman who's missing a few teeth, beams.

"How do you help women?" I ask, and then add, looking at Nana, "I mean, besides taking them out of bad hospitals."

Ayan puts down the chicken leg in her hand. "The Laurel Society exists to help women in any way we can. We give shelter to those who are fleeing cruelty or violence, and we help single mothers struggling to survive."

I think of Juda's mother. Did she ever receive help from the Laurel Society? And have all the women around me escaped from miserable households?

"But why don't you get caught?" I say. "Don't your husbands come looking for you?"

I look around the circle, and fear flickers in some of the faces. A thin woman with hollow cheeks and ears that poke out from her head like two slices of apple says, "We don't ever leave."

Ayan meets my look of surprise with a motherly smile. "We regulate the comings and goings very closely. We have a few Twitcher uniforms, and we use them wisely. If women were walking in and out of the building all day, we would've been discovered years ago."

Many of the women start to nod.

If I didn't feel claustrophobic before, I do now.

I sop up my remaining soup with bread.

"Take it easy, Chickpea. You're eating as if you'll never see food again." I look over at Nana. I want to be able to abandon the crumbs on my plate. But after the hours that the Ashers made me go without food and the day in the bunker with a jar of squirrel, I intend to finish everything within sight. If nothing else, I've learned that life is unpredictable, and I have no idea where I may end up tomorrow.

When I finally abandon my plate and sit back, my stomach is bloated and I'm afraid that I might actually be sick. Mostly, though, I feel exhausted.

"I think it's time that Mina learns your history, Ayan," Nana says. The women around me settle into their cushions as if they've been waiting for this moment. Ayan waves her hand, and two women start to clear the dirty plates. She licks her fingers clean, making tiny slurping noises. Even this uncivilized gesture seems refined when she does it.

When she starts to speak, she addresses the whole room,

not just me, causing all the other women to gather close to listen. "The symbol of the laurel leaf goes back thousands of years. It begins with the tale of Daphne and Apollo, a story created by the Greeks, and then retold by the Romans, and then interpreted by artists for centuries."

I smile, but I feel stupid, as if I'm already supposed to know what she's talking about.

"Daphne was a beautiful young maiden walking in the forest, and Apollo, the god of sun and light, saw her and fell madly in lust. He tried to force himself on her, so she ran away through the forest. But she was a girl and he was a god, and he quickly caught up to her, so she cried out to her father, the river god, for help. But did she ask him to strike down Apollo?"

The other women shake their heads and answer together, "No, she did not."

"No. She did not," Ayan repeats. "Did she ask him to quell the lust in Apollo's heart?"

Again they all shake their heads and say, "No, she did not."

"No. She did not," Ayan says. "Did she ask him to root Apollo's feet to the ground so that he would no longer be able to give chase?"

"No, she did not," the women say, more loudly this time.

"No. She did not." Ayan looks directly at me now. "Instead, she cried out to her father, 'Change and destroy this body which has given too much delight!' and her father heard her and answered her prayer. In that instant, he changed her into a laurel tree. No more voice, no more body to provoke sin, no more woman. And when Apollo saw that his love had been transformed, he plucked some leaves from a branch and made the laurel his symbol from that day forward."

"Bastard," Rayna says, a grumble just loud enough for us all to hear.

I sense a new alertness, a quickening rhythm in everyone's breathing. The energy in the room crackles with excitement and a mounting fury.

Ayan continues, her eyes on fire, as if she herself has been sprinting through a forest. "We use the symbol of the laurel leaf in order to reclaim it for Daphne. It was never Apollo's to have. A woman shouldn't be punished for the sins of man, for the lusts of man! If a man cannot control himself, it is *his* sin, *his* duty to answer to God, not ours!"

All the women nod, some murmuring assent.

Ayan is really worked up now. She's speaking more with her hands, causing her bracelets to clack against each other. "Wearing a robe and veil is no different from asking God to turn us into trees. The veil is a prison made of cloth that we have accepted as the will of God, and no one can break us out of these prisons but ourselves!"

The women nod; someone claps.

"Being silent, uneducated, nonworking members of society is the same as being dead stumps in the forest!"

The women clap and yell, "Death to Apollo!" and, "Long live the laurel leaf!"

"Do you understand, Mina?" Ayan says.

The women stare at me, but I'm tongue-tied. "I . . .

think . . . that the story of Daphne is very . . . It's wrong that she ended up as a tree." I look at Nana, hoping this is good enough.

Nana smiles but seems a little disappointed, while Ayan whispers, "Yes . . . yes."

Gray has started beating on a drum, so the chant picks up rhythm and volume. "Long live the laurel leaf" is whispered over and over, until it no longer sounds like words. Soon a middle-aged woman, with a wrinkled neck and braided hair, gets up and starts twirling. Everyone claps and urges her on. Her green skirt spins so that I can see her thick white legs underneath. She swings her hips back and forth and then closes her eyes and begins to undulate. I've never seen dancing like this. Her movement seems like something only a husband should see. She sways over to Ayan, leans in, and shakes her breasts. I'm shocked, but then everyone starts laughing.

The dancing woman then continues around the circle and grabs a tall, spindly girl with bushy brown hair and oversize glasses. Despite her height, the girl doesn't appear to be much older than I am, and once she begins dancing, an enormous smile lights up her face. She isn't lustful like the first woman. She's more like a puppy releasing pent-up energy after being inside all day. She holds both her arms straight out to the side, spinning. Once she starts, she looks like she'll never stop.

Herra then joins, as well as a handful of other women, all smiling and laughing. These women are so different from any I've ever known. They no longer have husbands, but it's more than that. They aren't looking over their shoulders anymore. They can talk and laugh and dance in this room without constantly glancing at the doorway, wondering when a man might enter to stop it all. For that freedom, they're willing to live underground and never leave.

Looking at me, Herra holds out her hands. I look at Nana, who gestures for me to get up, to join in the dancing. But I shake my head. I've never danced before, and I wouldn't want all of these women watching me, especially Rayna. I look for her, and, like me, she's still sitting down. On her stoic face I see the faint trace of a smile as she watches the dancers. She glances at me, and the smile quickly disappears. I feel bad that I ruined her brief moment of pleasure, but what can I do? My face gets on her nerves.

Someone has lit incense, making the air thick with smoke and the smell of burning pine. Can Juda hear us? Surely the sound of the drum and the chanting is reaching him, wherever he is. I hope his dinner was as tasty as mine, even if he had to eat it alone. Maybe I can sneak away soon and find him. It's only been a few hours since I saw him, and I already have so much to tell him. I wonder what he would think of this dancing. Considering that he was embarrassed to look at these women without their veils, I can't imagine he would survive this gyrating. I smile, thinking about how red his face would be.

I just can't believe that Nana won't give him a chance. A day ago, my fantasy would have been the two of them meeting and talking. And now they're both in the same building and Juda's being treated like a criminal.

The huge amount of food I ate has made me tired, so I snuggle into the mound of pillows. I try to keep watching the dancing, but my eyelids are so heavy that each blink is an effort.

Before long, I drift into sleep, the beat of the drum dictating the progression and texture of my dream. Damon is pursuing me, and I can no longer run, because my feet have grown roots that reach ten feet underground. Juda is there with an ax. He wants to cut the roots and set me free, but I beg him to wait. He doesn't understand that the roots are part of me, and that when he cuts them, I will bleed. I'm yelling at him, trying to explain, but he won't listen. He's too intent on saving me. He lifts the ax above his head and, with all of his might, slices me in half.

I jolt awake, crying out.

The women continue to chant and dance, taking no note of my distress. I look at Nana. She's singing and clapping her hands, immersed in the moment. She looks younger and less tired—beautiful, in fact. She's happy here. They're all happy here. So why do I feel miserable?

The answer is eating his supper alone in another room.

TWENTY-FIVE

I'M SURROUNDED BY A HEAVENLY SMELL, nestled in a field of lavender, and at first I think I can't possibly be awake. I sit up and find that I'm lying on a makeshift bed made of pillows and sheets on the floor of a small, plain white room, my clothes folded on a chair by the door. I wear a loose cotton nightgown that I don't recall putting on. My body is stiff and heavy, as if I didn't move once all night. I don't really remember leaving the room where we ate dinner.

Like the room where Juda and I first met Rayna, this one is full of cardboard boxes. These have all been pried open, so I crawl over to the nearest one and peer inside. I see lots of small objects, wrapped in dust-coated bubbles. I pick up one of the tiny packages, blow off the dust, and unwrap it slowly. The lavender scent gets stronger as I discover a purple bar of soap like the one I used on Nana. I put it up to my nose and inhale deeply. Heaven.

I move to the next container and find hundreds of cute boxes, cream-colored rectangles etched with the words "Chanel No. 5." I open one and find a delicate glass bottle filled with golden liquid. Perfume, I'm guessing. Father

gave some to Mother once. She pretended to be scandal-
ized. Perfume is forbidden, its sole purpose being to lure
men. But I could tell she was secretly thrilled. I would smell
it on her sometimes right before my father came home. But
she would rush to wash it off if anyone else visited the house.

This bottle is much larger than the one Mother had. I
twist off the pretty top, spray the perfume in the air, and
stick my nose right into the mist. I'm trying to decide
whether I like it, when I sneeze violently. I look around,
thinking that since No. 5 made me sneeze, maybe I'll like a
No. 3 or No. 4 better, but I don't see any other numbers in
the big cardboard box.

"Nice, isn't it?"

I jump at the sound of the voice, almost dropping the
bottle. I turn to see Ayan standing in the doorway.

"Be careful," she says. "That's worth eight thousand
BTUs."

My hands feel huge as I replace the bottle in its box.
"I'm so sorry. I was just curious."

"Don't apologize. We found the boxes here when we
discovered the cellar. We have no more right to them than
you do." She enters the room. "But sometimes when we
need money, we sell the perfume and soap on the black
market or trade them for food. We've been blessed."

I run my hands through my hair. I know I look half-
asleep, and her easy elegance makes me self-conscious.
"Where is everyone?"

"At breakfast. We thought it would be best to let you
sleep awhile."

"Where's Nana?"

"She's fine. She's eating, too." She clasps her hands in front of her. "I thought you could eat with Juda."

"Yes!" I stand up.

"Get dressed," she says. "I'll wait outside."

I throw on my clothes, thrilled to see a new bra that Nana must have found for me. I start to pull my hair back into a ponytail and then decide against it. Why not leave it down if no one cares?

When I'm ready, Ayan walks me down a long hall with doors on both sides. "How many rooms are there?" I ask.

"We didn't use to have many. It was one huge, open space. But that got inconvenient, so we started to partition it off."

"You did it yourself?" I ask, unable to keep the astonishment out of my voice.

"Yes," Ayan says, with a smile that's supposed to tell me that there's nothing the Laurel Society can't do. "I believe we now have at least forty rooms."

A moment later she starts speaking in a less casual voice, reminding me of the one my mother uses when she's about to give me an unpleasant chore. "You need to have a talk with Juda."

"About what?"

"About when he's going to leave."

I stop walking. "What are you talking about? You said he could stay."

"I said he could stay for the night."

My rib cage seems to narrow around my heart. "But I need more time with Nana."

"No one is asking you to leave, Mina. You'll be a welcome addition to our community."

"Can't Juda and I have more time? We need to decide what we're going to do."

"I'm sorry, but Juda's already making a lot of the women uncomfortable with his presence. I've bent the rules as it is." She starts to walk down the hall again.

"Please, Ayan." Grabbing her hand, I look into her eyes, gray-green like winter grass. "Just give me until tonight. Please." My voice catches on "please," and I'm embarrassed. The women of the Laurel Society find their strength in themselves, and I don't want her to think that I'm reliant on a boy. But I know if I ask Juda to leave, I might never see him again, and the idea fills me with dread, like a thickening of my blood that makes my body heavy and unwilling to move until she's changed her mind.

Ayan sighs, as if she's been pleaded with many times before. "All right. I'll give you until six o'clock tonight. But then you have to either send the boy away or leave with him."

Almost hugging her, I say, "Thank you." I didn't expect her to budge.

We arrive at a door at the very end of the hall, and she knocks.

After we hear a muffled "yes," Ayan takes a key from her pocket and unlocks the door.

"You locked him in?" I ask, trying to control my outrage, since she's just granted me a favor.

"The others wouldn't agree to his being here overnight unless they knew he was under lock and key. You can see why it's in everyone's best interest to send the boy home."

Home? If she could see the small concrete bunker full of rotten food, would she still be calling it that?

She opens the door. The room is piled to the ceiling with crates, boxes, bags, and mountains of folded clothing. At first, I don't see Juda. Then I spot him in the corner, nestled between two towers of shirts and pants, sitting on the floor on a mound of sheets and pillows similar to the one I slept on.

He waves. "Hi," he says. "I'd get up, but, uh . . ."

If he stood, his head would hit the low ceiling.

"This is ridiculous," I say to Ayan. "Why don't you give him my room?"

"We actually thought he would like it in here. He can take whatever he wants." She gestures around the room. "We don't need any of it, and he probably doesn't have access to these kinds of products."

She's talking about him as if he can't understand English or as if he's a vagrant they found on the street.

"What is it all?"

I ask him, not Ayan.

"Shoes. Pants. Shirts," he says. "Men's and boys'. I've never seen anything like it, actually. There are coats and scarves, hats, gloves. There are, like, thirty different kinds of underwear—"

"Take whatever you need," Ayan says, cutting him off.

He smiles his goofy smile. "Thank you. You're very generous."

Generous? How can he say that when they've locked him in here all night?

Ayan excuses herself and, as she closes the door, says, "Mina, come back to the main room when you've finished breakfast." Then she's gone.

"Huh. She left us alone," I say.

"They don't like men, but they seem to like rules even less," Juda says.

"Your mother left us alone, too. Does she hate rules?" I ask.

He considers this. "She thinks that rules have a time and a place. If your life is in danger, etiquette is not a priority."

I smile. My mother wouldn't agree. If my home were on fire, she would expect me to make a scrumptious meal for my husband before I ran out.

"I hope your mother isn't too worried about us," I say. I really wanted to leave her a note when we left the bunker, but, of course, she can't read.

He smiles halfheartedly. "I left the lantern at the top of the stairs so she'd know that no one took us by force. She won't be worried yet."

Yet.

I cross over to him and take his hand, squeezing it tightly. I sit on the floor next to him, seeing a tray with two plates of fried ham slices and more of the bread we ate last night, plus boiled eggs. Juda hands me a plate and silverware, and I dig in happily.

"I like your hair," he says.

"Thank you." My hand touches it self-consciously. I never know what to say after someone gives me a compliment. "This place is amazing. It goes on forever—rooms like this one, just on and on." When he doesn't respond, I say, "How'd you sleep?"

"Very well, actually, probably because I ate so much. You?"

"Fine," I say, slicing the ham.

"And how's your nana?"

"She's . . . I think she's in more pain than she's letting on. But she's relieved to see me."

"Of course she is," he says.

"She seems really happy to be here. Most of the women do," I say. I gesture to the piles around us. "So, you've found some clothes that you like?"

He shrugs. "I was being polite. Most of them have holes chewed through them. Moths, I guess." He takes a bite of toast.

Our conversation seems stiff and forced. Am I acting strange because of the discussion with Ayan, or does Juda feel awkward, too?

"What's that smell?" he says, leaning toward me.

I stiffen. I haven't bathed since we were in the bunker. "Uh . . ."

"Jasmine? No, more musky."

Oh! The perfume. I must have gotten some on me. "Do you like it?" I ask. "It's very expensive."

"I know. I once broke a bottle of Mrs. Asher's, and it cost me over a month's salary."

"So you don't like it," I say, feeling disappointed for some reason.

"I prefer how you smell on your own," he says, and then blushes.

I smile. What am I supposed to say now? *I like how you smell, too?* The truth is, I do. I love his combination of clean, earthy scents.

"And I don't like makeup," he blurts.

I raise my eyebrows, surprised at the declaration.

"You asked me before," he says, "if I wanted women to wear makeup, and I don't. I think you look great how you are, and you don't need anything on your face."

Now it's my turn to blush. "I'm sorry I was yelling at you in the Theater District. I just got upset, thinking of all those women—"

"I was raised by a single mother, remember? If it hadn't been for my uncles . . . who knows what would have happened to us, to her."

My mother screams at us a lot about how we could all end up on the streets, but I guess I never took her seriously. I knew she was afraid of having less money, of not being able to afford hot water or as many meat and sugar rations every year. I never thought she was afraid of being literally *on the streets*, but after she burned me, ensuring my engagement to Damon, she said, "You won't be forced to sell your body." She was trying to prevent me from ending up in the Theater District.

"Do you think your mother knows about the Laurel Society?" I say.

Tapping his egg on the side of his plate, he begins to peel away the shell. "I've been wondering about that. When I was little, there was a time when things were really grim, and my uncles were struggling, too. And just when we'd reached our last crumb, a neighborhood woman showed up with a basket of food. No explanation. Now I'm wondering whether she was part of the Laurel Society. If my mom knew about it, she never told me."

I wonder if Mr. Asher had anything to do with the emergency food basket. "I think if your mother knew about the women here, she would've told me about them yesterday, don't you?"

He shrugs. "She wants you to be safe. But she also wants me to be happy." Half his mouth turns up in a cynical smile. "I wouldn't have reacted well if she'd sent you away from me."

I can't imagine he's going to react any better if *he* is sent away from *me*. I inhale deeply. "Ayan says you have to leave."

He doesn't respond but keeps peeling his egg.

"Say something," I say.

"They've wanted me to leave since the second we arrived. I'm shocked I lasted this long."

Cracking my own egg, I peel it, leaving tiny bits of shell sticking to the surface. "She also asked if I wanted to stay."

He nods. "I figured that would happen, too."

"And what did you figure I would say?"

"I wasn't sure. I know that I want you to come with me. But if you're not sure, and you leave, then you'll be miserable."

I want to be here with Nana. I know that. But why does it have to be at the price of losing him? The choice is impossible.

I pick at pieces of shell, creating small dents in my egg. He offers me his peeled one, perfectly smooth, and I take it.

"I know what I want," he says. "I've had feelings for you since the first time we met, when you tried to stand up for that woman in Union Square and then made fun of me for cursing." Smiling, he looks into my eyes. "But then when I saw you ready to charge down here, down a pitch-black staircase into who knows where, because someone you loved asked you to, I couldn't believe how brave you were. That was when"—he pauses, taking a breath—"I knew I loved you."

I'm taken aback. My mother, my aunties—everyone—has told me not to expect love, that it's dangerous, that it will ruin my life.

He says, "Do you love me?"

I stare at him. I should want to answer right away, shouldn't I? But if I say yes, it will feel like a promise, like I'm choosing him over Nana. How can I leave her again right when I've found her? Or what if Nana's right, and as soon as I pledge my love, Juda becomes a tyrant?

My tongue feels thick in my mouth. One second goes by without my answer, and then another. And another. And then I know it's too late.

He picks up my egg, picking off the remaining shell. "You have to stay here, Mina. You won't be happy with me."

"You don't know that," I say. "I just need more time."

He nods.

"Ayan gave me until tonight. Can't you do the same?"

He nods again, but he still doesn't look up.

I eat some of his egg, but my mouth has gone dry and the yolk tastes like chalk.

"You met me," he says, smile gone, a bitter look in his eyes, "on the day of your Offering, about to be signed away to the highest bidder. Maybe I was just a way out, the only other option you could see."

"That's not true! Or fair!"

"Your feelings probably seemed legitimate at the time," he says, sounding pompous, like Damon. "Don't worry. I don't think you used me."

What in the name of the Prophet is he talking about? "What about you?" I ask. "What did *you* know about *me*?" A haze of anger and defensiveness clouds my vision. "Was it that Damon wanted me, too? Or just that you saw a girl in a tight dress with her breasts sticking out and had to have her?"

His confused face instantly makes me regret my words.

"I think you should leave," he says, his soft voice only guaranteeing I feel worse.

"I'm sorry. I—"

"Now," he says, more softly still.

Standing, I try to think of something to say. Our conversation can't end this way. I feel desperate to fix it, to make him feel better. He thinks he wants to hear, "I love you, too," but he doesn't. It will only make him feel worse, unless it's followed by "I'm coming with you," which I can't say. So neither of us speaks, and I walk out, letting the door lock behind me, leaving him a prisoner once again in a room so tiny he can't even stand upright.

TWENTY-SIX

I WALK ALONG THE HALLWAY IN A DAZE, TRYING to figure out whether I'm more angry at Juda or at myself, but soon realize I'm most angry at Ayan and Nana for wanting Juda to leave.

Nana said, "The boy seems important now, but I promise you he's not." How could she possibly know who on this earth is important? Did the Prophet seem important when She was first born? When She was a teenager?

Nana declared that Juda was unimportant because he's male. Is that not just as bad as deeming someone unworthy of an education just because she's female?

I look for Ayan, ready to plead my case. In the dining area I find Gray, who directs me to Ayan's office down the hall. As I'm about to rap on the door, I hear voices coming from inside.

Ayan sounds agitated. "This isn't a joke, Rayna. If it happens again, I'll ask you to leave."

I decide this isn't a good time to knock but find I'm frozen in place.

"Who else will do your recon missions?" Rayna says with confidence.

"That's my concern."

A snort. "It's everyone's concern. You'll be a submarine with no periscope."

I knew Rayna was trouble. I wonder what she did.

"I'm revoking your private sleeping quarters," says Ayan. "You'll go back to sleeping in the dorms, starting tonight."

There's a loud *thunk*, as if maybe Rayna has kicked a trash can.

Rayna says, "How can you just sit here month after month, doing nothing?'

"You think saving lives is nothing?"

"Do you know how many *more* lives we could save if we didn't hole up here like cowards?"

"Courage is about doing the moral thing, not giving in to anger."

"My anger is not immoral! How many more stonings will you let happen before you—"

"*Stop* painting the leaves," Ayan says. "Don't make me say it again."

Rayna is the one who's been painting leaves around the city?

The door flies open. If Rayna notices me, she makes no sign. She marches off, down the hallway.

Through the open door, I see Ayan sitting in a surprisingly spare room with a white desk and a clear plastic chair. She's staring straight ahead, breathing deeply. She turns to look at me when I enter, and she doesn't look pleased.

"Hello," I say, feeling awkward. When she doesn't respond, I continue, "I'm sorry to be nosy," I say. "I couldn't help but overhear . . ."

She raises an eyebrow, doubting me.

"I thought you should know that . . . uh . . . the leaves that Rayna sprayed helped me find my way to you. I never would've figured out Nana's clue without them."

She nods once. "We have a protocol. Leaves are to be painted in very specific areas where they won't be noticed by authorities. We want *women* to see them, *not* Twitchers. Rayna is trying to stir things up. And that is not her place."

Oh.

"Is that all?" she asks irritably.

I'm guessing this is not a good time to talk to her about Juda. "Do you know where Nana is?" I ask.

"Probably the library."

Seeing my confused face, she adds, "Turn right out this door, then walk to the end of the hall."

Leaving the office, I wonder what Ayan means by "specific areas" where women will see the leaves. Have I ever seen a leaf painted at a prayer center? I can't remember.

I reach the end of the hall and push through a swinging door, and for a moment all thoughts of leaves and Juda are swept away. The space is huge, bigger than the dining area. Low glass cases line the floor, like the ones the butcher uses to display his pig carcasses in the market. But these cases are not filled with meat. They're filled with *books*. Thousands of books.

The books are stacked on top of each other horizontally, books in all different shapes and sizes, their spines pressing up against the glass—paperbacks and hardbacks. I had no idea this many books still existed in the world, let alone that women were keeping them! I want to laugh and cry at the same time.

In the nearest case, I read the names on the spines: William Faulkner, Henry Fielding, Janice Fillmore, F. Scott Fitzgerald, Zelda Sayre Fitzgerald, Ian Fleming, Deborah Foiles, C. S. Forester—

"Mina! Over here!"

Following the sound of her voice, I find Nana sitting in a far corner.

"I can't believe it!" I say, giddy.

"Welcome to the library." Nana slumps in a frayed armchair, legs propped on a stool. As I readjust to seeing her so fragile, anger leaks out of me like I'm a draining bathtub. Next to her, on a plain chair, sits the tall, bushy-haired girl who danced last night. Between them, a blue-and-white tea set rests on a small table.

"This is Grace," Nana says. "She's the librarian."

Grace seems very young to be in charge. I sit down in a chair opposite the two of them. "What a wonderful job."

"Yes," Grace says, playing with a curl of hair as she looks at the floor. "I mean . . . uh . . . I'm not *the* librarian. We have . . . uh, several. Miriam is . . . in charge."

"Where did all these books come from?" I ask.

"The Laurel Society helps women in need . . . but its, uh, secondary mission, uh, *just* as important, is to collect and protect the books of our city." Grace doesn't seem to have a lot of practice talking to people. "This collection is, uh, one hundred years old."

Dumbfounded, I ask, "The Laurel Society has been in Macy's for a hundred years?"

"No, Chickpea," Nana says. "When the Prophet died and the Teachers outlawed reading for women, a woman named Maud Gayhill began to hide books in her attic."

"She was so brave," Grace says, eyes wide behind her big glasses. "She did all of it—uh, hid books, sheltered women—all with her husband, uh, living in the same house."

"After word spread about Maud, books started arriving from all over the island," Nana says. "Women carried them across town hidden in strollers or wrapped up like pork chops! And not just books—anything they could get their hands on, anything they thought might one day help their daughters get an education: newspapers, magazines, letters, even restaurant menus!"

"It must have all been, uh, very exciting," Grace says.

Grace has not had run-ins with many Twitchers if she thinks crossing the island with a book is "exciting."

"Ms. Gayhill, uh, moved the collection when it got too big. It went several places, including, uh, Carnegie Hall, before it ended up here," Grace says.

Amazing. I wonder what else women were able to save. What else is buried around the city?

"Would you like to see what Grace found for me this morning?"

Nana holds up a magazine. I can't believe it. It's the Primer. But it's like new.

"Look at her face, Grace," Nana says, handing it to me with care. "First time I ever saw her speechless in all my years!"

I run my hands over the cover, which is fully intact. "*Time Out*," I say, amazed. "We were both wrong."

"Yes, we were, Chickpea."

"We have many quality samples of, uh, that title, from the early twenty-first century. It was a popular guide to the city, published on a weekly basis, and many—"

"Shhh, Grace," Nana says. "Let her enjoy it."

"Oh," says Grace, sitting back. "Sorry."

Gently, I flip through the pages I know so well.

The best Jersey-style dogs.

Spanish dance-rock stalwarts.

Bioluminescent bay, full of plankton that sparkle a brilliant blue.

But it's the pictures that leave me wonderstruck. For years I've been forced to use my imagination to fill the blank squares, and here are the images, finally. Women dancing. Men singing. Men and women, *together*, drinking, eating food, or gathered in the parks. In the film section, people are doing all sorts of different things: arguing, kissing, running from an explosion. In the music section, they play instruments. A group of women stands holding guitars, wearing next to nothing, their faces smeared with color, their mouths painted to look like wet cherries. They wear high heels like Mrs. Asher's, and they're pushing out their breasts with pride. They aren't wearing much more than that woman in her pink underwear in the Theater District. If I were wearing so little, I would be humiliated. The women in the picture are smiling and laughing.

They don't look humiliated. They look strong.

Nana breaks my reverie, saying, "I was as surprised as you. I thought Ayan had given me the only copy."

My head jerks up. "What do you mean? Your mother gave you the Primer. And her mother gave it to her."

"Not exactly," Nana says, looking embarrassed. "I told you that because I had to make sure you would retrieve the Primer if something happened to me. I needed to make it valuable."

"So, it never belonged to your grandmother?" I say, confused.

"No," she says, with regret. "My grandmother learned to read when there were still a few secret schools for girls. She taught my mother using the Book when my father was at work, and my mother taught me the same way." She waits for me to respond, and when I don't, she adds, "Five years ago, I asked Ayan to bring me something that mentioned Macy's, and she chose our Primer. You'd think she could've given me the copy without the torn cover!" She laughs.

Grace raises a finger. "Actually, it makes perfect sense. Ayan would've wanted the more intact sample to stay in the permanent collection."

I'm unsettled by Nana's confession, but it's hard to say exactly why. "What about the pictures? If your grandmother didn't cut them out, then who did?"

"They didn't seem appropriate for a ten-year-old," Nana says, shrugging. "It seemed best to remove them."

"You damaged a piece from our library?" says Grace, shocked.

I guess Nana hasn't told her the fate of our Primer. I have no intention of confessing to Grace now.

Unsubdued by Grace's disapproval, Nana says, "Ayan made it clear that the Primer was a gift. It belonged to Mina."

I look at the *Time Out* in my hands, and I'm filled with sadness. "I would have gone to get it without the lie, Nana."

"I know that now. How could I have guessed when you were ten years old how you would feel?"

I wipe my hand across my eyes, stifling a sob.

"I'm sorry. I didn't know the story meant so much to you."

"It's not that."

"So what's wrong?"

"Everything."

She offers me a cup of tea. "That's not possible."

Grace reaches her hand out for the *Time Out*, seeming nervous I'll spill on it, so I hand it back to her. But I don't feel like drinking tea. "Ayan is making Juda leave."

"I know you'll miss him," Nana says, "but over time, you'll see that Ayan's decision is for the best." She sips her tea.

Annoyed that she thinks all decisions have been made, I say, "Miss him? I might go with him."

She sits up, stung. "You can't be serious. People don't come and go here, Mina. You won't be allowed to come back! I'll never see you again!"

"But why should I have to choose between you?"

"This isn't just about me. Look around!" she says, gesturing at the books. "Look at the education that's waiting for you. You have so much more to learn. You can't leave all this behind for a boy!"

Nana looks to Grace, signaling for her to speak.

Grace leans toward me, her too-big glasses sliding down her nose. "You'll learn to really like it here. Sometimes it can be, uh, kind of suffocating, I suppose. But everyone is nice, and the books . . ." She looks around, a bee surrounded by a thousand flowers. "The books are just so wonderful, I can't even tell you. There are so many I could give you to read . . . like the mythology collection that has the story of Daphne and Apollo! We also have oodles of newspapers and magazines and *stacks* of *Time Out*. And Miriam offers reading lessons on Wednesdays and Frid—"

"I can't wait for you to read your first novel!" Nana blurts.

I look at the *Time Out* in Grace's lap. Nana and I could sit here every day, reading to our hearts' content, never worrying about being caught or about Father arriving to say "time to go home."

"A novel, Chickpea, well, it just opens up your mind in a way you can't imagine. You get to feel things, visit places and worlds you would never know otherwise."

Grace says, "You have a very hard choice. The boy you came with, uh, he seemed nice . . . and he's, uh, very handsome."

Nana shoots her a look. "Thank you, Grace. Maybe you could get us some more tea?"

Chastised, Grace excuses herself, taking the teapot.

"Mina, I know you have feelings for the boy. But you're young and you're making a mistake that's going to get you killed!"

How does she know what will get me killed? She

doesn't realize what I've already survived. I'm sick of people underestimating me.

Now's the time to say what I came to say. "You just hate all men. Like Rayna. You hate all of them because your husband turned you in for reading. He betrayed you. And now you want me to hate men too. Why can't you—"

"He didn't turn me in!" she says, angered and surprised at my words.

"What?" I say, confused. "Then who did?"

A pain crosses her face that I've never seen before, a sharp and heavy heartbreak.

"Mother," I say, knowing the truth the moment I say it.

Torment is all over Nana's face.

"How old was she?"

After a while, she says, "Eight."

I'm dumbstruck.

At eight, I was still playing hide-and-go-seek with Sekena. My mother had what I always longed for, a childhood in Nana's house, and she threw it away—decimated it. Nana wants me not to judge people, to stop and consider the lives they've had, what shaped them. But in my mother's case, I believe she was born cruel.

"You must hate her," I say.

"I love her," Nana says. "Always." As her eyes water, I realize I've never seen Nana cry. "She was a child. She didn't know what she was doing."

The woman who set me on fire? I imagine she knew *exactly* what she was doing, even at eight. "Who did she tell? One of her friends?"

"Oh, no. On the way to the market, she stopped a Teacher in the street, and before I knew what was happening, she'd told him everything. He had me arrested on the spot. My Marga was always smart, resourceful like that."

I say nothing. Mother ruined her life. If Nana doesn't want to hate her, I'll do it for her.

Nana sighs. "You are my great love, Mina. You are everything Marga should have been. She was a coward. She loved to read more than you and me combined. Our lessons were her favorite part of the day. But her father would come home, treat her like a princess, talk about the men she could marry, and tell her how important it was that she be docile and pious. She started to fear that no man would want her if she were educated."

"At age eight?"

"Your grandfather convinced her that she would be worthless unless a man wanted her, and that using her brain was a sin."

"Grandpa Silna is a pig."

"In the beginning, I loved him very much. Just as you love Juda. I was in the Tunnel less than six months before he remarried."

I go to her, kneel, and wrap myself around her. "I'm so sorry."

"Don't be sorry. Just don't repeat my mistakes."

"Refill?" Grace is back, steaming teapot in hand, eager eyes darting back and forth between Nana and me as she tries to ascertain whether she should rejoin us.

"Thank you, dear," Nana says, giving her a warm smile.

Grace fills Nana's cup. The smell of chamomile fills the air.

"I was thinking, uh, about what you should read first," Grace says, her face vibrant. "If you'll come with me . . . I'd like to make a suggestion."

I look to Nana, not feeling that our conversation is over.

She says, "Go ahead," seeming tired. I'm not used to this new Nana who gets exhausted so easily.

When I kiss her on the cheek, she says, "Promise me you won't leave without saying goodbye."

"I would never," I say, knowing now that I won't be able to leave her at all.

"THE BOOK IS ONE OF MY FAVORITES, SO IT'S actually in my room."

Grace practically skips down the hallway. I can't match her enthusiasm; my head is so filled with confusing thoughts.

We enter what must be Grace's bedroom, but it looks more like a crazy market stall. A bed in the corner over-flows with dolls and fluffy animals, stacks of books and magazines cover every inch of the floor, and what appear to be shower curtains line the walls. One has a big map on it, another has a cherry blossom tree, a third has cotton clouds against an indigo sky, and the fourth has an old Manhattan skyline. Most strangely, in the corner, two mannequins, a young boy and girl, stand dressed in formal wear. He's in a gray suit with a navy tie, while she wears a frilly lemon dress trimmed with lace.

Wading into the chaos, Grace grabs a few books and sits on top of the stuffed animals on the bed. With a beaming smile, she says, "Join!" She throws a few dolls off the bed, creating a small patch of free bedspread.

Once I'm seated, she hands me a book. "This is my favorite, *The Secret of the Old Clock*." She hands me a second one. "But this one might be my favorite, too, called *The Invisible Intruder*. You'll have to let me know which you think is better."

"Thanks," I say. Grace speaks more confidently now than she did in the library. I'm not sure if it's because we're in her room or because Nana is gone.

"They're both about this amazing girl," she says, "named Nancy Drew, and she's a detective who solves crimes. She always catches the criminal because she's really smart."

As I flip through the first book, she says, "So what's it like?"

"What?"

"Uh . . . *being* with a boy."

I flush but don't look up. "I haven't . . . Juda and I never . . . Who's been saying we've . . . done it?" I bet it was Rayna, trying to turn all of them against us.

The color drains from Grace's face, and she looks like she wants to bury herself under her stuffed animals. "No. I meant . . . uh, what's it like to talk to him . . ."

Now it's my turn to cringe. "I'm so sorry. I thought—"

"I know," she says, stopping me from saying it again. "It's my fault. It was a weird question."

"It wasn't. It's fine." I search for a way to end the awkwardness. "How long have you lived here?"

"Always," she says with a shrug.

"You mean you were *born* here?"

"Almost. I came when I was, uh, a baby."

"What happened to your parents?" I say.

"My mother got, uh, pregnant out of wedlock. She was sent to the, uh, Tunnel, but she got me to Ayan before I was sent, too."

Her nerves are back. I can hear it in her voice. "I'm sorry," I say.

"Don't be. I have dozens of mothers."

And they're probably a lot nicer than mine. "But they never let you talk to a boy?"

She strokes the head of a worn stuffed elephant. "No boys ever, uh, come down here."

"And you never go out? *Ever?*"

"Ayan thinks it's too dangerous."

"You've *never* been outside?" Wow. Grace is worse than Sekena. Feeling bad that I embarrassed her, I say, "Would you like to talk to Juda?"

"I couldn't," she says, playing with her strand of hair. "I'd be too, uh . . . He'd think I was weird."

"No. Not at all. He'll like you." I stand.

"Now?" Alarm fills her face, like I've said we're about to meet Uncle Ruho. She pats down her bushy hair. "I should change."

"You look great." Looking around, I say, "Take him a book. I'm sure he'd be happy to have something to do."

She grins. I've found her specialty. After searching a few piles, she chooses one called *How to Win Friends and Influence People*.

"It's pretty useful," she says. "Especially when you're, uh, in a place where maybe people don't like you so much."

"Sounds good."

"I've read it three times."

I wonder how bad Grace's ability to speak to people could possibly have been *before* she read the book.

Soon Grace and I are walking down the hall, arm in arm, and I realize bringing her with me to see Juda is a genius idea. She can act as a buffer between Juda and me, so we don't have to talk about our fight.

But I don't have a chance to see whether my plan will work. When we arrive at Juda's room, Grace gasps. The door is wide open, splintered where the lock was, and when I walk inside, Juda is gone.

TWENTY-SEVEN

"WHERE ARE YOU GOING?" GRACE YELLS AS I race down the hall.

"To see if I can catch him!" I say.

I head back to the main room, leaving Grace behind. I run into the passage that brought us here yesterday, but it's black as a starless night. Without Rayna's flashlight, I doubt I can make my way.

I call out, "Juda!" Maybe the dark slowed him down, too. Silence.

Reaching to my left, I grope the air until my hands land upon cold cement. I slide my fingers along, years of dust coming with them. My foot brushes something that scurries across the floor, causing me to cry out and almost turn back. I slide my hands forward again, the grit coating my palms, and take another two steps.

What if he's gone? The last thing I said to him was . . . *Oh God*. I accused him of liking me because I wore a tight dress.

Of course he left. He hates me.

I slide my hands farther, when something comes barreling out of the darkness, knocking me to the ground.

A voice says, "Who's there?"

Moaning from the floor, I say, "Juda?"

A beam of light hits me.

"Mina, what are you doing here?"

I don't respond. I hear two clicks, then Rayna's voice. "I asked you a question."

She must be in her Twitcher uniform, and now she's removed her helmet to speak to me.

I sit up, a bit muddled. "I'm fine. Thanks for asking."

"Were you running away?" she asks, ignoring my sarcasm.

"Juda left."

"Good."

"You didn't see him outside?" I ask, impatient.

"No. But I did see several dozen Twitchers, and they have only one thing on their mind."

"What?"

"*You.*"

Grabbing my sleeve, Rayna drags me back to the main room, where she whispers in Gray's ear. Gray scurries around the room, murmuring to everyone, until no one is talking. They all stare up at the ceiling, as if they can see through it to the Twitchers patrolling above. One or two women look at me with disdain.

I don't understand. Isn't everyone here a Deserter? Aren't Twitchers looking for all of us?

Rayna once again grabs my sleeve, pulling me to Ayan's office. We enter without knocking, surprising Ayan.

"We need to talk about the girl," Rayna says, shaking me slightly.

"I've had enough of you today, Rayna," Ayan says, cool as ever. "We can talk tomorrow."

Releasing my sleeve, Rayna approaches Ayan and mumbles in her ear. I strain to hear her words but can't.

Ayan stands, smiles at me, and says, "Let's go to the media room, shall we?"

What did Rayna say that has changed Ayan's attitude so drastically?

We run into Grace in the hallway. "Did you find him?" she asks, touchingly worried.

Ayan says, "Juda's loose?"

"He's not a hamster," I say, annoyed. "He's a person. And he's left, so you can all relax now."

"I didn't pass him when I came in," Rayna says. "He must have used the south exit."

Grace pats my arm. "I'm sorry."

Rayna and Ayan say nothing, continuing to walk. They're content to let him disappear, another man they don't have to think about. But, as much as I want to blame them for Juda's departure, I know why he really left: I couldn't tell him what he needed to hear.

"Where are you going?" Grace says.

"The media room," Rayna says.

"Can I come?" Grace asks.

Rayna scratches her blue hair, smiles at Grace, and says, "Okay. But don't touch anything."

Wow. Rayna likes Grace. Nice to know she likes *someone*.

Soon we reach a green door, which Rayna unlocks. Several desks line the room, radios and random computer parts sit everywhere, and a large monitor hangs on the wall.

"This'll take a minute," Rayna says.

The rest of us sit down.

Placing her Twitcher helmet on a desk, Rayna grasps the wire running out of the back of her uniform—the one that attaches to the helmet. She disconnects the wire, laying aside the helmet. Then she tugs at one of the gloves she's wearing, exposing wires between her jacket and the glove. It feels like we're looking at the wrist of a robot.

"Don't pull too hard. You'll break them," Ayan says.

Rayna glares at her like a mother being told how to breastfeed her own baby. She separates the tiny wires until she finds the one she wants, and then she pulls it. The wire that was attached to the helmet moves through the jacket like a snake until Rayna holds the whole thing, nearly three feet long.

She plugs the loose end into the monitor on the wall.

She wriggles her fingers a few times, and a keyboard pops up on the monitor screen.

"What did you do?" I ask, amazed.

"Not a big deal," she says. "I just rerouted the Twitcher feed from inside the helmet."

"It's way cool," says Grace in a knowing voice.

I agree. Now, anything that would be on Rayna's Twitcher computer, we'll see on the monitor. As Rayna's fingers type in the air, we see keys light up on-screen. She says, "This is the main alert I saw when I was up top."

Information scrolls up the monitor, too fast for me to keep up.

```
Priority  One  .  .  .  Mina  Clark  .  .  .
Assault  .  .  .  Missing  .  .  .
```

"I saw at least two dozen Twitchers in the area," Rayna says, "I assume because she's 'Priority One.'"

"Why? She's not a threat to the government," Ayan says.

"Beats me," says Rayna. "But that's not the weirdest part." She types again.

More words scroll up, and one sentence flashes over and over in yellow at the bottom:

```
Offender  to  be  returned  UNHARMED  to  home
of  Maxwell  Asher.
```

I'm relieved that Juda isn't mentioned. Mr. Asher hasn't turned him in. I wonder when Juda will start to wonder why.

Ayan is staring at me. I can't tell whether her expression is one of concentration or suspicion. "My understanding," she says, "is that you're accused of dishonoring a marriage contract, correct?" I nod at her. "That means the Tunnel, at the very least. Together with the assault of your fiancé . . . you should be looking at execution."

Nana must have told her my whole story.

"Isn't this, uh, good news?" says Grace from the corner.

I agree. Are Ayan and Rayna disappointed that I'm not in worse trouble than I am? "'Priority One,'" Ayan says, "means Uncle Ruho is using all of his resources to find you."

Now I understand why the women in the other room were worried. I've put the Laurel Society in danger. That's why Ayan was so quick to respond when Rayna whispered in her ear. But I have no idea why Uncle Ruho is interested in me, or why he would show me leniency. He *loves* a good execution.

Ayan has similar questions. "Since when does Uncle Ruho want to help Maxwell Asher, a dodgy real estate man?"

"But he's not in real estate. He works at the Energy Department," I say, "like my father."

"Since when?" Ayan asks.

"Ummm . . . since they started to build the Cooper Water Plant, six years ago. He's the chief engineer. Father was really annoyed. He said Mr. Asher had never built anything like it and was unqualified."

"Why would Uncle Ruho want Asher to be involved with a water plant?" Ayan says. "Rayna, check Asher's bank accounts for a large withdrawal right before he started working for the Energy Department. Maybe he bribed someone to get the job."

As Rayna types, Ayan taps her fingers on a desk.

How do you check someone's bank account? Women aren't allowed to have them—we aren't even welcome in banks. The information must be on a computer somewhere. When I watch men go to an ATM to recharge a battery or a lightbulb, they insert a card that I assume holds their name and account information.

"Maybe Mr. Asher wanted to reform his reputation?" Grace says. "Do something for the city?"

Rayna rolls her eyes. "Once a scumbucket, always a scumbucket."

Grace laughs, then covers her mouth.

Numbers scroll across the monitor at such a speed, I'm amazed Rayna can make any sense of them. "There!" Rayna says, shouting with surprise, as she freezes the screen. "Ayan, it's not a withdrawal . . . it's a *deposit*, a big one. One hundred million BTUs."

"Uh, what does that mean?" I ask.

Ignoring me, Ayan pinches the bridge of her nose between her thumb and index finger. After a while, she says, "See if there's a public record of it. A sale in that amount. I suppose Asher might have sold his real estate business." She doesn't sound convinced.

Rayna types away. What does any of this have to do with the Twitchers who want to arrest me? I feel like Ayan is talking about squares when I thought we were talking about circles.

"Yes," Rayna says, and Ayan's head pops up in surprise. Rayna reads, "'City buys Mercury Recycling Plant from Asher Organization.'"

"Just one building? Why would Uncle Ruho buy some old plant for a hundred times what it's worth?" Ayan says.

"That recycling plant's been gone for years," Rayna says, confused. "It's just a muddy lot."

Ayan taps her fingers some more, saying, "I need to sit down."

"What's wrong?" Rayna says.

Resting in a chair next to me, Ayan stares at her hands

as if they belong to someone else. "Mercury . . . If you ingest it, it can cause infertility, birth defects, cancer. I think I might understand why the Convenes are getting sick." Her breathing becomes shallow. "If Maxwell Asher built the Cooper water plant using the pipes and infrastructure from the recycling center, he could have been slowly poisoning Convenes for the last five years."

"I don't understand," I say, but I feel my body go hot with fear.

"Uncle Ruho wants to wipe out the Convenes, and he paid Asher to poison their water supply." Ayan says this as if it's the most obvious thing in the world.

"*This* is causing the plague?" Rayna says.

"But why would Uncle Ruho want to kill the Convenes?" I say.

"He tells the Teachers it's to suppress an uprising," Ayan says, "but we believe he doesn't have enough food or fuel for the whole island, so he wants to cut the population in half."

"You're wrong! The water plant is *saving* lives!" But even as I say the words, I feel like I'm sinking deep into the floor. What was it I heard Captain Memon say to Mr. Asher? *I want to discuss your contribution to the Convene problem.* I assumed he meant a monetary contribution—toward finding a cure. Now I see that Captain Memon was thanking Mr. Asher for *producing* the problem.

I look back at Ayan, whose mouth has set in a hard line. Even Grace is staring at the floor, unable to meet my eyes. I say, "Father has no idea. He would be heartbroken. He's spent half his life finding a way to filter that water."

CAROLYN COHAGAN

Rayna watches me closely, probably trying to decide whether I'm lying.

"I have to tell him," I say.

Rayna and Ayan exchange glances.

"He would close the plant if he knew!" I say, looking at Grace. "He has nothing against the Convenes."

Ayan says, in her most composed tone, "This neighborhood is infested with Twitchers with one directive: to find *you*. So if you're prepared to be captured, to be married to a boy who tried to rape you, then by all means, walk out the door and go warn your father. But know that the Ashers will *never* let you escape again."

I look at Rayna, knowing that if I'm looking to her for help, my cause is lost.

She surprises me by saying to Ayan, "The plant will be shut down much faster if we have someone on the inside."

"Agreed," says Ayan. "But we can't risk the possibility that Mr. Clark is part of the plan. He would warn Uncle Ruho. We need to contact Jordan Loudz and the Convenes. They can deal with the water plant however they want and spread the word about contamination. This is bigger than the Laurel Society."

I thought the Laurel Society helped women in need! What about the Convene women who will suffer—who will still be drinking the poisoned water while word slowly spreads? My father could shut down the plant in one day. Now I understand what Rayna was talking about; how can Ayan be content to sit underground, watching all these horrible things go on in the world above? I know she's

314

helping people, but what about all the people she's failing?

"I'm sorry, Mina," Ayan says in a softer voice. "If your father truly doesn't know what his water is doing, then he's been ignorant and blind and he'll have to suffer the consequences. There's nothing we can do."

I hate her for reducing my father to such simple, pathetic terms. "My father has spent his *life* finding a new water source for this city," I say, seething, "so that in ten years we don't all die of thirst. I would hardly call that ignorant."

Ayan says, "I'm sure his intentions were once noble."

"They still are!" I cry. I want to pick up the equipment lying around the room and throw it at her. Why can't she have any compassion? Is it because it's my father? Would she be more understanding if I wanted to go help my mother?

I look at Rayna, praying she'll support me. "Tell her. Tell her we have to do more!"

Rayna grinds her teeth, but she says nothing.

"You girls should leave," Ayan tells Grace and me, her tone calm and unflinching. "Rayna and I have a lot to talk about."

That's it? End of discussion?

"Go spend some time with your nana. Or relax in your room," Ayan says. "I'll find you if we need more information."

"Gee, thanks," I say, heading for the door.

"Mina?"

I don't stop, but Grace says my name, too, so I turn around.

"Promise me you won't leave the building," Ayan says, somber. "If you're caught, you put us all in danger."

We stare at each other for a long time, but finally I give her a curt "fine."

Then I leave with Grace before I lose my temper again.

Numb, I walk behind her to my room, and soon we're seated on my bed, the scent of lavender now overly sweet and suffocating.

"I'm really, uh, sorry about your father," Grace says.

I reach for a bar of soap and run my thumbnail down the edge, leaving a long mark.

"I believe you," she says, "that he doesn't know what's happening."

"Why?" I snap. "No one else does."

She picks at a curl of her hair, splitting the ends, while I continue to scratch at the soap. I like the way the waxy substance feels under my nails, and I imagine digging away until there's nothing left but a tiny purple pea.

After a long time, Grace says, "I told you my mother had me out of wedlock. But I didn't tell you that, uh, the man who made her pregnant was her uncle. She trusted him, he was family—then he did that to her."

I stop scraping the soap. "But *she* went to the Tunnel?"

"Yeah. Nothing happened to her uncle."

"I'm sorry, Grace. That's awful." I stop feeling sorry for myself for a moment.

Anger flashes in her big brown eyes. "I don't think a person should suffer for another man's crime."

"Thank you," I say.

"For what?" she says, surprised.

"For being so honest. For believing me."

She smiles, her shyness returning. "Do you think . . . we can be friends someday?"

Now I'm surprised. "We're friends now!"

"We are?"

I nod, smiling as much as I can in my present mood. "Yeah."

She pulls her legs up under her, grinning. "Do you want me to tell you some Nancy Drew stories, for distraction? I swear they'll make you feel better."

"I have a lot on my mind. I think I'd just like to be alone for a while."

"Of course." She stands, looking embarrassed. She leaves without a goodbye.

Normally, I would worry that I'd offended her, but I have too much to think about. Tossing aside the soap, I lie back on the bed.

I've never felt so paralyzed. I want to talk to Nana, but I can't bear to see her relieved face when I tell her that Juda is gone, or hear her smug voice when she reminds me that she told me he would behave this way. And what will she say when I tell her about Father? Most likely she won't be surprised at all. She'll say that the evil of men perseveres.

I roll to my right, curling into a little ball, trying to ignore the question that's slowly pushing its way forward into my mind. I've created a barrier against it, a pathetic dam that's started to leak with uncertainty. The question repeats itself, and I can't hold it back any longer: What if Father *knows*? What if Ayan is right and he's been collaborating with Uncle Ruho and Mr. Asher from the beginning? He spends all day, every day, at the water plant. Could Mr. Asher really have pulled off something like this *without his knowing*?

I remember Father's face as he told my mother and me that the Convenes were giving him an award. I saw true pride in his smile. Could anyone be such a good liar?

My belly twists and turns at the thought. I've grown up expecting Mother to lie—to my aunties about my father; to my father about Dekker; to Dekker about me. If Ayan thought my *mother* was involved with the mercury scheme, I would probably believe her. Mother will do whatever she has to in order to get what she wants. But I thought Father was different.

Sekena asked if I thought Father knew about Mother and Dekker setting my cloak on fire. I said no, but, if I'm going to be honest with myself now, I said no because I couldn't handle any other answer. If he knew about the plan, if he condoned the burning of my flesh, I didn't know whether my heart could take the pain.

Lying here, stuck underground, I can't help but confront the possibility that he knew what Mother intended to do with that candle. He never came to visit me when I was recovering in bed. Why? Because he felt guilty? And if that wasn't the reason, there's only one other possibility: he doesn't love me. He didn't care enough about my injury to see me.

I sit up in bed, hot tears blurring my vision. I grab the

bar of lavender soap, but it's not enough now. I lunge across the room, my hand closing around a Chanel No. 5 box. I rip it open, yanking out the priceless bottle and smashing it against the wall. The sound of the glass shattering is satisfying, but not nearly as satisfying as imagining Ayan's face when she sees her precious Relic's been destroyed. I grab a second bottle and let this one drop casually on the floor. The third, I whirl around and throw toward the door, but it lands with an incredible smash on the left wall, the liquid leaving a terrific yellow stain that looks like urine.

As my eyes burn with the overpowering stench, disgust contorts my stomach. Breaking the bottles hasn't soothed my anger or misery.

I can't stay here. I run into the hallway, afraid I might retch. I'm amazed to find no one is running toward my room, attracted to the noise or the smell.

I make my way quickly down the hallway, toward the black-and-white bathroom where I bathed Nana.

Gray, the cook, emerges from a doorway, and I slow my pace, trying to look calm. Even though I feel disgusting, inside and out, I smile at her. She smiles back, her missing teeth making her look like an evil spirit sent to mock me. As she passes, her smile disappears, the powerful reek of the perfume surely assaulting her nose.

But she says nothing, and I continue to the bathroom, where I run to the bucket in the corner and proceed to empty my stomach of everything I've eaten for the last twenty-four hours. I heave and heave until I think I'll pass out from exhaustion.

Then I lie down, placing my cheek on the lovely cool tile. I thank God for allowing me to stop throwing up, for allowing me to live.

Why did I have to be sick in the only bucket of water in the room? Now there's no water left for me to drink. I've never been very good at planning ahead.

Should I take a nap in here?

Maybe. I can't imagine moving. I need Rayna to come carry me the way she carried Nana.

After several more long minutes on the hard tile, I decide that perhaps the cold bathroom is not the best place to sleep. I'm not comfortable, and someone will eventually come in.

But where can I go? Not back to my bedroom, which is full of broken glass and intolerable amounts of perfume.

Slowly, I pick up my wrecked body, leave the bathroom, and make my way to the small room where Juda was staying. The lock is still smashed, but I don't think anyone will bother me there. Shutting the door as far as it will go, I crawl over the piles of men's clothes until I find the large indentation where Juda slept.

I'm happy to be lying down again. I inhale deeply, hoping to smell a bit of him, but all I can smell is Chanel No. 5 and puke. Serves me right, I suppose.

I find a packet of "Adult-Size Men's T-shirts" to make a pillow for my head. It shows a picture of a handsome man in a very tight shirt, smiling, with muscles flexed. I suppose he's trying to attract the attention of a single girl. Nana said that when marriages weren't arranged, this was how it worked. Men and women had to win each other with physical attraction only.

I throw the packet back onto the pile.

Nana is right. Men are worthless, destined to lead women down a path of misery and destruction.

I thought Juda and I had a connection—that there were no lies between us. After everything we went through together, he left here without a word. Does he know how selfish and cruel that was? If he were standing here right now, I'd shake him until his teeth clattered. I'd yell, *You coward! You're a little worm, sneaking away without saying goodbye!*

Why are men so impossible to know?

Juda *and* my father—nothing like what I thought.

My stomach lurches again.

Last Searing Day, my family broke fast with Grandma and Grandpa Silna. Grandma Silna had fixed a special meal of stuffed pigeon, which I found inedible, the entire dead bird sitting on my plate.

Grandpa Silna, who considers himself superior to almost everyone, had decided to lecture us on the importance of piety and how the Convenes were suffering from the plague because they didn't pay enough attention to God or the Prophet. His lecture was exactly the kind of thing I would tune out, except that Father interrupted him, unusual in another man's home.

Father insisted that the Convenes were sick for scientific reasons, not religious ones, and that they deserved our support, not our judgment. Grandpa Silna got very red in the face but didn't say another word the rest of the meal. I was proud of Father, even though Mother berated him once we got home.

Remembering Father in this way, arguing with my grandfather, causes the swirling confusion in my brain to cease for a moment, as if the dam has stopped leaking and the doubt has decided to reverse course.

I know my father. I know what kind of man he is. And I'm not ready to give up on him yet.

I KNOCK AGGRESSIVELY ON GRACE'S DOOR.

After a minute, she opens up, book in hand. "Mina? You okay?"

I push by her. "I'm going."

"Where?" she says, pushing her glasses up her nose.

"To tell Father what's happening at the plant."

She closes her door, nodding, not nearly as shocked as I thought she'd be.

"I'm sure he doesn't know," I insist, but then add, "If he does, I'll know it the second I see his face. But I have to see him, Grace. I *have* to know."

She keeps nodding.

"I need you to get me out of here without putting the Laurel Society in danger. Ayan mentioned a different exit that she thought Juda used. Can you show me where it is?"

Still nodding, she closes her eyes, like a Herald in the middle of a powerful prayer.

She's probably deciding whether she's going to tell on me or not, and I can't blame her. The Laurel Society is her family, and I'm asking her to betray them by helping me.

"I'm asking a lot, I know," I say. "But I thought maybe after what you told me about your mom . . . you might understand why I have to leave."

She doesn't respond. I chew my lip. Maybe coming to her was a mistake. She could go tell Ayan my plan before I have a chance to do anything, and then who knows what'll happen? Unlike Juda, I'm not very good at breaking out of locked rooms.

"Never mind," I say, heading for the door. "Forget I was here. You shouldn't have anything to do with this."

Her eyes pop open. "Don't leave!"

I freeze.

"I was coming up with a plan." Seeing my surprised face, she says, "You need my help to leave without anyone seeing you, but once you're outside, you still need to be hidden, because if you get scanned by a Twitcher, you'll be arrested."

"That about sums it up," I say, wondering how this is a plan.

"What if you were imperceptible to the Twitcher?" Grace says, with a hint of mystery.

I assume she's about to tell me the plot of *The Invisible Intruder*, but instead she takes my hand and leads me down the hall. After several twists and turns, she stops at a locked door and, after looking both ways, pulls a set of keys from her pocket.

As she unlocks the door, I say, "Does being a librarian include owning keys to all the rooms?"

Smiling shyly, she says, "Growing up here has its perks."

I wonder what other perks she has but forget to ask as soon as I enter the room. Six Twitcher uniforms hang on the wall.

"From what I understand," Grace says, "Twitchers won't bother one of their own."

Hanging from hooks, the uniforms—jumpsuits with gloves attached—look like they still contain men, like they're about to reach out to seize us. Cables dangle out of collars and plug into batteries lining the floor. As I touch a helmet, which sits on a shelf next to three utility belts and three large handguns, my hands shake. I've never touched a gun, much less carried one.

"You're a real-life Nancy Grew!" I say, amazed at the boldness of her plan.

"Drew," she says, correcting me but smiling nonetheless.

"It's a brilliant idea, but . . . I don't know if I can do it, Grace." I run my hand down the slick fabric of a black jumpsuit. "Fool people on the street, pretend to be a man."

If only Rayna liked me a teensy bit, I could ask her for help. I suspect she supports my cause. But her feelings for me seem the same as for a pimple: an irritation she'd like to never see again. Sighing, I say, "I can't pull off this kind of thing on my own."

Grace grabs a helmet, plopping it on her head. In a muffled, metallic voice, she says, "Who says you'll be on your own?"

I couldn't be more surprised if one of her mannequins came to life and said it wanted to join me.

"It won't be like one of your books," I say, reaching

over to take the helmet off her head. "This danger is *very* real." Her hair, always big, has puffed up even more after being squashed by the helmet.

"I know," she says, hurt.

"I think you need to give it more thought."

I would never forgive myself if something happened to her.

"I've been thinking about it for *seventeen years*." Her face, usually so open and animated, has become dark and serious. "I've never been outside, Mina. *Never.* The closest I've ever come to seeing the ocean is the cover of *Moby-Dick*. I know it's dangerous. We may be arrested. Or killed. But I'd rather have one real day up there, with sun and trees and wind and strangers strolling in the streets and the possibility of something *new* happening, than a lifetime of safety and boredom down here."

I study her sincere face, so much like a child's. Is Grace really two years older than I am?

"I promised myself that if the chance ever came for me to go up top, I would take it. And I'm not backing out now." Her cheeks are pink with emotion. "Besides, how else are you going to know how to operate the stupid thing?" She motions at a uniform. "I've been watching Rayna get in and out of one of these for at least four years."

She's right. I doubt I'd be able to figure it out on my own.

Sighing, I say, "You promise you'll listen to me on the streets? And pay attention when I say there's danger? And if I say you have to come home, you'll come home immediately, with *or* without me?"

"I promise," she says gravely.

I hand the helmet back, hoping I'm not making a horrible mistake. "Okay. Which part goes on first?"

TWENTY-EIGHT

As THE SUN RISES, THE DEVOUT MEMBERS OF the Laurel Society tend to their morning prayers, while the remaining women savor their safe, comfy beds. Grace leads me to the south entrance of Macy's, which is supposed to be used solely for emergencies. She peeks out at the street from a concealed staircase to make sure no one is coming. I hear her make a small plea to the Prophet as we emerge onto 34th Street, the shortest Twitchers in Manhattan.

I look back at the hidden entrance, hoping to find a marker for when we return, and am amazed by how completely the rubble conceals it. "Will you be able to find your way back in?" I ask Grace, my voice metallic and strange.

She nods.

"Then we're off," I say, trying to sound braver than I feel.

We begin by heading west on 34th Street. *This is so weird.* I'm not sure how to walk. Should I swing my arms or keep them still?

We make a right on Seventh Avenue. The helmet allows me to see better than I'd hoped, but the rest of the uniform is heavy and stiff. The boots are cinder blocks on my feet. Grace fetched us each several pairs of socks so we could fit into the enormous shoes. We put on extra pairs, then stuffed the rest into the toes. We tried to cinch the utility belts low, to keep from emphasizing our girlie waists, but I fear the weight of my handgun, in addition to the small tools placed in attached pockets, will slide the belt down around my feet as I keep walking.

As morning prayers end, the city comes to life. I hold my breath for the first few blocks, ready to be scrutinized, but soon find that people want nothing to do with us. They look away and move aside. Grace and I are able to move up the sidewalk quickly.

As a girl, I'm frequently invisible to the world swirling around me. A walk through the market can take forever as men block my path or elbow me aside. But when one is a Twitcher, the sidewalks empty as if a plow were coming through.

I want to bar the women from bowing their heads to us, to lift their chins and say, "Stop." But I enjoy the men's deference. I thrill at the power of catching the glimmer of dread in their eyes. I never knew causing fear could feel good, and I'm disturbed by the revelation. Do I have more of my mother in me than I would like to admit?

I still can't believe we're doing this.

Leaves blow across the sidewalk as daybreak reveals a slate sky. We reach 40th Street, stopping for a light. Across from us, a woman struggles to hold a baby with one arm and lead a toddler with the other. As I watch her, the

computer screen on the inside of my visor says, Scan
Human Female?

Curious, I wiggle my right hand, as Grace taught me. A
keyboard appears. I hit YES, setting off a low hum that must
be my Senscan moving up and down. Data soon scrolls up
the screen. How do Twitchers walk and read this stuff at
the same time?

As a fingerprint flashes, I read,

> Lydia Ferall, 37, Deserver, 5'3", 130
> lb., history of high blood pressure. Two
> children. One miscarriage. 36 days
> pregnant. Husband: Henry Ferall.

I have a new prompt: Spiritual Scan?

Why not? I hit YES.

The Senscan hums. I see brief flashes of Lydia underneath her cloak, her face and naked body.

> Negative for: seditious materials,
> explosives, hidden devices.
> Negative for: makeup, nail polish,
> tattoos, piercings.

Oh my God. All those years, Sekena and I argued about
how much the Twitchers could see, and I was right. I saw
Lydia's *naked body*. I feel faint.

I want to run to Lydia and apologize.

I can't believe Twitchers can see so much about us
whenever they want.

How dare they?

Grace is saying something to me, but she's not turning her head; she's trying to look official. "What?" I say, also looking straight ahead.

"My feet hurt," she says, more loudly this time.

We've only walked six blocks. We have *nineteen* to go. "Are you having second thoughts?" I ask.

"No!" she says, with defiance. "It's the boots."

She's right. They're unbearable.

"Maybe we could take a bus?" I say.

I'm not very confident about my suggestion, having no experience with buses. Girls aren't allowed.

We trudge to Eighth Avenue, where I know the buses will be heading uptown, but then I'm stuck. We can't ask anyone which one to take without giving ourselves away.

I have an idea. I focus on one bus for a few seconds, and, sure enough, the computer gives me the option Scan Bus? I do this for several buses, until I find one that's going to Columbus Circle.

Grace and I join a line of men boarding the bus, but they fall back and let us go first. When we step onboard, all conversation ceases, while the driver looks away, demanding nothing. I relish the moment, the authority we hold, but soon insecurity takes over. Should we walk to the back or stay near the front? Should we sit or should we stand?

I choose two seats in the front, deciding the longer we stand, the longer these men have to notice our diminutive size. After we sit, no one stares, so I decide my decision wasn't too bizarre.

At 49th Street, a Herald climbs onboard, sitting across from us. His skin is yellow and gaunt, his expression sour. Despite his aged face, his hands are smooth and delicate, likely from staying indoors and reading all day. The Book rests in his lap.

He stares at me, seeming to look straight through my helmet. I try not to squirm. His gaze switching to Grace, he gives her the same inscrutable stare, as if he can see not only her face but every sin she's ever committed. I imagine he must be noticing the length of our jackets, how the too-long sleeves are bunched up around the elbows, or how our pants are triple-cuffed around absurdly oversize boots.

As the bus stops every two blocks, sweat accumulates across my body and down my face. My helmet shield is fogging, and I'm afraid I won't be able to see when I need to stand again. Will the Herald denounce us here or wait until we're off the bus? Or will he wait until there are real Twitchers in sight?

Since I've been watching him, I've been too nervous to notice the blinking prompt in my helmet that says, Scan Human Male? I hit YES.

Brother Harris Lampre, 63, Deserver, 5'11", 170 lb., Diabetic/Type I, Herald. SUSPECTED CONVENE SYMPATHIZER. TREAT WITH CAUTION.

My clenched body relaxes. Brother Lampre won't turn us in. In fact, maybe he'll help us if he knows we're trying to help the Convenes.

But the computer said "suspected" sympathizer, which is hardly definitive. Not enough to risk our safety.

A Spiritual Scan will show me if he's actually hiding anything subversive, so I hit the button and then realize with horror what I've done. I squeeze my eyes shut, but not before receiving a flash of Father Lampre's wrinkled, blue-white flesh, his brittle, childlike shoulders, and the tiny tuft of white hair on his sunken chest. A small squeal escapes my mouth, while I fight not to dig my nails into Grace's thigh. *Thank the Prophet I didn't see any lower!*

We reach Columbus Circle. I hold on to my utility belt, nervous it will fall around my ankles when I stand. As I rise, Brother Lampre says, "God be with you and the cause you fight for."

I'm so embarrassed that I can hardly nod my head. I exit the bus, barely able to see through my clouded visor, sure I am about to collide with Grace.

On the street, Grace asks, "You okay?"

"Avoid the Spiritual Scan button" is all I say. Mercifully, the outside air clears my screen and I can see again.

"The city is so beautiful!" Grace says, taking in the buildings and the statue of Uncle Ruho in the middle of the traffic circle.

"I'm glad you like it," I say, imagining her eyes big and excited behind her glasses. I'm astonished she can find beauty in such a bleak, gray day.

I point to my building across the street, stark against the charcoal sky. Toots and Buddy stand guard out front, and three Twitchers with machine guns have joined them.

How has my home, the one place where I thought I'd always be welcome, become the most perilous place in the city for me?

Regret grips me like a sudden fever. How can I fix it, make it all go away? I want to escape this dark sky, crawl into my warm bed, and hear my father say that everything's going to be okay.

A red light flashes in my helmet. ALERT. Robbery. Union Square Market. Suspect: male, late 30s, brown hair, 6'0", white tunic.

My heart is heavy; if the man is caught, he'll lose at least one hand.

"I think I should go in alone," I tell Grace. "Are you okay if I leave you outside?" If I'm going to get arrested or shot, Grace shouldn't be with me.

"I *love* being outside," she says, all cheer and energy.

I hand her the Taser I've been carrying in my pocket. "If anyone tries to grab you, just press this button and hold the front end against them."

"Against them where?"

"Anywhere," I say, fairly sure I'm right. "And then run. Go back to Macy's."

"I'm waiting for you," she says. "I won't need to run." She places a gloved hand on my shoulder.

I nod, saying, "I'll be right back." Then I pull away, not wanting the Twitchers across the street to see her unmanly gesture.

Keeping a quick pace, I walk in what I hope is a confident fashion as I approach the entrance to my building.

I'm more nervous than ever, afraid that the Twitchers will recognize a fake, like rats sensing a mouse in their midst.

I head straight for the glass front doors, and, out of the corner of my eye, I see the other Twitchers nod at me.

I nod back.

Toots and Buddy make way for me as I open a door. Too bad I don't have time to perform a basic scan. These two men have stood here my whole life, and I don't know one thing about them.

Not pausing, I pass Rab the doorman at the front desk and walk straight to the stairwell. He doesn't say a word.

I labor up the seven flights, and as I near the last one, I'm desperate to take off the horrible boots, to rip off the gloves and unzip my jacket, and allow myself some air. How do Twitchers survive in this gear all day? I think this is worse than the veil.

By the time I reach our apartment, I have a stitch in my side. I look down the hall, to Sekena's door, and think how much happier I would be to be visiting her. But I have one reason for being here, and one reason alone. I take a deep breath and knock on my parents' door.

TWENTY-NINE

MOTHER SEES THE TWITCHER IN HER DOORWAY, and her face goes slack. Amused, I walk into the living room while her head goes down in submission.

She follows, shouting, "Zai!"

I'm relieved Father hasn't left for work yet.

He takes his time coming downstairs, since Mother makes a habit of shrieking his name. When he appears, if he's alarmed to find a Twitcher in his living room, he doesn't let it show. Instead he says, "Peace" and stands tall, making it clear whose house we're in.

Releasing the latches on my helmet, I lift it off. I can only imagine my appearance—my face red, my hair damp and matted.

Mother must not recognize me, because she reaches for an umbrella leaning near the front door and is about to stab me with its pointed end. Luckily, Father says, "Mina?"

Mother freezes. "Mina! Good Lord in heaven! WHAT HAVE YOU GOTTEN YOURSELF INTO NOW?!"

She looks different. She's always looked angry, but I see a new anxiety in her eyes. Or maybe it was always there and I was too afraid of her to notice.

"I told you, Zai!" Mother says. "I told you she'd be back to beg our forgiveness. Where else does she have to go, the little heathen—"

"Be *quiet*," I say, tired of her voice already. "I'm here to speak to Father."

She's so shocked, she actually stops speaking.

I step toward my father. "You aren't supplying fresh water. Mr. Asher used bad pipes to build the plant—something to do with mercury. It's poisoning the Convenes."

My heart slows in my chest, refusing to beat again until I've heard his reaction.

He huffs, a wheezing noise escaping his throat. "How could you possibly know that?"

The shock on his face could be from my news, or from my knowing the news. I was sure I would know the difference straight away. But I don't.

"I . . . it's a long story," I say, having no intention of mentioning the Laurel Society.

"Tell me!" he says, becoming angry.

"What I can tell you is that Mr. Asher used to own a mercury recycling plant, and he sold the parts to Uncle Ruho for a hundred times their value, and then he became the engineer of your plant." I indicate my helmet. "It's all on the computer."

"No, no. That's not right," he says. His face is ashen. "That can't possibly be right."

"She's trying to manipulate you, Zai! Ignore her," Mother says.

Father keeps muttering, "That can't be right." His voice has begun to tremble, and he gazes at the floor.

I walk to him, putting my hand on his forearm and forcing him to look at me. "You always said Ruho was prejudiced against Convenes. And you couldn't believe he was putting the first new plant on the East Side."

"Show me what you saw," he says.

I hesitate. Not only do I not fully understand my computer, I also have no time to spare.

"She can't," Mother says, pulling Father away from me. "Because it's not true."

Father shakes her off. "Show me!"

After a few false starts, I manage to type "mercury recycling plant" into the keyboard. I hand my helmet to Father, its wire connecting us. I say, "Put it on."

After he does, I hit the ENTER button, knowing the information will scroll in front of him.

While Father stands with the helmet on, Mother whispers, "You think because you told him this he'll forgive you and let you come home?"

"Not at all," I say.

"The neighbors won't speak to us. The doorman won't even look at your father. Your brother has been searching for you nonstop!"

Dekker has never cared about me. I'm not interested in her lies.

"He's ashamed to show his face at the Lyceum! You've destroyed his career, along with your father's!"

Has Father already been fired?

Sensing I'm having a moment of guilt, she says, "Either you return to Damon this instant, or I'll have you arrested and sent to the Tunnel."

"You seem to be forgetting," I say, touching my belt, "who has the gun in this room."

I savor the look of fear that dances briefly across her face.

Father removes the helmet, looking sadder than I've ever seen him. I needed to know the truth, but I had no idea how painful it would be to see my father's dream destroyed.

"I'm sorry," I say.

"You were right to tell me," he says, handing the helmet back. His face is sunken and, if possible, looks older than it did when I walked in.

"Don't trust her," Mother says. "She's a nasty little liar."

"*I'm* the liar?" I say, stepping toward her. "You told me Nana was *dead*!"

"Ura's alive?" Father says, disoriented.

I nod, and he looks at my mother as if she's a stranger who has snuck into his house.

"I had no idea, Zai," she says, feigned innocence slipping into her voice. "A man came from the hospital and told me she'd disappeared. And you know how these things always turn out. Under the circumstances, it seemed like the kindest choice—I thought I would save Mina a lot of pain by telling her Nana was already gone."

"Save me pain?" I say, furious. "You haven't cared about saving me from pain a day in your life! You wanted Nana out of our lives. You wanted to leave her there alone to die like an animal!"

"This man," Father says, trying to wrap his head around Mother's story, "the man from the hospital, he never *told* you Ura was dead?"

Father's never been able to see who Mother really is, not like I have. How can such a brilliant man be such a fool?

"I *thought* he was telling me she was gone," Mother says, modifying her story.

I can see where this conversation is heading. I turn to leave.

"Don't let her get away, Zai. Not again!" Mother shrieks.

Father doesn't move, so Mother surges forward, grabbing my sleeve.

"Let go of me," I say, my patience with her at an end.

With her free hand, Mother slaps me across the face. Without thinking, I slap her right back.

She yelps in surprise. "How dare you!" she says. "*You* betrayed your family. *You* ruined us."

Taking a step closer, I get right in Mother's face, realizing I've grown almost to match her height. In these boots, I can finally stand eye to eye with the towering, terrifying monster of my childhood. "I've never understood why Father stayed with you."

She slicks back her hair to make sure no strands have escaped her taut bun. "On your own for one week, and now you know everything? Your father is an angel, and I'm the Devil? Is that it?" She laughs. "The day you were born, you know what your father said? 'At least we have one son.' And on the day of your engagement, he was in such high spirits, he said, 'Praise be to God, we're finally going to get our money back for this girl!'"

"Marga!" Father says.

"What?" Mother says, batting her eyelashes. "She craves honesty, so I told her the truth."

Spinning, I face him, knowing I have to ask my most dreaded question. "Did you know about the candle, Father? Were you in on it?"

His face is pure bewilderment.

I point at Mother. "She told Dekker to set me on fire at the Offering."

"That's . . . Why would she do such a thing?" Father asks. "That makes no sense, Mina."

"Tell him, Mother. Tell him all about it." My voice rises. "How you wanted Damon to see me without my veil. How you put me in that obscene dress!"

"Zai has never cared about how household business gets done. He cares only that it's done well."

Father gapes at her, face reddening. Does he disagree with this statement, or is he embarrassed by its accuracy?

"I was in bed for days," I say to Father. "You never came upstairs once to see how I was doing."

"Your mother said you were indecent," Father says. "That I should give you your dignity!"

I laugh. My dignity? He was preparing to sell me like a hog, and he was worried about my *dignity*.

He didn't know about the mercury. He didn't know

about Mother's plan with the candle. Why don't I feel better? Sadness encloses me like a winter fog. I tell him, "You dedicated your life to protecting this city. I just wish that one time you could have tried to protect *me*."

"It's not too late," he says, an unfamiliar shame filling his face. "Stay here so I can take care of you."

I think of Jordon Loudz and the Convenes, and what they will do once they learn about the water plant. "You need to look after yourself."

I walk to the door.

Mother snorts, a short, nasty laugh. "You're a stupid little girl, and if you walk out that door, you'll die starving in the streets."

"The sad part," I say to her, "is you think that Grandpa Silna and Mr. Asher and all men respect you because you act like them, treating your sisters and your daughter like dirt. But they see you just as they see every other woman— inferior, ignorant, and weak. Men think you're a joke, and women think you're a traitor. You'd better start being nicer to God."

She takes a step backward, as if I've shoved her. A frown appears on her face, and for a moment I wonder if I've actually unsettled her. But within seconds, her expression becomes hateful again. "You're not leaving!" she screeches.

"That's *enough*, Marga," my father says.

"By the way, Father," I say, opening the door, "Mother actually *does* know how to read. Nana says she was a star pupil. I would bet she reads everything in this house, including the letter that explains what a *loser* Dekker is. His career at the Lyceum may be in danger, but let's please be honest and agree it has nothing to do with me."

My mother jerks forward to seize me, but Father grabs her shoulder. She's still cursing at me as I walk down the hallway.

I fly down the steps, not overheated this time, light on my feet, aware that I will never set foot in this building again.

THIRTY

I'M NO FOOL. MOTHER WILL SEND SOMEONE after me as soon as she's able. I expect to hear her howling down the stairwell any second.

But I delivered my message. Father knows the truth.

Reaching the ground floor, I bang through the exit door and march through the lobby. Outside, rain batters the sidewalk. Drops hit my visor, making it hard to see as I scurry past the guards and Twitchers once more.

I'm thinking about how we can sneak back into Macy's and how upset Ayan will be with us when we get there, when I'm stopped dead in my tracks. Grace is standing exactly where I left her—but a Twitcher is by her side. He appears to be speaking to her. *Oh, Grace, what did you do? How did you give yourself away?* I imagine her standing under the trees, twirling in her uniform.

I don't know what to do. My instinct is to sprint as fast as I can to safety, but I can't abandon Grace. Although how can I help her? If I go to her, the Twitcher will soon know I'm a fraud, too, and drag us both to the Tunnel.

I'm still trying to decide what to do, when Grace spots me and waves her hand, signaling for me to join them.

The Twitcher must've made her point me out. Resigned, I cross the street, hoping that once I reach them, Grace will decide to use my Taser. The Twitchers in front of my building will surely notice, but then we can make a run for it. I pray that the Twitcher standing with Grace has not already filed a report on us.

Crossing the street, I approach slowly and notice that the new Twitcher isn't much taller than Grace. Before I have a chance to speak, the Twitcher walks up to me and says, "I have a message from your grandmother."

I recognize the voice. It's *Rayna.*

Thank the Prophet.

She looks back at my building, making sure no one followed me. "We need privacy," she says brusquely, walking away from Columbus Circle.

Grace and I scamper after her, but I'm so confused. What does Nana need to tell me that can't wait until I get back to Macy's?

"How did it go?" Grace asks me. "Did you tell your father?"

"Yes."

"And?"

"He didn't know."

"Do you feel better?"

Do I? "He'll do the right thing," I say, thinking, *If Mother lets him.*

We move rapidly across a Central Park South emptied by the rain. Wind lashes through the trees and whips up the street, sending drops horizontally through the air, rendering umbrellas useless. Most of the women on bikes have

disappeared, but one or two remain, their wet cloaks clinging like a second skin.

Pointing to Rayna, I ask, "How did she find us?"

"They all knew where we'd gone," Grace says. "She just
headed to your parents' place and looked around for tiny
Twitchers."

"Did she tell you what the message from Nana was?"

"No. She said it was 'for your eyes only.'"

Weird.

"Is Ayan furious?" I ask.

"Sounds like she's *not* happy," Grace says, with worry in
her voice, "especially since you promised you wouldn't leave."

"We were going to bring the uniforms back," I say,
penitent.

"Rayna says if we'd been caught—if we get caught now
—we'll expose the only means that the Laurel Society has
for moving safely around the city. If Twitchers start scanning other Twitchers, the Laurel Society will be trapped
underground."

I hadn't thought of that.

"I feel terrible," she says.

"We just can't get caught," I say, feeling terrible, too.

Grace says shyly, "After Rayna scolded me, she said she
was impressed that I'd come with you, and that coming up
top like this was pretty 'badass.'"

I'd have given anything to see Grace's reaction to the
compliment—I imagine her smile was a mile wide.

Rayna leads us another half block east, then ducks into
a garage full of taxis. A fat, bald man sits there, half-asleep,

listening to the radio: *Men are superior to women. Uncle Ruho is superior to men. God is above all.*

Rayna signals with her thumb for him to leave the garage, and he jumps up and scurries out without a word. One more advantage of being a Twitcher.

Rayna walks between the rows of yellow cars, and once she's convinced we're alone, she flips up her helmet shield, which has fogged up in the rain. Grace and I do the same. Rayna then removes a piece of yellow paper from her pocket and hands it to me. I recognize Nana's small, boyish handwriting.

Mina, my dearest love, my darling girl, my valiant granddaughter:

Ayan came to me this morning and told me you had run away. She explained about your father and his water plant. I'm sorry you didn't feel that you could come to me, because I SUPPORT your decision. Zai is a good man, and he's the only reason that I got to meet you.

I have convinced Ayan to show leniency to you and Grace, and the Laurel Society will welcome you with open arms if you return. But, Chickpea, DON'T COME BACK.

I want you to leave Manhattan.

I'm sure you're shocked at my words, but really, what could be so bad over that Wall that's worse than here? Uncle Ruho tells us that there are Apostates who want us dead, but have you ever SEEN an Apostate? TALKED to one?

We're taught that they hate us, but don't you feel hatred from the Teachers who educate our men? From the Twitchers who patrol our streets?

Are we sure that the Prophet built the Wall to protect us, to keep the Apostates out? Or did She build it to KEEP US IN?

Do you know why I was leaving my apartment the day I fell? I was going to buy food, for OUR escape. The day of your Offering had come. I didn't have any more time. If you got married, had children, you would never leave.

I know that yesterday I told you that I wanted you to stay with me forever, but I was being selfish, Chickpea. I wanted you to stay here because I love you, but this is the right choice.

How I wish I could come with you! But this adventure is for a young person, not an old lady with a broken hip and a bad knee. And you can do this on your own. You've always known how.

So go be an intrepid explorer, Chickpea. Eat the biggest piece of cake. Climb the highest tree. Ride your bike the fastest. Don't ever desire or expect anyone to make things easier

for you. Keep up with your education. Brush
your teeth. NEVER underestimate the value of
kindness. And—this is important—listen to your
gut instinct about people. It's usually right.

Don't worry about me. I'm in fabulous
company—more books than I could read in a
lifetime. And knowing that you are out there,
free in the world, will keep me alive and smiling
for a long, long time.

Love, Nana

I'm too stunned to speak.

I look up to find Rayna and Grace staring at me.

"Do you know what this says?" I ask Rayna.

"The gist of it," she says.

How can she be so calm? I hand the letter to Grace.

"It's completely crazy," I tell Rayna, sure that Nana has finally lost her mind. "You told her she was nuts, right?"

Rayna doesn't answer.

How can Nana tell me to abandon her again? I just found her! "The Apostates want us dead, Rayna. You know that."

She shrugs. "No one's attacked the city since I've been alive."

Because the Wall protects us!

I hear a gasp to my right as Grace reaches the absurd part of the letter.

"Mina," says Grace, "this letter is astonishing."

"It's bonkers, Grace. I can't do it."

Lightning flares outside, and I expect Grace to marvel at the spectacle, but the letter consumes her. "She's been planning your escape all these years," she says. "She's so brave. It's really sad she can't come with you."

Come with me? Has Grace gone crazy, too?

A clap of thunder makes me jump. The rain outside begins to come down in sheets, causing rivulets of water to flow into the garage. "And you've always known how to leave?" Grace asks, fascinated. "Why didn't you tell me?"

"I have no idea what she's talking about!" I say, mystified by the whole thing.

"I told Ura you'd be clueless," Rayna says snidely. "She was *sure* you'd know what to do."

"It doesn't matter," I say, "because we're going back to Macy's." I need to just *talk* about all this with Nana.

Grace nods. "You can always leave later, when you're better prepared."

Rayna shakes her head. "I promised your grandmother I wouldn't let you come back."

I hope the hammering rain has made me misunderstand her. "We're not stupid, Rayna," I say, sick of her. "We can find our own way back!"

She grabs the front of my jumpsuit. "You *are* stupid! Both of you. There's going to be a war, and you have to get the hell out of here!"

Grace is incredulous. "What war? What are you talking about?"

"With the Convenes," I say. "As soon as they learn that their water is poisoned. Right, Rayna?"

She nods, releasing me. "Whether they blame Uncle Ruho, the Deservers, or both, there's going to be a reckoning. And the smart thing to do is to leave the island before it begins."

"Then you should come with us!" says Grace, distraught. "The whole Laurel Society has to get out!"

"No way," says Rayna, her voice thick with disgust. "I'm ready for a reckoning of my own."

"I can't just leave Nana behind," I say.

"You *can*," she says, pointing to the letter. "That's what she just told you."

Without warning, my vision goes red. A message flashes across my screen:

```
Priority One UPDATE: Mina Clark . . . Age
15 . . . Impersonating a Member of the
City Guard . . . Armed . . . Shoot to
Disable, NOT TO KILL.
```

"Dammit," says Rayna.

"My mother—she probably turned me in," I say, knowing it's no excuse.

"Now you've ruined everything," she says, full of hostility. She turns to Grace. "See why you have to get out? Our *best* way of walking the streets is gone. Do you really want to spend the rest of your life trapped underground like a mole? Get out of here, Grace. Go have a Goddamn life!"

Grace looks about to cry.

"Stop yelling at her!" I say. "I don't know how to leave, okay? This conversation is pointless!"

Matching my irritated tone, Rayna says, "The subway, stupid!"

"Gosh, Rayna, if you knew, why didn't you just say so?" Grace says, handing back my letter.

I don't feel any more enlightened. "So, Nana gave you a map or directions or something?" I ask.

Rayna laughs. "No. She said you'd been memorizing subway routes for the last five years."

At first I have no idea what she means, but then I think of *Time Out* and the endless pages of restaurants, plays, museums, bands . . . and subway instructions.

> Joe's Pub, Subway: N, R to 8th St.—NYU; 6 to Astor Pl.

> American Museum of Natural History, Subway: B or C to 81st St.; 1 to 79th St.

I *have* always known how to leave Manhattan:

> Museum of the Moving Image, Astoria, Queens, Subway: R, E, M to Queens Plaza, switch to R, M for Steinway St.

I picture the remaining subway entrances around the city, their decaying signs covered in brightly colored circles full of letters and numbers that are supposed to mean nothing to me. No trains exist anymore, of course. I always assumed Uncle Ruho had filled in the tunnels or sealed them off.

But Nana must believe the tunnels are clear, and what did Juda say about the Ashers smuggling in diesel fuel? His theory was that the barrels weren't coming over the Wall; they were going *under* it. Some of the tunnels must lead out.

"You need to leave as soon as possible," Rayna says. "You're in a lot more danger now that they know what they're looking for."

"You too!" says Grace.

Rayna unzips the front of her jumpsuit, telling Grace, "I brought you a goodbye gift." She pulls out *The Secret of the Old Clock*.

"Are Apostate women allowed to read?" Grace asks, marveling at the idea.

"I don't know," Rayna says, "but if they are, don't you want to have your favorite book?"

Grace throws her arms around Rayna. "Thank you so much. I'll miss you."

Rayna looks like she might actually cry. While Grace zips the book into her jumpsuit, Rayna whispers something into her ear that I can't hear. Grace nods.

A noise comes from the entrance to the garage. Instantly, we all flip down our visors and become silent.

A man drenched in water, wearing the soggy blue tunic of a Student, ducks into the garage. Having found cover from the downpour, he looks relieved, until he spots the three of us. He quickly ducks out again.

We wait a moment, and then Rayna signals for us to

follow her. She leads us out of the garage and around the corner. We stand on the empty block, the relentless clatter of raindrops smothering our words.

"Mina, do you know the nearest subway from here?" Rayna says.

Concentrating, I tell her, "57th and Seventh. That should be the entrance for the R train." *What am I saying? Am I actually going to attempt this deranged plan?*

Rayna nods, and before I have a chance to give her a message for Nana, she's walking east, fading into the hard rain.

THIRTY-ONE

TURNING ONTO SEVENTH, I THINK WE HAVE
three blocks until we reach the subway station, but I can't
see far in the storm.

"Where will it take us?" Grace asks.

"Queens." If it's still called that.

"Oh, yes, of course," she says. "Queens was once the,
uh, largest of the boroughs, area-wise. Population-wise, it
was second to Brooklyn." She sounds as nervous as I feel.

She speeds up, ready to be off the streets, I assume. In
contrast, I find myself slowing down, having doubts. My
head is spinning with thoughts of Nana, Apostates, my
parents—and Juda.

Am I *actually* going to leave? And am I going to leave
Juda behind without saying goodbye? *Why not? That's
exactly what he did to you,* the bitter part of me says. But this
feels different. I am really *leaving*. If we go through that
tunnel, we'll never come back.

I shake my head, trying to focus on our plan, but
instead I see Juda worrying himself over my bruised hand,
offering me his laundry to sleep on, and drawing back
miserably when I couldn't say that I loved him.

"What's wrong?" Grace asks.

I didn't realize I'd stopped walking.

"It's Juda . . . ," I say. "Shouldn't I warn him about the poisoned water and the war? What if his mother or his uncles are drinking bad water?"

She doesn't answer. She looks up and down the street to see if anyone is coming.

"Never mind. Ayan will make sure everyone knows," I say, walking again. "Plus, he made it clear that he's done with me."

Now she's the one who stops. "You're kidding, right? He left to save you from making a decision! Like Marguerite . . . in *Camille?*" When I don't respond, she explains, "She tells her lover there's another man, when there isn't. She just thinks Armand will be better off without her. But she still loves him *madly.*"

I'm still not sure what love is. Is it the panic and pain I felt when Juda ran away from Macy's? The jittery, almost nauseated feeling I had being alone with him in the bunker? Why would I want to feel like that again? What if the women in my family were right and love is to be avoided at all costs?

I picture Juda's serious face and imagine the moments when he's been worried or disappointed in me. Then I envision making a joke, the small pause that follows, Juda's lips parting, and his mouth breaking into the most beautiful smile I've ever seen, followed by his deep, half-silent laugh that makes his chest convulse. He laughs as if he's used to doing it in secret, as if you're giving him forbidden pleasure. And *I'm* the one that can create that smile. *I'm* the one he's chosen to share that joy with, and the feeling is . . . everything. And I could live in it forever.

"I understand that you're torn, but you need to make a decision fast," says Grace, checking behind us again.

"We have to warn him," I say. "Or I'll never forgive myself."

Grace takes a deep breath. I'm sure she's about to say, "We don't have time," but she surprises me with, "It's very romantic."

"We'll hurry, and there shouldn't be any Twitchers in the Fields," I say, spinning and heading north.

She scampers after me. "*Camille* would have ended very differently if there had been Twitchers."

I BANG ON THE GATE WITH BOTH FISTS.

"Do what I do," I tell Grace, sounding more confident than I am. The gate guard on Fifth Avenue had no helmet or computer, but if this one does, we're sunk. At least the rain has started to let up.

The gate slides open. A guard is there, a farmer, like last time, and I walk right by him without explanation, acting on my growing theory that *no one* likes to interact with Twitchers. Grace mimics my arrogant stride.

The farmer, however, yells at us. "I'm sick of you guys pinchin' milk. I'm gonna complain to the Teachers!" I keep walking and tell Grace not to turn around. As I expected, the farmer doesn't follow.

I anticipated cornstalks, but we've walked into a maze of goat pens. Even though I have my helmet on, the smell is terrible. Rain has turned the ground into syrupy mud that sucks my boots downward. I have no idea where I'm going, but I don't want the gate guard to be suspicious, so I forge ahead, trying to ignore the bleating goats around me.

The pens are packed tight, with twenty or thirty animals in each, and they go on as far as I can see. I assume many of the unhappy creatures are supplying milk and cheese to the city, but I try not to think of the ones that will end up on dinner plates this week.

Their crying is overwhelming; there must be thousands of them. Do goats always sound like wailing infants?

My uniform is hot and stuffy again. I can't breathe. The raindrops on my helmet smudge the landscape, leaving nothing familiar. "This was a terrible idea, Grace. I'll never find him."

"At the moment, we're heading east," she says, her voice full of unthwarted energy. "Do you remember whereabouts in the Park his hideaway is?"

"How do you know we're heading east?" I say, skeptical. The sun isn't out, and Grace has never even been outside before today.

"Uh, the compass in my helmet," she says. She doesn't use a Rayna tone of voice, but I soon feel as foolish as if she did, because, sure enough, in the top left corner of my visor is a digital compass that says "E," with a little arrow.

"Can you tell me about his secret hideout? What you saw nearby?" she asks.

Not sure how it will help, I say, "It's under an old building."

"That's not, uh, useful."

"Okay." I concentrate harder. "There were kitchens. Juda said it used to be a restaurant."

"Good!" says Grace. "What else?"

"And there were . . . columns . . . and a porch on a lake."

"The Boathouse!" she says. "It's sort of in the middle, so we should walk north."

I look at her, amazed.

After I follow her for a while, she says, "*Breakfast at Tiffany's*, in case you were wondering."

"Huh?"

"I read it six times. Holly Golightly goes to the old Boathouse with the narrator and then decides to send her brother, Fred, some peanut butter. But Fred is really dead."

I nod, as if anything she's said makes sense.

We've walked for a while longer when she adds, "It's not really how I pictured it, the Park."

"I'm sorry," I say, knowing she must be disappointed not to see families having picnics on rolling green hills. Nana introduced me to Time Zero when I was ten, so I already knew what the real world was. I can't imagine what Grace is experiencing. To grow up surrounded by Time Zero—her books and magazines, the dolls and mannequins —and then to be confronted with . . . I look at the grimy, rank goats, the dingy sky above, think of the armed guard at the gate. She must regret having come with me.

Reaching the end of the goat pens, we pass through trellises filled with tomato plants, cucumbers, and what I guess are squash or zucchini. I'm about to ask Grace to tell me about Holly Golightly and Fred, when my helmet begins furiously vibrating. I spin around, sure that someone is holding a Taser up to it, but we're alone. Grace grips the top of her helmet with both hands, so I assume she's feeling the vibrations as well.

Dizzy, I raise the shield on the helmet, hoping some fresh air may help. I'm immediately assaulted by the booming gong of the Bell, as if it's three meters high and I'm its clapper. I slam the shield back down. Blessed silence surrounds me, the vibration all that remains of the insane clanging. I always wondered how the Twitchers survived the sounding of the Bell, and now I know—when necessary, their helmets are gloriously soundproof.

Grace keeps her visor down. She must have guessed from the look on my face that lifting it was a mistake. In the distance, farmers run through the rain to reach their prayer center.

My instinct is to hide; I forget that they're more afraid of us than we are of them.

When the vibrations finally end, I signal to Grace to keep walking.

It's strange that no one expects Twitchers to pray. They're always hovering outside the prayer centers, keeping an eye on things, but never in the prayer circles. Aren't they afraid of Hell? Maybe Uncle Ruho gives them special dispensations. He has the power to do that, to exonerate you from sin, although I've never heard of his doing it for a girl.

Since I've been with the Laurel Society, where devotion is optional, I've skipped my daily prayers, but I realize now that I've missed them. They're such a reliable part of the day, and even though I sometimes complain about them, I always feel better after I've prayed. It's very calming.

Crossing the remains of a paved road, we see the crumbling statue of a man with his hand stuffed in his shirt. Excited, Grace says, "Look." She's pointing through trees, but I can just make out a body of water. We follow along the edge of the lake for a few minutes, and it's not long before we spot the Boathouse.

"It's beautiful," Grace says. Exactly what I thought when I saw it.

From across the water, we seemed close to the building, but we have to traipse over several large hills and down the remains of a decaying staircase to actually reach it. My feet are killing me.

"I can't believe you talked me into this," I say.

"Me? You're the one who wanted to come," Grace says, indignant.

"I was ready to leave, and then you started talking about Camille and Armand."

"It's *Marguerite* and Armand, and it's hardly talking someone into something when she's already made the decision herself," Grace says.

"But I hadn't . . . ," I say in protest.

"I saw the way you ran after him when he left Macy's."

I have nothing to say in response. The rain has subsided to a soft mist, and bugs have started to reemerge along the shore.

"What do you think makes a person love someone else?" I ask.

"How should I know?" Grace says. "That's like asking why scissors don't work when you use them with the wrong hand."

I laugh, wondering what kind of boy Grace might fall in love with.

Finally arriving, exhausted, we approach the Boathouse slowly so Grace can take in the whole thing. She seems disappointed.

"I was hoping there would be at least a table or two left," she says, shrugging.

We walk back to the kitchen, where I show her the metal door leading to the bunker. Seeing it makes my heart lurch.

Grace insists on staying up top while I go down to talk to Juda. She thinks we need a moment alone.

Although she's probably right, I wish she'd come with me. I feel as frightened as if Captain Memon were waiting at the bottom of the stairs.

MY BOOTS THUMP ON EACH STEP. "JUDA?" I say, the name muffled by my helmet. "You here?"

When I reach the bottom, he's not in the room. The clothes that we slept on rest in two piles, undisturbed. No new food seems to have been opened. I'm bewildered.

I was so sure he'd be here, I never even considered a second option. I'm filled with disappointment and then shame for having made Grace come all this way for nothing.

What if Mr. Asher decided to report Juda after all? Juda could've been nabbed the second he left Macy's. Would Rayna have told me if the arrest report came up on her computer?

Remembering I have the power to check on his status myself, I wiggle my right hand.

I'm trembling as I type his name into my computer—J . . . u . . . d—when suddenly I feel a terrible blow to the side of my head.

I fly into the cement wall, my helmet hitting with a loud *crack*. The impact shudders through my skull; my teeth rattle; my head throbs. Through dizzy pain, I make out the figure of Juda, arms raised, ready to clobber me again.

"It's me! JUDA! IT'S MINA!"

He freezes midstrike, confused, horrified.

He puts down his arms.

I lean against the wall, waiting for the world to right itself. I catch my breath, then slowly lift off the helmet.

"Careful!" he says, helping me. He sucks in a breath. "You're bleeding!"

I note the metallic taste in my mouth. "I bit my tongue."

"I'm so sorry. I thought you were—"

"A Twitcher. Yeah, I know," I say, feeling the knot on my head. "Didn't you hear me say your name?"

"No! I hid the second I heard the door open."

"I hope you don't treat your mother this way."

"She knocks!" His voice wavers between anger and guilt.

"Where were you?" I ask.

"Under the stairs."

"It's . . . a good spot."

"Are you okay? I'm so sorry," he repeats. He now sounds quiet and gentle, reaching the tone I need—penitent.

"I'm fine. I'm not sure about the helmet." Seeing that the side of the helmet is cracked from top to bottom, I disconnect the wire that attaches it to my jumpsuit. "Not great quality, these things."

He looks at me with such concern and intensity that I become conscious of how terrible I must look, with my clammy face and matted hair.

"Are you okay?" he says.

"You just asked."

Grasping my head with his hands, he leans in and kisses me. I suddenly don't feel the spot where I bit my tongue. All I feel is him, as he gently kisses my forehead, my cheeks, my nose, and finally my mouth.

I gently pull back. "You left me. How could you do that?"

"The choice you had—it was too much, so I made it for you."

"No one asked you to."

"I know. I—"

"My whole life has been about people making decisions for me! Don't *ever* do that again."

"Okay," he says, taken aback.

"Do you still want to be with me?" I say.

"Of course."

His answer is so automatic, so clear, that instead of being grateful, I feel a wash of guilt. I hope one day I can be as brave with my heart as he is with his.

"Thank goodness," I say. "I was afraid maybe you'd fallen in love with Rayna."

He looks confused, and then that gorgeous smile appears, followed by the strange, soundless laugh that makes his chest tremble.

Before I know what I'm doing, I dive onto him, almost knocking him over. His kiss was tender and soft, but mine is rough and desperate, like I need oxygen and he's the only source.

He's caught off-guard, but once he regains his balance, he responds with equal fierceness, and soon he's pulled me down to the floor.

This is love. It must be—the rain, the gray, the alert for my arrest have all disappeared. All I can think of is how much I want his hands on me.

He wanted me to stay down here with him forever. Now the idea doesn't seem so bad. I know that eventually the room would've closed in, life would've become too small. But why couldn't I have let it last just a few more days?

After another few heavenly minutes, I stop kissing him and I stand and smooth my uniform. "How did it feel to grope a Twitcher?" I ask.

"Better than I would have guessed," he says, flashing the smile again.

"I left Grace upstairs."

"Who?"

"You haven't met her yet. She's . . . you just need to meet her." I have so much to tell him.

"One second." Standing, he kisses me again. "Thank you for coming. It was really brave."

"You'd do the same for me," I say, and I know it's true.

I redo my ponytail as I walk up the stairs, wondering how I'll tell him everything—about the water, the looming war, Nana's subway plan. I told Grace that I was coming here to warn him, but that was a lie. I came here because I want him to come with us. But how can I ask him to leave his mother and his people behind? It's too much.

But I don't know what I'll do if he stays. Grace won't be any help—this will be the first time she's ever talked to a boy. She's going to be *so* nervous. She's probably up there right now thinking of her novels, wondering which one it will be like.

I open the door, ready to ask her, and what I see makes me feel like I'm being thrown into another wall.

"Juda!" I yell back into the bunker. "You need to come up here. *Now.*"

THIRTY-TWO

A HAZE OF RAIN TRICKLES THROUGH THE HOLE in the kitchen ceiling and makes a puddle on the decaying floor. Grace kneels on the ground, hands in the air; her handgun and my Taser lie next to her in the pooling water. Beside her is Juda's mother, Rose, frozen in the same position, her veil clasped in her fist. Standing behind them, with a large, nasty smile, is Damon Asher, rifle in hand. No longer dressed in a hand-embroidered tunic, he wears a military-style jumpsuit with glossy black boots, and a gun holster crisscrossing his chest. His eyes gleam with self-satisfaction.

When Juda arrives behind me and sees his mother, he lunges toward her but stops when Damon aims the rifle straight at his gut.

"Be still," Damon says.

My mind spins. How can this be happening? We were minutes away from escaping. Did my mother manage to get a message to Damon already? But how did she know where I'd go? I look at Grace. The visor on her helmet is flipped up, exposing her tear-streaked face. How could I have done this to her? I should have left her at Macy's, safely surrounded by stuffed animals and shower curtains.

"Peace, Juda," Damon says.

Juda won't take his eyes off his mother.

"Don't be rude. You started this, after all," Damon says, redirecting the rifle at Rose.

"Peace, Damon," Juda says. His voice shakes, whether from anger or fear, I can't tell.

"Put down your firearm and get on the ground," Damon tells Juda. After Juda does what he says, Damon tells me to get on the ground, too.

Juda and I kneel close together by the bunker door.

Damon seems not to have noticed the gun at my side. I don't know how to use it, but I'm sure Juda does. How can I communicate to Juda that he should take it from me? As crazy as Damon is, there's only one of him, and there are four of us.

But as I'm formulating a plan, Mr. Asher enters the kitchen, and behind him is my brother, Dekker, who has a pistol.

There's no breaking free now.

Mr. Asher surveys the group. His eyes find Rose. She looks as if she's about to plead with him, when he says, "Well done, Damon." He looks at Juda. "It was Damon's idea to track your mother for a few days. I thought it was a waste of time. I didn't think you were the kind of boy who would endanger his own mother."

"And I didn't think Damon," Juda says, "was the kind of boy who would rape his own fiancée."

Mr. Asher puts a restraining hand on Damon's shoulder. Damon looks ready to rip off Juda's head.

"Dekker," I say, "you don't have to be a part of this!" I

can't believe that he's spending time with the Ashers. Surely Damon has treated him with nothing but disdain, a degree above a servant.

"Shut your mouth," Dekker says. "What were you doing down there, anyway?" He indicates the bunker door. "I don't even know why these people want you back."

"That's a good question," I say, looking to Damon. "You don't love me or care about me. Just send me to the Tunnel."

"Of course I love you!" Damon says, his face full of surprise and concern. "The first time I saw you, I recognized your beauty and knew you would make an adequate mother for my children. But now I know you're strong and ferocious and savage when you need to be. You're truly deserving of the name Asher. We're going to be the perfect couple, the envy of all Manhattan. And, Mina . . ." He becomes very solemn. "I forgive you."

I'm speechless. After I stabbed him and stuck a Taser between his legs, Damon still thinks we can be a happy couple. Even Dekker is looking at him like he's cracked.

"We have only one thing in our way," Damon says, aiming his rifle at Juda's head.

Rose and I both cry, "No!" Juda puts a gentle hand on my wrist, trying to calm me.

"No, Damon," Mr. Asher says. "We *discussed* this."

"*You* discussed this. And you were wrong. Captain Memon agrees with *me*."

"I'M YOUR FATHER, AND YOU'LL OBEY ME!" Mr. Asher says, his voice thundering across the room.

Damon doesn't flinch. He's empowered by his rifle. "No more talking," he says, cocking the gun and holding it at his waist.

Mr. Asher rushes forward, grabbing the muzzle in an effort to stop him, but the gun fires—a deafening *bang*.

Damon gapes at his father, who walks backward several steps. Mr. Asher turns, looks to Juda, opens his mouth, then collapses on the floor.

Rose speaks first. "Max!"

Her voice seems to wake Damon, who yells, "Father!" and then drops to Mr. Asher's side. A confused Dekker continues to keep his pistol trained on the rest of us.

From where I'm kneeling, I see red radiating out from Mr. Asher's stomach.

"Apply pressure!" Juda says.

"Shut up! Just shut up!" Damon yells at him, looking down at his father. "Why did you do that? You stupid old man! *Why did you do that?*"

"I h-had to," Mr. Asher says, struggling. He coughs violently, producing blood. "J-Juda is my son."

"What?" Damon says, reeling back.

My head snaps to look at Juda, whose face is difficult to describe—shocked, disbelieving, and angry all at the same time. He looks to Rose, who's crawling over to Mr. Asher.

She takes Mr. Asher's hand, blood pooling around him. "You saved our boy, Max," she says. "Thank you."

"I don't believe you!" Damon says, blurting his words like a young child. "You're all making this up!"

No one pays attention to him. We're all watching Mr. Asher, the color draining from his face, his breathing becoming increasingly labored. Another cough brings up more blood, thick and foaming.

Mr. Asher turns his head slightly to look at Juda. "It was better you d-didn't know. It made you the better man. I want you t-t-to—"

Juda goes to him as he struggles to finish the sentence. Mr. Asher is distracted, as if he sees something descending upon him but can't move out of the way.

Then his eyes go wide; his rasping breath stops. And Mr. Asher is gone.

Rose says a short prayer, tears running down her cheeks. Lifting her head, she says to Juda, "I'm sorry. We thought—"

"Don't speak to me," he says, closing his father's eyes.

"He's been lying to me my *whole* life," Damon wails, standing up. "He didn't want me. No one does. Why not? Why don't you want me?"

He's talking to me. I don't know what to say.

"I'm the richest, most handsome man in New York, haven't you heard?" he says sarcastically, tears pouring down his face. "I just wanted to love you. I was showing you love! And then my *best friend* clobbered me over the head! How about that, Rose? Your son is a *traitor*. He interrupted me having a moment with my fiancée, because he was Goddamn jealous." He points the rifle at me. "Come here, Mina."

"Don't go," says Juda.

I have no choice. He can shoot every one of us now. I

stand and walk toward him, wondering if I grab my handgun if I can figure out how to fire it, but I'm so frightened, I can barely focus on Damon's face.

"Good girl," he says, like I'm a pet.

When I reach him, he seizes the gun from my utility belt and cocks it while placing his rifle on the ground. Grabbing my wrist, he jerks my body toward him, until he has one hand around my waist. The other holds the handgun against my temple.

He puts his mouth against my ear so I can feel his wet breath. "All the trouble started with you. Before *you*, I had a friend and a father. I don't think I'm so interested in having a bride anymore."

"But we'll be the envy of all Manhattan," I say, trying to sound sincere. "The perfect couple."

"You think knowing how to read makes you smart? Or dressing like a man makes you powerful? You're like one of the goats out there," he says, waving his gun. "Infinitely replaceable."

He places the gun above my ear again. The world seems to freeze as I wait for the shot. I wonder about Paradise and whether the descriptions are real. Have I been everything God wanted me to be? Will he let me sit beside him and the Prophet? If he won't let me, then he won't let Nana, and wherever she's going is where I want to be. . . .

I hear the blast.

I wait for the pain.

I fall to my left, a huge weight taking me down. Blood is everywhere, and Damon is screaming. In my shock and confusion, several seconds go by before I realize that he's the one who's shot, not me. I look up to see my brother, his gun pointed where Damon used to be standing.

"Dekker?" I say.

"He was going to shoot you. I never . . . That wasn't the deal," he says, voice shrill. "He said he was . . . he wanted to marry you. Oh God. What did I do?" He wears the same expression he had the time he accidentally broke some of Mother's china.

"You saved my life," I say, awed. I was sure any feelings he had for me disappeared years ago.

"Yes," Dekker says, clearly as surprised as I am. He looks at his pistol, as if it made the decision on its own.

Damon writhes next to me, shrieking in pain. Dekker shot him in the thigh.

Rose stands, her cloak covered in Mr. Asher's blood. "The farmers will have heard the shots."

Juda won't look at her, but I say, "Yes, we have to go."

"Help me!" Damon cries. "You can't leave me like this."

"Of course we can," Juda says, lingering over the body of his father.

Damon moans, his face a ghostly white. I hate Damon, maybe more than anyone on God's earth, but seeing his blood pooling on the floor, the tears running down his face, imagining the excruciating pain he must be in . . .

I remember what Nana said about trying to have sympathy. His whole life, Damon never felt loved. He knew his father preferred Juda, but he never knew why, until today. He isn't an evil person; he's just . . . pitiful, and he doesn't deserve to bleed to death in this kitchen. "Do something," I tell Juda.

Juda scowls at me, clenching his jaw in defiance.

I glare back, saying, "If you leave him here to die, you'll end up in Hell, battling him for all eternity, unable to feel happiness or pleasure *ever* again. Is that what you want?"

He rolls his eyes and says sarcastically, "The Prophet would be proud of you." When he sees how serious I am, he says reluctantly, "Go downstairs and bring me back some clothes, the cleanest ones you see. Ma, go with her and bring up a bucket of water."

I do as he says, rushing into the cellar, barely seeing what I grab. When I return, he tears a shirt into strips and ties a tourniquet around Damon's thigh, above the wound. He quickly rinses the area around the bullet hole, which I can't look at without fear of being sick, and then leaves the bucket next to Damon so he can drink the water if he wants.

"That's the most I'll do for him," Juda says, finality in his voice.

"Thank you," Damon whispers, and I suspect he's about to pass out.

Dekker stands in the corner, grimly watching the whole process, his expression suggesting life might be easier if Damon didn't survive to explain his injury.

"Where's his rifle?" I ask.

Grace, who I hadn't even noticed was missing, walks into the kitchen. "I threw it in the lake."

"Good thinking," says Rose.

Grace picks her handgun out of the puddle on the floor and places it, dripping, back in her holster. She then picks up the Taser and presses the ON switch. When nothing happens, she looks at me and says, "Sorry."

I shrug. The Taser served me well when I needed it.

Grace then lifts my handgun off the ground, offering it to me, but I shake my head. What's the point if I can't use it but someone else can turn it against me?

To my surprise, Rose reaches out and takes it, raising up her cloak and shoving it into the waistband of her cotton pants. "Time to go, Udi," she says.

Juda kneels over Mr. Asher's body, whispering words I can't hear. Rose looks one last time at the motionless figure, the father of her child, before putting on her veil and leading Grace out of the kitchen. I couldn't read the expression on Rose's face—was she still in love with Mr. Asher after all these years? More and more, I'm astonished by people's supreme ability to hide their feelings.

I go to Dekker, touching his back. "You should come with us."

"No way," he says, pulling away as if I've pinched him.

"You just shot the heir of one of the most powerful families on the island!"

He refuses to budge.

Then I have a hard time pulling Juda away from the body of Mr. Asher. "This whole thing is . . . Why wouldn't Ma tell me?" he says. His voice is full of anger and resentment, and I wonder if I'll ever be able to confess that I knew, even if it was just for a short while.

"I'm so sorry," I whisper to him. "But we have to leave."

Juda says a prayer for the dead and then follows me out of the kitchen to join Grace and his mother.

Looking overwhelmed, Dekker stays behind, hovering over Damon's semiconscious body.

Because I'm sure I've seen him for the last time, I'm surprised to hear Dekker yelling for us less than five minutes later. We've almost reached the wheat fields, when he catches up, saying, "Where do you think you can go, anyway? The whole city is looking for you."

"I was just about to explain," I say.

THIRTY-THREE

————

ALMOST OUT OF THE PARK, TRYING TO STAY IN the shadows, we can't stop arguing about our plan. Juda and Rose understand that a Convene uprising is inevitable and that the island is no longer safe, but Rose believes the Apostates will murder us, while Juda worries that the subway tunnels are impenetrable. Dekker thinks we're all nuts and should hide out on Wall Street, where the homeless drug addicts live.

Grace, of course, tries to be helpful. "People have, uh, made it out before. Ayan once told me that it shows up on the computers from time to time."

"See?" I say, hoping I sound confident.

"The Ashers use the tunnels to smuggle fuel," Juda says. I'm encouraged the tunnels haven't been sealed off. "But most are flooded. Have been for decades. So I don't know how anyone is moving through them."

"By motorboat?" Dekker says, lagging behind us.

"Rising sea levels caused substantial flooding through-out Manhat—" Grace stops walking. "Uh, my helmet alert says bodies have been discovered at the Boathouse."

"*Nyek,*" Juda and I say at the same time.

————

"We should hide until dark," Rose says, quickly turning off the path. She leads us up a small hill into a grove of trees with nice coverage.

"It stinks," Dekker says, holding his nose, and he's right. The air smells like a litter box.

"We're above the toilets for the farmers," Rose says.

Not immediately visible in the fading light, a dozen brown plastic pods, each the size of my bedroom closet, stand in a ring on the other side of the hill.

"Great hiding spot," Dekker says, voice nasal.

Just then, a tired-looking farmer saunters into the circle of outhouses, prompting us all to step back into the shadows. The man disappears into a pod without looking our way.

"We shouldn't be stopping," Juda says, tense and jumpy. "The longer we're here, the longer they have to put extra guards at all the Park gates."

I'm not sure how we'll get past *one* guard. Juda and Rose are covered in blood, I'm wearing a uniform with no helmet, and I've just noticed that Dekker's covered in vomit. He must have gotten sick before he caught up with us.

Seeing my worried face, Juda says, "We have four guns between us. We'll be fine, as long as there's only one guard."

"So let's go," I say.

"What's the point if the subway's flooded with water?" Dekker says. He doesn't want to stay and he doesn't want to go. As usual, there's no pleasing Dekker.

"Can't we build a raft?" says Grace. "Like Huckleberry Finn?"

"Does this Huckleberry man know how to make a raft

out of goats and corn?" Dekker says. "Because those are the only things around for miles."

I'm annoyed at Dekker for being rude to Grace, but he's right. We don't have any useful materials. Didn't Nana know that the subways might be flooded? I'm becoming more wary of her plan by the minute.

"The *whole Park* is full of trees. Surely we can find some wood somewhere," Grace says.

"Fetch me an ax and some nails, and I'll have you a boat by Sunday," Dekker says with a smirk. I want to slug him and assume everyone else does, too. Even Grace has lost her perpetual smile.

Rose steps between them. "No time for bickering. We'll have to think of something else that floats."

If only we were closer to the Eleventh Avenue canals, we could find plenty of small boats, but we're miles away. Rose is right. We have to think of something else that floats.

"We don't have time for this. We need to get to the gate," Juda says.

I ignore him, thinking about metal and how it sinks, picturing old coins at the bottom of the fountain at Lincoln Center. Trash floats in the gutters after a rain, but that's mostly paper cups, leaves, wrappers—nothing that's going to withstand any weight.

"Who's going to take care of the guard?" Juda says.

"Not me," says Dekker.

"Styrofoam floats," Grace says. "And cork."

When I was a little girl, my mother used to wash me in a shallow bath of warm water. She'd scrub my head while I

played with soap or a washrag. I'd knock a shampoo bottle
into the soapy water and watch it floating on its side, imagining it was a ship on the Hudson surrounded by squawking
seagulls.

Plastic floats.

I study the toilet pods at the base of the hill. Aren't they
made of plastic?

The farmer emerges from his pod, door swinging behind
him, creating an instant silence among us. Check-ing my
utility belt for a screwdriver, I whisper, "Juda, I have an idea."

THE GATE AT FIFTH AVENUE LOOKS DIFFERENT
from the others, with a huge, modern fence curving inward
and iron doors in the middle.

Crouching behind some thick bushes, I watch as Juda
strolls toward the guard. The man is short but beefy, and
his thin hair sticks straight up, as if he's just pulled a shirt
over his head.

Startled, the man raises his shotgun, but his face relaxes
when Juda waves, saying, "Peace."

"Peace," says the guard. Dried blood coats Juda's uniform, but twilight makes it difficult to see on the black fabric.

"I'm the backup," Juda says.

"Wha . . . Why?" the man asks.

"You haven't heard? There's been a murder." Juda walks
to the man's left, causing him to turn away from our hiding
spot. "Maxwell Asher—shot over by the reservoir."

I can't see the guard's reaction, but I hear his voice

register surprise. Next to me, Dekker springs out of the shrubbery, and in no time he has his pistol in the small of the man's back. The man stops speaking as his body goes taut, his hair seeming to grow even taller in alarm.

After Juda has taken the guard's gun, the rest of us leave our hiding spot and Rose opens the gate with her pass. Juda uses handcuffs from Grace's utility belt to secure the guard to a tree, throwing the shotgun out of reach. Then we all go racing out the gate.

Both Grace and I carry large brown plastic doors (tomorrow a few farmers will find their outhouses are lack-ing in privacy). My door is unwieldy, threatening to trip me, but I'm determined to hold on to it. Seeing me struggle, Juda takes one end and we carry it between us like a massive serving tray.

I've removed my boots, abandoning them under a tree and convincing Grace to do the same. Finally free of their colossal weight, despite the hulking door, I feel light and fast as the wind. We're headed for the subway at Fifth and 59th and the entrance—thick stone columns topped by broken lamps—is only a hundred yards away.

Running, Rose rips off her veil and lets it fall to the sidewalk. I spot a few pedestrians on the street, but no Twitchers. The men and women quickly turn away from us, wanting no part of whatever we're involved in.

Darkness falls as we reach the entrance and run down the steps. We pass under a crumbling mural of birds and monkeys, and I know if Grace weren't so out of breath she'd tell me a story about it.

To my left, the derelict remains of a machine that says METROCARD sag against a wall covered in white tiles that, miraculously, still shine. Orange rust coats pillars that look like they've been holding up this station for millennia.

We reach some sort of gate, but it's strange-looking, with parts that poke out like a coat rack. It looks much more secure than it is, because Juda and Dekker yank out a rotted section in no time.

Juda says, "Grace, let me help you." He holds her plastic door as she wiggles through the small space. He then does the same for me. When it's Rose's turn, he supervises to make sure she's safe, but says nothing and doesn't offer her a hand.

We reach another set of stairs, but before I can get upset about going even deeper into the earth, I see that Juda was right. Water, brown and murky, waits at the base of the steps.

The tunnel is flooded.

I keep running, heading down the stairs with my door as if I've seen nothing, not because I'm brave, but because I don't have any other plan. When I reach the bottom, I splash straight in and keep going until the water hits my waist.

I'm woozy at the thought of my head going under, since I don't know how to swim. I haven't prayed for days, but I start now, placing the plastic door on the surface of the water.

It floats.

Thank you, God. Thank you, Prophet.

I smile back at the others. "C'mon!"

Grace scurries down next, placing her door in the water as well. I hope that two rafts will be enough for all of us.

I take a few more tentative steps downward and soon reach the bottom of the stairs. The water is up to my shoulders. The smell is ripe down here, mildew and urine mixed with gasoline.

"Don't think I like this," Rose says with apprehension as she joins us. She immerses her legs, tightly gripping the handrail. Her voice travels across the water, then bounces off the low ceiling.

"None of us does," Juda says. He walks down the stairs and into the water without offering her help.

"This is repulsive," Dekker says, wading in. "Do you know how many diseases are floating around in here?"

I give him what I hope is a withering look.

"Manhattan receives approximately forty-five inches of rainfall a year, so really, the tunnels should get flushed out pretty regularly," Grace says, smile back in place.

Dekker takes a few more steps, submerging himself to the waist. "Does it disgust anyone else that this water is warm?"

I keep moving, suppressing my terror that the water will become deeper without warning. Poor Rose, the shortest of all of us, has water hitting her chin.

As I move away from the stairwell, the blackness becomes impenetrable. My joy at the success of our floating doors fizzles. We can't cross the tunnel if we're *blind*. "It's too dark. We won't make it," I say, despondent.

Dekker leans over to Grace and says, "Unhook your helmet."

"Why?" she asks.

"Just do it," he says.

She does, and he snatches it off her head.

"My glasses!" she screams.

Dekker's hand shoots out, catching them just as they're about to hit the water. "Calm down, kid," he says, handing them to her.

She puts them back on, not amused.

Dekker examines the Twitcher helmet briefly and then hits a button on the side, causing a panel to open on top that reveals a blinding flashlight.

"You could have just told me about that," Grace says, irritation growing.

"But we'll all see better if the tallest person is wearing it, yeah?" Dekker says, disconnecting the helmet from the wire on Grace's jacket and plonking it on his own head. As he looks around, he illuminates the entire space.

He blinds Grace, who says, "Don't break it. It's our last one."

"Yes, Mother," he says.

I can't believe I left behind my own helmet and the chance for a second flashlight, but at least we don't have to abandon our plan.

Dekker turns the headlamp left, whistles, and says, "There she is."

The tunnel.

With the paltry light we have, all we can see is a gaping black hole, the toothless mouth of an Apostate devil, ready to swallow us whole. Water drips from a nearby pipe, while a low buzz resonates out of the dark lair, seeming to be the tunnel breathing back at us.

"Well, what does everyone think?" I say.

"I think we've got people in front of us who probably want to kill us," Dekker says. "We've got people behind us who definitely do. And a tunnel in between that might do the job for them."

"Your brother has a way with words," Juda says.

"Remind me never to invite him anywhere again," I say, unable to believe that I'm stuck with Dekker for the foreseeable future.

Dekker slogs ahead of me, saying, "You're lucky I—"

And then he drops into the water, disappearing and leaving us in total darkness.

THIRTY-FOUR

"WHERE'D HE GO?!" GRACE SAYS, AS I SHOUT, "Dekker!"

I hear a second splash. "What was that? What's happening?" I say, terrified of what might be under the water. "Juda?! Grace?! Rose?!" I reach out a hand, but even with my plastic door, I'm too frightened to move my feet.

"Here," says Rose.

"Me too," says Grace.

"Where's Juda?!" I ask.

"Just wait," says Rose, calmer than I feel she should be.

I hear another splash, bigger this time, and see a flickering light. Juda has burst out of the water, holding my brother, who looks like a giant, flailing newborn.

The light's okay! I think, instantly ashamed that I'm more relieved about the headlamp than I am about Dekker.

"Juda can swim?" Grace says.

Of course. He probably learned as part of his security training—in case Damon slipped inside his enormous bathtub or something.

Paddling past me, Juda heads back to the stairwell with Dekker, who grabs the handrail, gasping and coughing.

"What happened?" Rose says.

Juda stands, catching his breath, pushing wet hair from his eyes. His tunic is sticking to his body, and I'm disconcerted by how glorious he looks. "The floor ends about ten feet from here," he says. "Drops six feet." He looks at Dekker. "Thanks for figuring that out."

Dekker glares at him, hacking up the last bit of water from his lungs.

Juda looks over at the tunnel. "Judging from where the drop is, the train tracks were on a lower level than the platform where you waited."

I focus on his words. "So that means . . ."

"Rafts from here on out," Juda says.

"But how," Dekker says, recovered, "are we going to—"

"What's that?" Rose says, alert.

"What?" Dekker says, jerking his head left, then right, like a frightened canary.

"I hear something," she says. "Don't you?"

I hear the steady dripping of water and our own breathing gently echoing across the water, and then, straining, I hear a thumping sound.

"It's coming from the entrance," Grace says. I look up the stairwell and see a shadow moving above.

"Let's go!" I say.

Splashing toward the tunnel, Dekker rips the plastic door from Grace's hands, slapping it on the water. I assume he's trying to leave us behind, when he says, "Grab on!" to Grace, who leans in awkwardly and grasps the edge.

I look to Juda, the swimmer, for instructions on what to

do with my door. He says, "Hold on with both hands. You too, Ma." Rose and I get as close to the spot where Dekker sank as we dare. We grab opposite sides of the door, and Juda positions himself at the end, as if at the head of a table. "Kick, Dekker!" he says. "You have to kick to get moving, like this!" He tells Rose and me, "Time to lift your legs, ladies." He propels us forward, legs chopping the surface, his feet sending water cartwheeling through the air.

But Dekker and Grace don't move. Dekker thrashes and flails, pulling his end of the door underwater, and I fear he might pull Grace down with it.

I look back, seeing that someone has almost reached the bottom of the stairs.

It's Damon.

Face scarlet and smoldering, dripping with sweat, putting all his weight on one leg, he looks like he's broken out of Hell to find us. "Stop!" he screeches. "You'll never get away!"

Without turning around, Juda says, "We should have let him bleed to death."

What have I done? I'm the one who insisted Juda help him. It's my fault we're going to be caught.

"I'm coming for you, Mina!" Damon shouts, rabid as a dog, seemingly oblivious to the pain of his wound. His eyes are manic, searching, desperate for retribution.

"Don't you have guns?" I ask everyone, regretting that I let Rose take mine.

"They're waterlogged," Juda says. "If we fire, they could explode."

"Maybe you could've mentioned that before we all dove in," Dekker says.

Damon peers down at something in his hand and then looks frantically in our direction. Can he even see us in the blackness of the station? "Dekker, turn off your light," I say.

Dekker does as I say. A first.

"If you escape, I'll hang your families!" Damon shouts.

I can't see Rose's face, but I can imagine what she's thinking. She has brothers, Mal and Jiol. I think of Father with a sinking heart. Does Dekker care about him? Or Mother? I've lost all sense of what matters to him.

"The children, the old people, everyone!" Damon says, louder still. "Anyone who's breathed the same air as you will suffer!"

I block out images of Sekena, my aunties, the Laurel Society, and Nana, staying focused on Damon. He's not getting into the water, hasn't even waded down to the bottom step. Perhaps his wound is too painful. But if he's suffering so much, how did he walk here? He must have pretended his injury was worse than it was so that we would take pity on him. Or maybe pure rage and hatred are acting as anesthesia.

His mouth twitches into a snarl. All he wants is to seize and throttle us, and yet he recoils from the water like a rabbit faced with a boiling pot.

I allow myself a small smile as I realize *he doesn't know how to swim*. He must have assumed Juda would always be there to take care of any water-type situation.

"Come and get us, you spoiled brat!" I holler.

"Mina, what are you doing?" Grace asks, distress in her voice.

Ignoring her, I yell, "Where's your backup, Damon? Doesn't anyone like you enough to help you?"

He takes a step into the water. "Captain Memon is on his way!"

"Don't count on it," I shout, even more loudly. "Your father did him favors. And your father is dead!"

"Mina!" Rose says, shocked. I give her a look begging her patience but then realize she can't see me in the dark.

"Shut up, you stupid Saitch!" Damon says, fury pulling him forward. He roars as his wound hits the murky water.

Juda must have caught on to my plan, because he yells, "You'll never be the man my father was!"

"I'm going to hack out your heart and choke you with it," Damon shouts. He wades in farther, growing confident as he realizes the water is only waist deep. Pulling a shotgun from a hidden holster on his back, he fires at us through the darkness. The sound of the shot explodes around us like a cannon.

"Get down!" Juda yells.

Where? I'm grasping the door for dear life. If I loosen my grip, drop into the water any farther, I'll drown.

The gun has ruined my plan. I've made things considerably worse.

"I thought you got rid of his gun," Dekker whispers with anger.

"I did," says Grace. "He must've found the gate guard's."

"We saved your life! What's wrong with you?" I shout, amazed at his coldness.

"You DESTROYED my life. You MURDERED my father!"

What?

Now I understand. If he eliminates us all, there will be no witnesses to say that he shot his father. He can blame it on whomever he chooses.

Damon fires again. A deafening blast.

Grace screams.

"Are you hit?" I say, heart stopping.

"No," she says, terrified.

"Don't scare me like that," I whisper.

"Shhh," Juda says.

He's right. We're giving away our location. In the darkness, Juda reaches out, grabbing Dekker and Grace's door. He whispers to Dekker, "Kick under the water. At an angle. Stay quiet."

We move very slowly away from Damon, whom I can barely see now. He's up to his chest in water.

To my surprise, Rose yells, "Your father thought you were a pea-brained ass!" She must've figured out my plan, too.

Juda shifts us to the left as another gunshot fills the shadows. The bullet is so close I can smell the gunpowder.

The slur from his father's mistress too much to bear, Damon splashes forward. "I'm going to kill you last, you stupid slut, after you've watched me kill your son. And after I've killed you, I'm going to slice—"

But we never learn what he's going to do; we hear a

gasp and a slosh as he drops off the ledge and into deeper water, just as Dekker did. Except this time, Juda is not going to save anybody.

I listen for another splash or ripple. But there's nothing. We're alone.

Dekker flips his light back on, saying to Rose, "Did you do that on purpose?"

"What do you think?" Rose says dryly.

"Nice job," says Grace.

"Pretty cool," Dekker says.

"You okay?" Juda asks me, knowing I set the trap in motion.

I nod but have no idea whether I am. "It had to be done," I say. No one else speaks.

I tried to save Damon once, to give him a second chance. *Never underestimate the value of kindness*—that's what Nana said. Damon not only underestimated it but took advantage and tried to punish us for it. And look where it got him. I think of him struggling to breathe under the water, and it makes me feel sick.

We may end up with Damon in Hell after all.

"We need to know how he found us," Juda says, looking at his mother.

"How would I know?" she says, clinging to the raft precariously.

"We ran through the street with outhouse doors!" says Dekker. "It wasn't subtle."

"Mr. Asher said he was tracking you for days, Ma," Juda says. "We need to know how. There's no point in moving forward if a thousand Twitchers are going to follow us."

Rose looks angry, and I understand why. How can it be her fault that the Ashers followed her? But then she seems to have a realization and her expression turns guilty. She reaches underneath her sodden cloak and produces her necklace—the chain with the gold heart. "I'm sorry, Udi. I've had it for so long, it never occurred to me in a million years that it could be a collar. Max was so sweet when he gave it to me. . . ."

Juda, not wanting to hear any more, takes the necklace and tosses it into the water, close to where Damon disappeared. "It probably stopped working when it got wet. But if it didn't, maybe someone will find the body."

Rose says a prayer, so I do the same, although, to be honest, I'm not sure I want Damon to be found. His presence here will notify everyone of our escape route.

Juda begins showing Dekker how to kick again. "Above the water," he says. "Your legs should feel light."

"What about Captain Memon?" Grace says. "He's coming!"

"No way," says Dekker, moving his legs spasmodically. "Damon wanted to shoot us all and let us disappear like waste down his sewer. He didn't want *any* witnesses."

I agree, but it doesn't make me kick my legs any more slowly.

DEKKER AND GRACE MOVE FORWARD AT A stop-start pace. I try to kick under the water in a way that's helpful to Juda. We've lost sight of the subway station. I know that Damon *probably* didn't contact Captain Memon, but I still fear that at any moment we'll be caught in the bright beams of Twitcher flashlights and assaulted by gunfire.

But the deeper into the tunnel we go, the quieter and darker it gets and the more I can believe no one is following us. The only light comes from Dekker's headlamp, which creates a feeble triangle of visibility ahead of us. Steel pillars line the walls, while a vast barrel-vault ceiling looms above. Behind us, the blackness is thick but alive, an undulating darkness that warns against falling behind.

After around thirty minutes, Rose asks, "How far to the other side?"

"I don't know," I say. "It's two subway stops. More than seven avenues?" And under the East River. Water above. Water below.

She nods, looking prepared.

"You okay, Grace?" I ask, noticing she looks anxious.

Using an affected voice, she says, "*I have a hunch from reading about old passageways that there may be one or more rooms off this tunnel.*"

"Oh, honey," Rose says. "I don't think we're going to be seeing any rooms."

Dekker adds, "But if we do, we'll drop you off for tea."

"It was, uh, a joke," Grace says. "That was from *The Hidden Staircase*. Nancy Drew?" I can't see Grace's face in the shadows, but I bet it's bright pink.

"Who?" Dekker says.

"I thought you read at the Lyceum," Grace says.

"Not *lady* writers."

"Nancy Drew is the hero. Carolyn Keene is the writer."

"Still a broad."

"Maybe we should conserve our energy and not talk," Rose says.

"Great idea," Juda says.

I settle back in, concentrating on the rhythmic sound of Juda's and Dekker's feet. I watch Dekker's triangle of light bounce as his head moves.

The water seemed warm when we entered, but the tunnel becomes cooler the deeper we go, and the more my hands ache from holding on to the door. Passing pillars, I see strange markings, symbols written quickly in spray paint. They must be words, but they're nothing I can translate. How old are they? Are they warnings?

After about forty minutes, the tunnel widens and, once again, white tiles cover the walls. Grace says, "It must be the next station."

I'm opening my mouth to say I'd like to stop and rest, when Juda whispers, "Turn off the light, Dekker." Before Dekker flips off the headlamp, I get a glimpse of Juda's face, alert and tense. I realize he's worried that if Twitchers are looking for us, they might be waiting for us here.

The others must fear the same thing, because no one makes a sound. I wonder if they're holding their breath, like I am. The slow *swish* the rafts make through the water now seems louder than a taxi honking at rush hour.

The blackness is terrifying. I can handle the water, the fear of not knowing what's below me, but only while I know what's above me, in front of me. Now a hand could reach out to grab me and the others wouldn't see it, couldn't warn me. My teeth start to chatter, and Rose has to whisper for me to hush.

My back bumps against something, and I nearly cry out. I've hit the tunnel wall. Poor Juda can't steer without light. I push off the wall with my hand, hoping Juda will be able to right himself.

We paddle in the darkness longer than must be necessary. How big can a station be? But no one wants to be the one to break the silence, to reveal our location. Finally, after another ten minutes of bumping into walls, unable to stand the blackness one more second, I whisper, "I think we're clear."

Dekker clicks the light back on. We're deep in the tunnel, the station not in sight. To my left, Rose sighs in relief. The tunnel that was gloomy and ominous an hour ago now seems bright and welcoming. "Next stop: Queens," Grace says, and no one responds.

More time passes.

I wonder how much longer I'll be able to hold on to the door. Rose looks like she's going to pass out.

"Juda?" I say. Shaking himself out of a trance, he looks at me. I gesture at his mother.

"Ma?" he says, startling her.

"Yes, Udi?"

He holds her gaze for a moment, seems to decide she's in adequate condition, and says, "Nothing."

She looks crushed. How long is he going to be mad at her?

Juda looks at me. "What did your nana say about the people on the other side of the Wall?"

"They're not as bad as we think." I'm exaggerating. What Nana really said was that they couldn't be any worse than the people we already know.

If my childhood stories are true, heathens live on the other side. They don't believe in God or the Prophet, and they'll try to convert us to their heathen ways as soon as we arrive. And if we don't convert, they'll tie us to stakes and burn us alive.

"I once heard that there aren't any people left at all," Dekker says. "It's only robots out there, and they have laser guns ready to kill all humans."

"I think it's the opposite," Grace says. "No robots. No computers. No nothing. Just a bunch of dirt and grass and dogs and cats that have returned to the wild."

Dekker laughs, a low bellow that rumbles up the tunnel. "So you think the Apostates are a bunch of kittens?"

"No," she says, defensive. "I think the Apostates are long gone. They didn't have order, or the Prophet, like we did. And so their people fell, like the Romans."

"Like the who?" asks Dekker.

"Goodness, Dekker," Grace says. "What are they teaching you at the Lyceum?"

"That's Brother Clark to you," he says with irritation.

"I think we should brace ourselves for anything," Rose says.

"Nothing else can shock me today," Juda says.

"Are the guns ruined forever?" I ask.

"Nah," says Juda. "We'll dry them out, oil them up, and they'll be good as—"

Grace screams. "Something touched my leg!" she says. A second later, she shrieks, "There it is again!"

I say, "What do you think . . ." and then I feel it, too—something scratching my thigh.

"I felt it!" Juda says, his voice full of alarm. "Dekker, shine your light straight down into the water!"

We all look around, desperately trying to see into the black, dingy river.

Dekker says, "Over there—eyes! It's a rat!"

The second he says it, Juda lets go of the raft and starts slapping at the water. "Where?! Where is it?!"

Without his weight, the raft flips up, sending our end plunging into the water. The world goes silent as I lose my grip and my head submerges. I reach out but grasp nothing and keep sinking. Rats swim in the water inches from my nose, and I open my mouth to scream, causing water to flood my lungs. My chest burns like I'm on fire again. *Kick your legs*, I think. *Just kick.* But when I do, my legs are heavier than lead, convincing me that I didn't remove the Twitcher boots and now they're going to suck me down, as if the Twitcher they once belonged to is in the depths below, pulling me under out of spite. I keep sinking.

A hand grabs the neck of my jacket, pulling me to the surface. I try to help, but my body is an anchor. My lungs want to explode. My head finally reaches the surface, and I take giant gulps of air.

Juda is holding me. He pulls me in close, wrapping an

arm around me as he treads water. "Easy. Take easy breaths."

I cough, and once I start, I can't seem to stop.

"Is she okay?!" Grace asks.

I nod. Rose says, "She'll be fine," helping me back onto our raft.

"I'm sorry!" Juda says. "I didn't mean to let go. It was the rats—"

"He hates them," Rose says. "Always has."

"She knows!" says Juda, glaring at her, as if Rose threw me off the raft.

"Enough," I say, my coughing fit over.

"I know," he says. "I have to get over the rat thi—"

"STOP . . . being so rotten to your mother!" I say, sick of it all.

"What do you know—"

"You have years to punish her for lying to you," I say, catching my breath. "But . . . right now . . . we'd all like to survive the next few hours . . . so please get over yourself . . . and start acting like a human being."

He opens his mouth, ready to protest further, but changes his mind. "Let's keep moving," he says.

"He deserves to be angry," Rose says.

"Fine," I say. "But I'm cold and tired . . . I'd appreciate it if he could wait until we're out of this tunnel to deal with his grievances."

"Amen," says Dekker.

"You're no picnic either," I say. "The best thing you have going for you is that light on your head. And you stole that from Grace."

"Let's not turn on one another," Rose says. "If we need one thing, it's to be united when we reach the other side."

Grace speaks quietly. "So there's good news about the rats."

"*What?*" I say, snapping at her, too.

"They aren't fish," she says, so softly I can barely hear. "They can't swim for long, so we must be close to land."

As soon as she says this, I realize I'm barking at everyone because I'm terrified. I don't know if I'm ready for what awaits us.

Before I can apologize, I see a faint light ahead, proving Grace right. We're about to reach the next stop, Queens Plaza.

> This 6,000-square-foot, candlelit rooftop crowns the Ravel Hotel in Long Island City. The garden terrace is furnished with plush orange chairs and features clear views of the Manhattan skyline and the Queensboro Bridge.

For years, I've pictured Queens covered in candlelit roofs. If only.

Before I feel mentally prepared in any way, we reach the station. It seems bigger, more decrepit, than the last two, but it has the same rusted pillars, white tiles, and wide staircases. I'm surprised. I don't know what I was expecting, but I guess I thought this station would be different.

Juda steers us out of the tunnel and toward the stairs.

Be an intrepid explorer.

With trepidation, I take my hand off the raft and grab the rail of the stairs. I let my feet drift down until I find solid ground. Whatever hesitation I have about what is outside is now overwhelmed by my desire to get out of this unholy tunnel. The others must feel the same, because we slop out of the water, storm up the stairs, and race out to the light.

THIRTY-FIVE

WHEN I GET TO THE SURFACE, I'M BLINDED BY
the rising sun and I hear nothing, not even traffic. When
my eyes adjust, I see houses—lots and lots of houses—lined
up neatly in rows, painted in the most wonderful shades of
orange, lime, baby blue, and red, each with its own shim-
mering, emerald-green lawn. Queens is brighter than
Rose's fruit salad.

"Where is everyone?" Juda says.

"I told you," Grace says, "there are no people left."

"Yeah. Puppies are watering those lawns," Dekker says.

"It's barely first light," says Rose. "They're all asleep."

A grove of red oaks grows to our left, and a bird chirps
as it notices morning has arrived. Dekker looks as wide-
eyed as Grace as they glance around the strange terrain. I'm
sure I look just as astonished. I don't know what I expected
—an army of readied Apostates; Uncle Ruho with a drum of
oil; pile upon pile of ash and bone—but not this. This is . . .
beautiful.

Feeling sore all over, I stretch my exhausted limbs. I'm
chilly in my wet clothes, ready for the sun to grow hotter
and dry me off.

"So what first?" Juda says. I'm surprised to see that he's looking at me for instructions.

I'm about to say, "How should I know?" but, looking at everyone's nervous faces, I remember that they've never even seen a copy of *Time Zero*—*Time Out*, I mean—and that this was *my* plan. Juda is looking to me for leadership because *I have led them here*.

"Let's find some food," I say, letting my stomach guide my decision.

Everyone nods, and we survey the area. Grace, Rose, and I wander toward the grove, thinking of nut trees and berry bushes. Juda walks toward what looks like a pond to search for fresh water, but Dekker heads straight for a street full of houses.

"Dekker!" I say, as loudly as I dare. "What are you doing?"

He shrugs. "I hate wasting time."

And that's when I hear the sound—it's a low humming. At first I think it's in my head, maybe water in my ears. But as it gets louder, I know it's coming from nearby. The others turn in every direction, looking for the source.

I spot something in the sky heading toward us. The buzzing gets louder as it nears. "Juda . . . ," I say.

"I see it," he says, running back to us. "Get behind me."

"Watch your mother," I say, walking forward to get a better look.

Dekker sprints back over to us, joining Rose at the rear of the group.

Is it a hawk? It seems too large. In fact, it looks large enough to be a man. What if the Apostates can fly?

"It's an angel," Rose whispers, giving me chills. Maybe we died, drowned, and this *is* an angel, here to judge us and take us to Heaven or Hell.

"Should we run?" Dekker asks.

Where to? I think, but maybe he's right. Despite my exhaustion, my body is on full alert, ready to flee at the smallest sign of danger. I want nothing less than to get back in that water, but standing out in the open now seems foolish. I say, "I think we should head back down the stairs." I walk slowly backward, and the others do the same. None of us takes our eyes off the object in the sky.

The humming is louder, an engine sound, and the thing picks up speed. We begin to run, but before we can reach the subway, it swoops down and lands right next to Grace. She leaps away from it like it might explode, and I don't blame her. We all jump away.

But nothing happens. It just lies there—a big metal cube surrounded by a silver skeleton that branches into wings.

"What should we do?" Grace says.

"Talk to it?" Dekker says.

"Hello. My name's Grace."

"It can't talk," says a new voice.

I whirl around to find a small, serene girl studying us through enormous cornflower-blue eyes. Wearing a white T-shirt, white shorts, and pristine white sandals, she has shiny brown hair and a sweet freckled nose. "It's making a delivery," she says.

While the rest of us stare at her in fascination, Grace says, "Of what?"

The girl approaches the flying metal thing and opens a little door on the side. She reaches in, pulling out a peach, plump and ripe. "Want some?" Her accent is odd. I understand what she says, but it sounds more like *wuntsum*—one word.

The rest of us look at one another, stomachs grumbling, wondering whether anyone is brave enough.

"Picked less than thirty minutes ago," she says. "I *only* eat Georgia peaches." When none of us responds, she shrugs and takes a bite. She lets the juice run down her chin, and I see a drop land on her crisp white shorts. The smell is intoxicating.

Wiping her mouth with her hand, she says, "Are you more of the tunnel people?"

"There have been others?" I say. I shouldn't be surprised, given what Juda said about the fuel.

"Some. My brother's going to be very jealous that I found you," she says. "I can't wait for you to meet him. I'm Beth, by the way." She walks toward the nearest row of houses, munching her peach. "Let's go wake him up." *Wekkimup.*

Beth seems unfazed by our arrival in Queens. Perhaps Apostates are just pleasant and calm about everything. She's also very young, so maybe no one's taught her to be afraid of "heathens" yet. Either way, she's now happily marching up the street, ready to introduce us to her family.

I look at the others, wondering what to do.

I call out, "Beth!" and she turns around. She's surprised to find we aren't right behind her. "If we come, do you think we could get some food?"

She nods with enthusiasm. "Mama's a great cook. And she *loves* guests."

Smiling at Juda and the others, I walk toward her.

We follow her past a bright crimson house with white trim, and I'm wondering whether maybe I can live in a house like that someday, when Beth pauses and says, "Oh, wait, I'm supposed to ask . . . do you believe in the Prophet?" She looks up at me, her big eyes waiting in bright anticipation.

Listen to your gut instinct about people. It's usually right.

Deciding to take Nana's advice, I say, "Yes, Beth, I believe in the Prophet."

"Well, shoot," she says. "Then I'm afraid you're under arrest."

A siren sounds all around us, while flashing yellow lights rise out of the perfect green grass.

"If you guys don't mind," Beth says, pleasant as ever, "could you please lie down on the ground?"

"Run!" shouts Juda, his voice cutting through the alarm.

I sprint toward the subway station, assuming the others will do the same, but Dekker and Grace run toward the grove. Juda starts to run with me but then turns around when he sees that his mother is frozen in place next to Beth.

I'm trying to decide if I should turn around, too, but it doesn't matter, because I hear a zipping sound and a net lands on top of me. Clawing at it with my hands, I feel it entangling my feet, and soon I'm tripping toward the pavement. I cry out as I land on my hip with a *thud*.

I hear lots of people now, and someone, a man, picks

me up from behind and lays me down face-first in some grass. Cuffing my hands behind my back, he says, "Don't move, honey," and then walks away. I can barely turn my head. The grass is cool, wet with morning dew, and it prickles my face.

Soon I see Grace, Dekker, and Juda laid out beside me, all facedown and cuffed. I turn my head with difficulty and see Rose to my left. She looks angry and frightened but not hurt.

I turn back to Juda, who lies next to me. His eyes dart around frantically as he tries to survey our situation. "I'm sorry," I say, but he can't hear me over the siren.

I say it again, more loudly: "I'M SORRY."

He looks at me, confused. I can tell from his expression that he's trying to formulate a plan, but he can't possibly know how many men we're up against. We can't see anything, since we're facing the ground, and the siren drowns out their voices. It could be one man; it could be a thousand.

Grace is next to Juda, weeping.

"This isn't right—there's been a mistake!" I yell through the siren. Aren't they going to give us a chance to explain? It can't be over with just one question!

Juda is saying something to me, but I can't hear him. His expression is urgent and I think he's telling me to do something.

I shake my head, trying to express that I don't understand.

Two men come up behind him, about to seize him.

I try to warn him, to say, "Behind you!" but it doesn't

matter. The men pick him up, yanking him back as he resists, and take him away.

I don't have time to protest, because I feel hands on my own back, lifting me up and carrying me away from Grace, Dekker, and Rose.

I'm shoved into the back of a huge, shiny van. I search for Juda. My fear spirals as I see that I'm alone. As the doors close, I see Beth talking to a man who is also wearing all white. The two of them turn to stare at me, and Beth, before she can stop herself, waves goodbye, her half-eaten peach still in her hand.

"Wait!" I cry, but the doors shut and I'm thrown into darkness.

— End of Book One —

NOTE TO READER

Globally, 62 million girls are not in school.

Every year, 15 million girls are married as children.

Stoning as a punishment for adultery is still legal and occurring in over 14 countries.

———————

If you would like to help girls around the world like Mina, please contact any of the following organizations:

The Malala Fund
malala.org

Let Girls Learn
usaid.gov/letgirlslearn

Girl Rising
girlrising.com

ACKNOWLEDGMENTS

This book took many years, countless drafts, and a horde of willing readers. For all their help and brilliant insight, I would like to thank Amy Elliott, Steve Schrader, Emily Klein, Sam Lanckton, Elisa Todd Ellis, David Divita, Roberto Cipriano, Josh Jackson, Ann-Tyler Konradi, Michaela Watkins, Gabrielle Pina, Mark Richard, Mina Javaherbin, Robin Hopkins, Canan Ipek, Drea Clark, Zena Leigh Logan, John Sylvain, Alison Locke Nelson, Alexandra Smith, Evie Peck, Blakely Blackford, Susannah Luthi, Jinny Koh, Andrea Eames, Lynn Cohagan, and the USC Master of Professional Writing Program.

A special thanks to the librarians who read early drafts of this book and who continue to champion the cause of reading every day. Thank you to Neil Gaiman, whose line about the power of the novel I plagiarized. Thank you to the excellent film *Girl Rising*, which gave me the line "ignorance is the enemy of change."

If any writing in this novel is subpar, it is because Richard Rayner didn't get to read the final draft. He is a teacher extraordinaire who nurtured this book well beyond his duties as an advisor. Richard, I will *not* say, "Thank you enthusiastically." I will say, "Thank you, with enthusiasm."

If I left anyone out, then *nyek*, I apologize.

ABOUT THE AUTHOR

CAROLYN COHAGAN began her writing career on the stage. She has performed stand-up and one-woman shows at festivals around the world, from Adelaide to Edinburgh. Her first novel, *The Lost Children*, became part of the Scholastic Book Club in 2011 and was nominated for a Massachusetts Children's Book Award in 2014. She lives in Austin, where she is the founder of Girls With Pens, a creative writing organization dedicated to fostering the individual voices and offbeat imaginations of girls ages 9-17.

For more information about Ms. Cohagan, *Time Zero*, or Girls With Pens, please visit www.TimeZeroBook.com.

SELECTED TITLES FROM SHE WRITES PRESS

She Writes Press is an independent publishing company
founded to serve women writers everywhere.
Visit us at www.shewritespress.com.

Trinity Stones: The Angelorum Twelve Chronicles by LG O'Connor.
$16.95, 978-1-938314-84-1. On her 27th birthday, New York
investment banker Cara Collins learns that she is one of twelve
chosen ones prophesied to lead a final battle between the forces of
good and evil.

Faint Promise of Rain by Anjali Mitter Duva. $16.95,
978-1-938314-97-1. Adhira, a young girl born to a family of
Hindu temple dancers, is raised to be dutiful—but ultimately, as
the world around her changes, it is her own bold choice that will
determine the fate of her family and of their tradition.

Cleans Up Nicely by Linda Dahl. $16.95, 978-1-938314-38-4. The
story of one gifted young woman's path from self-destruction to
self-knowledge, set in mid-1970s Manhattan.

The Island of Worthy Boys by Connie Hertzberg Mayo. $16.95,
978-1-63152-001-3. In early-19th-century Boston, two
adolescent boys escape arrest after accidentally killing a man by
conning their way into an island school for boys—a perfect place
to hide, as long as they can keep their web of lies from unraveling.

The Wiregrass by Pam Webber. $16.95, 978-1-63152-943-6. A
story about a summer of discontent, change, and dangerous
mysteries in a small Southern Wiregrass town.

Pieces by Maria Kostaki. $16.95, 978-1-63152-966-5. After five
years of living with her grandparents in Cold War-era Moscow,
Sasha finds herself suddenly living in Athens, Greece—caught
between her psychologically abusive mother and violent stepfather.